Abigail's Summer

(The Curio Chronicles)

Robin John Morgan

First published (Paperback) in the UK in 2021

Violet Circle Publishing, Manchester, England, UK.

ISBN: 978-1-910299-27-2

Text Copyright © Robin John Morgan 2020.

Cover Illustration 'The Face of the Future' © Rin Zara Morgan 2020.

Cover background, digital images, and design. © Rin Zara Morgan 2020

All rights are reserved: no part of this may be stored in a retrieval system, reproduced or transmitted by any means, electronic, mechanical, photocopying, or otherwise without the prior written permission of the publisher, in accordance with the terms of licenses issued by the Copyright Licensing Agency.

All characters and scenarios in this publication are fictitious, and any resemblance to real persons, living or dead, is purely coincidental.

British Library Cataloguing in Publication Data.

A catalogue record for this book is available from the British Library.

All paper used in the production of this book are sourced only from wood grown in sustainable forests.

www.violetcirclepublishing.co.uk

Also by Robin John Morgan.

Heirs to the Kingdom.

Book One, The Bowman of Loxley.

Book Two, The Lost Sword of Carnac.

Book Three, The Darkness of Dunnottar.

Book Four, Queen of the Violet Isle.

Book Five, Crystals of the Mirrored Waters.

Book Six, Last Arrow of the Woodland Realm.

Book Seven, Bridge Of Sequana.

Book Eight, The Circle of Darkness.

The Curio Chronicles.

Part One, Abigail's Summer.

*For everyone, who has ever looked inside themselves,
and has struggled to be understood.*

Birch has always told me that life is a journey. She had
often told me as we sat in the dorm, that it annoyed her
that it was always referred to as a path of life. In her book,
it was river, and she had dropped the sail, and was enjoying
the journey, bobbing along, and going with the flow, and I
thought, I could do that too.

(Abagail Jenifer Watson)

Chapter 1

Approaching Summer.

There comes a time during those hallowed days of university, when you sit up rather abruptly, and the seriousness of the moment hits you bang in the face. I talk of that moment when through the haze of the wild days of leisure time, alcoholic binges, and the endless slipping between the bed sheets, with some spotty faced literature nerd, that the fog of your wonderful life clears, and you realise it's time to go home for the summer.

There is no doubt that this is that moment of crisis and panic, when the sudden realisation that all of this wonderful lifestyle, is about to end, as it grabs you and drags you back to the sobering cold light of day. Going home should be a happy, wonderful experience, but for myself, it felt like I had escaped from prison, only to be caught on the run, breathing the fresh taste of pure freedom, and I was about to be dragged back kicking and screaming.

Having spent the first eighteen years of my life, living in the heart of the southern British countryside, my rebellion had taken the form of packing my bags and moving north to Manchester, as far from the world of church fates, endless gardening, and the solitary baking of every type of cake, as I could possibly get. Don't get me wrong, I love my family and I am very grateful for the chances they have helped me to achieve, but if I am completely frank, I was never going to grow up to be a lace and frills sort of girl, living happily in my thatched cottage with Mr right. Okay, so I could do the thatched cottage, but from my point of view, I think I would possibly be better off being the odd old lady with cats, who the kids avoid as they think I am a witch, and to be honest, they would not be that far from being right.

I am not really complaining, but my life had been lived in the picturesque, post card village of Wotton Dursley, where the most exciting thing that had ever happened, was the vicar once gave his sermon wearing red socks.

Picturesque yes, it is very beautiful, but it can also be boring, especially if your mind is constantly filled with the fantasies of the books you read, and unfortunately that happens to be me. I consumed every book in the village, and lived my whole life in one long endless dream, to relieve the boredom of what in essence, was the quaint order of village life.

Fortunately for me, against the endless rhetoric of my accountancy father, reading had become my saviour, and with a set of Grade One A levels, I made it in to university to study literature, business, and public relations, where I had set my sights on working in the publishing industry, for some hip and funky independent company that published gothic fantasy.

With an acceptance from several universities, I looked at the map, and much to my mother's horror, I moved north to the cobbled streets and smog of Manchester, where for the last year, I have had my eyes well and truly opened to the world, and all of the joys it offers, and guess what, I have embraced it lovingly with both arms.

For the first time in as long as I can remember, I have felt as free as bird, surrounded by like minded individuals, who have no use of judgement, and are happy to join in with the madness with you, rather than sit back, point the finger and gossip, which is pretty much what life back home has always been like for me. Uni life has taught me that I am not different, but that I am creative and imaginative, even if loud at times, and the love of the written word, is a thing of great value to be relished and treasured. Looking at the size of my bookshelves in my dorm, it is clear to see, I have been changed forever, and there is no going back to the girl I was at home.

Actually, looking in the mirror, I think it's quite apparent there is no return. My sleek blonde hair, is now black with red tips, my powder blue eye shadow is now a heavy raven black, and the rosy cheeks of that fair yet golden tinted complexion, has become pale and whiter than the tissue hung in the toilet. I have undergone a transformation, from the south country prim and proper virgin nerd, to a fully dark night's vampire gothic geek, with matching black T Shirts, pants and heavy boots.

Most of this miraculous transformation had been the result of sharing my room with my now best friend in the world, Jemima Dixon, or Birch as she is more widely known, due to the fact that she is a Pagan naturist, with snow white hair that carries vague black patches, somewhat resembling birch bark.

Birch is a year older, and is also studying Literature as well as Psychology, but behind the mass of Shakespeare and Chaucer on her book shelves, she harbours a collection of fantasy that is five times bigger than my collection. Birch lives in the perpetual world of all things elven, and studies her white witchery with a passion, embracing every element of the natural world, and all its spiritual wonder. She preaches the freedom of the winds, and the power of the moon, and I was hooked from day one, listening to her talk of the freedom we all have locked inside, repressed from years of social oppression, indoctrinated into us from the day we are born. To put it simply, I didn't care if she was right or wrong, after living in the centre of the country, in a village where nothing ever happens, I was in the big city, with the sounds of the winds of freedom blowing through my soul, and releasing me from the oppression of home, and it made absolute sense.

Well at least it did until I realised that term time was over, and I had to head home for the next two months. To be honest, most of my transformation has until now, been internal. It's in the last term, it has become more visual if you understand me. I kept my appearance relatively calm looking for most of the year. It's just the feelings within me, have blossomed more and more in the last three months, and in a vodka induced frenzy, one wilder than wild weekend, everyone got a bit carried away, and my transformation to gothic loving geek became complete. I am not exactly sure how, I just know that it started one Friday evening, and by Monday I had the full black hair and red tips thing going on, and it just felt like a natural thing to borrow some of Birch's makeup to complete the ensemble.

Abigail Watson was no more, and I loved it. I looked in the mirror, and my eyes opened wide for the first time as I saw me, well okay, I have seen me every day, but that day I saw the real me, it was like I had been trapped in a chrysalis all my life, and finally I had awoken and broken free of the cocoon, and become the butterfly I was always meant to be, albeit one of Satan's by the look of me, but never the less, I felt I had finally conquered my inner demons, and had been reborn into whom I was meant to be.

It's a wonderful liberating feeling, to see yourself finally walk into a life you have always wanted, and actually be free enough to dress, and be any way you want to be, the only drawback is that suddenly, I have to return to the life I had before, and I am already starting to feel more than a little apprehensive. Let's be honest here, I live in a village that feels cut off from the whole world, it's a place where nothing has changed in hundreds of years. Every lawn is cut to perfection, every flowerbed including that of the village green is completely weed free, and filled with the most vibrant flowers you could ever imagine. The houses are spotless both inside and out, and the inhabitants go about their business like they are trapped inside some old fifty's movie.

This is the heart of England, where church is attended, and what you wear, and how you talk says everything about you. Gossip is the only thing faster than email, and reputation is everything. So suddenly I am finding the thought of returning home a little unsettling. I know, it's madness, I finally discovered my path in life, and now I am sat lost in dread, because the person I want to be, and actually have become, is the person who will probably be hung up in front of the church, or stoned to death for heresy, after having been tried and found guilty of being a witch, and worshiper of the northern horned god.

I had reached the bottom of my glass, and was staring into the abyss of my own demise, my stomach had been twisting and churning for days, and all those feelings had rushed up to the surface, as I stared at Birch, and her deep understanding green eyes. "Kill me.... Just creep up in my sleep and suffocate me with a pillow, I am telling you Birch, once I get home my life will be over."

Birch sat on her bed and smiled. "Come on Deads, it won't be that bad... Okay they may be a little shocked at first, but once they get used to it, they will accept it." She gave a chuckle, as her piercing green eyes twinkled. "They don't really have that much of a choice, do they now?"

I gave a long sigh sat on the floor, on the old worn rope rug, and leaned my head back onto the bed. "You have no idea of what it is really like... Honestly Birch, it's like the village of the dammed, only with neatly curled hair, tombola's, the Mothers Union and dark ages thinking. These people are not like us, they have rules for everything, and how it looks is the most important aspect of life. Trust me, if they met you, they would burn you at the stake on the village green, on Halloween."

Birch lifted her gin, and took a long swig of the glass. "Well maybe they should." I sat up and stared at her.

"What burn you at the stake?" Her eyes gave a sparkle, and her mouth gave a twitch into the slightest of smiles. It was a smile I knew well, the one I knew meant mischief.

"No stupid, I meant meet me, I must admit having listened to you for a year now, I am a little curious as to what it is really like. I fancy a chance to study the truly repressed, it could well help with my thesis."

It took a few moments for me to fully understand what she was actually asking, after all she was a Psychology major, with the goal of following her mother's footsteps into sexual dysfunction and relationship therapy. I cannot deny knowing her as well as I do, and how frank she could be, just the thought of actually saying the word orgasm out loud, back home in my village, was too delightful to contemplate, and I stared at her.

"You want to come and stay for a bit... I mean actually stay, Dad has the guest house, it is like a small flat, and empty since gran died. I can call him and ask him if you want?"

Birch gave a nod, and her long white, dark patched, hair swayed across her face. "I have nothing better to do, Kev is off with the band this summer playing gigs, so apart from a few things at home to sort, I am free for the summer. I could use some travel and fresh country air, and it will give you a little moral support. I mean let's be honest, if they think you are a freak, wait till they get a load of this."

She chuckled, and I felt the biggest wave of instant relief crash over me, I cannot deny the thought of facing my parents alone, was far greater a fear, than being burned at the stake as a heretic. I flopped my head back on the bed with a smile.

"You seriously are the best, you know that? I am so afraid of going home, my mum is going to absolutely freak when she sees me."

Birch got up and walked over towards the small table containing various bottles, and lifted the Rhubarb Gin bottle. She screwed off the cap, and poured a good size measure.

"As I said Deads, it will still be a rocky few days to begin with, even having me there won't make it easy. It will just be good knowing you will not be alone this time. If I am honest, it is about time you two faced each other and had a long talk, I think it has been coming for some time, you just ran away, maybe it is time you went back, and not only faced her, but faced yourself."

I turned my head on the bed, to look at her as she walked back, her long white hair swished upwards, as Birch flicked her neck, sending the hair back over her shoulders.

"How do you mean face myself?" She stood above me looking down, her naked skin as white as snow, looking like a towering alabaster goddess, and held out a refilled glass.

"I remember when you came here, you were awkward, shy, and completely introverted, you were the atypical village virgin, ready for slaughter. God talk about repressed, you had no clue who you were or what you wanted, your identity had been erased and replaced, with your training to become your mother all over again. My only hope for you was you loved books, I used to watch you whilst I was at the desk working, as you lived inside a book, fantasizing about living the same free life as your characters. You yearned to be free, and you had no hope of ever achieving it, which is why I stepped in, and look at you now." She smiled. "Three months ago, you were a true country bumkin with your long blonde hair, perfect skin, prim skirts, and the right designer shoes, and look at you now, so you tell me Sweetie, why the sudden extreme change?"

I took the glass, and she returned to sit on the edge of the bed. As I looked deep inside for the right words, nothing really came to mind, it was possibly the gin as my mind swirled. "She does frighten me, not so much because she is scarily aggressive, because she is not, it's just... I am not sure how to say it."

"She is far too orderly and controlling." I sat up and faced Birch.

"Yeah... She has a way for everything, and everything has

its place, and has to look just perfect." Birch gave a nod of recognition.

"And that is just not you, is it now Sweetie?" I had to chuckle, I had never realised living with her in this dorm room, she had noticed so much about me. I took a mouthful of the drink.

"Oh, I like this one, you can really taste the Rhubarb."

Something inside me was stirring, and I was not sure if it was the Gin or my soul. Birch had a way of doing that to me, I stared into the glass of light pink liquid, I had not realised my words had softened.

"I cannot be that perfect, I will never be that organised, life just isn't like that, it has frayed edges and disarray, and I kind of like the frayed aspects of life, they feel more real." I felt her hand ruffle the top of my hair; I had not even noticed she had stood up again.

"Come on, we are drunk enough. I have need of a hot elf like bass player between my thighs, and you my dark little gothic beastie, you need to find the solace of a drunken virgin, to sacrifice to the lords of your deep and dark desires. Tomorrow we have to clean this place up, and get ready for the Summer, so tonight we head into the darkness and hunt." She turned towards the door and I gave a laugh.

"Probably better if you wore clothes, I am not so sure your elf is ready for the band to observe you in your womanly seductive natural state." She looked down as she placed her empty glass on the side.

"Oops... Oh and by the way?"

"What?"

"For the sake of all the lord's Sweetie, put some clean bloody knickers on." I looked down at the red lace G string.

"Hmm see what you mean, give me a moment, and I will change."

Chapter 2

Harriet and Marjorie.

Summer was in the air, as the rain of the last week stopped, and the sun came out, lifting the temperature above Wotton Dursley. It was shortly past nine am, and already the small village was busy as the shops opened, and the bus stop, and train station, were left deserted. After over an hour of commuting, workers had made their way out of the village to the nearest town of Oxendale, nine miles away. Silence had descended over the village, apart from the petrol driven mower of Ronald Banks, as he traced the neat stripes into the village green, with his push along, chugging, mower.

This was a village that had a set routine, and every morning things ran like clockwork, Lillian Ford Baxter had the tea room open, as her business partner, Celia Thorpe Willingham polished the glass on the counter top, ready for the first customers of the day. Peter Saxon, was setting up postcard stands and a fresh vegetable display, outside the Post Office/ Village Shop, whilst his wife Mary, rolled up the security shutter on the small glass Post Office counter inside. Colin and Angela Peters, were in the bakery shop sorting out the orders ready for collection, and after a good weather check, Andrew Bosworth, was busy unfolding the large blue umbrellas, above the tables in the garden at the rear of Hunters Arms Hotel and Bar.

The main street was small, neat, and groomed to perfection, with hanging baskets filled with a riot of many shades of red, white and blue, hanging from every building and lamp post. It was as Abigail had always stated to her friend Birch, a small yet beautiful village, groomed and maintained by all the residents, and all organised by the local parish council. Everything was almost set for the day, but there was one last arrival, before village life for today could begin, and as always, she arrived precisely on the stroke of 09:15, with the clack of her patent leather shoes, on the road down from the church.

Marjorie Wallace, appeared on the main street, and made her way across the road towards the tea rooms, for the first of her day's engagements. She was the wife of the Vicar, Milton, and chair of the Parish Council. She wore matching tweed, and walked with an air of power and control, as she politely gave a nod, and greeting to each of the shop keepers, who all stopped their duties to greet her as she passed by.

Her task today was yet more council business, for summer was coming, and there was a long line of events to plan, in the hope of attracting tourists to the village, and much needed revenues. Clasped tightly in her arm, was a bunch of leaflets, printed out the evening prior, providing all the details and the agenda, for the upcoming planning meeting of the Parish Council's Summer program. She approached the Tea Rooms with its lace curtains, and powder blue surround, stopping to view the scene across the Village Green, and also ensure everything was in order and in its place, and with a glance like a hawk, to ensure nothing was out of place, she spun on her heels, adjusted her brightest smile, and pushed the door open to the ring of the tiny brass bell, hanging above it.

Her voice rung out across the green as she entered. "Lillian, Celia, good morning, and what a beautiful morning it is."

Across the green, outside the Hunter's Arms, Harriet Barker, gave a shudder and rummaged in her pocket of her long green canvas coat, for her packet of cigarettes. She lifted the packet out and slipped out a cigarette, then returning the packet to her deep pocket, she rummaged for her lighter. Crossing the road opposite the florist's shop, she lit the cigarette, and took and long drawn in puff of smoke, it was the first of the day, and having spotted Marjorie on her rounds she needed it.

To state there was no love lost between the two women, would indeed be a great understatement, she had spent her life teaching art at the local high school in Oxendale, was unmarried, and had every intention of staying that way. She lived her life for her art, and her home studio was filled with masses of paintings, and she loved the freedom it gave to her life.

To Marjorie it was considered unnatural, and she often ridiculed her for what she considered to be a wasted life of wanton sex with many men, and nights drinking in the Hunters, to which Harriet had earned the title of Village Harlot. She was also a known supporter of the Green Party, and proudly displayed her green party banner in her window, for months after the local elections, something Marjorie could not tolerate, as the village had elected a Conservative councillor for the last forty seven years.

Harriet waved to Ronald, as he walked down the green for the umpteenth time, and smiled as she drew in another long pull on her cigarette, blowing out the smoke, which was combined with her sigh of boredom, when suddenly there was a peep, and the small red shiny car of Felicity pulled up on the other side of the road. She smiled as the window rolled down automatically, and her voice bounced out from within.

"Hey you, I was just thinking about you, why aren't you in school?" Harriet smiled.

"I got two double free periods this morning, the GCSE students are finished, and all the other years are off on a field trip for geography, so there is no point being in, what you up to Flick?"

"I am off to collect a package from Mary, but I am free after, are you up for a coffee?" Harriet took a long pull on her cigarette.

"Just got to pick up some acrylic paint from Jessops, then yeah, I am pretty much free for a bit, but I will warn you, the Fascist is on the prowl, watch your back." Felicity glanced up the street.

"Alright Hatty, I will drop the car off, grab my package, and meet you here in a few minutes."

Harriet gave a nod, and flicked her spent cigarette out into the road, Felicity gave a moan. "Do you have to; you know she will have seen it?" Harriet gave a giggle.

"See you in ten." She turned and walked the three shops down, towards Jessops's craft supplies, as Felicity drove off to find a free parking spot.

Felicity Watson was Abigail's mother, she was a model of a perfect village housewife, and was probably one of a very short list of females, who willingly associated with Harriet. They had grown up together in the village, and had attended the same high school and eventually art college. Felicity was two years older than Harriet, but out of sheer boredom and loneliness, had found a mutual bond in art as students, and their friendship had blossomed into a lifelong friendship.

Harriet had always been a little on the wild side as a teenager, and on many occasions, had goaded Felicity into what were often much wilder situations than was in her comfort zone. Felicity was the first to admit, that without the regular bad influences of Harriet as a young woman, she probably would have led a very boring life indeed. All that had changed once she married Edwin, a very bright and skilled accountant, who had the golden touch with figures, and so she had slowly over time, become more and more settled, much to the often, derogatory sarcastic comments of Harriet.

Harriet on the other hand was a very free spirit, she saw everything in life as art, and had often challenged the system of authority, and lived her life to the full, which was where Marjorie found her distaste and disapproval in every aspect of Harriet, and her lifestyle.

Harriet was honest to a fault, outspoken, swore a lot, and very challenging, something she attributed to having to work with teenagers, who she viewed as artistic luddites, who had taken her classes expecting a free ride to a GCSE, which of course it was not.

Having parked the car, Felicity made her way into the post office to collect her package, Mary as always was happy and cheerful.

"No care package for the young one this week Felicity?" Felicity smiled as she pulled the small parcel addressed to her across the counter.

"Not today Mary, she has finished her exams, and will be coming home soon." Mary gave a big bright smile.

"Oh, how lovely, you must be so proud?" Felicity dropped the small parcel in her shopping bag.

"We are, she has worked really hard this year, and I cannot deny, it will be so wonderful seeing her again."

Little did she know of the endless sexually fuelled drunken

binges, and mass panic as the exams approached, which saw her daughter and roommate, locked in their room quaffing coffee for three days straight, as they tried last minute to cram for their final exams.

Mary gave another wide smile. "Such a lovely girl, so polite, prim, and proper, you rarely see a girl raised in such a decent fashion these days, you and Edwin have done a wonderful job." Felicity gave a smile; she was indeed, very proud of her daughter.

"She has grown into a lovely young woman; we are very proud of her."

Mary was a really kind woman, and Felicity liked her a great deal, but she knew how Mary had a habit of dragging out the conversation, and with Harriet and Marjorie on the same street at the same time, she knew she had to get away as fast as possible. "I really am very sorry Mary, I would love to stay, but I have a pressing engagement, so I will have to bid you a good day."

Without hesitating, and also aware that Marjorie could spring up at any moment, she turned sharply, and headed for the door, in the hope of not being spotted. As she made her way towards the craft shop and Harriet, Felicity made it three feet through the door, and spotted Harriet leaving the shop down the street, when that familiar cold feeling flowed over her.

"Felicity my dear, how lovely to run into you."

She turned to find herself confronted with the heavily powered smiling face, perfectly styled hair, and make upped to perfection Marjorie, and did her best to appear calm and composed, knowing Harriet was just yards away behind her.

"Hello Madge, how lovely to see you too." Marjorie held out two neatly folded sheets of paper.

"These are the details of Fridays council meeting at the Church Hall, it is very important we are all prompt on arrival, as we will set the agenda for the entire summer events list." Felicity gave a nod.

"Yes, we received the email, Edwin and myself will as always be there on the dot."

Her voice was a little strained, as she was well aware that Harriet would not miss the opportunity to join them, and it was very obvious Madge had spotted her walking up behind her, by the glare that was emitting from her eyes. "I am sort of in a hurry at the moment Madge, but we will have a little catch up on Friday after the meeting. Yes?" Madge gave a scowl and looked right passed her to Harriet, who was smiling at her.

"I believe you lost something, did you not?"

Felicity wanted to die on the spot as she saw the shadowed outline of Harriet, who was almost at her side on the pavement floor. Harriet smiled again, as Felicity glanced sideways wishing she was anywhere but here. Harriet's defiant hazel eyes glared back into the dark abyss of Marjorie's.

"The only thing I have lost in 47 years of life Marjorie, is my virginity."

Felicity felt the physical pain of her horror rip through her insides, why the hell did she have to always make a comment that would offend Madge, could she just for once be polite? Marjorie looked back at the art teacher with utter distaste.

"Well I am amazed you can remember so far back; I was referring of course to your recent case of littering; I do believe that item you so freely discarded, to soil our village, belongs to you." Harriet looked back down the street.

"Oh, that thing, it is fine Marjorie, it is biodegradable, if you don't believe me just ask Norman and Daisy."

Screams bellowed in Felicity's head, out of all the snide and rude comments she had to make, she had to pick that one. Apart from Harriet, who Marjorie despised with a passion, the only other people in the village Marjorie hated as much, were Norman and Daisy Merryweather.

Norman was the grandson of the late Group Captain Simon Merryweather, a distinguished veteran, and RAF hero of the Battle of Britain. On his passing, his land had been bequeathed to Norman, which included several acres of elaborate landscaped gardens, and a first rate Edwardian house. Marjorie had respected and admired the Group Captain, so when his grandson arrived, with his flaky new age wife, and converted the property to an off grid homestead, complete with full organic plant nursery, it horrified Marjorie, who referred to them as 'those vagabond beatniks.'

Mild panic rose inside Felicity, as she looked at the frowning face of Marjorie, and she gave an exasperated sigh, knowing she had to separate them as fast as possible, before it escalated into yet another public shouting match.

"I have to go Madge; I will see you Friday."

She turned and grabbed Harriet by the arm, and walked off briskly, half dragging the smiling and waving Harriet along with her, back towards the craft shop. Harriet sniggered.

"Good recovery, well done you." Felicity gave a long sigh, she felt flustered and embarrassed.

"Why do you always have to be like that, can you not just for once be civil?" Harriet shrugged.

"In her eyes I am the village whore, why should I care what she thinks? She is a fascist, who makes Nurse Ratchet look warm and fuzzy." Felicity gave a sigh and smiled.

"Will you ever grow up?" Harriet gave a chuckle.

"I work with teenagers, and it's not a requirement of the job... You know there was a time when you would have treated her with the same distaste, I remember the real Flick, I painted her remember?" Felicity gave a cough.

"I was young and stupid, and you had way too much influence, and the less said about those paintings the better." She stopped and looked at Harriet who gave a smirk.

"What?"

"I have to live here too, I left behind the scandals of our past, and I have worked very hard to be accepted again. Hatty, I love you, but please do not ruin this for me, it's all I have." Harriet gave her head a shake and her voice lowered.

"You are such a fool, you are an amazing artist, you could blow my stuff out of the water, and have such an amazing career, and yet you sold out everything for this fake bullshit village life. Don't you miss it Flick...? How the hell do you feel alive in the centre of all this? I have my art; I paint and sketch... I also fuck a lot too, how the hell can you settle for this? There is a massive world out there Flick, and it's not like this, it's modern, free, and filled with people who create. I know, I have taught them year in and year out, and as good as they are, not one of them has ever come close to the gift you have. Why settle for some backward thinking village stuck in the 1940's, it makes no sense to me at all?" Felicity looked Harriet in the eyes.

"I have a beautiful home, a wonderful husband and a daughter everyone is proud of, it is my life and I chose it, and whether you believe it or not, I am happy, now can we drop this and move on?" Harriet gave a sigh.

"You say the words, but all I hear in your tone is regret, I will shut up, but I will also say, it's never too late Flick, think about that."

It was pointless trying, Harriet had raised the same subject endless times, and she wondered why she even still tries. The answer was always the same, an unconvincing I am happy and have what I wanted, but Harriet knew different, she remembered all the dreams they shared, and how it had been Felicity that had inspired her the most to follow her own heart and focus on her art. It felt so disappointing to see her best friend in the world, sell herself out so cheaply, and as much as she wanted to understand, she had to admit, she did not, in this one thing, Felicity in her mind, defied all logic.

Chapter 3

Shock Tactics.

The train ride had been fascinating as I listened to Birch, who lived just on the outskirts of the quant village of Uppermill, in Saddleworth, on the far moorland boundary of Greater Manchester. Although many of the locals were unhappy to be lumped into the Manchester region, and still considered themselves to be Yorkshire folk, of which the boundary was a little way up the road. The town once was a hive of industry for textiles, which was mainly due to the terrain being so steep, with very acidic soil, making it difficult for farming.

In recent times, it had become a place where many who commuted to Manchester for work, found a little place of quiet clean air to come home to, and so the prices of property had soared, and the place was considered too 'Posh' compared with many of its surrounding towns. Birch's mum, Veronica, enjoyed the quiet restful place simply for writing her books on sexual discovery, sexual pleasure, and also sexual disfunction. Her books had helped her enhance her therapy practice, which was situated in the city centre of Manchester, and so like her husband William, who worked at the university, they would commute together daily on the train.

I cannot deny, I loved the grittiness of the place, which was built from Yorkshire stone, and had a real industrial vibe to it, which wove through the picturesque houses and tall viaduct, onto the wild and barren moorland. I loved this new northern feel and lifestyle, although I had noted, it had rubbed off on me far more than I had realised, especially when it came to bad language.

The village centre was busy and thriving, as all the traffic towards Huddersfield, trundled through in a long stream, and the stone cottages were filled with gift shops, and craft orientated small shops, which as Birch made very clear to me, also had an excellent off license, and a good few pubs.

Looking round, I noticed the similarities between my own village and this one, and yet it was clear that here, people were more at ease and relaxed, and certainly more friendly and less judgemental.

I could see where the naturally grounded attitude of Birch came from, and could understand how someone growing up here, would find a really strong connection to nature. The moors surrounding the town rose up on all sides, covered in trees and wild carefree swathes of heather, but there was a feeling of damp mystery to them, and I find it strangely alluring, and so different from the wheat and barley fields that surround my own village of Wotton Dursley.

The hill up to the house, which was situated on a small circular road, and built of brick, was very steep, as we both pulled our suitcases on wheels up it. I felt like my lungs would explode, and I stopped to catch my breath a few times, noting how unhealthy I have become since starting university.

Living at home, I would go jogging down the canal, more for escape and to relieve the boredom, than for the reason of getting fit. Birch appeared unaffected, and strode up them, with relative ease, like an Amazon marching home.

Finally, gasping for air, we hit the straight and level, and trundled along towards the place Birch called home, with a neat garden that flowed informally around the flower beds, which I was so pleased to see had a few dandelions growing in them.

The house was a large four bedroomed house, with a conservatory, a large back garden, a block paved drive to a garage, and a large front porch. The inside of the house was very down to earth and ordinary, except for the fact that the walls contained all sorts of eclectic artwork, and everywhere you looked there were piles of books, and files of notes, and I instantly felt at home and relaxed. It was perfect, and reminded me very much of the dorm I shared with Birch, just on a larger scale.

Birch filled the kettle as I stood in the kitchen watching. It was kind of odd seeing her in the kitchen being simply herself, we have spent most of our time in the cafeteria, or buying take out at Uni, and let's be honest, we always drank gin and vodka in the dorm, so just watching her make coffee was strangely fascinating.

"Grab some cups Sweetie, they are in the cupboard up there."

I turned, to grab the knob of the pinewood door, and as I opened it, I heard Birch give a huge explosive laugh, as I viewed the inside of the cupboard. It was a very startling surprise, as I gazed upon what my naive self, deemed to be sex toys. Just for a moment, I had no idea at all what to say, as Birch laughed and approached my side.

"Sorry about that, this is my mums' spares, we have so many we have nowhere else to store them."

I am not sure why, I mean it's not like I have not seen the real things in my year of lust filled adventures, but I was uncertain of what words I could use to express the strange sensations of shock I had at the moment.

"Shit Birch, how many does your mum need, is she really that horny?"

Birch gave a cackle, and lifted a long nine inch black rubber dildo out of the cupboard, and giggled.

"They are spares, mum gets sent loads for her work, she hands them out to her female clients, and they let her know what they think of them."

This was all just so natural and ordinary for her, as she stood there waving the thing in my face, and I could not help but think that if my mum found that in my room, she would throw a blue fit and then faint. I had to shake my head to stop being cross eyed, as I stared at the huge black monster waving before me.

"Wow your mum is cool, and kind of freaky and messed up, you know that right?"

Birch started to giggle again, as she walked down the kitchen towards the kettle, I followed still uncertain of what I was feeling, and noted the slight trembling in my legs. She reached up to another cupboard, and I have no idea why, but I averted my eyes, and was afraid to look, but I was certain I would think twice before ever opening a kitchen cupboard again.

Birch pulled two earthenware mugs from the cupboard, and placed them on the table, then turned for the coffee jar. "Mum is pretty cool, I am sorry about that, it is like our ice breaker to get people used to her job, not everyone appears to understand it."

"Ice breaker...Holy shit Birch, you could break more than ice with that thing, I mean. seriously do people really use those?"

I somehow felt I had a lot to learn about the modern world, and just how sheltered my upbringing had been. She smirked as she slid the drink to me.

"You would be surprised what people do to each other to get sexual satisfaction. I suppose for me this is all just sort of normal." I lifted my cup to my lips. "Mum and me once beat eggs for an omelette with one, you know, just for a bit of a laugh."

My windpipe restricted, filled with a mixture of coffee and oxygen, and as much as tried not to do it, coffee exploded out of my mouth, and sprayed all over the kitchen table. My lungs screamed for more air and less coffee, as I choked and gasped, and all I could hear between wrenching gasps, was the high pitched hysterical, cackling, laughter of Birch.

Aid came with a resounding slap on the back, and I gave a violent cough, as I tried to squeeze out the remaining tears in my eyes, and took a long inward breath refilling my lungs. The still laughing Birch, handed me a tea towel.

"Sorry Sweetie, I could not resist." She chuckled. "Are you okay?"

My recovery took several more minutes, as Birch wiped up the coffee still chuckling.

Finally, with what remained of my coffee, she took me upstairs to the guest room, which was still bigger than the dorm, and painted pastel yellow, with a matching duvet.

I put down my case, and looked out through the window, across the industrial rooftops, to the rising wild moors beyond. It was a vast rolling expanse of lone trees and pink heather, bound and stitched together with shrubs, grasses and wild flowers. Something about it stirred me deeply inside, something about its emptiness, its openness, its freeness. I found it breath taking, and moved by it, almost like looking out into the wild beyond, it made me feel like I was looking inside me. Birch came up at my side and looked out of the window.

"Many of the locals believe that to walk out on the moor, is to walk alone with yourself, and to know yourself." It made such sense.

"It is truly magnificent; I can see why it meant so much to

Bronte." Birch gave a smile.

"If Heathcliff ran around up there, he would more than likely get swallowed in the bog." I gave a chuckle, and felt her arm slip round my waist. "For me this is home Deads, and I want you to feel that way for the next week. Come on, and I will show you my room."

Leaving my bag for later, Birch took me down the hallway to the next door, and into her room, which blew me away completely, as it was wall to wall shelves of books. She had just about every fantasy novel I had ever heard of, let alone read, as well as all the classics of literature, and a very well stocked section of books on sexual dynamics and psychology. I noted fifteen books all bearing the name of Dr Veronica Gemma Dixon, on the spine.

"Wow your mum has written a lot of books." Birch sat on her single bed.

"Yes, she has worked with a lot of people, and done a lot of research, it really is a very fascinating subject when you dig into it."

I sat beside her, lustfully staring at her collection of fiction and fantasy.

"I would imagine it is, to be honest, I have never really thought about it, I only had sex once before I came up here, and have been doing my own research for my own personal reasons. I never actually thought about the motivation behind it all, I can understand why it fascinates you though." She lay back on the bed and relaxed.

"I have grown up with it, the house has been filled with sex related items all my life, I have no idea how many conversations have gone on in the background, whilst I was playing between my parents. For me growing up it was a normal thing to talk about, although it did have its drawbacks, especially at school when I corrected the sex ed teacher, and told her she was giving the wrong advice." I looked back at her.

"Ouch, how did that go?"

She gave a smile, and her eyes gave off that familiar cheeky twinkle.

"My mum came into school and re-educated the teacher and proved I was right."

I couldn't help but laugh, and I loved how close she felt to her mum, it was something I had struggled with for the year before I started university. Thinking about it, I wondered if we would ever be able to talk again without having blazing row after blazing row.

"My mum would never do that, she would back the school, even if they were wrong." I felt a soft pat on my back and heard Birch's soft voice.

"Not every parent gets it you know, they struggle to let go of what they see as their helpless child, it is hard for some mums to let go and allow their daughter to become an independent woman. Sadly, the only way you will truly get your freedom is by standing your ground, and talking things out like a grown up. The more adult like you are, the more she will start to see it, trust me Sweetie, I will be there when you are ready to do it." I gave a soft sigh.

"You remind me of one of her friends, she said something similar to me before I left." Birch sat back up at my side.

"Really who? Tell me more about her?" Her bright green eyes twinkled at me, and she smiled.

"She is called Hatty, she is mums' best friend, I used to go see her and watch her paint, she is a really cool artist. Her and mum grew up together and went to art college together, so she has known her longer than anyone. She has often talked to me, and always encouraged me to walk my own path. She is the only one in that village who I think understood the pressure my mum put on me, she has tried to talk to my mum many times to get her to see my point of view." Birch nodded understanding me.

"She sounds like a pretty cool and down to earth person." I smiled.

"Yeah, she is, although my dad hates her, I am not sure what happened, but she decided to get her own back on him a good few years back, and she knows how much he hates cleaning the pool. So one afternoon just after he finished cleaning it, she got his younger brother in the pool, and had sex with him. My dad went crazy and threw her out, I mean I shouldn't laugh really, because she had no clothes on, as they had been left in the house. She just smiled at him, and then walked naked up the drive and home. I loved her for that, he was absolutely lost for words, sadly though, she could never come to the house again whilst he was home."

"She sounds pretty awesome; will I meet her when we are at your house?" I gave her a big smile and nodded.

"Oh yeah, I really want you to meet her."

I did, in fact I had been thinking about it quite a lot since Birch had offered to come home with me, although understanding Birch and Hatty, I knew they would hit it off straight away, and that bothered me a little. Hatty was forty seven and wilder than most girls I had met in Uni, and the thought of combining her with Birch, in one of the most frustrated and repressed villages in England, worried me more than you would imagine. I knew for a fact my dad would not be happy at all.

The front door banged downstairs, and Birch jumped, a gruff voice shouted from the hall.

"You home Jemi?" Birch slid off the edge of the bed.

"Oh shit... Guard your vagina?"

"Huh?" She turned and winked.

"It's Bev from next door, she takes care of the cats when mum is at work, she is a lesbian with a particular taste in new lipstick lesbians, sorry but to her you are fresh meat, no matter what I say go with it, okay?"

I nodded feeling somewhat panicked, actually why did I suddenly feel in danger, and just what exactly had I just agreed to?

"Am I going to be raped?" Birch started to laugh.

"Oh Sweetie.... I will save you."

I nodded, suddenly feeling utter panic, as I heard a heavy clumping on the stairs, Birch looked round flustered.

"Oh crap, she is coming up."

I felt my heart start to pound in my chest, what the hell was so big it made such a loud clumping, did she wear big boots, or was I about to raped by a female gorilla? I swallowed hard, and gripped the duvet, not that it would prevent me from being dragged to the floor and molested, it just felt reassuring, as I was becoming more and more alarmed at the thought of what these Northern women were really like. Birch turned to me as she slid open a draw and pulled out a towel.

"Quick, take your pants off and lie back on the bed."

I felt the sudden onset of complete fear course through my

veins.

"WHAT! ... Screw you Birch, let her have your vagina, mine is staying all male only, no teeth allowed." She lowered her voice, and started to giggle.

"Deads, please trust me, I am not about to feed you to that vulture, I have seen what she does to young innocent girls. Just go along with me, and for god's sake hurry up."

She grabbed my pants round my ankles, and gave an almighty tug. I fell backwards on to the bed feeling utter terror, as the cooler air hit my bare legs, and my black jeans came clean off. Birch grabbed my legs, and spread them wide, and I panicked even more, and felt my legs instinctively turn inwards, as they naturally wanted to snap back together.

My ears pounded with the rhythm of my heart, which appeared to match the clumping feet coming down the hall way, I was starting to sweat.

Birch was swift, as she threw the towel over my waist to hide my black satin and lace panties, and then she leaned in between my legs, and for a second, I felt I was not completely safe from Birch, let alone whatever beast was lurking outside the door.

I stared over Birch's shoulder, my eyes locked on the door to the hallway, my heart two beats away from cardiac arrest, and then came the knock, and that same gruff voice, and I think my heart stopped or time froze.

"You in there Jemi?" Birch winked at me, and looked back at the door.

"Just a second Bev." The door opened, and I almost peed on the bed. I breathed my thoughts quietly out in a whisper.

"Holy shit, I wish I hadn't quit the choir now."

Bev was big, actually scratch that, she was frigging huge, one of her tits was bigger than my waist. She had the smallest head I have ever seen, which was covered in bright purple spikey hair, and her face was covered in piercings, I was utterly terrified, and felt my vagina recoil in fear.

Birch was amazingly calm, she turned to looked at Bev, as she gently pressed the towel down to hide my terrified pussy, and then looked back at me and smiled. Just for a moment I wasn't sure if I was about to be sacrificed to the purple turfed Chuff

Chomper of Uppermill, as Birch ever so calmly said.

"Oh, it's okay Sweetie, you just have a bad dose of clap."

My head went into free falling melt down, from fear of rape, to 'I had the clap!?' Wait... What, I have the clap? How the frigging hell did that happen he wore condoms, screamed in my brain, as I was momentarily paralysed at the mouth?

Birch nodded, and turned to look back at Bev, who was looking a little disappointed having broken into a grisly smile, when she had first spotted me, lay legs akimbo on Birch's bed. Birch pushed the towel down further, and stood up and winked at me.

"I will get my mum to bring you some antibiotics home tonight, don't worry it will clear up in a week or two, although it may smell a little funky down there for a while."

I nodded and swallowed hard, and suddenly understanding I was saved from the hell of the beast, I relaxed and tried to speak a hoarse few local words.

"Thanks mate."

Birch turned, and walked to the door, where she embraced Bev.

"Bev Sweetie, lovely to see you."

She turned and pointed at me lay relaxed and trying to regulate my almost exploding heart.

"This is my mate from Uni, she is called Deadly, or Deads for short." She lowered her voice a little. "Bit of trouble with her pipes down there, I was just checking her over for mum."

Bev nodded looking concerned, hell she was not as concerned as I had just been, Birch turned back to me.

"Get yourself dressed, and I will put the kettle back on, come join us when you are ready."

Birch guided Bev back through the door, and closed it behind her, and I heard her chatting and chuckling with Bev as she accompanied her down stairs. I gave a huge sigh of utter relief, and just lay on the bed looking up at the ceiling, and the huge poster of Gandalf the Grey.

It was several minutes, before I was able to sit up, and find my discarded jeans, which were on the floor over the other side of the room. I took a huge breath, and tried to induce calmness into my being, knowing Birch was the truest friend I ever had, and I had just survived a fate worse than my mother or Marjorie Wallace. I looked down.

"Shit, I did wet my panties."

I picked up my jeans and walked back to my room, and took my time, and dressed in the clean big white knickers my mum bought me, which I usually saved for that time each month. I figured maybe they would serve as insurance, just in case Bev changed her mind.

For a few moments I looked out of the bedroom window again, and gathered my composure, and then made my way down the hallway to the stairs. I stopped at the top as I gathered my thoughts. "Hell, the north can be a scary ass bloody place, I am almost looking forward to going home."

Chapter 4

The walk of Shame.

I sat back in the seat, of what was going to feel like a long journey by train. We had changed at London, and were Wotton bound, and my apprehension was building deep down inside me. Birch had hoped we could borrow a car from her friend, but sadly it had failed its MOT, and so taking the train for now was our only option.

It was not long before Birch dozed off, after all, our last night in Uppermill had seen us encounter a leaving party, hosted by Birch's wonderful parents, and a drive out with Bev to the local reservoir, and upper lake, where she proceeded to strip, and dive into the water to skinny dip.

Birch appeared to have no issue with it, and soon followed, and so being the only one left on the water's edge, I had no choice but to join them, and plunge into the icy water. Northerners are way hardier than I first thought, and I almost froze my ass off, but I cannot deny it was great fun, and after a week of becoming accustomed to life again away from University, I was feeling alive, and filled with hope for a future of many more free encounters.

Watching Birch sleep in front of me, as the train in the background, clickety clacked on the tracks, my mind shifted back to what had been a wonderful week. Those first moments in Birch's house had been testing, I honestly thought I was going to be raped by Bev, but over the week I had grown really fond of her. She was actually a really placid and caring person, who adored cats and plants, and I really learned to be more open and understanding when meeting new people. It is so easy to judge a book by its cover, which felt a little bit ironic, because I knew the moment I arrived back in Wotton Dursley, everyone would feel those same judgemental feelings I had, when first confronted by Bev, and it was so wrong of me.

I had really grown to like Veronica, Birch's mum. It was not that hard, as she was almost just an older version of Birch, I watched them talk and interact, and at times had felt an ache inside me, and I have to admit I felt envious, because I knew that I would never really have that sort of closeness to my own mother. She had insisted I call her Roni, which felt odd at first, apart from Hatty, I had addressed everyone by their full name in the village, it was just the way things were, and yet another example of how out of step the village had become with the modern world.

Mid week, Kev had stayed over, as his band were playing at the local pub named, 'The Railway,' and that was yet another eye opening experience, to see how laid back and cool her father was with Kev. At age thirty, I am sure my father would not let a male stay in my room, unless I was married to them, for me it was just another reminder of how strict my parents had been, and also how little I really understood about the world outside the village.

I am nineteen, and I have never seen a live band in a pub before, so for me it was just an epic experience. It was crazy as people piled in close, and the music was so loud, I had to shout at Birch and Bev just to be heard, but oh my god it was the most thrilling night of the whole week, and I made a mental note, that I really had to get out more, and experience life among the masses.

I was definitely missing out, this place had so many special and kind people, for a reclusive book worm like me, it felt like being yanked out of my safe snug comfort zone, and tossed into a wild adventure. As scary as it was at first, just being in the pub surrounded by smiling strangers, was a mind blowing and amazing experience, although Northern ale is strong, and I did puke several times on the way home, much to the amusement of Birch and Bev.

I will never forget that night, as the three us left Kev to pack up, and we walked through the dark, slightly chilly night, on the empty streets, laughing and talking as we all linked arms, I think this really was my first time truly understanding the joy of having proper true friends.

A memory slid into my brain of the previous day's morning, as I sat at the kitchen table alone with Roni eating breakfast, whilst Birch was still flat out in bed.

"My daughter has grown very fond of you; I am surprised at how close you two have become." I had frowned unsure as to why she had said that.

"What do you mean, she is just being herself with me?" Roni smiled.

"Believe or not, Jemi is not that at ease with people, apart from Bev. She is really good at faking it, especially with strangers, but she has not really had that many close friends in her past."

It felt like a complete shock to hear it, and I cannot deny, I did not fully understand why, because at Uni, she was so popular with everyone. Roni smiled.

"It is not easy growing up with two professionals like us as parents, my work especially attracts a lot of attention, especially the books I publish. Jemi was raised in the shadow of them, and she took quite a lot ridicule for it, I almost considered giving up my practice and becoming a teacher because of it. Will convinced me to talk things through with her, which I did, and as a result we made it through, but the cost of that was she bonded deeper with me, and rejected those her own age. I was so happy when she began to email me little snippets about the really cool girl, she shared a room with."

It came as a massive surprise to me, and I had no way of responding, yet Roni appeared to understand and just smiled. "Jemi has told me some things about your home life, she is worried about you going back alone, which is why she asked if she could go with you. I am not sure if you are aware, but you are pretty naïve for city life, Jemi has been carefully controlling your exposure to new things, so it does not freak you completely out. She is an extraordinary girl, who has formed a deep bond with you. I am not sure you are fully aware of how important you are to her, but as her mother, I can tell you, that girl will have your back for the rest of your life."

In a way I had felt that always with her, and I smiled at Roni.

"I am glad you told me, and hope you know I feel the same way, I would never have made it through this year without her. I feel I owe her so much; I am not sure I could ever repay her for what she has done to help me adjust." Roni stood up and simply patted my hand.

"Trust me, you have already paid her, and me in full, just being there has made all the difference."

I turned to the window as the trees passed at high speed, breaking occasionally for a river or planted field, my thoughts drifted around in my head, as I processed my free life away from home, and the value it had brought me. With flying trees, and the sway of the carriage, my mind wandered all over, until suddenly I was snapped out of it with a jerk, and turned to see the mass of snow white hair with dark patches, and those bright green eyes close to me.

"Hey sleepy, we are almost there, you better get your things together."

I sat forward in the seat, and looked at my files on the table beside my phone, I had meant to read through some notes, but had been so lost in the thought, I had dreamed and slept the journey away. My mind was still fuzzy as I packed everything into my shoulder bag, and lifted my case off the luggage rack, and then like a cold chill running down my spine, I heard it on the platform, as the station master shouted it out. "Wotton Dursley... Wotton Dursley!!"

I felt a soft firm grip on my arm, and turned to Birch with her bag on her shoulder. "Are you ready for this?" I swallowed hard, as my stomach twisted and swirled, and shook my head.

"Not really." She gave me that familiar smile.

"You survived the rugby team hitting on you in the student's union, trust me, if you can get though the year without sleeping with any of them, you can survive anything, those buggers are persuasive and relentless." I smiled.

"Good point."

When I stepped off the train, my legs turned instantly to jelly, Birch showed our tickets to the station master, and linked my arm for extra support. I suddenly felt really sick, and then like a flash I remembered, and I turned to Birch.

"I need the ladies." She gave a nod, and steered me towards the lady's toilets, where I quickly rummaged in my bag. "I meant to put them in on the train, I just forget, give me a minute, will you?"

Birch gave a frown, not completely understanding, until I

rooted around for a few seconds, and I produced the case that contained my black contact lenses, and she instantly understood. "You are everyone's blue eye girl; I get it now." I smiled.

"Not for much longer." I opened the case, and tried to unscrew the bottle with the liquid in, but my hands were shaking too much. Birch gave a soft sigh.

"Here let me do it, in this state, you will probably blind yourself."

It took much longer than normal, Birch had never worn them, and so had little idea of how to put them in. Fifteen minutes later, and having suffered a poke in the eye, I ended up knelt on the floor with her foot on my shoulder, and her gripping my jaw like a vice to keep me still, and several curse words from both of us, we emerged from the ladies with renewed confidence, as I blinked in my contacts to adjust to the brightness.

The thing I love about wearing contacts, is it feels like wearing a mask. I think it is more psychological than anything else, but just knowing with my hair dyed and a fringe, which I have never had in my life, and different coloured eyes, I felt few would have the ability to recognise me, and that alone felt comforting. At the gates to the station I stopped, I still felt sick and my stomach was reeling, Birch turned to me. "Here drink this."

"What is it?"

"Dutch courage." She gave me a big smile. "I thought you would need some."

I looked at my hand, and the little bottle of brandy, lying in it. Birch unscrewed the cap for me, as I was trembling so bad, and raised her bottle in salute. I lifted mine and we chinked them together.

"Here is to the walk of shame."

She gave a little giggle and lifted the bottle, and downed it in one, I quickly followed suit, and felt my throat explode with fire and coughed.

"Jesus that's strong." She winked.

"Only the best for you my dark little beastie."

She turned, gripped the handle of her pull along case, and then took a deep breath. "Okay.... Let's bloody do this before the brandy wears off."

Without another word, she linked my arm, and took a huge step forward, and we set off up the hill towards the road, and the left turn towards the main street of the village.

As we boldly strode up Station Road towards the cross roads, with Green Street, and the Main Street, I felt confident and pretty happy, but maybe that was the brandy kicking in. As we turned left onto the main village street, I felt my legs tremble, and I gripped Birch tighter. Birch gave a little gasp.

"Holy shit Deads, I only thought it was two or three shops, not this bloody many. When you said village green, I thought you meant like room size, you know big enough for a good sized picnic, but that bugger is as big as a football pitch." I swallowed hard trying to keep my eyes down, and my face hidden from view.

"Keep walking, if we stop Birch, I am running back to the station."

She patted my hand, and we began what would be indeed our walk of shame once my identity was revealed. As predicted two strangers in the village of dubious description hit the gossip network within a second, and I could hear the beeps of text messages going off all across the green.

In the tea rooms, the lace curtains were twitching, and Marjorie was on full alert, with Lillian and Celia at her side, as they typed at a fast rate into their phones. The 'transient alert' had been activated, and all eyes were on the main street.

Understanding the way the village worked, I was fully aware that every single person in the village had stopped what they were doing, and all eyes were on us. Birch did not seem to mind, she smiled and nodded to each person she spotted, staring out from behind their shop window displays. Birch leaned into me as I looked at the floor, and quietly spoke.

"It is far more beautiful, and a lot bigger than I pictured it, but I also see what you mean about village of the dammed, I am sure if they stare any harder, our heads will explode."

All I could do was count the shops, as I saw the bottom of the doors pass by. We had passed the news agent, the bakery, the gift shop, and were level with the florists. My heart was racing inside me, and I felt all the eyes on me, even though I could not see them, I knew they were there, and it brought back all the feelings of walking with my father age ten.

"Children should be seen, and not heard, a respectful quiet child, is a child worthy of praise."

I walked behind him in his shadow, I was his shadow, and unable to step forward, and be seen. Walking at the side of Birch, all I wanted was to be that unseen shadow again, out of sight, hidden from view and not the centre of the village's attention.

I remembered the scarecrow in Sutton's wheat field, stared at and alone, everyone was aware of them, but no one cared enough to really know them, a lonely figure in full view. That was me, it had always been me, I gripped Birch's arm tighter.

"I think I am going to cry Birch." Her arm squeezed back.

"Don't you dare, you are better than all of these, lift your head Deads, and walk proud, don't let these buggers get to you."

I couldn't, my legs were trembling, and the fear was too great. I looked at the floor and the shop doors, thank god we were past the sweet shop, and was level with the craft shop, when a loud 'TING!' echoed in my ears as we passed, and my heart, which was once again beating at an alarmingly fast rate, almost failed, as a voice stopped it dead.

"Abby?"

I closed my eyes tight, and I wanted to die, I heard the footsteps, and then right in front, the bright light through my eye lids faded. Whoever they were, they were right in front, and I swallowed down the raging panic in my throat. I opened my eyes, and there in front of me, blocking out the light, was a pair of heavily patched, and paint covered dungarees. Birch stopped as the stranger blocked our way. My head was spinning with panic, as I recognised Hatty, and then she gave a howling laugh.

"Well fuck me, you absolutely beautiful child... My god, I am so proud of you at this moment."

I had stopped breathing, and as I lifted my head up, I started to breathe again, and saw the widest beaming smile I had ever seen on Hatty's face.

Hatty lifted her hands to the sides of my face, and leaned in, and kissed my cheek, and whispered.

"Bloody good for you kid, you shook em all off and found your real self, and my god, it is fucking outstanding." She kissed me again.

Birch leaned in. "By the way, I am Birch, and you are?" Hatty gave a beaming smile.

"Very pleased to meet such a great friend of Abby's. I am Harriet, but call me Hatty, everyone I like does, which is two people currently, and now three, you have earned it Birch."

I was still shaking and unsure of what to do, but I was so relived it was Hatty, and not one of the others. My voice was quiet, as I did not want anyone to hear it.

"Hatty, mum does not know I am home, she is not expecting me until tomorrow." She gave a nod.

"Need a place to hide?" I shook my head.

"No, it is today or never." She understood, she looked me up and down, taking in the long black flared skirt, the tight top, the lack of a bra, the red tipped hair and dark eyes, and she beamed a huge smile.

"Oh, Abby darling, I highly approve, wow, you have blown me away, and made my year." She looked at Birch. "Do you have a smart phone?" She shook her head. "Daft question, you are young, it goes without saying." She gave Birch another smile. "Can you do me a favour?"

Birch shrugged unsure of what to say. "Er...Sure...What?"

"Film Edwin's reaction when he first sees her, my god it will be sheer gold to see that." Birch gave a nod not fully understanding.

"Okay!?"

Hatty looked up the street, her eyes fixed on the small group outside the tea rooms.

"Get going Abby, the Fascist is out, and on the prowl, and don't forget, I have a spare room if it gets too rough. Oh fuck, here she comes, go on git, let me handle her, and don't worry, I won't say a word about it being you. Call me if you need me."

I did not need telling twice, Hatty was my only ally, and if she said get going, I was going. I yanked on Birch's arm, and dragged her forward with force, Hatty winked at Birch.

"Take good care of her for me, will you?" Birch nodded, as I dragged her forward, and walked as quickly as I could without appearing like I was running, and Hatty wore her best smile as she walked away from me towards Marjorie, who was already on route and level with the gift shop.

It took moments before they faced each other, and I was moving as fast as I could in the opposite direction, and saying thank you over and over in my head to Hatty. Marjorie craned her neck, and tried to swerve past Harriet, but Harriet changed her course blocking her path, Marjorie scowled at her with utter hate.

"Know them, do you?" Harriet frowned.

"Who?" Marjorie pointed down the village street.

"Them... Those transients you were just talking to?" Harriot gave a nod.

"Oh... Them... Nope, no idea who they are, why is it important?"

Marjorie was visibly infuriated that they had spoken to Harriet, before she could get to them, her eyes glared at her, she sniffed something fishy, and aimed to get to the bottom of it.

"What did you talk to them about? I know you, and you are up to something Harriet Barker."

Harriet shrugged. "They were hunting those weird poky things; you know the little invisible monsters you track on your phone?" Marjorie frowned.

"What on earth are you talking about, what nonsense are you concocting now?"

Harriet grinned at her; she knew she had her on the ropes.

"You know that Japanese game thing, it is one of those new fangled apps you use on your smart phone. It allows you to see invisible monsters, and you get points when you find them. I told them not to worry about the invisible ones, I warned them not to loiter, as there were a few alive and living monsters in this village, which they should most definitely avoid."

Marjorie had no clue whatsoever about smart phones, her only use was text, and that was a recent discovery taught to her by her son Nigel. "Why can you not just talk straight, why is everything you say utter gibberish?" Harriet shrugged.

"It's an artisan thing, you would never understand it."

She turned and looked back to see Abby had made it past the shops, and crossed over the road, and she was heading on to Manor Road, within the next ten minutes she would be home safe. She had successfully fulfilled her duty as god mother, and given Abigail the time she needed. She turned to look back at

Marjorie who was also watching.

"Have you finished; can I go home now?"

Marjorie was lost in thought for a moment, as she stared at the two girls disappearing out of sight, and on to Manor Road.

"What? Oh yes...Yes, go home, you are making the place look untidy."

On the corner of Manor Road and out of sight, I stopped and leaned against the wall. I was shaking from head to foot, and my heart was pounding, and I was finding it hard to breathe. "Wait a moment Birch, my heart is coming out of my chest, I think I am having a heart attack."

I held my hand close to my chest, feeling like my throat was going to restrict and suffocate me, I leaned forward and put my hands on my knees and tried to breathe. Birch crouched down and took my hand.

"It is alright Deads, it is just a mild panic attack, squeeze my hand, I am here and I am not leaving, just breathe." I pulled the air in and out of my lungs, I desperately wanted to cry.

"I am so sorry, I really am sorry, I don't want to be like this Birch." I felt the tears welling in my eyes, and squeezed them closed.

"I was fine, honestly, all year I have been fine, I should never have done it, I should have stayed as I was."

I felt Birch's hands on my shoulders, as she lifted me upright, and before I could blink, she was around me, pulling me close and tight. Her breasts pressed into me, and her hand on the back of my head pushed me into her shoulder, and just feeling her warmth, her love, was simply too much, and the tears flowed. Birch spoke very quietly.

"You wonderful sweet girl, what the hell have they done to you, to end up like this? Come on, let it all out, you cannot let that live inside you."

I hated myself for crying, but I just could not stop as I buried my head in her shoulder, and felt it erupt out of me like a volcano.

"This is good Deads, you must let it all out and take the pressure down. I am sorry, I never realised it was this bad before, but please have no fear, I am with you, and I am here for the Summer. We will do this, we will do it together, and you will be free, I promise you Sweetie."

I am not really sure how long I cried, I felt exhausted when I finally finished. Birch wiped my face, and whipped out her make up, and did a very rapid make over for me. I just stood there, unable to really think or speak, as she took control, watching her green eyes flash as she followed her hand doing the makeup. Every now and again, she would look at me and softly smile, and I saw something deep inside her pupils, and it made me feel calm and relaxed.

"I have never met anyone like you before, do you know that Birch? You really are quite amazing?" She stood up and smiled.

"All done. I have my mum's DNA; it does show on occasion." She looked down into her bag, and dropped her hand inside.

"I have been holding this back, but I think it is time we pulled out the big guns, what say you Sweetie?"

Birch lifted out a bottle of toffee flavoured Vodka, held it up, and smiled. "Sugar rush and Dutch courage enhancer."

I gave a giggle and felt a little better. She unscrewed the cap and took a big swig from the bottle, then handed it over, as her eyes screwed up.

"Here... Wow!"

I lifted the bottle and took a long swig, it entered my mouth, and felt sweet, and yummy. I swallowed and suddenly my body erupted in fire, and I coughed as my eyes closed.

"Jesus Birch." She laughed and winked.

"Not completely sure he would approve, but we need reinforcements, and this stuff feels like it came straight from hell, a bit of bad ass is all we need to move onward, so grab your shit girl, we are about to face Armageddon, come on let's go."

Birch grabbed my hand, turned, and walked off, and all I could do was follow, I felt the fire inside me and a new ray of hope, I had known her for a year, and I thought I had seen it all, but as I walked along at her side, watching her lovely long white hair with patches, sway across her back, I knew there was still a cavern of hidden talent deep within her, and all I could think of was her mum, and her words, and yes, I think it was going to take me a life time to really learn everything about her.

Harriet walked back down the main street; her mind slipped

into the past. For a moment looking at Abby, she had seen
something she had not seen in a very long time. A girl she had
thought she had lost, and yet there she was, unchanged and as
equally determined. It felt painful to remember her, and she gave
a long sad sigh.

She crossed the main street walking slowly, and lit up a
cigarette, and then turned and walked onto Manor Road, towards
her home at number three. Fumbling in her pocket she pulled
out her key, and slipped it into the lock. Just for a moment she
hesitated, and looked back to where Waterside Lane started.

"Seriously Abby, if you even date an accountant, I promise you,
I will drown you in the bloody canal." The door opened, and in
she stepped.

Waterside Lane was where the richest people in the area lived.
The houses are large and set back in large plots of land. Most of
the inhabitants work in London, and are usually something to do
with the financial markets. It took a few seconds to understand
this is where the elite lived, and Birch was really surprised to find
I had grown up here. Things were starting to make more sense
to her, but she was here for one purpose only, support, and she
aimed to do the best she could for her best friend Deadly, and she
had no idea how grateful I was.

High walls were the fashion, gardens the size of parks filled
with trees were in vogue, and electric gates came as standard. I
stopped and looked across the road, Birch stood close.

"Are we here?"

She could feel the tension rising up out of me, as I lifted my arm
and pointed across the lane.

"That's it, the one with the black iron gates. I made it Birch, I
am home, just please stay close, I think the brandy and vodka is
wearing off."

Gripping my arm tightly, she leaned in to me and whispered.

"Come on then let's do this, let's get it over with. Remember
that girl who left here a year ago, she no longer exists, no matter
what they say or what they do, this here at my side, is who you
really are. No one has the right to tell you who you are, or what
you need to be, you can be only you, so go in there and show
them the real Deadly, because Sweetie, if they reject you, it's fine,

you will be living in Uppermill from that moment on. Okay deep breath... Let's do this, and then I say we get drunk to hell, are you in?"

Chapter 5

Transient Watch.

Mrs Perkins peered out of the window from behind her net curtain, her phone pressed close to her ear, as she viewed the two transients in front of her house. One was completely dressed in black, the other wore a long green tie dyed skirt, with a long burgundy top, and had a yellow lace shawl wrapped around her waist as a belt. She whispered into the phone, even though the windows were shut, and no one outside could actually hear her.

"The black one is pointing at Felicity's house; you must let her know to lock all her windows and doors."

Back in the Tea Rooms, Lillian frantically dialled Felicity on her mobile, as Marjorie continued her conversation with Mrs Perkins. Felicity was in her bed room tidying up, when the cordless phone at the side of the bed rang. She crossed the room and picked it up.

"Wotton 591." The voice of Lillian in full panic, blurted down the phone to her.

"Felicity... Felicity, you must lock all your doors and windows, we have transients on your lane, and they are pointing to your house. Hurry and lock everything you have away."

Felicity frowned, and walked over to the window to peer through the nets. She moved back to the side of the window, as she saw the two strangers across the road. She held the phone to her ear.

"It's alright Lillian, everywhere is locked, and I have the security gates."

She peered through the curtains, watching their every move, the one in black moved forward, and the other followed, she let the phone slip from her ear, as she leaned further out to watch. They were coming her way in a diagonal across the lane, and heading right for her gates, she felt the mild panic, and was unsure as how to react. Lillian's voice squealed into the phone down by her waist, Felicity lifted it quickly and heard Lillian.

"You must be calm Felicity, we are going to send help, fear not we are with you, and aid is on the way, so stay calm, they are probably just gypsies selling pegs and fortunes." Felicity nodded feeling reassured, as the two transients reached her gates.

Birch looked at the large heavy iron gates. "Wow you live in a fortress; I take it your dad is richer than I thought, and felt the need to protect his stash?" She chuckled. "So, what now?"

The moment had arrived, and there really was no going back, I took a huge intake of breath and smiled at Birch.

"Too late now, time to face the music." I lifted the small panel on the brick post at the side of the gate, revealing the digital key pad, and pressed the buttons 2-0-0-1. There was a slight buzzing noise, and the large heavy gates gave a sudden shudder.

"OH MY GOD THEY ARE HACKING THE GATES!"
Marjorie turned with a look of abject terror, Lillian felt faint and rocked back on her heels.

"She will be raped, I said it would happen to one of us one day!?"
Lillian's eyes fluttered, as she rocked back, and was caught in the arms of Celia, who grabbed the phone, and lifted it to her ear, as two customers rushed, and grabbed Lillian in her swoon, and guided her to a chair, Celia was deadly serious.

"Felicity darling, listen very carefully, you may not have much time, they have hacked the gates and are coming for you, you have to stall them until we can get someone there, I will not allow a friend of mine to be raped in broad daylight."

Stood alone in her bedroom, and knowing there were transient rapists in the neighbourhood was terrifying. She fumbled the phone away from her ear, and moved back against the wall, clutching the phone with both hands to her chest.

As her breathing increased, her mind swirled at the horror that was about to befall her. She took several deep breaths as she tried to calm herself, somewhere in her chest mumbled words of reassurance, were spoken by Celia, but lost to her ears, when suddenly she heard the clank of the winch on the gate's mechanism, and the familiar squeak as the gates separated. Her heart almost stopped; they were in!

Birch linked me by the arm, and gave me another reassuring smile as the gates separated, and we grabbed the handles of the wheeled suitcases, and took our first step forward. I was so glad just to have her at my side, and even though my stomach was wrenching and reeling with some form of satanic butterfly, just having her with me gave me hope in the knowledge I was not on my own this time.

We were five paces inside, when suddenly my mum's bedroom window burst wide open, and Birch jumped with surprise.

My mother hung out of the widow looking desperate, and red in the face, as she looked at us frantically waving her phone.

"We have no need, sorry, no pegs required, no fortune telling, we have all we need, so on your way you go."

I stared at her in disbelief, she did not even recognise me. We both stood still staring at her as she waved her phone like a lunatic, it was Birch who spoke first.

"Huh!?" Birch looked at me and shrugged.

"Is your mum crazy, and you were just too embarrassed to say so?" I hunched my shoulders, and looked back at my mother.

"Mum... What are you doing?"

I suddenly realised my mistake, in this house mum was a word for the common people, I quickly corrected myself, as I looked at the crazy stare in her eyes. "Mother...What's going on?"

The noise that came for her was a little weird, it kind of sounded like the air rushing out of a balloon, and her eyes opened wider than I have ever seen, and she started to shake slightly, almost like the first tremors of an earthquake to come. Birch sniggered and leaned into me.

"And there it is.... The penny has dropped.... Wait for it."

Her voice was soft and really quiet, I had to strain to hear it, almost as if she was in a trance, and whispering it.

"Abigail... Abigail?" Birch sniggered.

"Oh, look she remembers you?"

I couldn't help but smile, and nudged her in the ribs as she started to giggle, Birch took the lead as always, and lifted her hand to wave.

"Hello Mrs Watson, I am Dead... Abby's friend from university, it's very nice to meet you."

My mum blinked, shuddered, and then as the understanding hit her, she looked up the lane with wild eyes, and then back at me.

"Oh my God they are coming... You must get inside, Abigail hurry... Hurry, they must not see you."

She disappeared through the window like someone had grabbed her legs, and suddenly pulled, and Birch gave another giggle.

"You know what, I think we are in for a fun summer?"

I shook my head, I was feeling the complete opposite, but I was happy that at least Birch had the chance to take notes for her thesis, I pulled at the case, and we headed for the door.

Back in the Tea Rooms Marjorie turned with a satisfied smirk, and looked at Celia, who appeared to be in minor shock and had blurted out.

"Oh heavens, it is Abby."

"I KNEW IT! That Harriet Barker was up to no good, I could smell the deceit on her, that harlot is involved in everything that is indecent in this village."

Celia blinked, and looked at Lillian who had recovered a little.

"Lillian it is Abigail...Oh my, what have those northerners done to her, our precious rose appears to have been... Violated?" Marjorie snatched the phone out of Celia's hand, and lifted it to her ear.

We were half way through the door, and the gates were swung shut behind us, as my mother came tearing down the stair in abject panic. We had no time to say or do anything, as she grabbed us, and frantically pushed us up the hall towards the kitchen.

"You cannot be seen if they get here, for the love of God Abigail, what have you done to us?"

Birch lifted her hands in surrender, and walked quickly in front; our cases remained abandoned just inside the door.

"You must stay out of sight, you cannot be seen, good god what will neighbours be thinking, to see you walk here, looking like that?"

Once in the kitchen mum spun on her heels, and without a word, pulled the door closed behind her with a bang, and she was gone, and we were alone. Birch gave a giggle.

"I will give you this Sweetie, you do not disappoint."

I smiled, but I had been here before, and knew what was to come. It was not that hard to predict, my mother would be in the study peeping through the curtains, making sure the coast was clear, and then would come her eruption. Birch walked round our large spacious kitchen.

"Wow this place is amazing Deads, so what next, coffee, or Toffee V?" She pointed to her large shoulder bag hanging just above her waist. I gave a long sigh, and made my way over towards the kettle.

"Just for now let's play it safe, my mother does not wholly approve of women drinking, unless of course it's sherry with the vicar."

I filled the kettle, Birch lifted her bag, and dropped it on the counter, and walked round having a good look at the kitchen.

"Wow Deads your home is gorgeous, I take it all the cupboards are safe to open, that will be novel?"

She chuckled, and even I had to smile, she walked over to the large folding patio doors, and looked out on the huge garden, complete with very large stone patio, excessive loungers, and of course the full size swimming pool.

"Whoa this place is like a luxury hotel, I thought I had it good, but this is something else. I take it that is the guest house?"

I gave her a nod as I sat down at the breakfast bar, feeling drained.

"I prefer your house, you have a real family in it, and it is not as sterile as this place, this kitchen has always reminded me of a hospital."

I looked round at the room with its pale grey marble floor tiles, white tiled and scrubbed walls, with its off white fittings and cupboards, where everything had a place, and nothing could be seen. It was a vast bright porcelain and marble, clean space, and it felt as unlived in as it always had. Birch turned and leaned back on the glass doors.

"So, while it is quiet, what should I expect?"

It was quiet, in fact I felt it was a little too quiet. I was not really aware of what my mum was up to. I had no idea she was sat on her bed, back on the phone trying to do damage limitation, and smooth things over, because her daughter had brought shame to the family. I looked at Birch, and the kettle rumbled at the side of me.

"Mum will be calling off the dogs." Birch frowned.

"What do you mean?" I sighed.

"Transient alert... Hatty would have stalled them, but these people are as relentless as the rugby team. They will not be happy until what they see as transients, are removed from the village. They have a neighbourhood watch that is more equipped, and better trained than the SAS." She understood.

"So Hatty is a transient?" I shook my head.

"Nope, she is the Village Harlot." Birch leaned off the glass, and walked over as the kettle clicked off.

"That is a bit mean, she is an artist, I have never met one yet that is not free spirited, and as for Harlot, I hate the way the world says women cannot be sexual or enjoy sex. I have watched my mum smash that myth to pieces for years, and it still won't die. Wow this place really is like stepping back in time." I stood up, and reached for the coffee.

"Seriously... You have no idea of what you have walked into, that train was not really a train, it was a time machine back to the past."

I spooned out the coffee into the cups, as I silently counted the seconds in my head. An eruption was coming, and it would not be much longer before the top blew off. I slid the coffee across the counter, and lifted my cup with both hands.

"Thanks Birch, I feel better having you here, but you do not need to stay if it gets too hot, you can go over to the guest house and relax, what is coming will not be nice." She shook her head.

"I am going nowhere Sweetie, in my book your parents and this village are all lab rats, and I aim to study them closely, this shit is awesome for my thesis." I frowned not quite understanding what she meant.

"I thought your thesis was on sexual repression?" She smiled.

"From what I have seen to date, the only person bouncing the bed springs round here is Hatty, she is way to calm to be sexually frustrated, and looking at the faces peering out of the windows of the shops today, I would say a dammed good orgy on that football field you call a green, would possibly loosen the whole village up."

I could not help but smile, she leaned over the counter towards me and whispered. "Hey... When do you think your mum and dad last screwed?"

I burst out laughing, as she smiled a wicked grin, she sat back in her seat and winked.

"Looking at your mum, I bet it's been a long time, I would even bet she has cobwebs down there only Bev could reach."

I exploded with laughter, just the thought activated my fit of giggles, as Birch sat in front of me with her arms crossed, her eyebrows raised, and wearing a very cheeky smile. I wanted to stop, but my belly was wobbling as the giggles rose up, and as hard as I tried to push them down, I could not. Birch sniggered.

"You know my mum has shit loads of tablets to help guys rise at home, I think I will text her to send a few dozen boxes, your dad might thank me for them."

I really wanted not to laugh, but she started with her cackle of a laugh, and I was gone beyond control. Both of us sat there on the edge of Armageddon, waiting to be hung drawn and quartered, laughing hysterically like little girls. The kitchen door burst open, and my mother walked in looking like she was about to murder someone, well actually she was, me. I tried to stop laughing but once I saw her, Birch gave a loud grunt of a snigger, and as hard as I wanted to keep my face straight, I simply couldn't.

I have come to realise that at times talking to Birch is lethal, as she had this weird way of planting little seeds into your brain that germinate. My mother marched across the room like a sergeant going to battle, and stood three feet away glaring at me. I fought to suppress the smile on my lips, as she stood there, arms folded, and legs slightly apart, in a stance of power that I knew well, and all that I could think of, was that was probably the widest her legs had been apart in years. Her stare burned into me, she was really pissed off, and it showed.

"So, you find all this funny, do you?"

I fought the urge to look at Birch, who had her lips locked together, and was fighting the impulse to laugh. I was trying my hardest to hold it in, but could not control my lips. which were in a fixed natural smirk, she was becoming more and more irate, as her arms unfolded and she pointed at my hair.

"Just what exactly is this monstrous mess? Have you any idea of the trouble you have caused young lady, turning up here looking like a gypsy, have you no shame at all?"

I swallowed hard, but before I could say anything, I heard Birch's calm, quiet voice.

"I am sorry Mrs Watson, but how have we caused trouble, all we did was walk from the train station to here, just how exactly is that causing trouble?"

She glared at Birch, but as I have seen her do a thousand times with others, she changed her tone.

"I am sorry young lady, I forgot your name, but what you both fail to see is that here in this village we have standards, admittedly they are higher than in northern towns, which is why we strive to be well raised and conduct ourselves in a manner befitting the likes of the people who live here." Birch gave a nod of understanding.

"So, what you are saying is transients and harlots like me are not welcome here?"

Even I gasped in shock, wow Birch was so direct, and my mother was completely put on the back heel. Birch was so like her own mother, calm, collected and precise, I was in awe. My mother stammered a little.

"I... I ... I would not call you that." Birch sat back in her chair.

"You said we looked like gypsies not two minutes ago, is that different?"

I could see the impatience rising in my mother, she did not lose many fights, and I was sure she was about to bounce back; I felt my teeth clench, as she looked at me and glared.

"You do look like a gypsy, WHAT THE HELL WERE YOU THINKING?"

It was at that moment, she spotted them, and she almost went nuclear. With the speed of a viper, she reached out and grabbed my head with both hands, and dragged me out of my seat, and up to her face.

"OH MY GOD, YOU DYED YOUR EYEBALLS TOO!?" Her face was beetroot, I heard Birch snigger.

"Mother they are not dyed!

"OH MY GOD, YOU TATTOOED THEM?"

Birch sniggered again, I tried to pull my head away, and my mother let go, and lifted her hands to her mouth, and stepped back in utter horror. I took a deep breathe.

"Mother they are not tattooed."

She took another step back looking even more mortified, and shook her head in disbelief, her voice dropped, it was as if she talking to herself.

"I knew it... I knew it."

She stepped further away; it was almost as if I had some sort of contagious disease. I tried to step forward and reach out to her, but she jumped back, and then fell to her knees, shaking her head.

"I warned Edwin it was a risk, I told him, but as usual, he just would not listen."

I had no idea what she was talking about, as she knelt on the floor shaking her head. I took a step forward.

"Mother?" She looked up at me and her eyes glared, and her voice dropped to icy.

"It's drugs isn't it... Oh Abigail please tell me it's not that Crack or... OH MY GOD IT'S HEROIN ISN'T IT?"

Birch sniggered, even louder, and I stood as still as a pillar, trying to understand what had become of the deranged workings of my mother's mind. It came out more as a natural reaction, having spent a year at university in Manchester, as I looked at her in utter disbelief.

"What the fuck Mum? They are black contact lenses, it's not drugs, we would not do that." Birch shrugged sat alone behind us.

"Well a few spliffs here and there, but it was nothing untoward."

My mother's eyes opened wider, and her hands came together almost as if she was praying. I turned to Birch who smiled.

"Not helping Birch." She winked.

"Sorry my bad."

Coldly and quietly, she rose to her feet, and the temperature in the room plummeted. Her voice was sharp, and icy, and her face looked like stone.

"Abigail Jennifer Watson, you will show our guest to her dwelling, then you will go to your room, and stay there until your father returns. We will then debate what has happened, and get to the bottom of this monstrosity of a dress code. I have already arranged for Delphine to pay a house call, where your monstrously ugly hair will be fixed back to its natural state, and you can remove those abominations from your eyes. This is not University, in this house there are rules, and you will follow them. I will speak with your father later, and look into how to arrange a transfer to a more suitable and reputable institution. Am I quite clear?"

I have no idea where it came from, was it the Brandy and the Vodka mixing, was it a life time of oppression, was it just having Birch close by? I really had no idea, but I knew in that second that my year of fighting to find myself was not going to waste. I looked my mother right in the eye and gritted my teeth.

"I am nineteen, and you have no frigging right to control my life any more, just because you threw your own life away, you are not destroying mine. I AM QUITE CLEAR MOTHER!?"

She took two steps back, and I honestly thought she was going to faint; her gasps came out with her words.

"I have never been spoken to in such a way ever!" It was as if the air had run completely out of her.

Birch gripped my arm lightly, and looked at my mum with a confused look. "Seriously... Wow Mrs Watson, now that actually does surprise me."

Birch led the way, as my whole body boiled into numbness, she guided me through the door and down the hall. I felt numb, but elated, never in my life had spoken so forcefully to anyone, my world exploded in my head, what the hell had I done? Birch squeezed my arm.

"Well done you... Are you alright?" I was slightly dazed.

"I think so... I am so sorry."

"Nothing to apologise for, I think you stood your ground wonderfully... So how big is the bed in the guest house?"

"Huh?" She smiled.

"Double or single?" My mind was blank.

"Double I think." She smiled.

"Okay, you are sleeping with me, just don't tell Bev, she will never forgive me." I smiled.

We got our things, and Birch guided me out of the front door, and round through the side gates, across the garden and into the guest house. She sat me down on the large king sized bed, and then went into the tiny kitchen area for a couple of glasses.

Digging around in her bag she pulled out the toffee vodka and poured two good measures, then reaching into her bag she lifted out a can of lemonade, opened it, and poured it into the two glasses.

I sat on the bed trying to find the right words, I was at a loss, Birch handed me the glass.

"Don't talk, just drink, we are living the gypsy lifestyle, just us two harlots together. Don't sweat it Sweetie, when the time is right the words will come." I stared at the glass, and felt the tears forming in my eyes, Birch softly smiled. "Tears are good too."

Chapter 6

History in the Present.

For the second time that day, the sounds of arriving text messages echoed across the village green. The gossip network had been fully activated, and was in full swing, as Marjorie went to work with Lillian and Celia. It had not taken too much to work out that the female dressed in all black, was in fact Abigail, and Marjorie intended to capitalise on this latest scandal, and use it to her advantage against her greatest rival in the village.

Sat alone at home on her bed, unaware that Marjorie was at work doing her best to stay ahead in the game, Felicity picked up the phone, wiped away her tears, and dialled the private internal number of her husband. It rang for almost a minute before Edwin picked up the phone and answered.

"Felicity, I hope this is important, I am about to go into a very important meeting."

His voice was as always, calm, aloof, and devoid of all emotion. She felt the tears build up in her eyes, and pulled the tissue box with a frilly cover closer to her.

"Oh Edwin, everything is awful, I am not sure how to tell you, but Abigail has come home with her friend, and everyone in the village has seen her."

Edwin felt impatient, he noted his secretary gathering his notes for the next meeting through the window. His tone was very matter of fact.

"Well I would hardly say that is a reason to disturb me, I mean the whole dammed village has watched her grow up, they must have seen her a million times to date."

Felicity was struggling internally to control her emotions, she knew how he hated emotional outbursts, but how was she to tell him that their whole family had been shamed in front of the entire village? Her tears flowed even faster, and she felt everything inside was building to an exploding point.

"You do not understand, it is how she looks. Oh Edwin she has changed."

He could see his secretary point to her watch, and he was close to being late, something he absolutely hated.

"Felicity, can we not discuss this when I get home, I hardly think she has changed so much, she could offend an entire village. Don't you think you are being a tad overdramatic?"

His secretary shook her wrist at him, displaying the watch he had bought her for Christmas last year. It was just too much for Felicity to hear, Abigail had turned on her with a devastating effect, and it had been simply too much for her handle, and she needed someone to care. Her pain, anger, frustration, just came from nowhere.

"SHE LOOKS LIKE MORTICA ADDAMS, AND HER FRIEND LOOKS LIKE GRANNY MUNSTER, YOU ARE NOT HERE, YOU HAVE NOT SEEN HER!"

Edwin stumbled a little and looked at his phone.

"I beg your pardon?"

"Edwin, she has black hair, her eyes are also black, and she is here with a white haired transient type, AND THEY BOTH HAVE NIPPLES!"

"Pardon?"

He looked out of his window, and waved his secretary to come into his office.

"Felicity just give me a second."

He covered the mouth piece of the phone, as his secretary entered the room.

"Angela dear, I have a small issue of a domestic nature about my daughter, could you just let them know I will be along shortly, give them some coffee or tea, this won't take a minute." He put the phone back to his ear. "Felicity, for Pete's sake get a grip will you, every woman has nipples, what did you expect, they are both young women?"

Felicity lifted another tissue and tried to wipe her eyes.

"You do not understand, you never do, I can see them clearly through their clothing, and they are moving." He frowned at the phone.

"What the hell are you blabbering on about, of course they move they are flesh for Pete's sake."

"THEY ARE BOTH BRALESS, AND THAT FRIEND OF HERS HAS A STAR OF SATAN ROUND HER NECK, AND THEY WALKED THROUGH THE VILLAGE TODAY, AND MARJORIE SAW THEM. DO YOU UNDERSTAND ME NOW?"

"Oh my god… did Ronald, Peter, and Colin see her?"

"YES, YOU BLATHERING IDIOT, THE WHOLE VILLAGE SAW HER!"

"What about the Vicar?"

Felicity took a long deep breath, and tried to compose herself, she took another long intake of air, and then lowered her tone.

"Edwin our daughter and her friend, got on a train this morning and took a four hour train journey. They arrived in the village, walked from the station to our home, and for the entire time her breasts were clearly visible through her shirt to everyone she met, do you now understand why this is a catastrophe? Whether the vicar was one of them or not, is somehow irrelevant, if he didn't, everyone else did?

"BLOODY HELL FELICITY, WHY DIDN'T YOU STOP HER?"

"Edwin she was supposed to arrive tomorrow, how could I, when I did not bloody well know she was coming today, for god's sake man keep up with me."

He shook his head trying to contemplate the idea that every living man in Britain, had free access to his daughter's breasts, to say the least, he was appalled. Felicity gave a sob.

"She shouted at me too."

It was simply too much for him to deal with. "She did?" Felicity answered with a feeble voice, and then burst into tears and wailed into the phone.

"She has never shouted at me like that before, but she positively screamed at me, oh Edwin I am sat in my room and don't know what to do."

His tone became more the cool, calm, tone she was used to.

"Leave this to me Felicity. Look I have to go, I have a very important meeting, which is worth a lot of money to us. I will get through it as fast I can, and then get away as quickly as possible, where is Abigail now?"

"She is in the guest house with her friend, and for all I know, they are on their knees praying to Satan."

He gave a long sigh, as he saw his secretary returning looking anxious.

"Leave her there for now, you have a little sleep, it will make you feel much better, and I will deal with this when I get home. I am quite sure a few prayers will not make that much of a difference to the horned god. Alright I have to go; I am already three minutes late."

He did not even say goodbye, he just terminated the call, and Felicity heard the long tone through the receiver. She clicked the button and the phone went quiet, then sat on the bed, and burst into yet more tears.

Birch looked at Abigail fast asleep on the bed. "Poor lamb you are exhausted."

She picked up the empty glass from where she had dropped it, and placed it on the unit at the side of the bed. Carefully lifting her, she slipped her top up and over her head, and then folded it neatly. Moving to the bottom of the bed, she leaned over, gripped the waistband of her skirt, and then pulled it down her legs, and slipped it off. She stood back and gave a soft smile, and she looked at Abigail out cold in just her black lacy panties.

"What a rough and bloody awful day for you."

Pulling the duvet over from the other side of the bed to cover her, she walked into the other room, and picked up her laptop, which she set up on the small table by the window, and switched it on. The laptop came to life and she waited, entered the password, then allowed it to boot up fully.

A few moments later, with her own glass refilled, she clicked the video call button, and then clicked on the icon for her mother, the familiar ring tone played, and then her mother's image appeared smiling at her from her office at home.

She gave a big smile. "Hey mum."

"A call this soon must not be good news, how is she?"

Harriet sat at home in her garden with a worn-out sketch pad, and looked at her drawings from many years ago, where a woman of extreme beauty stood in a pose in her studio.

"My god you were pretty Flick, what the hell happened?" Her phone gave a long bleep.

"Oh god, not another message from that bible thumping witch?"

Harriet had ways of making sure she knew everything Marjorie was sending out to the rest of the village.

She picked it up and stroked the screen up, and was a little surprised to see the name Flick. She opened the message and read it. 'I need you.'

It was not like it was completely unexpected, she had sat there for hours waiting for some response, she hit the small dialogue box, and started to type. 'Canal, ten minutes, usual spot.' Then she hovered her finger over the button, and gave a long sigh before lowering it, and pressed send, as she muttered to herself.

"I am a better friend than you deserve, I hope you realise that Flick?"

Birch sat back in her seat watching her mother on the laptop. Veronica was thinking about all she had been told by her daughter.

"What is her father like?" Birch shrugged.

"Not met him yet, her mum just threatened her with the wait until your father gets home line." Her mother gave a nod.

"From the little she has spoken about him, which let's be honest is very telling, I would say looking at the fact he has London offices and works in finance, he is probably money driven and power mad, which can only mean one thing." Birch gave a nod.

"Control freak?" Her mum smiled.

"No doubt about it, I would say you will see some narcissistic traits, and if he is as cold as you think he is with his wife, well I think it is highly likely he is banging his secretary, or at least someone he works with, it does fit the type don't you think?" Birch gave a nod.

"Not sure Deads could handle knowing that if he was, especially at the moment." Her mother completely understood.

"Jemi darling just remember, when he gets there, you must under no circumstances leave her completely alone with him. If I am right, he will control himself better with an audience, so stay high visibility. I think that will actually create a space for dialogue between them, and if she starts to struggle, chip in and help her out. She is such a lovely girl, I really like her, and I think she is good for you too. This is great stuff for your thesis, I hope you are making lots of notes?" Birch smiled.

"Not made too many yet, it has been a bit frantic and I am really tired, but I will." Her mum smiled.

"Good girl, okay, look I have a client in ten, so keep me up to date, and I will send you those things, and we will talk soon, give Deads my love and hug from Bev, I love you darling."

"Love you too mum."

The call ended and Birch sat back, as the screen returned to the menu. She closed the lid and then stood up, and walked into the room where Abigail was still sound asleep. She lifted her top and pulled it over her head, and then pulled down her skirt, revealing her naked body, then she slid onto the bed at the side of Abigail, and closed her eyes. It had been a long day of traveling, and she yawned, finally the booze was taking effect.

Two hundred yards past the bottom of Manor Road, where it met with the main street, there was a bridge under which ran the canal. A few minutes' walk down the tow path, the wall moved back, creating a small paved space, into which a bench had been placed bearing a brass plaque, carrying the name of Alice Barker.

It had been placed there by the Parish Council in memory of Harriet's mother, who spent many years fund raising for the Church Restoration Fund, on behalf of the W.I.

Harriet sat on the back of the bench with her feet on the seat smoking, as she watched Felicity pace up and down the pathway.

"Come on Flick, what did you expect?" Felicity spun on the spot.

"Well not that... You have seen her, how could she?"

Harriet flicked her cigarette, and then took another drag of it, she breathed out watching the smoke flow into the air.

"Yeah, how bloody inconsiderate of her, she has no right growing up, and finding a place in this world where she can just be herself." Felicity gave her a stern stare.

"Your sarcasm is not appreciated, thank you very much."

"You used to love it before you married that drip, hell you once swore like a sailor, and had the tongue of a whiplash. You learned the hard way to stand your ground and didn't let anyone put you down, what the fuck has happened to you Flick?" She gave a frustrated snort.

"We have done this too many times, when are you going to

stop?"

Harriet took a long pull on her cigarette, and flicked the last part of the stub into the water.

"When you start listening to me, like you used to."

Felicity watched the cigarette stub float on the water.

"You do realise that is littering?" Harriot shook her head.

"Yeah, Madge informed me earlier today, my god Flick can you hear yourself, because I am not sure your aware, but you are starting to sound like her?" She scowled at Harriet.

"That is not true… And it is hurtful." Harriet gave a nod.

"Maybe." She paused for a second, and she looked at the bench where her feet rested. Her voice lowered.

"I will tell you what is hurtful Flick." Felicity looked at her and snapped back.

"What exactly?"

Harriet lifted her head, and there were tears in her eyes, just for a moment it caught Felicity completely off guard.

"I walked out of a shop today, and walked right into a young girl, dressed in the most amazing Gothic dress. Her hair, her makeup, her stance, just blew me away, because there right in front of me was a girl I knew better than anyone. You see she was my best friend, and I loved her with all my heart, and she left me, and yet there she was again right in front me, exactly as I remembered her. It was like she just stepped out of the 1970's to greet me, but it wasn't my best friend, was it?" The tears rolled down her face, and Felicity felt a lump in her throat.

"Please Hatty don't do this, I am not sure my heart can take anymore."

Harriet gave a sniffle and wiped her face on her sleeve, she looked up with red damp eyes.

"She is you; she is exactly the same, just as beautiful and just as determined, and filled with an abundance of life. Yes, she is your daughter, but hell Flick, I almost had a heart attack, she had black hair and heavy dark makeup on her eyes, and there was no way on earth anyone would recognise her, but I did. I caught the tiniest glimpse of her as she passed, but I knew in an instant. Christ Flick, she is your double." Harriet gave a snort, as more tears rolled from her eyes.

"I went home broken hearted, because I knew this was coming,

I knew that cold fish of a husband would break her the way he did you. I sat in my garden, and I cried my eyes out for her, because she had to go all that distance away from you two, just so she had enough space to breath, and discover the truth of who she is."

Felicity shuffled her feet, and she looked at Harriet with tearful eyes.

"This is so not fair, it isn't Hatty, I given my all for her, this is not fair, you should know better than to bring all the past up to beat me with." Harriet sniffled and nodded her head.

"I agree with you, it isn't fair, but this is not about the past is it Flick? This is about Abby, it is about now, and who she is, and what her future will be. For Christ's sake Flick, she is only nineteen, she has her whole life ahead of her, and just as she takes her greatest step forward, you have dragged her back, just like you always have. Flick you are forty nine years old, two years on from me and look at you. Honestly tell me, is this what you want for her?" Felicity frowned.

"Just what exactly is wrong with me, I do my bit to stay fit?" Harriet gave a long sigh.

"I hate to say this, but these days you are acting a good thirty years older than me." Felicity looked enraged, she lifted her finger and wagged it her.

"Now just you steady on, there is no call to get personal."

"Isn't there? You should ask your daughter the same question, because I would say that what you said to her today was beyond personal. Face it Flick, you full on attacked every aspect of her looks, have you forgotten, Amanda Drinkwater?"

Felicity gasped, and her voice rose several octaves higher.

"I cannot believe you would even dare to bring her up in a conversation with me, how could you Hatty, you know how she made my life a misery?"

"I remember her well, I see her occasionally, she lives near the school in Oxendale. I remember her taunts at poor frail Felicity Montgomery, and how she ridiculed your hair for dying it black, and laughed at your heavy dark eye makeup and mascara, do you remember the name she called you, do you?" Felicity put her head down.

"I hate you at times, I really do, you never fight fair." Hatty shrugged.

"Well not with her I didn't, she was a tough bitch. What did she used to shout before I took her teeth out with a hockey stick? Oh yeah that was it."

"I mean it Hatty, stop!"

"Monstrously Abominable Montgomery, that was it wasn't it?"

Hatty slipped off the bench and came up close to her, as Felicity stared at her with horror in her eyes. She lowered her voice to a soft loving tone.

"Flick, you looked at your stunningly beautiful daughter, and you said those very same words today. Hell, after all you went through, all that pain and despair, and yet here we are thirty years on, and you became that rancid bitch because your daughter has done exactly the same thing you did."

"STOP IT... I MEAN IT HATTY... JUST STOP IT!"

Hatty slipped out her arms and embraced her tight pulling her close, and Felicity burst into tears.

"I didn't mean it, honestly I didn't mean it Hatty, she is everything to me, you know that." She gave a sigh.

"I didn't mean it, how familiar. She said that too when I took her teeth out, or at least I think she did, it wasn't easy to understand through the slurs and spitting she did." Felicity wailed in Hatty's embrace.

"God forgive me, I didn't mean it." Hatty gave a soft nod.

"You know that, and I know that, maybe you should make sure Abby knows it too. I think you need to face the facts Flick, and you two need to sit and actually talk, instead of shouting at each other."

Harriet Barker, stood on the tow path of the canal with her best and oldest friend, held tightly in her arms, as she wailed into her shoulder. It was a scene not unlike one earlier that day, where Birch held Abigail equally as tight.

It took a good ten minutes before Felicity was calm enough to talk again, and together they walked back down the path towards the bridge, and the steps back up to the road. Felicity looked at Harriet as they reached the road.

"I am sorry Hatty." She looked at her and smiled.

"Yeah, me too, I hate falling out." Felicity gave a nod of understanding.

Side by side they walked along the road to the corner of Manor Road, and turned. It was a short walk up towards Waterside Lane, where they stopped, it was almost 7:30pm. Felicity took a deep breath.

"I hate you when you are always right." Harriet shrugged.

"Me too, I am supposed to be the fucked up one." She gave a giggle.

"You know how much I love you Hatty, I mean you do know?" Harriet smiled and nodded.

"BFF... Bolshy friends forever, I have not forgotten. Will you be alright?" She gave a nod.

"I have a lot to think about, and more to do, but yes, I will, as always be fine."

"You should get some sleep." She gave a slight chuckle.

"That was Edwin's advice too." Harriet grinned.

"Then stay awake, you know where I am if you need me?" She turned and crossed the road.

Felicity took another deep breath, and then walked up Waterside Lane towards home. When she arrived at the house, the gates were open, and Edwin stood by the car holding his brief case and several files of papers. She looked at him as she approached, he carried his familiar unphased appearance, she was exhausted, and did not want any more trouble, his eyes followed her as she walked to the door.

"Well?" She put the key in the door and then looked back.

"Well what?" He blinked.

"Good grief Felicity, Abigail of course?" She gave a long sigh.

"We need to talk Edwin." He nodded as he stood there by the car holding his papers.

"Well damn right we do, we cannot have our daughter running wild and looking like a freak, what on earth will everyone say?"

Felicity turned round, as the door swung open, and faced him.

"Edwin, we need to talk, but not to Abigail, leave her alone with her friend for tonight. Have you eaten?" He nodded.

"I had something at work."

Felicity said nothing, she walked into the house leaving Edwin to lock the car, and then head for his study as normal.

Harriet turned at her door and looked back, but Felicity was out of sight.

"Maybe I should show Edwin how good I am with a hockey stick; he could then compare notes with Amanda." She gave a slight chuckle, and then her door opened, and she stepped in.

Chapter 7

Girls Talk.

It felt strange to wake up in a double bed, with Birch naked, and curled around me, in a strange room. Actually, it was not really a strange room, I have always known it as 'Grannies Room,' but in my time away, it had been decorated and remodelled. I wriggled free of Birch's grasp of my right boob, and then lifted her leg off me, so I could slide to the edge of the bed and sit.

My head felt fuzzy, and my insides unsettled, it somehow felt unfair, how many of the people I know at University have gone home today, to be warmly embraced by their mother's and father's? Not me that was for sure?

I stood up stretching, my whole body ached like I had been in a fight, well I had, just not a physical one, and yet my limbs felt the same. Was this the stress that attacks the body that Birch is always writing about? I did not know, but it had certainly been stressful, of that I had no doubt. I walked into the living area, the sun was still up, and the clock read 20:15, I had been asleep for four hours. I stopped on route to the toilet.

"Dad finishes work and is home by half seven, where is he?"

I felt my bladder throb, dad could wait, peeing was far more important. I hurried into the small side bathroom, and just about got my panties down in time, before my bladder erupted.

I feel there is a certain joy in sitting on the toilet, or so I discovered in that moment, just relaxing and letting the flood gates open felt somehow therapeutic. I leant forward just letting the long stream do its own thing, as I contemplated the thought, maybe I should talk to Birch, she may find it to be some new way to relive stress. I started to chuckle, as a vivid image of squatting women in a field came to mind, all screaming out their anxiety, whilst urinating, maybe I was on to something?

I turned to the roll holder. "Oh Shit!"

There was no loo roll, I looked round the bathroom, at the small bath and sink, nope nothing. The door was open, and there on the unit at the side of the small flat screen TV was a box of tissues. I stood up, my panties still round my ankles, and shuffled like an escaped convict in leg irons towards it. I grabbed a tissue, opened my legs and began to wipe.

"What ya doin?"

I looked up to see Birch stood in the doorway leaning on the frame.

"What does it look like?" Could she not see, I am sure every woman alive wipes like this? She gave a sigh and walked into the room.

"God Deads, if you are going to masturbate, lie on a bed with your legs wide open, and take your knickers off for god's sake, don't do it in front of the window." She walked through to the toilet.

"Huh?"

I looked to the right, and I was right in front of the window in full view.

"Holy Shit!"

I quickly shuffled back towards the toilet, where Birch was sat down, and having a similar experience to my earlier one. She smiled with delight as I stood in the doorway watching, yep, me and her were very alike, and somehow that mattered, I pondered sharing my theory.

"Sweetie I love you, but watching is making me anxious, it's sort of screwed up don't you think?"

"What... Oh shit.... Sorry!"

I turned around still holding the damp tissue, I noted her flow increased, maybe my new theory had flaws that would need ironing out first, before bringing it up with Birch? The flow behind me stopped.

"Oh Bollocks."

"What's wrong?"

"No loo rolls."

"Yeah, I know."

"Well?" I turned to face her.

"Well what?" She smiled.

"May I have a tissue to wipe please, I have no wish to do it in front of the window like some people I know?"

"Oh crap, I meant to bring them in here."

I turned, and did my convict escape walk back across the room towards the tissue box.

"REALLY!... Deads take your bloody knickers off." I looked down and smiled.

"Oh yeah."

I lifted my right leg and shook it free of my panties, then walked back to Birch as she chuckled at me, and I handed her the box.

"Thank you, Sweetie."

The toilet flushed, and Birch came out of the room, she pressed her stomach.

"I need food."

I heard the groan within her from the other side of the room. I looked out of the window towards the house.

"Mum has probably put some stuff in the cupboards for us, although she prides herself on cooking at meal times, it is odd that she hasn't."

I picked up my phone, I had several texts, I saw one from Hatty, and tapped it open. 'The word is out your home. I talked to your mum, you did better than I thought. Talk to her Abbs, she is not your enemy, even if it feels that way.' There was another text from her, and I opened it and read. 'P.S. I still think your dad is a prick, be careful xx' I laughed as Birch leaned over to see what I was reading.

"Still no love lost there then?" I shook my head.

"She really hates him." I closed the message and saw a text that surprised me from 'Deb's'

Debbie Wheeler was my high school friend, actually she was the only real friend I had in school. She had lived in Oxendale on the council estate until her mum remarried, and she now lived on the same lane as me, just farther up. Her step dad was pretty rich, so when he married a girl from the council estate, there was to say the least, a lot of objectionable comments in the village.

Debbie had a rough time at school, as many of the girls in the village bullied her, I defended her a few times, and the sad thing was, she was a really clever girl. Her step dad, adored her and treated her really well, as she did him, her real dad was a real jerk. At home or my house, she was happy, but everywhere else growing up in the village, she hated.

I opened the message and read. 'Is it all true, are you home and shameful, I hope so?'

I had to smile as I read it, she was really down to earth and understood village life as well as I did. I clicked the dialogue box, and began to type. 'It's all true, I am to be burned at the stake after church tomorrow x.' I pressed send.

My phone started to ring and I swiped up, and put it to speaker phone for Birch to listen. "Hey you."

"Oh my god... Oh my god you really did it, you are the talk of the village, you are now equal to Harriot in status. I am of course completely delighted, and offer you my hearty congratulations."

Birch gave a smile as she pulled her case into the room, and lay it flat on the floor and opened it, she looked at me.

"I like this girl." Debbie's voice came back through the phone.

"Is someone with you?" I realised she could hear everything.

"Yeah, it is my friend from Uni, she is called Birch, we have you on speaker."

"Oh right, Hi Birch, so I take it you are the green witch that was walking with Abby? Gotta say, love the name, it sounds all earthy."

"She is Deb's, I think you and her will really get on."

"Hey what are you two doing, I was going to book at Pemberton's, it's a bit slow there tonight, you guys want to join me?"

I looked at Birch, my stomach had just twisted again, I could not deny, I was not in a rush to head into the village so soon. I had sort of planned laying low for a while. Birch appeared to understand, but there again, I knew her, and how much she stood up for who she was, I was apprehensive as I looked at her.

"What do you think Birch?"

She was holding up a pair of pants, she put them back on the case, and looked at me with those bright green eyes, and before she spoke, I think I already knew her thoughts.

"Honestly, it's up to you, but I am not one to hide Deads, if it was me, I would walk out proud, and not hang my head, so why put yourself down for them, you are who you want to be, so own it like you did earlier?"

I turned back to the phone, although my heart had begun to race a little.

"Okay we are in, what time do you want us there?" A wild screech came from the other end of the phone.

"Okay I will ring them now and book us in at 9:30, it's open till one, so we will have bags of time, it's curry night is that okay? Don't worry about getting there, Dad just said he will pick you up, and drop us off, oh wow this is going to be fantastic, I have so many things I want to ask."

I could not help but laugh, as I heard her excitement, it really felt like she had not changed since school.

"What you going to wear Debbie?"

"No idea... You are not going to dress down are you, oh god I hope you won't give in to them?" Birch leaned over to the phone.

"Oh, Sweetie, it is beyond us. It is my first night out here, so as tradition states clearly in the females guide to University, it's tight pants, tits out, and boots up, are you game?"

Another loud squeal of laughter came from the other end of the phone.

"I cannot wait, I shall grab you in twenty, okay?"

The phone cut off, as Debbie ended the call, and I sat back and looked at Birch.

"She is really sweet, but she has to live here remember, we don't, well only for summer, and then we head back for another year."

Birch stood up, and slipped on her black satin pants, then stopped, and looked back at me.

"Look Sweetie, you had a chance to make your own choice, you did it because you were around someone who gave you the space and support to do it. What if Debbie is looking to you to do the same for her? I sort of got the feeling you have done something she has never dared to do alone, and maybe; you will be the example that drives her towards exploring herself."

Up until that moment I had never thought of it that way, I had never realised Birch had been aware of that part of me. I cannot deny for almost a year I had admired her openness and bravery, and to a degree, it was because of her, I had found the strength to finally be myself.

Deb's had always been excited when I had talked about who I wanted to be, and what I wanted to do with my life, but never for a moment, had I thought she had the same dreams too. It was quite a surprising revelation. I sat pondering it as a pair of black satin pants hit me in the face.

"Stop thinking and start dressing. Those pants and this scandalous top should do the trick. Go with the red eye makeup, I have always thought it brought out the blue in your eyes, no contacts tonight, we are not hiding, we are flying the freak flag with pride."

"Thanks Birch." She held up two pairs of boots.

"No problems Sweetie, now what do you think, I think, black leather prostitute boots... Agree? After all I want the glamourous hooker look tonight?"

I could not help but giggle, I have no idea how I would survive without her, and I am sure she had no idea of how special she was to me.

The change was frantic, as we raced against the clock, but when the message came, she was on her way, we were ready, well just about. I looked in the mirror with red surrounded eyes, to match the tips of my hair, and I cannot lie, if I was gay, I would Defo sleep with me too.

Birch as always, had booze, I had forgotten her traveling liquor stash, which she had in the bottom of her case. Gin was out of the question, no mixers left, so she opened a large bottle of Southern C, and we took a straight double, screwed up our eyes, had a little shake, and we were ready.

We fell out the door laughing, and I noticed my dad stood at the patio doors, as we walked up the garden, deep inside my stomach churned, but with Birch at my side I continued to walk straight, he opened the door as I approached the side gate.

"Abigail... Can I have a moment?" I carried on walking.

"Hi Daddy... Sorry we are off to meet Debbie, and we are running a little behind, got to dash, oh this is Birch by the way." She waved.

"Good evening Mr Watson, thanks for letting me stay, your guest house is beautiful."

I walked right past the side of the house, through the side gate, and headed for the metal front gates without looking back, Birch smiled all the way.

Debbie was stood at the gates; her dad was in the car with the engine running. She squealed again when she saw me, and as soon as the gates parted, she was inside and wrapped around me in a suffocation hug.

"You have no idea how excited I am to see you." Birch chuckled.

"I think the squeals gave you away somewhat." She moved to Birch, and gave her a hug too.

"Wow you guys look amazing, I did my best, what do you think?"

She stood back and gave a twirl. Debbie was wearing tight black jeans, which did show the shape of her bum off very well indeed, she also wore a long black silk top, and had put heavy mascara on her eyes, which matched well with her long flowing wavy brown hair. Birch gave an appreciative nod.

"Nice boobs, and good butt, you're in the club."

She beamed with masses of excitement, and held her hand to her mouth and whispered.

"I am not wearing knickers, it's my first time ever!" Birch smiled

"Well done you, walking on the wild side." Deb's beamed with pride.

The drive was not that far, the restaurant was over near the station, so it was a short trip, which entailed Deb's sat sideways in the front seat, looking back at us in the back, saying things like, 'I think you look cool,' and, 'I am so thrilled you did it' over and over.

There were several selfies of her pointing the camera to catch us in the shot, which she assured me were going on 'Insta tonight.' Until finally we made it, and the car pulled in, and we piled out on to the pavement outside the restaurant. I took a deep breath, the place did not look too full, so prepared for my debut as 'Village Freak' mark two, after all, Harriet was still the crown holder.

Deb's said goodbye to her dad, and let him know she would walk back, and we turned to enter, when her father's voice came from inside the car.

"Abigail, have you got a second?"

It came as a surprise, as I stopped in my tracks, and turned to see him leaning over the passenger seat. He gave me a smile as I bent down, unaware of my loose top and showing the depth of my bosom.

"I just wanted to say, good one, I think you look absolutely stunning." He winked and looked down my top.

I have no idea why, but I felt my cheeks burn, and a jolt of happiness ran through me. I could not deny, I was afraid inside, because I have seen in my life how horrible this village can be to people who are not like them, but Mr Wheeler was one of them. Actually, he was one of the richest, and largest property owner in the area, and that counted for more than he realised to me. I stumbled a little in my surprise.

"Thank you, that means a lot." He sat up straight.

"Don't let them break you Abigail, stay your course, it is the right one for you. Let me know if your dad gives you a hard time. I know Edwin of old, I am a very large account holder, I can... Let me say, apply pressure where needed if you need it." He gave another wink. "Have fun, it's your first night of freedom, see you soon."

He drove off to turn at the station, and return home, and we all waved him goodbye. The three of us stood there looking like a hooker's convention in the eyes of the village, but we were smiling. Birch as always was taking note, she looked at Deb's at her side.

"I like your dad, he is pretty cool, I bet he is good in bed too. A guy with a twinkle in his eye like that one, you know he has what it takes to please a woman."

Deb's went bright red, and I laughed and grabbed her hand.

"That's Birch, don't worry, you will get use to her."

We turned, and all of us entered the restaurant, which had a nice hum of conversation, until we stepped inside, and total silence descended.

On entering the establishment, we were met by Chole, youngest daughter of the restaurant owner, Derek Pemberton. She was my age, I remembered her from school, because I gave her a black eye for picking on Deb's when I was sixteen, and got grounded for six weeks.

Like most things in this village, she had not changed at all, she was as snooty as ever, and plastered in makeup with eyebrows that had possibly cost her the price of a side of beef. She looked me up and down, so there was no change there, and then announced.

"Oh, it's Abigail, I am sorry, I hardly recognised you." I smiled, hating the bitch, as much as I always had.

"Whereas you have not changed a bit, well your eyes are back to being the same colour I see?"

She pursed her mouth and inhaled. She turned as Deb's sniggered.

"Table at the back out of sight, was it?" Birch stepped up at her side.

"We like dark corners, but I think that one there is more suited to us, not high profile, but everyone should have a reasonable view if they crane their necks... Thanks Chloe." We followed her down the room towards the back, and the seats Birch had picked out.

Like everything in the village, Pemberton's reflected the people who lived around it. It was highly tasteful, with the right décor, the right curtains, just the perfect vase with flowers on each perfectly laid table and so on, I was starting to find it all quite irritating, was there nothing in this village not quite in vogue and out of place? Oh, I forgot, I guess that would be me.

We had a corner seat, which actually I was a little bit relived about. I sat in the corner, Deb's sat with her back to the other customers, and Birch as always sat so she had a full view of everyone in the room. Chole delivered the menu, and Birch went straight to work ordering drinks, and a bottle of wine.

I was really nervous at first, I could see the other customers were staring, and there were a lot of silent conversations going on. Birch led the conversation with Deb's, who appeared to be far more excitable when alcohol was added.

There was an influx of people as our meal arrived, and I could have been wrong, but it felt like the word was out around the village, and people had starting flocking here just to see the villages latest attraction. I did a quick check on Instagram, and discovered the truth of the matter, Chole had taken a picture of me secretly and posted a big 'OMG Guess who just walked in' hashtag, with my name next to it.'

I will not deny, I was upset, I felt the pang inside, and slid back into the corner, Birch's hand came across the table to mine, and she softly held it. She was looking up the restaurant, her eyes fixed on the now full seats and quietly spoke.

"Sit up, and don't let them get to you, they came for a show, let's make sure they get one."

Birch turned to me. "Have your camera ready Deads, pay back is a bitch."

"What?" She winked.

Chloe came out of the kitchen door with a tray full of meals, and as quick as a flash, Birch gripped the edge of the table, and quickly lifted herself slightly up, then slid out her leg. The tray lurched, Chloe staggered, and then went head first to the floor.

There was a horrendous crash, Deb's screamed and brought her hands to her mouth, and the whole place fell instantly silent, as Chloe turned on the floor, her white blouse covered in hot food and curry. Birch was standing, and my heart was half way to cardiac arrest. Chloe's face burned bright red, as Birch took a step forward, and offered her hand, Chloe stared at her with hate.

"YOU DID THAT ON PURPOSE!"

One or two sniggers could be heard mixed in the silence, as Birch leaned over her. I was lost for words, half way between heart failure and laughter. I tried so hard, but it was impossible not to smirk, as Deb's turned to me still holding her phone, with her camera app open, her eyes wide and her mouth open. The door swung open as Birch grabbed Chloe by the wrist, and pulled her off the floor, Mr and Mrs Pemberton came in followed by their other older daughter Edwina. Birch was all apologies.

"I am so sorry, I was just getting up to go to the ladies, and I never expected you to come through the door. Oh, Sweetie please forgive me, what a terrible thing I have caused."

She turned to her parents, as Chloe glared at her with hate, Birch was still holding on to her wrist.

"I am so sorry, it was a complete accident, let me help clean her up."

She yanked on Chloe, whist still apologising, and dragged her into the lady's toilet. I sat there panicked, what the hell was Birch playing at? I was upset, but I could handle it. Mr Pemberton and his other daughter started to clean the floor. Deb's looked at the picture on her phone.

"I am framing this." She smiled. "Wow your friend is beyond

cool."

Inside the toilet, Chloe hit the wall hard, and Birch, who was in high heeled boots, and much taller, moved in very close to her face.

"If you ever pull a stunt like that on Abigail again, this will feel like a picnic. I am from the north, and up there we do things really different. I know a real big butch lesbian, with bright purple hair, who eats up posh little lipstick totties like you, and if I hear one word, or you pull any more stunts on Insta, like that on Abby, I will be inviting her to come down for a bit. You can trust me, you will not be able to hide from her."

Birch pushed her hard, back against the wall, and lifted up her phone as Chloe's eyes filled with tears of fear, she stepped back and took a picture of her covered in food and crying.

"I am going to What's App this to Harriet, screw with Abby again, and she will know just what to do with it, and just so you know, I will be here all summer, do you understand?" Chloe shook her head, Birch turned and walked out.

In the restaurant Mr Pemberton was almost finished cleaning, as his older daughter Edwina, was apologising to Lillian and Celia, as it had been their meal that had taken the dive with Chloe. Birch appeared and spoke to the ladies.

"I am so sorry ladies, it is one of those freak accidents that happens, but I feel bad your meal will be delayed."

She slipped her hand round her back, and pulled out an express gold card, and handed it to Edwina.

"Put their meal on my bill please, it is the least I can do."

She turned to the table and leaned down, her top fell open, revealing her ample breasts, and she smiled at the two ladies.

"Treat yourself to a nice bottle of wine with your meal on me also, and I hope the rest of your evening is very enjoyable."

Her green eyes twinkled, but the two ladies missed it, they were enjoying a different view.

Deb's turned back in her seat and looked at me. "I do not often swear, but your friend in my book is a fucking legend."

She gave me a huge smile, and I could not help but smile back, she was, she was an unbelievably cool person, but I had thought that all year. Cool and calm Birch returned to the table.

"Now, where were we?"

Deb's sat there smiling and tilted her phone round to show her picture, Birch grinned and lifted her own phone up, with the picture of the terror stricken Chole. "Beat ya." Deb's gasped with shock.

"Oh hell, send me that...What did you do to her?" Birch looked at me and winked.

"I simply showed her some northern hospitality, and gained a little added insurance in the deal."

The rest of the night went without hitch, Deb's asked hundreds of questions, especially after the story of Chloe, and Birch's reference to Bev. It was not far off one in the morning, and the place was almost empty, apart from Lillian and Celia, and two other couples. With the bills paid for both meals, we decided to leave. I gathered my things feeling a lot more relaxed and happier, and made my way to the door. I gave a smile to Lillian and Celia as I passed, and I enjoyed the fact they never took their eyes off me.

Deb's and myself arrived at the door, and waited for Birch, who again expressed her apologies, and handed Mr Pemberton a twenty pound note to take care of cleaning the blouse. She turned, and came up the room with a smile, and stopped at Lillian's side, she slipped a business card out of her back pocket, and placed it on the table in front of her.

"If you ladies ever feel the need to tell the village, my mother has a lot of skills in that area, look her up, she wrote a really good book about it. It was titled 'Les be friends.'" She winked at Celia, "Nice boobs."

With her cheekiest smile, she walked on and waved back. "Night ladies, have fun." And she joined us at the door.

Outside in the night air, we laughed all the way up Station Road, and onto the main street of the village. Deb's who had no idea about Lillian and Celia, and to be honest, very little idea about anything at all related to sex, with or without a man, was fascinated, and asked question after question.

By Manor Road, I told her my story of meeting Bev, which she found hysterical, and Birch told her about the first time she met her, which involved her staggering drunkenly into a room to find Bev going down on a girl. When Birch explained that Bev was going at the girl faster than a set of wind up teeth, Deb's almost peed herself laughing.

By the time we reached the gates, Deb's was staying over in the guest house, and had sent a text to let her dad know, and so us three girls staggered into the front door, making shushing noises, and trying not wake anyone up.

We had a surprise to find my mum sat in the kitchen waiting, as we giggled our way in, she was holding a glass in her hand, and I felt a pang as I saw how sad she looked. Birch looked at me.

"You and Deb's go on, I will be there in a while, I need to sort a few things out about my stay here, okay?"

I felt really guilty, but I knew with Deb's about, my mum would not create a scene, and so I shepherded Deb's out of the door, and left my trust in Birch. We giggled our way down to the guest house, and once inside, I grabbed the bottles of booze, as Deb's sat in the only arm chair raving about how cool Birch was.

Birch looked at Felicity, and watched as the tears rolled onto her cheeks, she did not hesitate, she crossed the kitchen and folded her arms around her.

"It's alright Mrs W, she does not hate you, just give her time." Felicity gave a massive sob, and pushed her face deeper into Birch.

Chapter 8

It's a Birch Thing.

It was several long minutes before Felicity stopped crying, and settled down filled with apologies.

"I am so sorry, I am not normally like this, it is very rude of me to impose on a guest in such a way."

Birch shrugged as Felicity sat down at the breakfast bar, Birch decided to join her.

"Maybe you should cry more often, I have told Abby a few times, it takes the pressure off." Felicity looked concerned.

"Has she cried that much?" Birch shook her head.

"Only in the last day and half, she has been really happy at university, I was surprised when she broke down after arriving here." Felicity looked a little guilty.

"My fault I take it?" Birch shrugged.

"A little bit, and the pressure of being judged by everyone here."

Felicity took a drink and emptied her glass, and looked into the bottom of it, Birch smiled.

"How many is that?" Felicity smiled.

"Just two."

"Oh, that is not good, firstly you never finish on an even number, and secondly, if your drinks amount to 'Just' well that means you have not finished yet." She smiled at Felicity. "Where do you hide the bottle?" She gave soft snort, and got up out of her seat.

"You my dear girl are far too wise for your years. I hide it down here behind the bags of flour."

The lemonade was already on the counter, Felicity opened the bottom cupboard, and pushed the bag of self raising flour out of the way, revealing a green bottle. Birch leaned over to look.

"Oh, I have something far better, grab a glass and try this."

She opened her large bag and pulled out a bottle of marshmallow flavoured gin.

"This stuff is all the rage back home." Felicity eyed the bottle.

"I have seen the flavoured stuff in the supermarket, I never thought it would be worth drinking." Birch winked.

"Give it a try, Dead's and me try each one as it comes out, we have sampled pretty much all the new flavours, but we are always on the hunt for a new one." Felicity sat down with the lemonade.

"Deads? Do you mean Abigail?" Birch suddenly realised.

"Oops, yeah that is her nickname at Uni, you know, gothic, darkness, satanic rituals and all that." Felicity swallowed hard.

"She is a Satanist? Oh god how will I tell the Vicar?" Birch sniggered, as she poured out the gin.

"No, she is not a Satanist, you are quite alright her soul is safe. She reads a lot of gothic novels, which let's be honest, all contain dark creepy graveyards, and some element of the devil, it was just a convenient nick name for her, and she sort of enjoyed it." Felicity gave a deep sigh.

"Thank heavens for that, I was half expecting to find slaughtered chickens in the garden when I saw that round your neck." Birch looked down and understood.

"Oh, yeah I get it, this is nothing satanic, it's a pentagram, a star of protection, it is a pagan symbol." She understood.

"But I thought pagans were into the devil?" Birch shook her head.

"The Christian church would have you believe that... No offence by the way... But the truth is Satan is a creation of your religion, not mine." She nodded.

"I see, so you are a pagan, is that why you are named after a tree, its beech or something is it not?" She gave a giggle.

"It's Birch, my real name is Jemima, if you are more at ease with that, most people call me Jemi. Birch is my nickname, you know because of the hair, white with black splatters, sort of like birch bark?"

"Oh, I see, I think that is actually quite wonderful, yes, it makes complete sense. I do also think it suits you. I feel you have a very natural way, a little like Hatty does with people. She calls me Flick, she is the only one who does, it is rather a shame, because I do like the way it sounds when she says it."

"Well if you are okay with it, I would love to call you Flick?"

She smiled for the first time since Birch met her, it was clear how like her in looks Abigail was.

"Yes, I do believe that would be nice." Birch smiled.

"Try your gin, it is good stuff."

They sat together for far longer than Birch had anticipated, the gin was a hit, and had to be tasted a few more times. Birch gave her more information on her daughter's life at University, and pointed how hard she studied, she admitted there were parties, she played down the sex, just revealing Abigail had lost her virginity in the village before Uni, was enough she thought for one day. Having established a repour with Flick, she moved on to other things, when Flick pointed to a large box on the counter top.

"I have stocked the fridge and the cupboards in the guest house, but I only did it with one in mind, but I feel Abigail will not really be using her room while you're here, dorm life and all that I suppose? I was going to take it down while you were out, I am sad to say I lost my nerve after Edwin mentioned she dismissed him, although it does not surprise me, I mean those two have not really got on well since she was a young teenager, he is not good with teenagers, too set in his ways." It was understandable.

"I have money, I can buy my own food, and I would like to contribute to the cost of living here, I feel it is only right."

Flick was enjoying the gin, probably a little too much, she frowned and waved her glass.

"Good grief, I will not hear of it. You are the guest of my daughter, and she also stayed with your parents, I bet they did not charge her?" Birch shrugged.

"That was for just a week, I am going to be around for most of the summer, I am happy to pay my way." Flick shook her head vigorously.

"I wouldn't hear of it, let us just say this is my thank you gift to you, for taking care of my precious child. She has told me often how good you have been for her, and to be honest, if you excuse my French, she would never have had the balls to come back with that hair, if it was not for you." Birch gave a titter.

"I am not certain her father agrees with you, he looked at her in a very disapproving manner when he saw her. I am sure his opinion will come out at some point." She frowned.

"I called him off for today, tomorrow is church, so he will be too busy buttering up the parishioners for accounts. I assume you Satanists will not be in church with us?"

She gave of a squeak of a laugh, and then grabbed her mouth, and she shook in her seat.

"I think I am disappointed, that would put the wind up Marjorie's knickers." Birch giggled, as Flick gave a mighty laugh.

"I think if we entered church, we would probably end up burnt at the stake on the village green, with the way they feel about us at the moment."

Flick gave of a wheezy giggle, and held her mouth.

"That would be hilarious, they could throw Hatty on as well, and rid the village of all sin at once."

She gasped in air, and carried on her wheezy laughing.

"I can just see Marjorie in her puritan dress and her white bonnet, striking the flint with a smile on her face. I think she would be in heaven, if she could get away with it."

Birch laughed with her, Flick was becoming very red in the face, she looked at the clock.

"I fear I got you tipsy, and it is getting late, maybe bed would not be such a bad idea?" Flick drained her glass, and placed it on the counter, still chuckling to herself.

"I believe you are right; I am a little more off kilter than normal, and nothing could be worse than our vicar's tedious sermons with a hangover."

She stood up, and wavered a little, Birch got up with her.

"Will you be alright?" Flick patted her sleeve.

"I am fine, I have been worse, you are a nice girl beech, I like you." Birch gave a smile.

"I like you too Flick."

She gave another bright smile, and staggered across the kitchen towards the door to the hall.

"Goodnight dear child, don't forget the box."

Birch quietly followed her just to make sure she was fine, and when she was certain, she grabbed the box filled with food, and a gave a big smile.

"Excellent we have loo rolls." She closed the door quietly, taking the box in both hands, she carried it down to the guest house.

Deb's was passed out on the bed when Birch arrived back, I looked at her splayed across the bed.

"What do we do now, it's normally me passed out, and you taking care of me?"

She put the box down, and joined me in the bedroom.

"I suppose put her to bed, it is what I do with you normally."

There was a slight hitch in the plan, which obviously Birch had not spotted, I looked at Deb's sprawled across the mattress, and pointed out the obvious.

"Birch she is not wearing knickers under those jeans." Birch shrugged.

"So what?"

Understanding Birch, I was slowly starting to realise was an acquired skill, which involved living with her day in and day out. She was a pagan, a naturist, and a training psychologist, and I cannot deny, they are admirable qualities. My only problem was when you added her attitude of total acceptance, and her slightly eccentric approach to life, and to the life of everything else, and then applied it to all normal people, culture clashes occurred, like this one.

I carefully considered the situation, and tossed it around my mind. How could I put it in a way she fully understood that whilst she was a very happy nudist, Deb's probably was not, and it appeared to me, that waking up nude, would probably freak her out.

"Er, okay... Look at this way, we have to undress her, but if we take her pants and top off like you do with me, she will be in bed wearing a bra, with no knickers on... No matter how you look at that, it's frigging weird." She understood.

"Yeah, I get it... Okay then, we simply take her bra off as well, it's better nude than half nude don't you think?"

Once again, I had to correct what in my brain was the obvious facts.

"Listen Birch, this girl has never had any kind of sexual experience." She nodded her head in agreement.

"To be honest Deads, if you screw her when she is asleep, I am sorry Sweetie, but that would be just wrong, I am really not sure I could float with that."

"For god's sake Birch, I am not going to screw her, hell I am not Bev. If I am honest, I prefer people awake when I do it with them." She looked at me not completely understanding.

"Then what is the problem?" I gave an exasperated sigh, I was right back to square one, so now you see the problem.

"If we leave her dressed like this, it will be uncomfortable for her. Yes, the bed is big enough, and we have slept together in a none sexual kind of way after a night out many times. The problem is she has not, so if she wakes naked in bed with us naked, won't she think we all had sex? I mean you spent all night telling lesbian stories, she is going to go there, you know that?"

The moment arrived and logic returned to Birch.

"I get it, I say let her sleep naked, and then let her form her own conclusion in the morning, and if it is the wrong one?" She gave an evil looking smile. "I say we run with it for a little while, it could be good fun." I shook my head.

"You are a very bad influence on me, but that is an awesome idea."

I sat Deb's up, and Birch pulled her top up, and then snapped her bra open. It was not the easiest task. Birch looked at her.

"Shit Deads, her boobs are freaking huge, how can someone so small have such huge knockers?" She lifted one up in her hand. "Have you seen the size of that, holy shit, no wonder she is so short, all her height went into her tits."

I started laughing and grabbed her pants. "You are absolutely sure you are not a lesbian right?"

Birch undid the buttons on her jeans, she started to giggle, as I pulled them off, Birch stepped back as we accomplished step one.

"Holy shit, there hasn't been a bush like that since the 1960's, you really need to show this girl how to trim."

She grabbed some of it, and pulled it out, it was at least a good three inches long. I tried very hard not to look, but could not help looking, and I can only say it was impressive.

"Birch leave it the hell alone, you know I am not sure I want to get in bed with you these days, you hang out with Bev way too much, I am not sure I am that safe anymore."

Giggling and struggling, getting her under the duvet was a hard fight, she weighed a tonne, and was hard to move. Birch looked at me.

"Best put her on the side of the bed, you know just in case she pukes, plus I want the middle."

"Why the middle?" She smiled.

"I like to cuddle, so either way I get something to grab on to." I thought about it for a moment.

"Probably better if you cuddle me, I am used to it, not sure Deb's will want to wake up in the arms of a naked girl, hugging her tit."

Finally, after wrestling her into the right place, we both retired to the living room to sort out the food. A couple of drinks later, and all the food stored, I yawned and headed for the bed room. I striped and got ready to get in bed, Birch somehow beat me, and slipped naked into the middle of the bed. She looked at me.

"Where you going?" I did not really understand.

"To bed, why?" She sat up in the bed.

"Not like that you are not, she is naked, I am naked, so knickers off."

I gave sigh, and then slipped them off, turned out the lamp and slid in. It was a big bed, but still cramped, but I was drunk and exhausted, and as I felt Birch snuggle into me, I felt happy and relaxed. I turned slightly feeling Birch slip her hand round onto my left boob.

"Is my mum okay, she looked really sad, is it because I said those things, Birch I hated myself, and I feel really guilty, did you tell her I am sorry?" Birch lifted her head to my shoulder.

"She knows Sweetie, I filled her in on a few things, she will be fine now, but seriously, you two need to talk at some point."

Birch snuggled in more, and I felt the warmth of her body against me, somehow it felt comforting.

"Thanks Birch, I knew she would be fine with you." Birch gave a slight twitch.

"My bad." I rolled back a little to see her bright green eyes twinkle in the darkness.

"What have you done?" Her eyes flashed.

"Well... Deads Sweetie, it kind of slipped out she likes gin." I felt the tension jolt inside me.

"Oh god which flavour?"

"Marshmallow." I closed my eyes in the dark, and felt the dread growing inside me.

"How pissed was she?"

It was dark, and I could not really see it, but I just knew she was swaying her head from side to side as she evaluated the situation.

"I would say…. Not that pissed…. Drunk enough to sleep well, yes she will sleep."

I knew it, leave her alone with a bottle and she is dangerous, hell this is probably the only girl alive that could get the Pope pissed.

"Birch… When you say sleep…Are we talking like Deb's, or not as bad?" She moved in the bed.

"Christ, not that drunk." I gave a sigh of relief.

"Thank god for that, I was panicked for a minute." She gave my boob a tweak.

"Go to sleep Deads, she will be fine… Night Sweetie." I reached back and patted her leg.

"Night Birch." I felt my eyes flicker and I was gone.

Felicity was stood in the kitchen in her best dress, and wearing her best hat, when Edwin walked in. She was also hiding a bad headache, no doubt curtesy of Birch. Edwin looked at her and gave a long sigh.

"Are you ready for this, we cannot hide the fact that our daughter has shamed the whole village, we must face this head on, and take what they throw at us. I am assuming our newly reformed Satanist will not be coming?" It was pointless to even comment.

Outside across the village, the bells were ringing, and all the village bar a few, of which the three of us lay flat out from our night of drinking, were included, came from every direction. The good sheep flocked to fill St Augustine's Parish Church, under the guidance of, Rev Milton Wallace.

He stood at the door, a bald kindly looking gent with large front teeth, and he welcomed each and every member of his flock.

This was a scene I knew by heart; it had happened without fail every Sunday in my life for eighteen years, and no one in the village, could possibly understand the joy of waking up in a University dorm every Sunday around midday, like I had for the last year.

To say I did not miss church, was an understatement. In the

words of what hopefully would be the famous writer of the future, Abigail Jennifer Watson. "I dammed well despised it."

It was one long service of boredom, watching the fake people of the village kiss each other's arses, and pray to be forgiven, for the very things they would do the moment they stepped off the grounds of the church.

If I never heard the Rev Milton give another hourlong drone of a sermon, with bad diction and no structure again, I would be a happy person indeed. This vicar had ways of sending you to sleep, anaesthetists had not even discovered. Hence, I will add, having a pagan naturist witch in the house, was a huge bonus, and there again, for my friend Deb's, who did not know her as well as I did, maybe not so much.

I lay in bed listening to the church bells, having been woken by them at the ungodly hour of 10:30 in the morning. I lay there in bed thinking, please god, it's Sunday, tell them all to start later, and while you are at it, create a way of drinking alcohol that does not leave a headache, when Deb's suddenly sat upright in bed, and squealed.

"CHURCH!"

I closed my eyes and pretended to be asleep, well half closed them, as I wanted to see her reaction. She was not fully awake, and with three of us in the bed, it was really hot under the covers, so she did not at first feel Birch's arm around her waist, and her left leg, which was straddling hers.

Debs rubbed her eyes and slowly came to life, and then suddenly it hit her, she lifted the duvet, realised she was naked, and being hugged by another naked girl, who had spent the previous night telling lesbian stories. She dropped the duvet and gave a huge gasp of sudden awareness. Her voice was a mix of shock, surprise, and strangely enough euphoria, but quiet, so as not to disturb us.

"Oh my god, I am no longer a virgin... And... And I gave it to a woman!"

She lifted the duvet and took a second look. "Oh Christ, yep, I have done it, I freed my female chastity, not to a man as I always thought, but to a woman, but which one did it?"

I sat up in bed, and she turned to look at me, I moved very

slowly so as not to shake the delicate contents of my head.

"What?"

"What did I do? Oh, hell did I do it with you when Birch was not here?"

I wanted to shake my head, but felt it best left still.

"Hate to disappoint you Deb's, but my vagina is men only, and I fail to have the ability to move my jaw at the speed of clockwork teeth."

She gave a sigh of relief; I was not sure if I should feel insulted. I dropped my legs over the bed, and got up. The church bells were ringing, and I knew there would be no more sleep for me.

"You want a coffee?" She nodded and regretted it, and flopped back on her pillow.

"Oh, Christ my head is banging."

I gave a laugh, as I walked towards the kitchen, she was a lightweight when it came to drinking, which reminded me of my first weeks with Birch.

"Hang on, I will go find the paracetamol."

The house smelt of curry and alcohol, Birch as I was well aware, was well known for her ability to expel gas in her sleep. I walked to the door, and opened it to change the air.

I instantly regretted it, as the sun was out, and it felt like my eyes were being burned out of their sockets. It was a moment of clarity, when I realised Bram Stoker must have experienced this, which influenced his writing of Dracula.

Ten minutes later, I returned to the bedroom where Deb's lay still, her hand covering her eyes. I put a cup of hot coffee on the dresser and opened my hand to reveal the two tablets.

"Here take these it will help."

She sat up and opened her eyes, and looked at the tablets, or at least I thought she did.

"Jesus Abigail, why the hell is that so bald? You have the vagina of a child."

It was just too early for me, I was struggling with being awake, I pushed the tablets back towards her.

"If you must know I shave it, guys like it that way." She gave a gasp.

"You can do that?"

"You're the new lesbian, you tell me."

I couldn't help but smile, as I picked up my knickers, and headed back into the living room, where I grabbed my long top, slipped it on, and then went straight for the door with my coffee. I sat on a lounger with my back to the sun and relaxed, it was nice and warm.

I was out there for a long while before Deb's appeared, she brought with her a plate of toast, which I greatly appreciated. I had wondered if she had found it hard to release Birch's iron clad stranglehold on her, but I felt it was best not to ask.

Coffee and an end to the bells, as the service started helped restore my hunger. She had found her clothes, although I noted her lack of bra, as she sat in the lounger at my side. We lay quiet for a long time, and then she began to tell me about her university course, I had always been a little disappointed that Manchester was never one of her options. As she finished and the conversation trailed off, I turned and looked at her.

"I hope you enjoyed last night?" Some of her bubbly self, had returned.

"Are you kidding me, it was awesome." I was happy to hear it.

"Thanks Deb's, it meant a lot to have at least one person here like me." She understood.

"I always felt guilty you know... I mean you always stood up for me, like you did that time with Chloe, I never stood up for you. I have always felt bad about that because you have always been there for me, you are my best friend you know that don't you?" I smiled and patted her leg,

"I know, you never needed to say it, you showed it, just like you did last night." She looked so serious.

"I have really missed you Abby, I am so glad you are back for a while. I like Uni and all, and training for bio chemistry is brilliant, but it's not the same as it was at school, there is no one like you there. When I heard you were back, and what they were saying about you, I got so angry, I talked to dad about it. He was the one that told me to message you, actually it was his idea to go out last night, he told me you would need someone close, someone at your side, and you must not hide from them. I wish I could say it was all me, but he gave me great advice and I took it."

"Deb's when I really needed you, that was when you showed up,

I am really grateful to know you had my back last night, it meant a lot to me." She gave me a huge smile.

"Really?" I smiled; I was still not ready for nods.

"Really, honestly Birch is an amazing friend, but she really has no idea what this lot can be like, you do, you lived through it with your mum. When you showed up, I knew you above all others really understood what it is like to be attacked by them, and having you there last night, was a massive help."

In the background the church bells began to chime again, church was over, and they would all troop out, thank the vicar, and then carry on as always, being mean to each other. I lay back and just relaxed, I knew at some point I would have to face my dad.

A very naked Birch staggered out of the door, and shielded her eyes as she looked for us. She spotted us by the pool.

"What the fuck is it with those fucking bells, why the fuck are they so loud, you can hear them in Manchester? I fucking hate country folk, they never fucking sleep."

She staggered across the grass towards us by the pool. "Is there no sanctity in this fucking awful place?" She looked at the pool. "Water is sound proof right?" She looked at the water, walked up to edge. "Fuck you vicar." She dived in, and I started to laugh, as did Deb's

"Ignore her, she has a hangover, it's Birch, you will get used to it."

Chapter 9

Vicars and Gnomes.

On Sunday morning after church, was the one big chance of the week to meet and gossip. In front of the gates on the roadway, groups would form, and the service would be discussed, followed by the latest hot news, and there was no mystery as to what that would be, especially after last night's incident involving Birch and Chloe.

Admittedly, Lillian and Celia were actually very complimentary, about the strange northern girl who had arrived with Abigail. Marjorie who had yet another chance to attack Felicity, felt a little wrong footed, as she heard Celia talk with great admiration for Birch. She frowned at her.

"We are talking about the same person are we not, you know the slightly taller one with the green coloured dress on that day, I believe she was dolled up to the nines in black leather last night?" Celia corrected her.

"Don't listen to the gossip Madge, we were there and saw it all, and I cannot deny, I thought both the girls were dressed very lovely. I will admit they were modern by our standards, but designer is designer, and all their clothing had the right labels." This was too much for Marjorie.

"I heard they attacked poor Chloe, I mean picking on a defenceless girl like that, it's disgraceful." Lillian shook her head.

"They attacked no one, it was a simple accident, just like last year when Harry collided with Margret. You know they have been told several times that door is dangerous. To be completely honest Madge, I felt Chloe was very rude, her manner and attitude were simply terrible, and that poor girl Birch, she was nothing but apologetic and helpful." Celia chipped in.

"She even took Chloe to the ladies to help clean her up, and paid in cash to have her uniform cleaned, I saw it with my own eyes." Lillian gave a hearty nod.

"Beautifully spoken, her punctuation was excellent, and I should know after 40 years teaching English. No, I am sorry Madge, I felt they acted like real ladies, especially Birch, she looked stunning, she is a very attractive girl. Her hair is simply delightful, I have never seen anything like it. She came to the table and actually apologised to both of us for delaying our meals, we did not see or hear a word from Chloe after that. No, she sent her sister out to apologise, and as you know, that is unacceptable." Celia chipped back in.

"She paid for our meal and thanked us for being patient, and she did so with a gold card. Now you tell me, what sort of common northerner would have one of those? You do know her mother is a very influential and famous therapist, don't you?"

This was all news to Marjorie, she had heard nothing of this from the others, she had no choice but to concede defeat, she folded her arms.

"Well, I stand corrected." Lillian gave a slight nod.

"Rightly so Madge, gossip is gossip, but false rumours are dangerous."

Harriet was six feet away leaning on the wall listening, she smiled, and spoke quietly under her breath.

"Smart girl Birch, I knew I liked you."

As the gossip died, the groups parted for another week. Felicity who had been stood at the side of Edwin for almost forty minutes, gave a sigh of relief, as he finally said his goodbyes, and began his journey down Church Rise, at the side of the village green. Felicity looked at him as she trotted along at his side.

"Did you really understand the sermon today? I cannot deny I was lost, it made very little sense to me, I did think the vicar was a little all over the place."

Edwin strode forward, his eyes always towards the bottom of the rise.

"I found it very inspiring, yes indeed, I think our vicar has deep insight to all things."

A voice a few feet behind spoke.

"It was all utter bollocks, that bloody idiot vicar has the insight of a wholemeal loaf. Christ Edwin, you are full of shit." He closed his eyes for a second, and gave out a long, irritated sigh.

"Frankly Harriet, your ill informed opinions do not concern me." She smirked.

"Obviously not, if they did your IQ would increase."

He spun round looking angry, and Felicity jumped back.

"Why are you here? I thought I made my feelings quite clear about your proximity to myself and my wife." She gave a nod, and then held her arms out wide.

"I have obeyed your rules, but sadly they do not apply here, unless your tax dodging firm has managed to buy this street, which I doubt it, as the Parish Council would have mentioned it, and I would have opposed it." He glared at her with hate.

"God you are irritating, don't you have a man to bed?" Her face was dead pan.

"No, he is giving his sermon at St Marks in Oxendale about now." Even Felicity gasped.

"That is uncalled for Hatty, Edwin's brother is past history, you should leave it where it lies." She shrugged.

"Yeah, it was in my bed for two years and not his wife's. I would say he was more of a man of the sheets than a man of the cloth, wouldn't you Edwin?" His face was purple.

"If you were a man, I would hit you." She smiled and wagged her finger at him.

"Now, Now, Edwin, don't let my sex put you off, we have equal rights, but best not show all these good church going folk, your true colours. I have no idea what they would say?" It was simply too much for him to tolerate.

"I am going to the Hunters, I will stand her no longer Felicity, you bloody well deal with her."

He stormed off in a rage, and Felicity gave an angry glance at Harriet.

"Why?"

"What?"

"Why bring that up again, you know how protective and proud he is of his younger brother. Oh, Hatty at times I find you quite impossible, it is no wonder you never married." She laughed.

"Having seen how he treats you is why I never married, and I like screwing more than sharing my studio."

"I sometimes despair, I really do Hatty, why I put up with you I have no idea." Harriet walked up to her side, and bumped shoulders with her.

"You know Abby and me are the only people who really love you, that is why you put up with me. I am a lost cause, and you are sucker for them. Not to miss the fact that my house is the one place you can run to when you need to, you know he will never knock on my door, well not if he wants to live."

She gave a smile and slipped her arm round her.

"You are so naughty, poor Jeremy, you should not pick on him so much." She gave a little giggle.

"There was nothing poor about Jeremy, what he lacked in brain skills, he certainly made up for in bed skills." She looked at Harriet.

"Really?" She winked and raised her eye brows. "Oh heavens, he was that good?" Harriet walked with a beaming smile.

"I must admit, I have missed him since his wife found out, there are few who have matched him. I am telling you Flick; you married the wrong one." Felicity started to giggle.

"I would never have guessed, wow Hatty, you certainly kept that one quiet." She walked on continuing to smile.

"You fancy a brew? If you do, tag along, it's not like Edwin will be back any time soon." Felicity looked a little worried.

"I am not sure; I did ask the vicar to call round and talk to Abigail."

Hatty started to laugh. Felicity did not quite understand.

"I am not sure why you find that funny at all."

Harriet could not help it; she already knew more about Birch than Felicity did.

"Oh, come on, Abigail is a big girl now, and she has Birch with her, I am sure the vicar will find it a very informative experience. You know those two being very modern and all that." Felicity looked at her with a suspicious glance.

"You know something, don't you?" Hatty shrugged.

"I don't really know anything, except Abby had her reasons for leaving the choir, and that Birch is or was Wiccan." She did not trust Hatty at all.

"What exactly does that mean?"

"Come for a brew and I will tell you." She started to chuckle.

Having enjoyed her swim, eaten some toast and drank several

cups of coffee, the still very naked Birch stretched out on the grass, as the sun was gloriously hot, and so she decided she would top up her vitamin D, and try to get a little colour on her skin.

Birch had finally come clean ten minutes before she had to leave, and confessed to Deb's, that her desire was overwhelmed by the booze, and so sadly, Deb's was still in fact a virgin.

Deb's appeared relived and disappointed at the same time, so Birch gave her a few URL's for her to look up online, just in case she felt the need to explore her sexuality more. Deb's left with a big smile, and promised she would be back as soon as she could.

With the house empty and feeling a little tired, I decided to join Birch, and tan out on the grass for a while. Lying in the sun as nature intended is without doubt one of the most liberating things I have ever experienced, and as I lay at the side of Birch and talked, the stress and the exhaustion of yesterday seemed to melt away. I felt calm, composed, and completely stress free.

"Oh, this is so wonderful."

In front of me was a tall cool glass of cola, my phone, and a few good books, just in case I needed one.

"I can see why you love being naked Birch, I must admit I always feel better when we chill in the dorm with hardly anything on."

"Hmm, it is your natural state, it's mad that so many do not understand that. This is how we were meant to be all a long."

My back was warm, my limbs felt relaxed, and my mind felt still and calm. My phone gave a loud bleep! I stretched up and grabbed it, and brought it close to my face, it was not easy to read in full sunlight.

"It's a text from Hatty." Birch turned her head to face me.

"Oh yeah, what does it say?"

I opened it up and read the message, and suddenly there was no longer enough sunshine to keep me calm.

"Holy shit, the Vicar is coming!" I was on my feet in a flash, Birch gave a sigh.

"You mean that twat with the bells?"

My mind was racing, I was not sure why he would want to come when my mother was not here. Suddenly it dawned on me, I was not in church, he was coming to see me... And I was naked on the grass... And it's only frigging Sunday. My brain screamed at me.

'Move your frigging ass Abigail, the bloody vicar is on route.' I panicked.

"Birch we have to get dressed, come on."

I moved towards the guest house and my suitcase, and looked back, Birch was still lay out on the grass, I felt the panic intensify inside me.

"Birch for god's sake, the bloody vicar will be here any minute."

She moaned, and lifted her head to look at me.

"It's your church Deads, this is mine right here, and I communing with it."

My heart was again beating so fast, I thought it would explode, I hadn't realised I was running on the spot and getting nowhere. I was starting to feel desperate.

"Birch please do not do this to me, I know how you hate them, just go with the flow and work with me here." She sat up and gave a long sigh.

"That twat woke me up ringing his fucking bells, and what the fuck is that all about anyhow, can they not find a quieter way to summon their customers? I mean you don't see a bloody great bell tower on Marks and Sparks. Their customers know the opening hours, and procced accordingly. I mean, why does half the neighbourhood have to suffer those horrible things clanging away, because your vicar's god needs souls?" She stood up. "It's a bloody liberty you know?"

I had no time to argue, the vicar was on route and we were both still naked, she strolled causally across the grass towards me.

"It is a very bias system you know, and I would say it discriminates against those not Christian. We should complain to the Church of England, and tell them to shut the fuck up on Sundays."

I nodded agreeing with her, she was almost at the door, and I needed to at least get her inside.

She finally made it, and I rushed into the bedroom and grabbed my suitcase, I yanked it open, and saw Birch in the living room looking at her clothes, my panic was lessoning. I grabbed a short black skirt and top, and hurriedly dressed. I listened out for the buzzer, and knew I had a key pad in the guest house, so all was well and moving forward.

Having dressed, I ran into the kitchen and filled the kettle, my eyes scanned the shelf for tea bags, I had no idea why, I just assumed Vicar's liked tea. I spotted them, and snatched them down, then gathered three cups. Phew, I was getting there, all I needed now was to calm down and breathe, before he arrived.

I turned in the kitchen to check on Birch, and my heart stopped dead.

"WHAT THE FUCKING HELL ARE YOU WEARING?" Birch smiled and gave a twirl.

"Isn't it great?"

She stood in the centre of the livingroom wearing a long black robe with a pointed hood, and fluted sleeves, which had little moons embroidered around them. She looked like the Grim Reapers completely insane aunty, crossed with Hermione's gay brother.

"Where the hell did you buy that, Hogwarts?" She gave another twirl.

"My Wiccan friend made it for me for Yule, I thought I would wear it as a dressing gown, it's really snug, and so easy to get out of."

She pulled at the front of the robe and it opened right up, and she was still naked underneath. Suddenly the buzzer went off, and I rushed across the room, and pulled it together quickly, the bloody vicar was here, time had run out. It was quite clear it had eloped with my last straining nerve. I was panicking as I looked Birch deeply into her bright green eyes, which sparkled with devilish magic.

"Birch please, I really love you, I do, and I know you hate vicars, but please just for me, be nice, alright?" She gave me a beautiful smile.

"You really love me?"

I nodded, the sweat running down the side of my face. She opened her arms and her robe opened wide, as she pulled me into a hug. The buzzer went off again.

"I love you too my dark little beastie." She kissed me on the side of the cheek. "Yuk! Salty."

I pulled free, and headed to the door breathing hard, and pushed the call button, it was too late now, I had done the best I could.

"Hello, who is it?" My heart was pounding inside my head.

"Oh, hello Abigail, it is Rev Milton Wallace from the church, your mother asked me if I would call for a little chat."

I looked back at Birch, who was still showing her nakedness in the gap in her robe, muttering something like 'Bell Twat" under her breath. I knew my odds of surviving this were about one in two hundred million. I was panicked, extremely stressed, and I had to keep the peace between a completely stupid and mad vicar, and one very tired and hungover Wiccan, with a passion, for psychoanalysing vicars, because they ring bells on a Sunday. I pushed the button.

"Hi Rev Milton, we are in the back, please come on though, the side gate is open."

I looked back at Birch, she appeared happy in her robe, I was just worried, because knowing her love of fantasy fiction, for all I knew she had a scythe hidden in it somewhere, and she aimed to use it on whoever pulled the bell rope.

There was little more I could do, so I walked out of the door, and headed up the garden to meet the vicar, talking to myself.

"I am definitely going to hell, if this goes wrong, this will be a one way shot to Beelzebub, and I will be abandoned by my parents."

The vicar came smiling through the gates, or at least it looked that way. I cannot say I have ever known for certain. His teeth have always appeared far too big for his mouth, and his over bite is so big. The kids in Sunday School used to say he would eat food off his chest.

It took him several paces to reach me, in which time I heard the sniggers of Birch somewhere behind me. I glanced back to make sure she was covered, she was sat cross legged on the lawn, with her hood up, and it was shaking, as she was clearly laughing at the first site of the vicar.

He took my hand and shook it, spraying his greeting all over me, much to the added amusement of Birch.

"So lovely to see you again Abigail, we have certainly missed you at choir practice."

I wiped my face with an already prepared tissue.

"So nice of you to say Vicar, but I had very good reasons, and with me being in University now, it was impossible to continue."

I held out my arm to guide him round toward the long patio table, I figured I could at least sit him out of spitting distance.

"Won't you come this way please Vicar?"

He happily followed holding on tight to a small leather bag. I kept Birch in my peripheral vison, considering her mood, and how well I had come to know her mischief, I did not trust her one bit, but for now she was remaining as still as a rock. The vicar chatted away quite happily.

"Such a sweet voice, yes…yes, I must say, we have missed your harmony in the middle, Martin has often said, it has not sounded the same since you left."

He chatted away happily, as he walked along behind me, almost as if he was talking to himself.

"I mentioned it to him today, he appeared quite happy to hear you were back, he even said it would be lovely seeing you in front and centre of the choir again." I felt the cold shudder run down my spine.

I got him to a seat, it felt like a victory, Birch was still in place, that was two for two, I was starting to feel calmer, and a little more relaxed. It looked hopefully, like maybe I could pull this off. I sat at the other end of the large glass table, and I was out of range, score, this was going better than expected as the vicar rambled on about the choir.

"Yes now let me see… Oh yes your mother… Well you see the reason I came was for two things really… Firstly your mother is concerned for your welfare, after all you have been away for some time, she thought maybe I could be of some help to get you adjusted back to village life."

Birch suddenly straightened up, her hood fell down her back, and her eyes opened really wide. She looked panicked, but I had no idea why. I tried my best to ignore her, she was slightly behind the vicar on the lawn, so she was well out of his eyeline.

"The truth is Vicar; I am really alright."

Birch opened her robe and started frantically pointing at her vagina, I tried to ignore her efforts to put me off.

"Yes, when I came back, I was very tired, you know long hours revising for my exams, followed by a very long train journey, I think it just took it out of me."

Birch looked more and more concerned, and became more erratic with her movements, and opened her robes again, and began pointing between her legs, with a long fluted sleeved hand, I frowned trying to work out what she meant. The Vicar noticed.

"I say are you alright?" I smiled.

"Sorry Vicar, I noticed my friend over there."

It was at that point terror struck my heart, he turned, and she was still pointing downstairs, my heart skipped several beats. Birch was like lightening, she flipped her head, and her hood popped up and her robes shut, and she sat as still as rock on the lawn. I had been holding my breath, as the vicar scanned the whole garden, he turned back looking confused.

"Is she really... Where?"

I was in utter disbelief, was he fucking blind, he had looked right at her? How the hell could he miss her? I mean it was so obvious, Birch was there sat crossed legged on the lawn, in her black robe, with a pointed hood, with fluted sleeves. She looked like a giant satanic garden gnome that has arisen from the lawn, to steal the souls of all the petunias, how the hell could he miss that? I had no choice but to go to plan B.

"She has probably gone to make drinks."

He appeared happy with that so I moved on, feeling the sweat run down my neck. "What was the other thing you wanted to see me about?"

He gave it a moment of thought, and then remembered.

"Oh yes of course, it's about the youth group activities for Summer, we do have a wide range of events."

Birch suddenly stood up, I felt more than a little apprehensive, what was she up to now? The vicar was babbling on, but I was lost watching Birch, as she suddenly lifted her hands to her mouth and then tried to mouth some words to me. I watched her lips not understanding her at first. She spoke slowly and I started to get it. 'You have got gnome kickers on' It made no sense until the vicar suddenly said.

"Yes, I have some leaflets in my bag down here, just a moment I shall get them."

Birch opened her robe, and pointed right at her vagina, and mouthed the words to me. The coldest trickle ran down my spine, as I suddenly understood her. 'you have got no knickers on' it all came flooding back in an instant.

In my abject panic, I had grabbed my short summer skirt and my top, thrown them on, and ran round like a mad person, but I had been sunbathing naked, so had forgotten to put any knickers back on.

As the vicar's head went down, and passed the edge of the glass table, heading for his bag, I gave a squeak, grabbed my short skirt, and swung my legs sharply away from the table, and crossed my legs.

When the vicar came back up with his paper and still talking, I was sideways on, leaning on my arm, which was on the table, with my head resting on my hand, and still smiling, as my heart raced and the sweat dripped off my brow.

He passed the leaflets across the table, and I gave a long exhale understanding I just survived flashing the vicar my shaven pussy by a hair's breadth, no pun intended.

"Here we go, you will find there is a much more on offer this year than ever before, and I do hope you will consider bringing your friend along. I have heard all sorts of interesting things about her, I am sure she will find spiritual guidance amongst us."

I was almost there, all I had to do now was convince him I was fine and happy, and he would leave, when Birch who during my moment's attention to the vicar, had gone.

She suddenly reappeared out of the guest house with a tray, and my heart sank. I was never going to get rid of him now he had a pagan to play with.

Birch walked up with her big beautiful smile, and all I could see was the antichrist of my nightmares, carrying my death on a tray.

"Hello Vicar, I am Birch, would you care for some tea?"

I have to admit, at first, I was pretty unsure if he would even see or hear her. I had been starting to think he had some sort of pagan blocker built into his Christianity, like my computer has to stop pop ups. I mean the old badger had looked at her sat on the grass, and not seen her, so I had my doubts that when she spoke, he would even register her voice. He looked right at her.

"Oh, there you are?"

What the frig, he saw her... No frigging way... How the hell did he miss her the first two times? I had to wonder if Wiccan came with a cloaking device, they could switch on and off?

She put the tray down, and sat at the table between the two of us, and began pouring tea out of my granny's old tea pot. I was highly suspicious of her change in personality. I sat there waiting for either my death or his.

My death by one wrong word from Birch, which was highly likely, or his from a hidden Scythe, concealed within her robes. The only thing I knew for sure, was Birch and the Bell Twat, were sat together, and this was not going to end well. It was not long before my death approached.

"Tell me my dear, I hear you are following a Pagan life?"

Yep, here it comes. I will just sit back and accept the blood bath of my demise. Birch smiled a cute smile, I made a mental note of that, 'Cute smiles are not to be trusted.'

"I am, I was involved heavily in Wiccan, but now I walk more of a solo path."

He nodded appearing actually far more interested than I thought he would be.

"So, you are seeking spiritual guidance at the moment?"

Wow this vicar drops JC's business card quicker than a Japanese business man.

"Not really, I am exploring more earth based experiences."

I almost laughed, alcohol and screwing men in fields, you cannot get more earth based than that.

"Oh, so interesting, and if you don't mind, could you tell me why that is, did you not enjoy your experience in your pagan group, I would be quite happy to get on my knees and pray with you.

Oh no, Birch's expression changed, here it comes, I am dead, I will be burned on the village green any day now. She gave a slight smile which was not good.

"Oh no, it was actually quite fun, I really loved cutting the heads off chickens at midnight, running naked through the woods, and the wild sexually deviant orgies. I can promise you, when I went down on my knees in the woods, all I was praying for was that he would last long enough to pleasure me back."

AND I AM DEAD!

The Vicar sat back in his chair, and I expected him to have a stroke right there and then. He smiled.

"Well, well, how extraordinary... I must say, I really should try and stay more up to date with modern practices, you are an extraordinary woman, and I am grateful to have spoken with you."

I was lost for words, all I could think of was, if Birch was extraordinary, the fact I had survived without blighting my family name once again, was a bloody miracle. Although I think the only thing the vicar needed to stay up to date with, was reality, how the fuck did he buy into that?

A few minutes later, after his drink, he gracefully excused himself, and thanked me for my hospitality, and made his way happily out of the garden. I bolted the gate behind him, and turned to see Birch back in her spot naked in the sun. I walked down towards her and she looked up and smiled.

"No more Bell Twats, okay?" I had to smile.

"Yes, I hear you, I will try to keep them as far as possible from you."

"Good... Next time I won't be that polite." I looked at her in disbelief.

"That was being polite?"

All I heard in the back of my head was my own voice, and it simply said 'That is Birch, she is like that, but don't worry, you will get used to her.'

Chapter 10

Kitchen Mischief.

Sunbathing was something I used to do a lot before Uni. I suppose it is the greatest advantage of having a large back garden, our boundaries on both sides were lined with mature trees and shrubs, and at the far end of the garden behind the greenhouse, we had the woodland that ran down towards the canal. The good thing about the properties on this lane, is that land around them is so big, none of the houses overlook each other, which simply put, means absolute privacy.

Having survived the visit of the vicar, I returned to the side of Birch, and lay beside her on a heavy tartan rug she had found in the bedroom, and once again relaxed. After the trauma of Birch, and as she referred to him, 'The Bell Twat,' all I wanted was some peace and quiet. Lying in the garden, stretched out in the sun felt familiar, and for the first time since arriving back, it actually felt like home again. It felt so natural that I had also forgotten to take into account we were both completely naked. Birch rolled over onto her back.

"I am cooking, this is wonderful... Although!"

I lifted my head to look at her. She was flat out with her legs spread, not the most lady like pose for this area.

"What?" She turned her head to look at me.

"No sunglasses, it never occurred to me to bring some."

"I got a few pairs somewhere; do you want me to go look?" She yawned.

"Why, where are they?"

"In my room of course."

Birch sat up quickly. "Oh my god! I have not seen your room yet, Sweetie, I want to see it, come on."

Birch jumped up looking excited, and set off across the lawn, in all the chaos that had been my life over the last day, I had completely forgotten that apart from the kitchen and the hallway, Birch had not actually seen any of the house. I jumped up off the blanket, and followed her, she glanced back, giggled and started to run.

"Come on slow coach."

I ran after her, and we raced laughing towards the patio doors, Birch made it first, grabbed the handle, and slid open the door, as I caught her up giggling, both of us came staggering through, unaware mum was standing at the counter peeling potatoes.

"Abigail!"

I bumped into the back of Birch giggling, and then suddenly it hit me, and I realised we were both naked, as I saw the look on my mother's face. I gasped a deep breath of air, and stood still next to Birch, as I stared at her feeling the horror of what was to become. My mind raced, I felt suddenly very awkward.

"Mum.... Er Mother?"

I was ready for the lecture, she looked me up and down, and gave a sigh.

"I was going to make a roast dinner, but I got waylaid with Hatty after church. I realise it has been tradition in this house to sit round the table on Sundays to a family meal, but your father as usual encountered Hatty, and has gone to the Hunters. I am making a shepherd's pie, I thought I would bring it down to you girls when it is done, if that is alright?"

No shouting, I was caught off guard, what could I say?

"Are we not eating at the table?" It was her turn to look surprised.

"If I am honest, I thought you would not want to." She waved her hand towards me still holding the peeler.

"Not very bohemian enough." Birch gave a slight chuckle.

"I like to sit crossed legged on the chair, if I can do that, I would be up for eating inside." I nodded in agreement.

"I would like to eat inside too." She gave a slight smile.

"Then I will let you know when it is done, and the table is ready." I made the effort and smiled.

"Thanks Mu...Mother." She looked at me.

"Oh, for heaven's sake Abigail, if you really have to, call me Mum, I am sure it will not be the end of the world." It was a token of peace, and I know for her, a huge step, I was taking it.

"Only on one condition." She gave a slight frown.

"I refuse to call you Deadly; I am sorry but there is a line, and I really am doing my best here, but black hair and shaved downstairs, which I have accepted as the new modern way, are as far as I can go."

Birch pursed her lips and tried not to laugh. I took a step towards her feeling uncertain and a little nervous.

"I will call you Mum, if you call me Abby, everyone else but you do, and it has always felt strange. Abigail should only be used when I misbehave, it's like a warning shot across the bow."

I know how hard that will be for her, for someone like my mum, having standards, and having everything appear proper is massively important. To most families outside the village, it is simply a normal formality, but here in this dark age thinking place, it is considered common, and simply not done. She put down the peeler and gave a sigh.

"I can see that studying business at University is paying off, your negotiating skills are greatly improved."

She looked me in the eye, I still thought she had the most amazing blue eyes, they had such depths. I could see Birch looking right at her, and watching her every reaction, I also noticed how she gave a very slight but subtle nod.

"You ask a lot for someone like me Abigail, as you know round here it is not that easy, but I will meet you half way. I will try, I make no promises, but when we are alone, I will call you Abby, just not in the village.... At least not for now."

Crazy as it sounds, it felt like a massive victory, and there was no way I was going to refuse it. I felt it was a huge show of effort on her part, and I was not turning it down. It felt like this was the first time in almost two years, we had actually had a conversation with real meaning to it.

I felt the warm hand of Birch on my bum, she pushed, and I stepped forward, I understood the message. Cautiously, I walked towards her and smiled and I held out my hand.

"It's a deal."

Her eyes glistened, as she wiped her hands on her apron, and she reached out and took my hand and shook it.

"Deal."

Then something unexpected happened. She pulled my arm, it jerked, and I felt myself go forward, and before I really understood what was happening, she pulled me close and into her embrace with a sniffle. I was caught off guard, and instinctively slid my hands round her, I felt her embrace tighten, and leaned into her, and before I really understood why, I was saying the words.

"I am sorry mum; I did not mean what I said." She gave another sniffle.

"I know, I was wrong too."

She held me far longer than I expected, but considering the last day and half, I let her take the moment. Her words were soft in my ear.

"We have to stop fighting, it is bad enough he shouts all the time, we cannot be like this, we are all we have, and we must stick together Abb....y."

I felt her hug soften, and she lifted her hand, I looked up as she took a deep breath, and turned her face away to wipe her tear from her eye. I lifted my hand to wipe the tear from her other eye, and she turned with sparkling blue eyes and looked at me, I smiled.

"No more tears mum." She took another deep breath and smiled.

"I realise it's off the subject, but I honestly can say, I never thought I would be stood in a kitchen, in the heart of the village of the dammed, peeling spuds in the buff. It feels sort of liberating don't you think?"

Birch stood on the other side of the counter waving the peeler, holding a half peeled potato in her dirty hand, wearing a very philosophical expression. My mum looked at her with those sparkling green eyes of life, and burst into laughter. She smiled at me with one of those intense smiles, and then winked, and I could not help starting to laugh with my mum, and all I could think of, was Birch, you are absolutely lovely, and thank you. She looked at me as I stared at her.

"What?"

She looked back to my mum and then me again, and my mum

just carried on laughing. It was probably the most absurd thing that had ever happened in the village, but it was here, and it was home, and it was Birch. I looked at my mum as she giggled.

"Trust me it's a Birch thing, you will get used to it." Birch smiled at us, and carried on peeling the potato.

It took a few minutes to settle down a little, before she understood we were going to help, she looked round the kitchen, and went straight in to her work mode.

"Right, if this is to be a team event, Abby, you can shell those peas, I will grind the beef, and we will need to chop some onions."

Without stopping to think, we all fell into our roles, and it felt nice. I was used to cooking with mum, we had spent hours in the past baking all day, but just having Birch involved made it feel a little more homely, although she was a messy worker, and yet I could see my mum biting her lip, and holding back.

I had seen Birch cook with her mum when I had been there, and I remember thinking at the time I wish we could do that here, but I never for one second thought it would happen.

The fact it was, made a huge difference as everyone relaxed, and just for a moment I thought, this has to be something to do with Hatty. She alone is the only person I know who can influence my mum enough to make big changes, and as I sat at the counter popping peas, with Birch opposite, I was really grateful to her.

I popped a really big pod, and the peas went everywhere, one dropped off the counter and landed right between my legs, I looked down and saw where it had wedged itself, and looked up to see Birch leaning over the counter looking at where it was. Her eyes moved up to look at me.

"I hope you are going to eat that, we are having beef with this dish, not fish?"

She smiled, and I heard my mum snigger. I gently removed it from outer labia, and popped it in my mouth with a smile, Birch gave a shudder.

"Oh god, you have been in Manchester way too long, and it's starting to rub off." I winked.

"Bev would have eaten it." Birch gave a snort.

"She prefers hers mushy." She gave a cackle of a laugh.

Mum looked at me not understanding the joke, I felt for now

considering the current cease fire, Bev was best left for another day. I was intrigued though, and considering we were all getting on so well, I dared to ask.

"You know mum, I have to ask. Does it not bother you with us being naked, I mean if I am honest, I thought you would be mad at us?"

She was seasoning the meat, and gave me a look of exasperation.

"My god girls, I was not born in the stone age, hell I once danced naked to Hawkwind at Reading Festival with Hatty. It may come as a surprise to you Abby, but you know, I too was young once. It would surprise you what Hatty and I got up to in the 80's, we had our days of liberation, you mark my words, as for being naked, I have never had an issue with it, I think it is quite natural."

Just for a second a wicked glint crossed her eyes, as I saw the fixed attention of not just myself, but also Birch, who was riveted. Mum was considering something, and I thought she was daring herself to say it. I felt a sudden excitement, it sounded mad, but just thinking she had been naked with others like I had, made me feel for the first time in ages, we had something in common. Birch was dying to know more.

"Come on Flick, spill the beans." That was my second shock, Birch called her Flick, my mum gave a nervous giggle.

"I have skinny dipped too." She gave a giggle like a young girl who was proud. I was actually really surprised, and gave a gasp.

"You have?" She nodded.

I was delighted and shocked at the same time, but actually why was I shocked, hadn't I done the very same thing just a few nights ago with Bev and Birch? Birch looked at my mum with a smile and deep admiration.

"Go Flick, you little devil you." She wiped a tear from her eyes, and then squealed.

"Oh crap!" She turned away from the counter holding her face, I panicked.

"What is it?" My mum gave a giggle as Birch looked at the ceiling stamping her feet.

"Frigging fascist onion got me."

I did not know what to do, my mum was on hand, as Birch

stamped and wiggled. She came round the counter and grabbed a tea towel, she grabbed Birch's face to lower it, and then dapped the towel in her eye, and wiped it.

"Good grief Birch, what a lot of fuss and nonsense." Birch wiggled like an eel.

"Ow...Ow... Ow, it stings like a bitch!"

"I thought you were a witch? Oh dear... Slain by a little onion juice, I mean seriously girl, what a scene?"

I could not help but giggle, as Birch's hands waved about in the air, as my mum dabbed at her eyes.

"Abby darling, get me some damp kitchen roll?"

I slid out off my seat, and ran round the counter, and yanked a piece of flowery kitchen roll off the holder. I reached over and turned on the tap, held the towel out to dampen it, then turned, and handed it to mum, as Birch continued with her yelps and dance. My mum chuckled as she replaced the tea towel, and dabbed her eye with cold water, tutting as she did so.

"What a baby, and here I was thinking you were all grown up?"

The kitchen door opened, but we were unaware, such was the racket made by Birch, and my father stood just inside the kitchen looking outraged.

"WHAT IN THE BLAZERS ARE YOU PLAYING AT?"

We all jumped out of our skin, Birch who had hold of the paper towel against her left eye turned and waved.

"Hi Ed, sorry I got attacked by a rouge organic onion."

I bit my lip, as I saw his utterly shocked face, my mum sniggered at my side. He looked furious, and lifted a shaking finger to point at us. I suddenly realised, two nude young women, and a fully clothed mother in an apron, dancing like maniacs attending to Birch who was making a racket, was possibly not the best way to earn his approval. I felt my hand slide across towards my vagina, my mum gripped my wrist and stopped me. I thought he was going to explode.

"NOT THE BLOODY ONION, ALL THIS, WHAT THE HELL DO YOU THINK YOU ARE PLAYING AT?"

Birch was still and calm, holding a towel to her eye, she smiled.

"We are making tea... oh no sorry, down here it's dinner... Surprise!!"

She waved her free hand in a jazz hand motion, my mum gave a snort of a snigger, and I tried, but it was impossible holding back the grin that painted my face. He was momentarily lost for words; my mum gave a long sigh.

"Oh for god's sake man, the girls were sunbathing, and then came in to help prepare a meal, what the hell is all the fuss about?"

I thought I heard his jaw hit the floor.

"Fuss... Fuss... I will tell you what all the fuss is about. THE GIRLS ARE NAKED, THAT IS WHAT ALL THE FUSS IS ABOUT!" Birch looked down.

"You noticed huh?"

I tried, honestly, I did, but I just could not hold it back, as I saw the look of utter confusion cross his face, it rushed up my wind pipe into my nose, and I snorted a huge snigger. I felt my mum jerk at my side, and could feel her holding hers back, and my father wrestled for the right words.

"Do you not feel ashamed at all?" Was all he could manage. Birch looked down.

"Well I always wanted bigger boobs, and I have not had a chance to wax since I got here, but I think I am okay with what I have got."

She turned to me; my eyes were bulging, as I fought back the laughter.

"What do you think Deads?"

I could not speak, and just twitched my head sideways several times, as I fought the inner compulsion to go hysterical. Birch was just on a whole other level of relaxed, and he just did not know how to take it. My mum took charge.

"Really Edwin, it's not like you have not seen naked women before is it now, I mean for god's sake man, we swam naked in the Riviera?"

It was my turn for my jaw to drop, I looked at her.

"You did!?"

I looked at my dad, and he was clearly on the back foot, and looked very embarrassed.

"It... It was a long time ago... Your mother and I were young and silly." I was annoyed, Birch answered before I could speak.

"I am young, and I can be silly, and I am not ashamed of who

I am, if you find my body shameful, then don't look at it. I have done nothing wrong today, except have a lovely time cooking with your wife and daughter. I understand this is your house, and I am trying to be respectful, but we did check with Flick, and she was fine with it, so I am not going to apologise for helping them do something nice for you, by making your meal."

Holy shit she used the guilt card like a pro. I looked at my father and it was clear, it was game, set, and match to Birch, he took a step back, and reached for the door handle, he looked embarrassed.

"I am simply not used to walking into rooms to be confronted like this, the fact remains this is not Bohemia, it is Wotton, and so therefore not expected. I was just very surprised; I am very sorry if my insensitivity offended you Birch."

He pulled the handle and retreated down the hall to his study, I thought I was going to faint, I stared at my mum in shock.

"What just happened?"

She gave a small gasp of a chuckle, and looked at Birch with admiration.

"You are just like her, I cannot tell you how happy I am Abby has a friend like you, I know the true value of it." She turned to me. "If her and Hatty join forces, you and I are in a lot of trouble."

I smiled at Birch, as she dabbed her eyes and then blinked. My mum clapped her hands.

"Okay, if we intend to eat, we need to get on, I will finish the onions, and then we shall, start on desert, the gauntlet has been thrown down girls, we need to make a meal that old misery will not forget."

Birch and myself looked at each other across the counter, and just smiled at each other, mum was right, and yes since being back home, I had really come to understand the value of her friendship.

Across Wotton, Harriet sat on the wall, with a pint of larger, smoking a cigarette, outside the Hunters Arms Hotel, which was the reason Edwin had left, and was now sat in his study at home, working on his speech for the Key Note address, at the conference he would be attending all week in Brighton.

Derek and Margret Pemberton came across the green, followed by Chloe and Edwina their daughters. On Sunday their restaurant was closed all day, and having spent the week cooking, it had become family tradition for them to eat out at the large hotel dining room.

Derek and Margret both gave a respectful nod to Harriet as they passed, and as their children approached, Harriet looked Chloe right in the eye.

"Have you got a moment Chloe?"

Chole looked like she was about to faint, her sister eyed her suspiciously, but Chloe stopped, and nodded to her sister, it was alright, and to go on. Harriet smiled at Edwina.

"I won't keep her more than a moment."

Edwina walked past looking intimidated, she had also been a student of Harriet, and the fear of her from school was still apparent. Chloe stood still looking awkward.

"How can help you Mrs Barker?"

"It's Miss, I have never married and neither wish to. I just wanted to offer a word of advice if that is alright?" The girl looked terrified.

"I have not said or done anything, honestly." Harriet gave a smile.

"Look Chloe, I was one of your teachers, you were in my homeroom for two years as I recall?" She nodded an agreement. "I would like to think I did a reasonably good job; I actually pride myself on being a competent teacher believe it or not? So, with that in mind I just wanted to say this. There are times in this village, where people jump to the wrong conclusion, and as a result people get hurt, I am sure you remember Debbie Ford quite vividly?" Chloe swallowed hard, and looked down.

"Debbie was from the local estate, and she worked very hard to get her qualifications, she was a bright girl who was top of the year. If I am honest, I feel she earned that spot the hard way, because life at home for her was not that easy at the time. In her last year of high school her luck changed, and yes because her mother remarried, her fortunes changed, I am sure you remember it well?"

Chole was very nervous and nodded her head.

"I do." Harriet looked at her intently.

"Yes, you do. What I want to say is there are people in this village, who shall remain nameless, who took a very wrong view of her situation, and ridiculed her mother and herself for it, of which, as I remember you were one of them?" Chloe was looking more and more unsettled.

"What happened to Debbie was wrong and very ill informed, the girl deserved the better life she got. Now I am sure you feel that what happened to you the other evening was equally as wrong, and I cannot comment as I do not know the full facts, but I am sure you are aware that Abigail Watson is my God Daughter? However, what I would like to say, is simply that if we form an opinion without knowing the facts, as I taught you in school, we do ourselves a great disservice, and we act out of ignorance, instead of informed facts. You were a bright student, and so I know you understand what I am telling you." Chloe took a deep breath.

"I do Miss." Harriet knew her well enough to know she understood.

"Okay then, I won't keep you much longer, so I will tell you only this. Birch, Abigail's friend is highly intelligent, but she is also street smart, she comes from the north, and they show little fear when confronted, as I am sure you are now aware. My advice to you would be, either avoid her, or be civil. The mistake you made the other night was you were disrespectful to three of your customers, and unfortunately one of them was a northern lass as they say. Next time be more respectful, and do not always assume those in higher spots in this village are correct. Think for yourself in future. Okay, go on and enjoy your meal, and take good care of yourself."

Chloe gave a hurried nod, and moved on through the gate towards the Hotel, Harriet turned.

"Oh, and Chloe?" She stopped.

"Yes Miss?"

"I realise you work long hours, but keep your sketching up, you do actually have some talent, don't waste it on dishes, focus on college, you have a very bright future."

"I still sketch Miss; I have not stopped." Harriet smiled.

"I am pleased to hear it, maybe you will bring them round at some point like you used to, and by the way, for fuck's sake call me Harriot, you left school three years ago." She smiled.

"Yes Harriet."

She turned and hurried into the Hotel. Harriet pulled another cigarette from her packet, and then hunted for her lighter. She lifted out a cigarette and smiled as she lit it, then dropped the lighter back into her deep pocket.

Chapter 11

Secrets.

Cooking with mum and Birch was great fun, if not chaotic at times. Considering this was my first time cooking naked, and it was also with mum, I was feeling wild and free. and completely liberated, and at ease, sort of similar to being back in the dorm in Manchester.

Like all good things, it had to come to an end, and after everything was cooking, and we had washed, dried and put everything away, which by the way, is a mammoth task when you cook with Birch, mum asked the one question we had not thought of.

Mum had opened a bottle of red wine to breathe, my father was a bit of a wine connoisseur, and was insistent procedure was followed. It was something in our house that had become standard.

Unfortunately, Birch was not one of us, and so seeing a wine bottle open on the side, she naturally assumed it was drinks time, and so poured out three good glasses. After a giggle and a short explanation, we opened a second to breathe, and sat at the counter enjoying our first glass of the day, when mum remembered.

"By the way girls, why were you racing to the house earlier?"

That was the moment the penny dropped, and Birch and I both looked at each other, and at the same time said.

"Bedroom!"

With glasses in hand, and filled with giggles, we were off, flying down the hall way, skidding round at the doorway, as we raced up the stairs, and I ran screaming and laughing for my room, hotly pursued by Birch. As we reached the top of the stairs, my father came out of his study to complain, only to see two very naked sets of buttocks disappearing in the direction of my room.

Edwin was up, and in the hall, so made his way to the kitchen to get a coffee, when he arrived, Felicity was outside on the patio having a cigarette. He poured his drink, and walked out of the door to join her. Felicity stood smoking, staring down the garden into space.

"Smoking again I see, how long has it been, I thought you had finally conquered it?"

Felicity blew out a long smoke filled breath, and flicked the ash on the lawn in front.

"It's been a rough week, hell it's been a rough year, and just for the record it has been eight months."

"So, you are talking to Abigail again I see, how did that go?"

She took another long pull on the cigarette, and held the smoke in, it was as if it was a requirement in order to answer, her tone was bland.

"She is my daughter, and you may not believe it, but that is the one hope I have in her. If you were home more, you would understand who she is, and who she will become." She turned to look at him stood in the doorway holding his cup.

"Do you remember the girl you married Edwin, hell do you even remember why you married her?" He frowned.

"What the hell is that supposed to mean? Of course, I do, I am looking right at her." Felicity flicked her ash and shrugged.

"You know there was a time when you looked at me the way you looked at her today." Edwin gave a sigh.

"Don't be ridiculous, she is my daughter, I would never see her the way I did you back then, just the thought is sickening. Christ Felicity I cannot believe you at times." She blew out another long plume of smoke.

"I was talking about Birch!"

Just for a second, he looked shocked, she smiled and turned back to look down the garden.

"It is alright Edwin, she is very beautiful, and she does have an amazing body, I do not blame you for looking, I won't deny, even I caught myself admiring her. I suppose when we reach our age, we admire youth more, simply because we have lost what we had."

Edwin walked out of the doorway, and stood a few feet to her side. He turned his head to glance at her.

"I have told you before, you are too hard on yourself, you are still the best looking woman in the village. Look Felicity, I realise I am not an easy man to be around, I am quite sure your wacky and meddlesome friend tells you more than often, but look what we have built here, we have done fine to get this far." Felicity laughed.

"Best looking woman in the village, but that is the problem isn't it, all your little indiscretions don't live in the village, do they?"

She took the last pull on her cigarette, dropped it on the floor, and ground the stub in with her toe. She turned and looked directly at him, and he looked guilty.

"I have no concrete proof, but a wife knows these things, you just know you know, and you have no idea how. I suppose being married you just get to know your spouse so well, that it shows, and you pick up on it." He tried to talk.

"Look Felicity."

"No, you look. Look at me Edwin, open your bloody eyes for once, just take a really good look around and see what you have, because it is only here because I have dedicated the better part of my life to maintaining all of this, you were never here. All those times that you complained about the burden my mother was, and yet you did nothing to help. I was the one running around for her, and it was the same raising Abby, and yes, I call her Abby now. Do you want to know why...? Because she asked me too, and I was thrilled that my daughter wanted me to treat her the same as that beautiful girl, who is her best friend. Crazy as it sounds, I wanted to cry, because it is the nicest thing that has happened to me in this house for over a year." He looked wretched and uncomfortable.

"What exactly are you saying, are you asking for a divorce?" She gave a frustrated sigh.

"You won't get off the hook that easy, I am not giving this up, all this is mine, and I earned it the same way you did your precious bloody business. Honestly, I don't care about your other women, it's madness but I don't, and just for the record I know Abby saw you two all those years ago." He gave a frustrated gasp.

"That bloody Hatty..."

"No... That bloody Abby." He looked stunned.

"What do you mean, did she tell you?" Felicity shook her head, and gave a frustrated sigh.

"My god you are unbelievable. I knew she told Hatty that she had seen you with that woman, but Hatty promised she would never tell me, and she has been true to her word, oh I have tried, trust me, I have tried to get it out of her. I did again today, but she is loyal to that girl in ways you will never understand. If you want the truth, I overheard Abby crying on the phone to her, you see that was when I found out Hatty confronted you about it, and you punished Abby for it, with your new rules and tougher penalties. I always thought you threw Hatty out of here because she screwed your brother in the pool, how bloody stupid am I?"

Edwin stared at her with his eyes wide open, Felicity gave a slight laugh, and shook her head slowly.

"God I am such a fool, I was so wrong, I never saw it, actually no, I refused to see it. You were pissed off that she was screwing poor Jeremy and not you, that was the real truth. You punished Abby for telling, and you punished me for not letting you have Hatty. I can handle you punishing me, I made my choice to be here, but Abby, she was innocent, she did nothing wrong. How sick can a person get? She was fourteen Edwin, and she was heartbroken, and you made it worse for her, no wonder she ran off to Manchester at the first chance she had, and tried to erase everything that reminded her of home."

Felicity pulled another cigarette from her packet, and slipped it in her mouth, Edwin just stared as she lit it. Felicity's bright blue eyes flashed with anger, but she kept her voice down, as upstairs Birch and Abby were laughing.

"You asked me what I want, well I will tell you; I want some truth. I am tired of all the bullshit; I am tired of the lies and the secrets. It is madness, because Hatty has been pointing it out for years, and yet it took a beautiful, kind, no nonsense girl like Birch, to really open my eyes and see everything for what it truly is. I watched her today Edwin, and she floored you in seconds just by being honest and respectful. That is why when she walked through the village yesterday with our daughter, they labelled them freaks, and why when she defended our daughter in that restaurant last night, her honesty and respect shone like a beacon, she showed this village for what it really is." Edwin swallowed hard.

"And just what is that exactly?" She laughed.

"It is just like you, they all are filled with bullshit and fake superiority, with their lies and their secrets. You know I really admire Bradly Wheeler; he is richer than any of us here, and yet he married a girl with no background and no breeding, and when all those hate filled bullies attacked her, what did he do? He stood by her, and he stood up for her, and he fought for her, and for her daughter, now that is a real man. Tell me Edwin, what did we do when our daughter came home, did we fight for our child? I am ashamed today, because instead of standing by her, we joined them, and my daughter saw it and she called me out on it, and rightly so."

Felicity took another long pull on her cigarette. Edwin shuffled his feet and took a sip from his mug.

"Look we did a lot of damage control last night and today, you know what this place is like, it will all die down it time."

"That is my point, we should not have felt like we had to, we should have stood by her."

"Well I... I wouldn't go that far, I mean come on, she does look bloody extreme, I mean my god, she looks like she just stepped out of a vampire novel." Felicity gave a nod of agreement.

"Yes, she does, I watched her today, she was naked and at ease, and loving just cooking with Birch and me, she had such a wonderful time. I looked at her with her long jet black hair with its red tips and a fringe, I mean, she has never had a fringe in her life. I just looked at her smiling. I thought what a beautiful child, I am not sorry to say that actually I prefer her like this, she can run naked and screaming all over the house all summer if she wants, because be honest Edwin, how long is it since she did that? Five, six years now? I love how my daughter has turned out, and I am really proud of her, and if as her father you cannot accept that, then bugger off to Brighton with your mistress, and leave us alone to have fun. It is getting late, I have to set the table and serve our meal, which I may add your daughter helped cook, will you be joining us?" Felicity walked towards the door; Edwin turned.

"If it helps, I am sorry." Felicity scoffed.

"Not really, and just for the record, have you forgotten my all time favourite book is Bram Stokers, Dracula?"

It was fun showing my room off, it is actually a lot bigger and tidier than Birch's room, although to be honest I have not been home for a year, and this was my first time in it since I came back.

My ceiling was plastered with Avril Lavigne posters, which probably did explain some of my attitude, although there were some of Zeppelin and Motley Crue as well. Birch loved having a good explore of my book shelves, and massive collection of DVD's, all of which contained the best of gothic/steam punk related movies. Deb's loved steam punk, and I loved the clothing, we have had many nights watching them on the computer.

Birch loved my wardrobe, and we spent ages dragging out stuff and trying things on. Our hips are pretty much the same size, her legs are a little longer than mine, but after swapping and changing, we found some long in the leg pants that fitted her really well. I love big baggy tops, and she grabbed quite a few, I figured we had been sharing clothes for ages, and I had worn most of hers, so it was my turn to let her take a pick. We looked less goth and more upper class bohemian, but hell it was fun, and we both thought we best dress for dinner.

I was mortified when she opened my toy cupboard and found my large collection of dolls. It had been so long since I had played with them, and yet I have never had the heart to throw them away. Birch took the piss a lot, then proceeded to put them in weird sexual poses, and asked me if I had done any, it was hilarious, and I rolled around on the bed, as she discovered the male doll, and added him to the mix of bizarre sexual positions.

We laughed so hard, and we eventually ended lay side by side on my single bed giggling like little girls, it was the best fun I had since coming home. She looked at me and as I lay at her side, and gently stroked the hair from my face, her bright green eyes sparkled with life, I smiled.

"Last time we did this Bev wanted to rape me, so are you going to have your way with me now, after all, we are alone, and I know you love my boobs?" She looked deep into my eyes; her voice was soft.

"I do love risk, but no Sweetie, you are a risk too far."

I really did not understand her, how could I be a risk? I felt closer to her than anyone I know, and as weird as it sounds, because I really am not into woman, if Birch had wanted to make love to me, I would have willingly let her have me. I stared back into her eyes.

"I am not sure I understand, why am I a risk?" She smiled.

"Do you want to know my biggest secret?"

Okay, so I know this girl and she is pretty wild, and very honest, and her morals can at times be somewhat looser than most of us. I thought about it for a second, could I really handle the workings of the mind of Birch? Yeah, I had fallen for it, some deep dark part of me that has a habit of looking into the void, and scaring myself had awoken. I stared into her deep beautiful eyes that inspired me so much.

"Tell me."

It was insane, what was she going to say, because in truth, I was actually afraid to know. Birch sat up, crossed her legs and faced me. I lay there looking up at her, as her long hair hung down in front of her.

"I love the all the lesbian jokes, I do, it's fun, especially with Bev and you, because you are not offended, and know I mean no harm by them. I have never been sure if I could go that way, I think it is possible, all women have a bisexual side, it is a lot more common than you think, but honestly Deads, I have only thought about doing it with a woman once, for the rest of the time I just wanted a good cock, as you know, I do enjoy them?" I gave a chuckle.

"But?" She smiled.

"As I said, I have only thought of sex with a woman once, and it was you." I felt the jolt run through me like electricity, and I swallowed hard.

"Me... When?" She leaned down and stroked my hair off my face again.

"It was a few months ago, in the dorm. It was when you were reading your essay on the humanity of the monster in Shelly's Frankenstein." She giggled. "I know sort of weird, I get it, but just sat watching you read really turned me on, I got so wet watching you, I cannot explain it, but I just wanted to throw you back on the bed and bury my face into you."

I was riveted, and wanted to know more, but I felt my heart beating faster and suddenly I felt warmer than I normally do, oh my god was I getting wet too? Birch sat there, so honest and so sincere, I had to stop myself from just reaching up and kissing her. I know, how messed up is that? I love men, actually scratch that, I freaking love men, I was too intrigued, and had to know more.

"So why didn't you?" She gave a sigh.

"Simply put Sweetie, it was you."

"Huh?"

I really didn't understand at all, I am quite sure had the role been reversed, I would have gone for it without a second thought. I suppose the one thing I know is, this is Birch's mind we are talking about, and as much as I have spent just about every waking moment with her this last year, I still know there is a huge depth to her I have not even scratched.

"Honestly I am bamboozled, you wanted me, but did not do it because it was me, I have to say Birch, I am lost." She adjusted her position.

"It was fear, plain and simple fear Deads, I cannot deny I fear little, but that day, I terrified myself." I gave her a frown.

"Screwing me would be that bad then?" She giggled.

"I didn't mean it that way. The truth is, I know a lot of lesbian couples, and most of them have not lasted, and as a result I have lost some good friends because they got heartbroken, and moved on. Deadly I really do love you, honestly, I do, you will probably not understand, but this, me and you, it means everything to me. It's why I am here, and I was terrified I would lose you, real unfiltered living terror, so I sat there and I watched you read, and I said nothing, and later that night when you went to sleep, I frapped like hell, and got it out of my system."

She gave me a big smile. "It was a good night." She laughed and I chuckled and understood, I sat up and nodded.

"Yeah, I get that, I don't want to bugger this up either, but honestly Birch, you missed the hump of a life time."

We both started laughing, and she lifted the pillow and hit me with it. I looked at my digital clock.

"We should go down; it is almost time for dinner... That is tea time in Manchester." I sniggered, and jumped off the bed, and the pillow missed me.

We came out of the bedroom into the hall, and I pointed across to the door.

"That's my mum and dads' room."

We walked further down, and passed the stairs to the next door on the left, I grabbed the handle and opened the door. "Bathroom and shower." She gave a nod, and then turned and walked further down to the door on the right.

"This is the guest room, it was almost where you would have been staying, but dad thought you would prefer your privacy, hence the guest house." I walked into the room and she followed.

It is not a huge room, but it had a good sized bed, and is reasonably spacious. I looked round, it has been ages since I have been in here, I grabbed the door of the large double wardrobe.

"Mum puts loads of her old stuff in here, sometimes I look at it and nick it, especially her old jeans."

I opened the door to show her, and felt a jolt to my system, Birch leaned in, it was filled with my dad's clothes, and I did not understand why. I just stood there and stared at them; Birch grasped the olive branch long before I did.

"Okay Sweetie, I have seen it, come on let's go and eat."

She pushed the door shut, and I turned and saw my mum at the door, she had a sad look on her face. My mind raced, I did not understand it at all, I stared at her as she stepped into the room.

"Why are dad's things here?" She gave a sigh.

"Sit down Abby darling, we need to talk."

I felt lost in confusion, I stepped back, and just flopped on the bed as my mind went into freefall. Birch stepped back, as my mum came closer and sat on the bed at my side, Birch made to leave, my mum looked up at her.

"It's alright Birch, you may as well stay, Abby will talk with you either way." She looked at me, and I felt completely out of it.

"Mum are you getting divorced?" She smiled and took my hand in hers.

"No darling we are not... Abigail let me put it this way so you understand. You went to University to find out who you were, I really do understand how important it was for you to have some space to work out who you are."

I gave her a nod, I wanted to talk, I just could not find the right words. She patted my hand and took a deep breath.

"Abby, life is not as easy as you think, there are lot of bumps in the road, and at times it is hard to navigate them. I think you have already learned a little of that, well after your grandma died, and then you went University, your father and I realised that we had hit a lot of bumps, and things were not really right. Both of us needed the space, like you, we had to work out what had happened to us. I suppose we needed some time, and some space. This was our solution, both of us were clear that we would find a way to work everything out, and we have been trying to do that. I suppose we said nothing because you were away, we really did not need to bother you with it."

I understood, she made sense but it felt so wrong, I felt shaken, it was like the ship I had sailed on to new lands, had suddenly ran into ground, and I was about to be abandoned on a deserted island. I tried to grapple with the reality of it, but I needed assurance.

"You are staying together, neither of you are going anywhere?" She smiled and patted my hand.

"It is a work in progress, but relax we are both staying put." I gave a long sigh of relief.

Dinner that night felt strange and surreal, we had spent the day naked, had dinner dressed, and all sat round the table like nothing had happened. Life was moving exactly as it always had, but it wasn't, it was fake, a lie, a deceptive secret.

I had always admired my parents, because no matter what they made it through, and yet as I sat there watching them talking just like they always had, it was hard for me to understand, and all I could think about was, is this how Birch sees the world?

Birch has always amazed me by the way she reads situations, and picks up on things I simply don't. My thoughts drifted back to the restaurant, and how she had just slipped a card on to the table, because she saw that Lillian and Celia, were hiding a big secret that could never be raised in the village.

It got me thinking, how many more secrets do these people have, and is that the reason they fear everyone new, oh hell, are they afraid Birch and me will expose them, is that why they hate us? I was so close to the truth, and yet I had not realised it, but who am I to talk, I have my own secrets too.

Birch told me something private, something deep today,

something I never saw, and as I sat there watching her being so natural, so honest and open, all I could think of, was I want to be like that, but I am not quite ready, but when I am, she will be the first to know.

My father talked of his Key Note Speech for the conference in Brighton, we both talked about University and our studies, although my father was more than interested in Birch's parents. I figured he wanted their accounts, after all, her mother has made a lot of money off her book sales, but watching Birch, it felt like she was already aware of that.

When dinner was over, we cleared the table, and loaded the dishwasher, and finished off the wine in the kitchen, where mum talked more, and absolutely promised me nothing at home would change. Eventually Birch and myself headed back to the guest house, with a couple of extra bottles of cola, and we lay in bed talking and drinking vodka. Birch turned on her side and looked at me.

"Will you be alright?" I lay on my back looking at the ceiling.

"Yeah, I think so, it has been one hell of a weekend." She chuckled.

"It is certainly not boring here." I turned to look at her.

"I am glad you told me about that night in the dorm, I have lay here thinking about it, and I think it was right. Promise me Birch, if you feel like that again, you will talk with me. I like that we are honest, especially when you think of the lies and secrets this village is filled with. I need one person who is straight with me." She nodded.

"I will... So, you are not disappointed with me then?"

"What because you chose not to sleep with me...? No, I felt it at first, but I am okay with it now." Birch slid over, and straddled me, and looked down as she smiled.

"So, about that?"

"Huh?"

She kissed me softly between my breasts, and then I felt her foot between my ankles. She dragged my legs apart, and slid in between my legs, and then looked at me with lustful eyes. I felt my pulse start to race.

"Birch!"

Her head slipped under the duvet, and I felt a hot soft kiss on the bridge of my ribs.

"Birch!"

I pushed my head back in the pillow. Another kiss landed on the top of my stomach.

"Hah... Birch!"

She slipped her hands down between my thighs and spread my legs wider. Oh god, I am not mentally prepared for this. Her lips touched my belly button, and I felt her tongue wriggle into it.

"Oh shit.... Birch!"

My mind raced, as she wriggled her tongue within my belly button, and I felt my heart start to race even faster, my calves were trembling, and my brain started to swirl. I could feel the heat in the bed rising rapidly, and her head lifted slightly, I was breathing faster than a jogger running up hill. I pulled my arms out from under the duvet, and grabbed on to the headboard.

"Oh shit... Oh shit... Oh shit... Birch!" I felt her hot breath on my vagina, and I closed my eyes.

"Oh, god, I am going to cum!!"

The suspense was a nightmare, any moment now, Birch would use her tongue to enter the man only zone, and I really did not know if I could handle her tongue, in a place where only men had ever roamed, my voice rapidly rose by several octaves.

"BIRCH!"

I opened my eyes, and gritted my teeth, my toes curled, and then she slid off the end of the bed, and out from under the duvet, and stood up with a huge smile on her face.

"I need a pee, ha, ha, Sweetie I got ya!" She turned, and ran to the bathroom cackling with laughter.

"You Bitch!!"

I was sweating like crazy, as I relaxed into the pillow, and took a long deep breath, my heart was racing, and in the background in the toilet, all I could hear was Birch laughing her head off. I let go of the head board, and let my arms flop on top of the duvet, I have never been so bloody scared in all my life.

Chapter 12

Petal.

My first weekend home had been to say the least, 'Stressful.' I had arrived back home with Birch, a shamed woman, a transient, the embarrassment of my family, and disrupter of restaurants. I had argued with my mother, ignored my father, discovered the two old ladies in the tea rooms, who I had always thought were best friends, were in fact sleeping with each other, almost flashed my shaved childlike vagina at the vicar, and had to try and subdue one of Satan's garden gnomes, who was a hater of Bell Twats.

At that moment when my head felt already full, and unable to cope, and my last nerve was as frayed as my new fringe, I discovered I could cook naked, my parents were sleeping in different rooms, and I was about to become the resident bitch of a pagan, naturist, apprentice lesbian. In the words of my dear sweet insane friend Birch.

"It had not been boring."

As a result of what I considered to be ample trauma, which had sent my subconscious into melt down, having finally fallen asleep, after way too much vodka, I was certain everything was finally done and dusted, but oh no, more was to come. I awoke at some God forsaken hour, dripping in sweat, having 'I hope' fingered myself in my sleep, whist having the nightmare that some female was going down on me, only to lift the duvet, and see the lust filled face of Marjorie Wallace eating me out, in a manner befitting Bev.

The scream that came from my mouth, was a tad louder than I expected, and I watched my beautifully naked sleeping friend Birch, go from the peacefully lay down position in the bed next to me, to upright in one swift motion, where she stood brandishing a fucking huge knife, facing the door, like a combat ready assassin, and all I could manged in my terror was to say.

"You sleep with a fucking knife!!?"

Still half asleep, Birch looked round the room, shrugged, and got back in bed. She turned in the dark, with her white face and hair, looking like an apparition, smiled, and told me.

"It was in my bag Sweetie."

She then flopped back on the pillow, and started to snore. Needless to say, I was dreading Monday, and the added fear of being chopped up in my sleep, by my now lovely and adorable, psychotic roommate.

Monday arrived in the shape of Deb's, my wonderfully cuddly, and exceptionally excited friend, she burst into the guest house, bounced into the bedroom, announcing.

"HI! Your mum me let me in," to which Birch and myself jerked awake, somewhat like corpse's being stimulated with high voltage, at which point Birch sat upright, rubbed her eyes, and made the request to Deb's of.

"Why are you ten times frigging louder than a Bell Twat?"

One hour later, having had plenty of coffee and paracetamol, we found ourselves sat in the sun, relaxing naked. Mum joined us in her bikini, and I sat with her on the loungers close to the pool, while Birch and a surprisingly naked Deb's swam in the pool. I could not help but note, that Birch appeared fascinated by Deb's much larger boobs, and their role in her buoyancy.

My dad had left in the early hours for Brighton, and would be gone for the week, which left me most of the morning quietly talking to mum. She was so much more relaxed than she had been over the weekend, and whilst the other girls frolicked, she talked in more depth about how she felt, and where she wanted to be in life.

I could not help but think of all the conversations between Birch and myself, and the scary thing was, I heard my mum saying the very same things I had. It was such an eye opening experience for me, and I started to see that as much as I messed around and had fun, I was also growing up. Watching Birch with her mum, had made me a little envious, but here I was having the same close experience with my mum, and I was really enjoying it.

Dad was not here, which meant only one thing, and much to my delight she turned up, having heard there was a pool party. Hatty arrived full of cheer, and stocked with gin, vodka and beers, she took one look at Birch and Deb's in the pool, and without batting an eyelid, she stripped on the spot, and dived in, much to the delight of everyone, especially my mum, who was again the only one dressed, albeit scantily.

Drinks were frequent, and fun was to be had, especially when my mum walked along the side of the pool, and Hatty pulled the laces on her tie up bikini, and as it slipped to the floor, Hatty pushed her in, with the comment.

"Remember camping in Scotland?" It was hilarious.

We ate outside as the evening moved on, sat at the table on the patio, and we gathered round with yet more drinks, and Hatty told us the story of their camping adventure, and how when they reached a twelve foot wall above a natural pool, she picked up my mum, and tossed her in to cool her off. She then stripped, and dived in herself. That was the tale my mum had tried to tell us in the kitchen on Sunday, it was her first experience of skinny dipping, as she had to lay her clothes out to dry, and once she had been in, she just stayed naked and swam.

With three in a bed, and an assurance from Birch no knives were anywhere within arm's reach, feeling more than tipsy we passed out until noon Tuesday, and woke in a calmer setting, as Deb's had the same hangover we had.

Birch resumed gnome duty under the big willow tree reading, and Deb's and myself relaxed in the kitchen with mum. That night we all pooled in and cooked another meal, and after we had eaten, we just sat quietly in the garden. It was relaxing and stress free, and I was loving it until Deb's reminded me just before bed.

"Have you been into the village yet?"

I was busted in front of everyone, they had realised I was avoiding what was in fact the inevitable. To date, I had manged to stay off the radar of Marjorie, and I wanted to try and keep it that way. Mum and Birch had been discussing her suggestion during cooking that fresh herbs were so much tastier than dried, and so it was decided by a unanimous vote, that it was time to instal a herb garden, somewhere in the yard.

My heart sank as mum decided that tomorrow we would walk into the village, and then head down Station Road, towards Merryweather's Organic Nursery. Deb's went home to check in on her parents, and promised to return the following day to join with me in showing a united front, just in case we encountered the Fascist on her rounds.

I lay in bed that night, with Birch curled round me nervous and afraid. Marjorie carried a lot of weight in the village, and I knew she would be doing her best to find a reason to ridicule my family.

I just did not want any more trouble, in the last two days the bond with my mum and me had grown stronger, and I really did not want anything to spoil it. I drifted off to sleep to the sound of Birch, softly breathing on the pillow at my side, and more apprehensive than the day I had arrived home, tomorrow would be testing, and I was simply not ready.

I woke up to the soft sound of my mum, who sat on the bed with a tray, which contained freshly made bacon sandwiches. I sat up rubbing my eyes.

"Hi Mum." She smiled.

"Here, eat these." Birch sat bolt upright in bed, and sniffed the air, her eyes still closed.

"Bacon?"

Mum gave a chuckle, as she got up off the bed, and lifted a plate, and placed it in Birch's hand, as she sat there, eyes closed, still smelling the air, and leaning into me.

"I have the kettle on, I will bring you some coffee."

She headed for the kitchen, and we tucked in. Birch gave a happy moan, as she chewed and opened her eyes. She shouted across the room.

"Flick, you are a goddess."

Chuckles came from the next room, and she soon appeared, placed our drinks on the tray, as we enjoyed breakfast in bed. It took a little longer than normal to get up, I think mum sensed I was stalling, Birch too. She decided to dress me, which involved her black leather jacket, black pants decorated with studded seams, and my leather black studded boots, it was a full on, goth/ biker chick look, I actually really liked it.

Birch wore similar pants, matched with a black tight top she had pinched from my wardrobe, and soft leather boots, we stood together on the patio, and my mum who was in casual slacks and a cream blouse smiled.

"You look really bad arse… That is the right saying, isn't it?" I had to laugh.

"Almost mum, it's 'Bad Ass,' and you have to say with attitude."

It was not very long before Deb's arrived, and it was very clear that the influence of Birch was taking effect. In a spurt of new found courage, and encouraged by her father and mother, she wore a tight woollen crop top, no bra, and a short black check mini skirt, on which she had attached her steampunk brown leather braces.

To finish off the whole look, she had on black thigh highs, brown fingerless gloves, and grey baseball boots. Birch was impressed, although she did walk round behind and lifted her skirt, just to make sure she was wearing knickers this time, which she was, black lacey ones.

Deb's beamed with delight, and swished her long brown hair back into a pony tail, which she secured with a small set of tiny goggles, as a bobble. The girls were dressed to kill, and ready to face anything they encountered. Mum gave the signal, and it was 'girls on the town day,' or in this case, the three renegade misfits of Wotton, and Felicity.

Walking down Waterside Lane, and on to Manor Road, I felt fine as we happily chatted and giggled, but as we turned the corner, and the village came into view, I felt my stomach twist. I would be on display in full daylight for everyone to see, and knowing how they have treated others in the past, I was to say the least vary wary. Birch appeared to sense it and linked my arm, it helped me feel a little more secure, and as she leaned in and quietly whispered.

"Let's get this over with, and screw what they think." I did feel a little better.

It was the school holidays, and the full Wotton Summer program had kicked in. On the green, two marques had been set up, which would serve many alternating purposes until after the Summer Fete. Today they were arts and crafts tents, so children from all around the village, could come on down, and join in doing many different things, from painting to basket weaving. I had attended several growing up, and so understood the whole set up. I walked slowly and filled in Birch, who was actually really interested in it.

At the base of the green, a new Wotton Dursley, village notice board, had been erected, after the last one had finally rotted away, and Deb's wanted a closer look, as one of her dad's friends had made and donated it. We crossed the road at the lower end of the street, and walked onto the grass to inspect it. Deb's leaned on the side of it.

"What do you think, I am impressed with the workmanship?"

I looked at the board, which now displayed and advert for the Village Fete, and I had to admit it was pretty good.

A voice called out behind me, I turned to see Hatty with her camera, she smiled at me.

"Stand next to Birch, I will capture the transients of Wotton."

Birch grabbed my arm and pulled me to her, and we larked about, making the horned god symbols of metal, it was fun, as Hatty took several snaps, and I felt a little calmer inside. Hatty walked over checking the shots on her camera, and appeared happy with them, Birch leaned over her shoulder to view them with her.

"So why the camera, I thought you were a painter?" Hatty gave her head a nod.

"I disagree with a lot about this place, but I still do my bit for the community, today I am officially photographer, and documenter of the day's events for the web site." Birch gave a chuckle.

"I am not sure those pictures will get used, unless they use them for a group wanted poster." Hatty gave a shrug.

"I record everything, whether they want to see it or not, I shall give this one the title of 'The Face of the Future,' That should put the wind up the fascist."

The village was a lot busier than normal, there were a lot of parents, who were killing time, as their children attended the craft tents. Outside the tea rooms tables and chairs had been set up, as Green Street had been blocked off for the week. The pub garden was also fuller than usual, and down each side of the green, people stood talking or were looking in windows, or taking advantage of some quick shopping. On the large green, several groups had laid out blankets, and were happily sitting enjoying themselves, and the whole feel of the village had a sense of happiness, it helped to calm me inside.

Mum had gone off with Hatty, she was going to pick up a few things, then head to the nursery, the three of us wandered around taking in the sights, after all for Deb's and me, this was all normal, but to Birch it was a whole new experience. I felt a tap on my shoulder, and was surprised to find it was Chloe. My defences went up instantly, she looked very uncomfortable.

"Can I have a word with you?"

Birch was already on one side and Deb's on the other, Chloe looked warily at Birch.

"I do not want any trouble; I just want to talk." Birch gave a nod, her face looking quite stern.

"Alright, just say what you wanted to, we will hear you out." Chloe swallowed hard.

"I did just want to talk to Abby." Birch stood resolute.

"We come as a trio, it's all of us or none of us, so what do you want?"

I actually felt a little sorry for her, she appeared terrified of Birch, which in itself felt funny, because I knew her, and she could come across as ferocious, but deep down she was the kindest person I had ever met, but there again, Chloe did not know that. I had to give her some credit, she came alone, and was summoning the courage to talk.

"Look Abby, I don't want us to be enemies, to tell you the truth, the other night I was jealous. I do not have the courage you have; I would love to have hair like yours, and I want you to know, I actually really admire you for it. I mean look at me, I have the right top, the right skirt, and the right shoes, so as not to offend the old ones. I have a wardrobe at home full of great clothes, but I cannot wear them here, I have to sneak into Oxendale on my night off to wear them. So, what I am saying is, can we be friends, I have been a total bitch in the past, especially to you Debbie, and

I want you to know I do regret it, and I am really sorry to all of you." I felt Birch soften a little.

"Chloe, friendship is earned, and I cannot deny, I am not in a rush to add you on Insta, some friend's requests are surveillance, how do we know you are not setting Abby up?" She shook her head.

"I would not do that." Deb's stepped forward.

"You already did though, didn't you?" She looked down.

"I took it down after talking to Birch in the toilet, I really am sorry, I honestly took it because you all looked so cool. I did not think others would see it, I don't have a huge list of friends on there, if I had known, I would never have posted it." She looked me right in the eyes.

"I loved your top and pants, honestly? Edwina really roasted me that night, she is a better person than I am, and then Harriet gave me a talking to the other night, and it really made me think. I want to make it up to you, but I really don't know how to."

It was clear to see she was trying, and I felt it inside, if the truth be known, I had enough enemies in the village, one less would be helpful. I glanced to Birch, and then Deb's for guidance, it was Deb's who took the lead.

"You were more than a bitch to me, if you want to make it up, you will have to prove it. Show us you are serious and we can have a truce, but if you try anything again Chloe, you will regret it." She gave a long breath of relief, I nodded to agree with Deb's.

"I have enough problems here Chloe, if you are not one of them, we can be friendly, I am not making any promises, but it will be nice to know not everyone here is against me." She smiled.

"To prove it I will say this just to you Abby, be careful, the CM wants you back, and he is pushing hard, I know you know what I mean?"

My heart felt the chill run through it, did she know something, it was hard to know?

"I am not coming back ever." She gave me a knowing look.

"I won't be around for it after the summer either, you made a good choice, stick to it."

Birch frowned and looked at me, Chloe looked to the top of the street, swallowed hard, and stepped back.

"I have to go, be careful, and I will see you around." I nodded.

"Yeah, look after yourself."

I turned and looked behind me to where she had looked, and could see the vicar talking with the choir master, and the verger. All three of them were looking at me, Martin smiled, and I felt a cold shiver run down my spine. Birch had turned round to look.

"Who is that Deads?" I felt the goosebumps on my arms.

"No one important, come on let's go and find mum."

By the time we arrived on Station Road, my heart was racing. I was walking as quick as I could without looking obvious, and to everyone on the planet I was pulling it off. Well, all except one person, and she just happened to be at my side, and had detection skills not discovered by the CIA yet. Birch linked my arm, and her voice was soft, as Deb's walked along chatting with my mum. We were past the station, and almost at the gates to Merryweather's Nursery.

"You may fool them Deads, but not me. If you don't want to talk, I get it, and can float with it, but if you ask me, you need to talk to someone, and soon. I will wait, but I am here, I am with you, and you know you are safe with me."

I really did not know what to say, we were halfway up the pathway into the Nursery, and all I wanted to do was run away, but I knew I could not.

"Birch... I can't, not today, I am not ready."

"Okay Sweetie."

We walked out into what had once been the gardens of the estate, which was now a fully functioning off grid organic nursery. Mum headed straight for the herb section, Birch and me followed.

Inside my head was spinning, my stomach was reeling and I was fighting the notion to talk with Birch, but considering the last week of my life, I knew that all I wanted to do was lay low, and get through the coming summer with as little trouble as possible.

I was aware of Birch linking my arm, but little else, as my mind wandered around, when suddenly I felt a sharp jerk and staggered sideways, Birch had grown suddenly very excited.

"Oh my god.... Holy shit, have you seen that beauty?"

I came out of my thoughts, and looked round. I saw the store hut, which was built of wood and tin sheets, compost piles, a few wheel barrows, a rusty old car, some hay bales, but no plants or things that would deserve the title of beauty. I looked at Birch who was stood still and smiling, with the biggest smile I had ever seen, and yet nowhere in sight, was there anything I would deem that interesting. She looked at me.

"Isn't it fantastic? I have not seen one like that in years."

I was looking at an old iron shed, and I had no idea why.

"Birch it's a bloody shed, how the hell is that worth getting excited about?" Her eyes were sparkling.

"Are you nuts… God my knickers are so damp at the moment, I mean come on Sweetie, series two, I'd say what 1966-7, possibly Cyprus from the colour, and there is no doubt it's ex RAF."

I stared at her like she was a lunatic, nothing she said fitted the description, I looked around and then realised, and I looked back at her, and then pointed.

"Please tell me you are not talking about that bucket of shit… You are seriously getting wet over that, hell Birch you need to talk to your mother if that turns you on, you are obviously in need of therapy?"

She was staring at the oldest crappiest vehicle I had ever seen, and judging by her face was not that far from having an orgasm.

"You are seriously messed up do you know that?"

"Oh, Deads baby, you have no idea at all, that is a premium collector's piece, and you are wrong, I don't need my mum, I need to talk to my dad. Oh man he is going to be so jealous."

"What… Of that pile of shit?" She gave me a nod, and started to walk towards it with a big smile on her face.

"Oh yeah, because that pile of shit as you call it, is a 1966-7 series 02 Land Rover Defender, and is ex RAF with its original bridge plate, and I aim to buy it if I can."

Sanity had left the village, and I was staring at the cause.

I stood and watched, as the bubbly side of Birch appeared. She approached the car, and began to chuckle and sparkle, as she danced on the spot staring at the car with love and adoration, it was sort of messed up.

As she approached, the bulbous figure of Mr Wilkes the garage owner appeared. He was checking it over, and he looked at the tall blonde, with patchy hair, in tight black designer clothing, who was dancing and laughing, clasping her hands together, and generally moving in the direction of having a climax, with a curious look in his eye. Birch was happily looking round it, skipping, whilst going over a very detailed list of the vehicle's specifications.

"Abigail!?"

I turned for a moment as the tall figure of Norman Merryweather, walked up the path, he gave a big smile as he approached.

"Oh yes... Oh yes... Oh I love that."

To be honest, I wasn't completely sure whether he meant the car or me, and I had to wonder if I was missing something. Was everyone in this village this orgasmic about cars?

"My god your hair is amazing, oh Abigail, I think you look absolutely fantastic."

I smiled; it was actually nice to meet someone round here who got the look. He came up with a beaming smile.

"Bit of a gothic biker chick look eh, fantastic?" I had to admit, I felt really good inside.

"Thanks Mr Merryweather, not everyone gets it."

He stood in front of me with his arms folded, towering above me, his legs parted, in a stance of appreciation.

"Good grief Abigail, call me Norman. Ignore those who fail to see the change of the times Abigail, it's people like you who have the power of mind to move forward that shapes the future. I often tell Daisy, ignore the stuffy old bats, they had their time, this time belongs to the younger generations. You look stunning, and I may add so does your friend, it's about time we had some modern ideas in this place, god knows it needs it." He looked at Birch, who was dancing, and lovingly admiring the rust bucket.

"Your friend over there appears very excitable."

I gave a laugh, although I must admit, she was starting to worry me, she was becoming way too giddy considering the trash heap she was looking at. Birch spotted me with Norman, she came walking at a fast pace towards him.

"Are you the owner of that Land Rover?" She had a tone of urgency.

"Hello, I am Norman nice to...." She pointed behind him.

"That manic is going to buy it and strip it, you have to stop him." Norman blinked.

Yep, she was way to giddy and becoming unstable.

"This is Birch, she is my friend from Uni." He smiled.

"Nice name, very natural, I like it, I do intend to sell it Birch, it belonged to my grandfather, but it is not something we can use, we have the electric van for deliveries."

"HOW MUCH?" I felt Birch was a little too direct, she was still pointing behind her at the car. "I WILL BUY IT." I looked at her with wide eyes.

"Are you mad, Birch it's a piece of junk." She stared at Norman.

"WHAT HAS HE OFFERED?" Norman looked very surprised.

"He says it started first time HOW MUCH?"

I was shocked, and I began to really understand that she was in fact completely serious. I saw that determined look in her eye I had seen many times before, and I knew Birch well enough to know, when she got that look, she was going to prevail.

Norman looked mildly amused. "We have kept it running, I remember it as a young boy, so I am rather fond of it, but it needs a lot of work, and as hard as it is, we have decided to let it go.... The tyres are like new, we found a spare set in the shed. Mr Wilkes has offered to take it away...."

"HOW MUCH?" Hell, she was going overboard a little. Normal gave a giggle.

"Such passion young lady, I like it.... If you must know he has offered me the scrap value of £200.00. for it."

"WHAT!?" Birch spun on her heels, and looked at Mr Wilkes. "YOU ROBBING OLD GIT!"

She turned, back and thrust both her hands into her large floppy bag, she rummaged around shifting its copious contents, which I cannot deny concerned me, as I have recently discovered that somewhere in the depths of her bag, mixed in amongst the bottles of vodka, southern C and Gin, she does in fact have a fucking big knife. I felt a little alarmed, and wondered if she was going to attack Mr Wilkes with it, I became a little nervous.

Norman watched with amusement; a large smile painted across his face. Birch rooted in her bag, as she did some sort of mental calculation in her head, and whispered to herself. I watched intently thinking, in forty years she will not have changed, and will actually be like that bag lady that accosted me in Piccadilly Railway Station last winter.

She suddenly pulled her hand out of the bag, and I flinched, if I am completely honest, I expected a big fucking knife, but felt the air run out of my lungs, as she waved a huge wad of bright purple twenty pound notes in front of Norman.

"I got £2435.00 I will buy it now cash."

"What the hell Birch, are you insane?" She looked at Norman.

"With the right care and a full restoration, it's worth four times that, but this is all I have on me, if you want more I will go and get it, just give me half an hour."

She was actually serious, I stared with utter disbelief. Norman broke into a howling laugh, I was as my northern mates constantly say to me 'Gob Smacked.'

"Shit Birch, do like rob banks on your day off, where the hell did you get that from... And why are you walking round with all that in your bag?"

Still holding the cash in front of Norman, she looked at me and smiled, and in her usual sweet and lovely manner, she spoke.

"Deads Sweetie, I can protect myself; you know that."

Norman looked at Mr Wilkes, he shook his head.

"It is a better offer than I will give you, she knows her stuff alright, spares for these things move fast, which is why I was going to break it up." Birch turned back with hate in her eyes.

"LUDITE!" He gave a chuckle.

"Maybe love, but it is folks like you that will pay for the bits I rip off, and no doubt you will be fixing her up, and I got to say, I admire that, I just don't have the time. The engine is a good one, and it runs, so you have a good shot of making her pretty with some time and money, take it if you love her that much, we need more folks like you, who love patching up these old beauties."

"I have money, and I know just the guy to get her back to life and looks." Mr Wilks smiled and looked at Norman.

"Half her offer, it's a fair price for how she looks now." Norman gave a nod and looked at Birch.

"Well I must say Birch, I love the way you love her, I must admit, I would really like to see her back to her former glory. I think Mr Wilks is a fair man, so why don't we say £1200.00 and call it a deal."

He held out his hand. Birch gave a huge smile, and her eyes sparkled like green emeralds. She grabbed his hand and shook it, and then thrust the money at me.

"Pay the man Deads." I took hold of the cash.

"Huh?"

Birch turned and look at Mr Wilks, as I counted the cash into Norman's hand.

"She needs an MOT, and I have to arrange insurance, how much to tow her to your garage, get her passed, and then drop her off at Deadly's... I mean Abigail's?" He walked towards her.

"She may fail you know; she has been here a while, I would say new brake pads for sure, and a few other bits, but give me £400.00 and we will start there, I have a few spares at the garage if she needs em. I already have spare wheels, and as you can see hers is missing the spare, I do a lot of these, as farmers like em." Birch nodded her head....

"Pay the man Deads." She looked at Mr Wilks as he stood looking happy.

"Sorry about the old... No offence." He laughed.

"So, I am still git then?" She giggled.

"£200 for that, you are a bigger git than you realise." He leaned back, and gave a roaring laugh.

Norman and Birch went off to the office to finalise the deal, and collect all the documents. I wandered back into the Nursery to find mum and Deb's, who had amassed far more than just herbs. I had actually forgotten the dangers of allowing my mum to run free around plants. I made a mental note that Deb's was not to be trusted, her natural enthusiasm just encouraged mum more.

Within seconds of finding them, Daisy gave a screech, and threw herself round me, and then raved about my hair, my pants, my jacket, it was clear she was delighted with the new look. It felt nice to actually be around people so accepting, but it was even nicer that my mum could see it all. She stood smiling, her blue eyes sparkling at me, and I felt a warmth deep inside me.

Mr Wilks rang for a tow truck, and once we had sorted out delivery of the plants with Daisy, Birch returned, and we all stood back as she raved about her new car. The tow truck appeared on the roadway towing the Land Rover, and Deb's looked stunned, she looked at Birch in complete astonishment.

"You bought that piece of shit... Seriously have you gone mad?"

Birch smiled, a look of complete love in her eyes.

"Wait until next summer when I have finished her, I will make you eat those words Deb's." Deb's looked at Birch.

"Honestly Birch, I love you to bits, and the way you look at the world is inspiring, but I have to tell you, because it is for your own good. If you polish poop, it's still poop."

My mum chuckled, Birch just stood watching as her new car was towed away, a look of inspired determination in her eyes.

"You will see Deb's... You will see."

Walking back to the road along the driveway of the nursery, I hung back with Mum as Deb's tried to convince Birch she knew a great car dealer; mum gave a sigh.

"I really do think Birch is such a lovely girl, I admire her completely free spirit, but Abby darling, I cannot deny she worries me at times." I gave her a glance and smiled.

"I told you, it's a Birch thing, you will get used to it."

Just up ahead, Birch stopped and looked at the big sign for the nursery. It was a large board with the name 'Merryweather's Organic Nursery' on it, and decorated with lots of bright and colourful flowers, she looked back at me as I came walking up, and her eyes sparkled with happiness.

"I am going to call her Petal."

Chapter 13

Face Off.

Birch was deliriously happy, as we walked along Station Road back to the village. I was roasting hot, and even though I was wearing nothing under my jacket, I was starting to understand why Joan Jett always wore thin black T shirts.

I get my boobs are not that big, I was proud of my 34B sized boobs, after all it had taken them nineteen years to form, but I was starting to understand Deb's more, as the heat of the day was rising from the concrete floor. To put it in a nutshell, I had boob sweat, and I was not enjoying it, and I could only wonder, how I had become such a slave to fashion?

It bothered me that Deb's with her jiggle, which was pretty impressive, and had garnered the attention of several smiling men, appeared completely relaxed and unaffected, I considered the point as I watched them bouncing up and down.

"What ya doing?"

Oh, crap, Birch had noticed me staring at Deb's boobs, she leaned in and giggled.

"If you are thinking of doing naughty things with her, I am totally up for watching, I may even film it."

She slipped her arms round me for the fiftieth time since purchasing Petal, and kissed me on the cheek. I had not worked it out, so deferred to higher power of all things related to the female body and perversion related.

"Why aren't Deb's boobs sweating, mine are a tenth the size of hers, and I can feel it running down to my pants?" Birch gave her a glance.

"Breathable wool."

"Huh!" Birch shrugged.

"Breathable wool, her top is thin, and air flows through it keeping them taters real cool, whereas you on the other hand, are wearing my leather, I feel bad, sorry. It is great in the winter, I just forget how hot it would be today, take it off."

It made sense, well at least her first piece of advice did, the second half not so much, the last thing I needed was to be topless in the main street. I mean seriously I just dyed my hair, and most of the village want to lynch me, could you imagine what would happen if I walked topless across the green?

"I have nothing underneath remember?"

"Oh shit, yeah I forgot."

I gave a sigh. Birch for the second time today stopped walking and disappeared into her huge bag.

"Stop girls, we have an emergency."

Mum and Deb's looked round, as Birch rummaged through god knows what, all I knew was the list was growing, ranging from lethal weapons, assorted alcoholic drinks, and wads of cash, I smirked.

"If you ever pull a rabbit out of that thing, I must warn you, we won't be surprised."

Mum and Deb's giggled. Birch obviously found what she was looking for and produced a packet of baby wipes, I frowned as she held them out with pride.

"Baby wipes? Are sure you have told me everything about your life Birch, I mean, baby wipes?"

"Huh... Oh.... Are you frigging serious? These things are a girl's best friend, have you any idea how many uses these things have? Deads Sweetie, your life depends on them."

Birch handed me the packet to hold, and pulled one out from under the thin clear vinyl that kept them sealed. Without warning, she grabbed the zip of my jacket, pulled it down two thirds of the way, and dived into my bosom with the wipe.

She gave me a huge smile, and raised her eyebrows, as I felt her slide over my boobs and wash them. It was damp and cool, and it made me tingle between my legs, as she stared at me with those beautiful green sparkling eyes. Her hands moved softly over my nipples, and I felt a tremble run down my legs.

"Pack it in you pervert."

Deb's was staring at me, with an envious look in her eye, Birch winked, and then tweaked my nipple, I gave a short gasp, as her eyebrows lifted, and she smiled in a very naughty and perverted way.

"Okay that is enough."

My legs trembled again, as she gave it one last tweak, and then pulled her hand out with a giggle. I gave a shudder, as she dropped the packet back in her bag, and she winked.

"So my dark little beastie, just how wet are you about now?"

My mum was giggling with Deb's, and I felt a little embarrassed.

"Screw you Birch, it's embarrassing, I am not wearing panties." She stepped back with a gasp.

"Really... Well done you, why the sudden change?" I felt awkward in front of my mum.

"Well last time we went out Deb's didn't, but I did, so I figured she would again, so I left mine off." Birch understood.

"Okay that's two with, and two without, I can float with that it's even." My mum shuffled her feet.

"Actually?"

I gasped with shock as it was now her turn to look a little flustered, I think Birch was even surprised, she spun round on my mum, and reached round and slid her hand right round her slacks clad bottom, my mum gave a sudden yelp. Birch stood upright and looked at Deb's, who was starting to look panicked, my mum gave a sigh, as I looked at her with my mouth open.

"To be honest, Hatty has never worn any underwear, and well, her bum has always looked so fantastic in pants, so I stopped wearing them with pants years ago." Birch smiled.

"Well then, there is little else to do, Deb's, you have to lose the knickers."

"WHAT.... NO FRIGGING WAY, I AM WEARING A SHORT SKIRT, ARE YOU INSANE?" Birch looked at her with devilish delight.

"Sorry Deb's but the rules are the rules." Her hands slid to protect her nether regions.

"I can't, I just can't, not here. I... I ...I might catch cold." Birch sniggered.

"Oh Sweetie, with the amount of thatch you have down there, you have no fear of that!"

I cannot deny, stood there watching, even I was starting to panic, Birch was asking too much, mum was curiously calm, but there again, she grew up with Hatty, so enough said.

Deb's looked petrified, as she stood there staring at Birch, and then the craziest thing I have ever seen happened. She was breathing really fast, but I saw as she gritted her teeth, and then!

"FINE!"

I gasped with shock, no frigging way, was she going to do it, and yet there in the middle of the street, on a busy summer day, my shy introverted friend Deb's, looked Birch right in the eye, slipped her hands quickly under her skirt, and pulled them down. I gasped with utter disbelief.

Deb's lifted her right foot out, and stepped back leaving her black lace panties on the floor, I could not believe what was happening. She gave a gasp, smiled, and looked at all three of us.

"We stick together, we stand together, and we fight together, and the rules are the rules."

She let out a long flow of air, turned, and leaving her panties on the floor, she walked with her head up, back towards the main street of the village.

I was struggling for words, as Birch stooped down and picked up Deb's panties, and dropped them in her bag, my mum who had silently observed everything looked at Birch.

"You didn't think she would do it did you, it was just a test?" Birch gave a smile.

"That girl has more guts than I thought, honestly I was just messing with her, but hell, she is seriously awesome in my book at the moment." I could not believe it.

"Birch she is in a short skirt, and just took her panties off, are you telling me it was a bluff?" She nodded.

"Yeah... I mean, Christ, there is no way I would walk round this place in a skirt that short with nothing under it, she is frigging braver than I am." I watched as Deb's stopped a few yards ahead of us, and looked back.

"Come on, I thought we were going to the Tea Rooms?" My mind was blown completely.

With the road closed, and extra tables set up outside on the road. The Tea Rooms was busy, but mum spotted a table inside, and we headed indoors. Deb's was doing fine, although she rushed to the table, and made sure she sat with her back to everyone, that way, there would be no way of being noticed by anyone. Birch rooted in her bag.

"In celebration of the saving of Petal from the jaws of Mr Wilks, this one is on me."

She grabbed my arm, and pulled me towards the counter. As we approached the queue, she turned and grabbed my jacket zipper, and slipped it down. My boobs were not huge, but my small round mounds, were clearly visible between the open teeth of the zip, and the small gap that had opened. She winked with devilish delight.

"Give the ladies a treat."

It's crazy, I have been here a thousand times, and yet suddenly understanding that Lillian and Celia, were in fact in a same sex relationship, and I was stood there offering them a peep at my under developed, and none existent cleavage, made me really nervous.

Birch led the way along the line, and as we approached Lillian, who was serving, she leaned over the counter, and looked Lillian right in the eye.

"Three coffees and a tea please." Her voice lowered to a sultry tone.

"What do you have that is seductively tasty Lillian?" Lillian gave a slight whimper.

"Oh dear!"

Birch turned, and ran her finger down the inside on my jacket, right between my breasts, I felt the tray rattle as it tickled, and again between my legs there was a deep throb. Lillian stared at my partially exposed mounds.

"Look I brought Abigail in for you to see her new get up, what do you think?"

Lillian looked very flustered, and her breathing changed. She swallowed very hard, and her voice was lightly breathless.

"I think you look... Oh my... Very beautiful Abigail."

She gave another hard swallow, and the tea cup on a saucer in her hand rattled. Birch leaned over and grabbed it, and as she slipped it out of her hand, I noticed how she extended a finger and ran it down Lillian's wrist.

The poor old lady looked more flustered than I have ever seen, she glanced over to Celia, who was filling cups with coffee, and staring lustfully at me. Even I felt suddenly hot and had to swallow hard.

The tray was filled, and with trembling hands I turned, I did not want to look back, but heard Birch whisper quietly to Celia.

"Wow Abigail has an amazing ass." I almost stumbled and dropped the tray.

Celia moved to the till, and Birch smiled at her.

"We wanted to come in and say thanks for standing up for Abby the other night, you know... Show our appreciation, if you understand my drift?" Celia gave a gasp; her voice was also quite breathless.

"Oh, we appreciate it, she is a very lovely girl, we would be happy to do... Er... Help her any time." Birch smiled.

"Just for that, I will give you lovely ladies an extra treat, can you see Debbie at the table?" Celia swallowed hard; her voice was almost a whisper.

"Yes!"

Birch leaned in very close to her and whispered, Celia stretched her neck out to hear it.

"She is not wearing any panties." Lillian dropped a plate, and it smashed on the floor, Celia fanned herself with her hand.

"Oh Really?" Birch gave a nod and winked.

"Mums the word." She handed them a ten pound note.

"Keep the change."

I watched, as Birch turned, and walked slowly smiling, swinging her hips, back to the table. I could see Lillian peeping over the glass counter as she cleaned, and Celia stood frozen staring at Deb's. I looked at her as she sat down.

"You do know you are going to hell, right?"

Birch gave a giggle as she stirred her coffee, Deb's had noticed Celia, and leaned in to look Birch right in the eye.

"You told her, didn't you?" Birch chuckled as my mum stirred her coffee.

"I knew it, you definitely told her I was not... Well, you know, I cannot believe you told her, she is looking at me like I am piece of meat." My mum giggled, and Birch winked.

"Deb's everyone is someone else's reason to masturbate." Deb's sat back with a gasp, and went red in the face, she looked at her plate.

"It's... Well, you know... Weird." Birch shrugged.

"Why, we are all born sexual, and 90% of sex happens in the brain, what, you think because they are of a certain age, they should not feel the same as we do? I got a news flash Deb's, those feelings never go away, no matter how old you get."

It sounds sort of odd, but I had never thought of it that way, and actually it made perfect sense. I never want a time in my life where I do not feel all these amazing feelings, I was having on a very regular basis inside me at the moment. Birch looked at Deb's.

"My mum had a client that worked in a care home, and she used to buy all the old ladies those hair brushes with the thick ribbed rubber handles, so they could discreetly take of themselves."

My mum gave a sudden explosive snort into her cup, and almost dropped it, she coughed as the cup went back on the saucer, and reached for her pocket, as she gasped and coughed even more. She pulled her hankie up, and held it to her mouth, and coughed. Her voice was strained.

"Birch... You bitch!" I could see her laughing, and spluttering behind her hankie. Birch raised an eyebrow.

"Something you want to share with the group, Flick?" My mum coughed and wiped her mouth.

"You should come with trigger warnings." She giggled as she straightened her cup on the saucer.

"Oh, how nice, you are having time with your girls Felicity."

That cool superior voice ripped through me, and I went cold inside. I looked up to see Marjorie eyeing me carefully.

"It is so nice to see you finally made it out of your house, and back into the population Abigail, although I am surprised to see you in this establishment, from what I have heard, I would have thought the Station Pub would be more you style these days."

It was a well known fact that in the village, that the poorer end of the population frequented it. My mum rose calmly from her seat, Birch looked up.

"Marjorie isn't it. We have been there, but found it was not crass enough for us, so we thought we would brighten up the atmosphere in town considering it's a summer event." She looked right down her nose at Birch.

"I take you are the Birch woman?" My mum moved forward.

"There is no need for this Madge."

I felt so small in that moment, and I just wanted to shrivel up, and get swallowed into the floor, I felt Deb's take my hand, I could feel the tears well up in my eyes. This was all my fault, and now mum would have to face the consequences, and just after things were really getting good between us. The tears dripped onto the table as I held my head down. Birch stood up, my mum held her hand back to tell her to hold off, and stared at Madge.

"We have paid to be in here, and we are doing our bit for this community by supporting this establishment, and event, as we always have." Madge smirked.

"You are correct, but in previous years your family has enhanced the reputation of these events, not lowered them as they have today. We have standards in this village, and you used to support them, not help lower them with your transient looking child and her friends. My God Felicity, what has happened to you, I once respected you?" That was too much and Birch moved up out of her seat.

"Why you old witch, I will...."

"Back off Birch!"

My mum held Birch back with her hand on her chest, there was complete silence in the place. Deb's leaned over and put her hand on my chin and lifted my face, as the tears streaked my make up, and I looked like Alice Cooper. She slowly shook her head and mouthed 'no tears, we are all girls together' I tried to smile, but this was awful and all my fault.

My mum took a long breath and composed herself.

"I understand you have a high bar set for this community, and yes, I have always played my role as vice president of the Parish Council to uphold it. I am exceptionally proud of my daughter; she is a first class university student with a kind and compassionate heart. As are her friends, regardless of how they look, which I understand meets with your disapproval. You know what Madge, I love her new look, and over the short time Abby and her friends have been in my home, I feel I have learned something very important from them." Marjorie gave a snort of derision.

"And just exactly what is that Felicity Watson?"

She turned and saw I had looked up, and was watching her, she reached out to me, and I lifted my hand and gave sniffle. My mum took it in hers and held it, as she turned back to Marjorie.

"Times are changing Marjorie, and you may not approve but take a good look, because here sat before you, is the future of Wotton Dursley. Without them, this place will disappear forever, and that legacy you boast so much about, will be worthless. I almost won the last parish council vote, even you have to agree it was very close. If this village does not keep up with the times, that will be your doing, and how will the people see you then?" Marjorie looked horrified.

"All talk and no policy, that is why you lost, and you will again." Somewhere behind her another voice spoke out.

"No she won't, because I will be campaigning with Abby, Birch and Debbie for her, and we will be raising modern issues that matter to the community, so that it does not get left behind." Marjorie turned to see Hatty holding her camera. Felicity smiled.

"You see Marjorie there are more modern views within this community, and we need to cater to them. I understand that you find it difficult to change, but if we want to survive, then we will have to at some point. We have a summer of events to organise, so I will say, let us get on with that, instead of spoiling this day or any other event, because even though we have opposing views, we will all need to work together to keep this village thriving."

She had clearly been out matched, and she knew it, her face was filled with fury, and her temper was boiling, she raised her hand and pointed at me, and I swallowed hard, she really does scare me.

"I will never accept that." Birch gave a snort.

"Then like all dinosaurs, you will die out." Marjorie looked at Birch and scowled, Birch just smiled, and her eyes sparkled with utter defiance.

"Oh, by the way I have money, it's northern, but probably more than you do, if that helps clear things up for you?" Marjorie gave a curt smile.

"I have things to attend to, some of the council are very busy today working for the benefit of the village, so I will bid you good day." Birch winked at her.

"Such a trooper, carry on soldier."

Marjorie turned, and walked out of the Tea Rooms. I stood up, and my mum pulled me into her arms and hugged me hard.

"Are you alright darling."

I just wanted to cry again. Lillian and Celia arrived to comfort me with a free cake, and Celia topped up our coffee. Celia fussed around me clearing the empty cups.

"Don't let this spoil your afternoon Abigail my dear, just sit back and enjoy your drink, you have done nothing wrong, ignore her."

Birch sat down and noted the frequent eye contact between Celia eyes and the inside of my jacket. Lillian had a cloth in her hand, and was wiping up the coffee my mum had spilt on the floor when she coughed, and suddenly the table bumped, and Deb's realising why, jumped with a gasp, and snapped her legs back together, a muffled

"Oh my… Oh dear," came for under the table, and then Lillian appeared looking very flustered, as Deb's when bright red. Birch started to giggle as Deb's stared daggers at her.

"I could go off you at times Birch, it will be all round the village in the morning." Lillian patted her shoulder.

"Have no fear dear, you secret is very safe with me."

Deb's went an even deeper shade of purple, as Birch sniggered, she looked at her across the table.

"I hate you Birch." I started to giggle.

Thirty minutes later, having had Birch redo my eyes, we were back on the main road, which was a little less busy. Birch suddenly remembered she needed sunglasses. Without thinking, I grabbed her arm, and swerved towards the Post Office/Shop. What the hell was I thinking, before I knew it, I was confronted with Mary. Birch just dodged her, and headed straight for the rack, where she grabbed at the glasses and started trying them on.

Mary smiled, but it was easy to see her disapproval, and in a strange way I found it hurtful, I had always liked her, because she had been so sweet to me, but things had changed. I knew I had to accept that, but even so, I felt sad inside.

Birch was trying on every bright flowery pair on the rack, and for once, I knew I had to do something. I flicked my hair back, and it flowed over my shoulder, and Mary frowned. I had to take a leaf from Birch's book, I had to stand on my own ground, after all Deb's took her panties off in the middle of the street, my mum faced out Marjorie, and Birch faced my dad out naked, this time I had to rise up to the level of their bar. I looked at Mary, as she frowned at me.

"It is okay if you do not approve Mrs Saxon, I know a lot of people round here don't, but you see the thing is, I did not do this to win the approval of you or the community. Mary, I love my hair, and my clothes, and you probably will not understand, but all my real friends do as well. I did this for me, it is who I am and what I wanted, and it has shown me who cares about me, so as far as I am concerned, it was worth it."

I turned round, even though my stomach was twisting and my legs were trembling, I walked out of the door and back onto the street. As soon as I hit the street, I gasped for air, and took a long deep breath, and just held the air in my lungs. I was scared inside, but I also felt good.

Ten minutes later, Birch came out smiling holding eight pairs of glasses, all of which were bright and colourful, I looked at them.

"You know, I pegged you for round mirrors." Birch shrugged.

"I got them at home, I want something to match with my ideas for Petal." She put on a pair of bright flowery glasses.

"I think these will set the vibe for my ride."

She gave me a huge smile, and pulled her glasses down half way, and winked. "What you did in there Deads, it made me real proud of you."

We walked down the road towards home, I felt a little relived, I will not deny I had felt some strong emotions today, but all in all, it went well. Birch linked my arm, and walked along saying little which was odd for her, but she smiled a huge happy smile. Hatty walked with my mum, and Deb's slipped her arm into Birch's. My mum glanced at Hatty who wore a big smile.

"You look smug, what have you done?" Hatty gave a happy sigh of contentment.

"Well if you want to know, I did not take a picture of Marjorie." Deb's gave a moan.

"Aww, Hatty, I really wanted a copy of that." Birch gave a chuckle.

"Oh, you clever girl Hatty." I looked at her.

"Why, a picture of her being confronted, and losing would be priceless?" Birch glanced over towards Hatty.

"Are you going to tell them or should I do it?" Hatty shook her head.

"No, I want this one, let me just say it has been a dream of mine for so long, don't spoil it Birch, I want to savour it." Felicity gave a sigh.

"If you two are done, will someone please tell me what is going on?" Hatty lifted her camera.

"This is a high quality 4k digital camera, not only does it take stills, it is also a video camera."

It took a moment before I realised just exactly what she had said, and then it hit me.

"Jesus Hatty, you filmed it?" She just smiled.

"You girls are good, but you still have a lot to learn, before you surpass me."

Chapter Fourteen

Revealing the Cage.

Wednesday had been a hard day, we arrived home hot and sticky, and headed for the cool shade of the guest house, Birch did not make it past the pool, she just stripped and dived in, and to be honest I could not wait another second to peel off the leather, and soon joined her.

Debs was not far behind, and we just lazed around in the pool cooling off, until Hatty and mum arrived with drinks. The rest of the day was a lazy day, just after six, Daisy arrived with the plant delivery, and Birch rushed inside to video call her parents and tell them of her new purchase. Debs had to leave to go home, and so I ended up alone, chilling out in the pool whilst Hatty and mum talked on the loungers.

I got out of the pool and lay on a towel in the sun on the lawn, and lazed on my phone, updating posts to my social media accounts. Chloe had started to follow me on Insta, so I looked at her profile, and was surprised to see her new pics, which she had taken of the three of us around the green. She had written on her post 'Coolest kids in Wotton # wish I had the guts' It really made me think.

I thought about Mary, it still hurt a little, but then my mind moved to Chloe. She had told me her sister Edwina had balled her out, and it made me wonder, just how many people lived in the village who were like Chloe?

Was Hatty right, if mum could swing those people on to her side and look to modernise, would they vote Marjorie out? It was an interesting question, Marjorie had been in her seat for seventeen years, she commanded a powerful influence on everything, and if I am really honest, I cannot see her losing so easily. I decided to wait, and then ask Birch her thoughts, she did have an uncanny way of looking at things.

With Birch busy with her parents, and then the insurance for her new vehicle, I drank way more than she did, and as I walked back into the house at nine, I was drunk and exhausted, she was once again busy on her laptop, and so I slipped into bed and just crashed out.

Before I knew it, morning had arrived, and I had no intention of going into town, so I headed out doors to find Deb's, Birch and Mum working on what was to become the new herb garden.

I spent the day lay on the rug sunbathing, and drinking gin, and flaked out early, with a drunken Birch, and before I realised, I was climbing out of bed, and it was one in the afternoon, and Friday.

Tonight, was the big village meet to outline all the plans for the summer, and everyone would be there, but once again the thought of being closed in, and in full view at the church hall, made me very nervous.

Mum had said I should go, and from past experience, I knew that just about the whole village would be there, so I begrudgingly said I would, but in truth, I just did not want to be there, I wanted to be here, safe and away from the nasty comments and gossips.

At 5:45pm, Birch, Hatty, Debs, and myself walked into the Church Hall. We were met by Marion Butler Davis, who instantly turned her nose up at the sight of us, she handed me a program.

"I am surprised to see you here; some people know no shame."

Birch and Hatty were both on high alert, Birch took a program and looked at her in her floral dress, and her perfect hair.

"If you had ever fucked in a field, you would understand why."

She smiled, Marion gave a gasp and lifted her hands to her mouth, her cheeks went pink, and Birch chuckled.

Hatty gave a giggle and took a program, Marion looked at her.

"Not only do they have shameful looks, they have potty mouths." Hatty gave a sigh.

"Potty mouths... Is that the best you can do Marion? Grow up, we all stopped using that term round here when we were six."

My heart was racing, I could feel the sweat on my back, and I was dressed in lighter clothing than the other day. I had put on my black top and black jeans and boots. Birch had done my eye make up in red, to match my hair. Two rows from the back sat Ellen and Bradley Wheeler, and so Deb's yanked on my arm, and dragged me in behind them on the next row. Ellen leaned back to look at me.

"You look stunning, I am so glad to see you here Abby, and I have heard a lot about your friend Birch, ignore the others, just be you, because you carry it off beautifully."

I needed that, but I think she knew it, after all she was Deb's mum, and so I was sure had been given very detailed updates. We sat down, Birch was on one side of me, and Deb's the other. I looked down the large hall to the stage. Ronald was up there by the council table testing the sound system, and then for many rows in front, people were talking, quite a few were looking our way, it was almost as if it had been expected.

Chloe and Edwina were sat with their parents several rows down, when they saw us, they got up from their seats and came to the back, and then slipped in from behind to sit next to Deb's.

Birch and I leaned forward to say hi, Chloe smiled as she sat down, and I noticed both of them had black jeans and boots on, with long tops, but it did not miss Birch's scrutiny, and she smiled and leaned into me.

"They are both braless, are we setting a trend?"

I had no idea; I was just glad there were some here who wanted to publicly support us. Out of nowhere a tall slender young man appeared. It was Anthony Robertson from high school, or at least he was when he was in my form. These days he worked for Delphine in the salon, and went under the name of Antonio.

Birch looked at him suspiciously, as he walked on to the row in front, and stood right in front of her with his arms folded, staring at her. He had long flowing highly stylish bleached hair, a tight fitted suit of burgundy velvet, and white small collared shirt with small flowers on it. He looked at me with a critical eye.

"Abigail, it is so nice to see you, and I must say darling, your hair is exquisite, you must tell me who is your stylist, I will look them up." I gave him a smile as I noted the gold around his neck and wrists.

"Hi Anthony, it's been a long time, and thanks, I appreciate your compliment." He offered a limp wrist to Birch.

"Well hello, I am Antonio, and I must say, I have been watching you very carefully. Your dress style is unique, and vibrant, and has real flair, I think you have the presence of a goddess." Birch leaned into me, and whispered.

"Who the hell is this, he is creeping me out?" I whispered back.

"He is called Antonio; he is a stylist."

"So, a gay hairdresser then, because he sounds like a stalker?"

"The locals deny that he is gay, they just say 'affected.' Round here, as you have seen, it's frowned upon. He is harmless, he was a really nice boy in school, but he was really badly bullied, because he had nervous ticks, and as you will find out, the local lads can be rough." She gave a nod and lifted her hand up, and shook it loosely.

"Nice to meet you, I think."

He gave an exaggerated high pitched squeal of a laugh, and leaned back and twitched. Deb's sniggered at my side. Birch looked back at him.

"You're a hairdresser here, right?"

He looked shocked, and rolled his eyes, in a very dramatic manner.

"My dear, I am a little more than a hairdresser."

"No shit, I worked that out straight away." Hatty looked at the floor and sniggered.

"I am a stylist, the best in Wotton." She leaned back to me and whispered.

"There are just two hairdressers here in the village, right?" I nodded.

"Yeah." Birch looked back up at him.

"It must have been a struggle for that particular crown, well done you, do you do your own hair?"

He swept his arm round in a sweeping motion, then ran his finger through his long hair, as his face gave little twitches.

"Delphine does it for me, she is my business partner by the way." Birch just nodded, he looked right at her.

"I l-o-v-e, love your hair, tell me was it styled by a professional?" Birch thought for a moment.

"To be honest Antonio, I cannot deny I am not too sure, I was really pissed when she did it, but hey it looked great, so I left it." He appeared unhappy with her.

"It is alright, you can keep it secret, I would too if I had such a talented stylist, after all it is such a competitive game. Tell me Birch, may I touch it and feel the rhythm of the cut?"

"I have a knife and I don't like my hair touched, I am sure you are very attached to your fingers, let's keep it that way and stay friendly."

He gave a huge high pitched squeal of a laugh, and patted the air in front of him.

"You are so hilarious, oh honestly you are so adorable." Hatty gave a sigh.

"Sit the fuck down Anthony, it will be starting soon." He tutted at Hatty.

"It's Antonio, and you should let me sort out that hair, I have told you before Harriet, that hack in Oxendale does your features no justice."

He plopped down in the chair in front. Birch leaned back into me.

"I think Hatty H-a-t-e-s, hates him." Deb's and me both started to giggle.

The people entering slowed down, and Marion came in, and pulled the doors closed behind her, she saw us and walked to the row on the other side and sat down. The place was pretty full, and the only two rows that had free seats, just happened to be the ones we were sat on, it was like the whole village were afraid to sit near us, just in case they were infected by us.

The members of the parish council walked on stage and took their seats. One chair was empty as my dad was away on business. Madge sat in the middle, with my mum on her right. Peter Saxon from the post office, Lillian and Celia were sat either side of them.

Marjorie leaned into her mic and began, and she droned on and on, and I realised I had forgotten how boring these things were. I lost track of how long she had been talking, was it twenty minutes, was it an hour? I had no idea.

Deb's was leant forward, leaning over Chloe as she faced Edwina, and they all whispered to each other, and I heard occasional sniggers. I looked at Birch, she was still as a rock watching every movement, and gesture of Marjorie, her bright green eyes focused, in the same way she did in the dorm, when she was writing her essays.

I sat watching her, as she sat back attentive to the stage, her long white hair, cascading down across her breasts, hanging just above her waist, her black pant legs, crossed, and the slight lean of her back, that moulded her into the chair.

I felt many feelings of affection, and safety, I knew her one motive tonight was to learn, and she was watching and studying Marjorie in ways only a therapist would, because I had started to realise, that Birch was starting to see Marjorie as a threat, to not only our liberty, but also to her own identity.

I knew of no other free spirit like Birch, there was an element to her that was pure, open, and transparent, but I was starting to see, she was seen as highly dangerous to a community like this, and Birch had already realised that.

I watched her white face, her defined soft cheeks, her shapely mouth and pale lips, my god she was so stunningly attractive, and I could not believe I was thinking it, but just watching her filled me with joy, and a sense of safety, it was a startling realisation.

Oh Christ, am I becoming a lesbian, is this how it starts? My mind reeled, holy shit why am I damp down there? I snapped my head forward, and tried to clear my thoughts. I took a breath and tried to focus, come on Abby, you like men, yes, I love men, although it had been well over three weeks since I had actually had sex with one.

I calmed myself, calm down girl, it's just feeling horny from the dry patch, it is nothing to worry about, I am fine, think of dicks, and it will just go away, yes that was it, all I needed to do was remember all the men I had banged in my head. That will fix it, but all I could think of was my last sexual encounter, and that was lay on my back with Birch kissing my stomach.

Oh, Christ I am in your church hall, for god's sake hear me, cleanse me of this feeling, I am not mentally prepared to be a lesbian.

For an hour it was report after report, as my mind wandered through the fields of sexual conflict, until finally Marjorie reached the part of the Summer Events list, and handed over to my mum.

My mum read down the list. The Oxendale College players would be doing a performance of Six sovereigns for Sister Sarah.

Birch smirked.

"Sounds about right, hanging pagans from trees, that should really turn Madge on, I am surprised we were not cast in it, it would make for another exciting Summer Event."

There was a talk on the rain forest by an explorer I had never heard of, a fund raising barbeque at the vicarage, a choir evening in the church, and a brass band concert, and then came the Village Fete.

Peter Saxon took the mic and went through an exhaustive list, of events, stalls, food set ups, and entertainments, none of this applied to me at all. I had already decided I was not going, Hatty leaned forward almost as if she had read my mind.

"Wait for the twist Abby, because it is coming next."

I did not understand, and as Peter finished, the mic went back to Marjorie. She leaned into the mic.

"Well what a fun packed line up of events. Now as all of you know this fete more than any other event, is massively important to the health of this villages finance. Without it we would lose very important revenues, and so we expect every one currently resident in this village to play their part and get involved. Hatty leaned forward and smiled.

"That is you two." Birch frowned,

"Why us, we technically live in Manchester." Hatty shook her head.

"Currently you live here, in the guest house, you are seen as residents. Welcome to the village, and welcome to her web my little flies."

"What if we say no Hatty?" She scoffed.

"You said no to the choir two and half years ago, and yet only days ago the vicar tried to get you to reconsider. Come on Abby, you know how it works here, they want you on stage for the lead solo at that choir evening, and if you refuse that, they will drag you in elsewhere. Madge wants to make you an example, and she will move heaven and earth to show you who has the power here." Birch listened carefully, she looked at Hatty.

"If she thinks she can hurt Abby in public, she will have another thing coming, I am tired of her politics and mind games, but if she really wants to play, then I say we play, because if she really wants us there, then we will be, but on our terms not hers." Deb's leaned forward.

"Count me in, it's all us girls together, we stand together, we stick together, and we fight together." I looked at her and smiled.

"Yeah, all girls together." Birch looked at Chloe and Edwina.

"So are you two in or out?" Chloe looked positively thrilled.

"We are in, you can bet on it." Birch nodded.

"Okay, so we will all be there, and it will be tits out, and boots on for all of us. Chloe and Edwina, you will be coming out for this event, it is time you used your wardrobe for home. I want your phone numbers; I will set up the communications channel." They looked at each and nodded excitedly.

It all came to an end, people got out of their seats to stretch their legs, and formed into groups. The talk started all over again, more stares, and more gossip. At the front there was a refreshment stand serving drinks and food. It was tradition for this to be a social event, and so everyone had drinks, and mulled around talking.

I heard my name repeatedly, and each time I felt a jolt, which added to the twists inside of me, others looked as if they wanted to say hello, but were afraid to in front of everyone else, we all stayed seated, but slid our chairs back so we could talk facing each other.

We were all chatting when the gorky tall figure of Nigel Wallace appeared with a clip board. I did not see him straight away, but Birch did, he stood in front of her with his clipboard, and stared at her like she was some kind of freak. He was wearing a plain white shirt with a blue bow tie, and neatly pressed pants.

"I am Nigel." Birch was not impressed.

"Really…? You have my condolences… What the hell have you got round your neck, you are aware the war is over, and we have all moved into the modern age?" He looked shocked.

"It's a tie, and we do not like potty mouths in here, a lady should conduct herself with dignity." She nodded as I turned round, and noticed him, Birch looked at me.

"Who is this prick?" I tried not to a smile.

"This is Nigel, he is Marjorie's son… Hello Nigel." Birch gave a sigh.

"Suddenly no further explanation is required." Nigel appeared to act all jittery and coy.

"Hi Abagail, it's been some time since I saw you, I hope you are well?"

He grinned from ear to ear, and his teeth, which were smaller, but were not unsimilar to his father's moved, I think. Birch leaned over.

"Seriously this boy sees you in his fantasies every night, you are aware of that aren't you?"

I wanted to laugh; the truth was he had asked me out so many times I had lost count.

"He has always had a thing for me, it is a long story."

Birch looked at him, he was staring with adoration at me, which was actually pretty creepy. He had not changed a bit, and was still as besotted as he had always been. Birch looked up at him.

"Is there a reason for the clip board, or should we just sit here and guess?" He did not even hear her; such was his attention to me. She clicked her fingers.

"Hey! Earth to Nigel, are you receiving me?" He jolted and looked at her and she smiled.

"Please try to focus on something other than Abby's boobs, it's off putting, because mine are bigger." He swallowed hard and went red. "Nigel... What is with the clipboard, do you need something?"

He looked down at the board, and then realised why he was there.

"Oh... Er... I need to know if you will be participating in this year's fete?" Birch looked at us all looking to her for guidance, she gave a sigh.

"Yes, we will be... We will be demonstrating a particular northern skill as a group."

He nodded and started writing. Birch shook her head.

"Write this down, exactly, as it is important to ensure it is right. We will require a tent with a full view of the event, comfortable seats."

He began writing every word she said.

"Seats for all five of us, okay? We will also require a good stock of alcohol, and then we will demonstrate the Northern Specialised Art, of taking the piss. I hope you have all that?" He looked up and scowled as we all started to giggle.

"The committee won't approve that."

"Oh, such a shame, it truly is a sight to see... Okay then answer me this Nigel, which contests did your mother win last year?" He looked at her suspiciously.

"I don't like you, or trust you, mummy says you are dangerous, but if you must know, cakes, jams, and flower arranging, why do you want to know?"

"Enter all five of us in each of those sections then." He started to write; Birch made sure he got it right.

"Abigail Watson, Debbie Wheeler, Chloe Pemberton, Edwina Pemberton, and I am simply Birch. Have you got all that, and if you have done that, can we go now?" He nodded.

"I am not stupid; I study genetics at university." Birch stood up.

"That makes so much sense to me Nigel, I am a training sex therapist, I am sure you have questions, so keep me in mind. Girls we need a drink."

I was so glad when we got outside and away from everyone. I was hot and sticky, and feeling a little shaken, and being out in an open quiet space was a joy. We walked out on to the green; Antonio came running out of the door.

"Wait for me don't you dare leave without me." He caught up with us as we headed towards the Hunters Arms. "You are the first people here I have ever identified with; I want to be included." Birch shrugged.

"Come on then and join the party, I need a good pint actually, several pints after all that." Edwina looked at Birch.

"You do know the Hunter's closes its bar at ten on Friday's don't you, it is why all of us go to Oxendale?" Birch stopped dead in her tracks, and looked at her watch, then Deb's and me.

"You cannot be frigging serious, its 9:45 what kind of dark age shit is that?" Deb's shrugged.

"That is what it is like here Birch, the Parish Council has a long arm, they get to make the rules, and to avoid disorder, the bar's close early Friday, Saturday, and Sunday."

I nodded at her, Deb's was right, Hatty was known for trying to change that rule, but the sad truth was, the parish had a fourteenth century law that let them over rule certain aspects of life, and Marjorie had ensured that no one would ever be drunk on the streets of the village, after ten. Birch looked at me in shock, I shrugged at her.

"Now you understand everything I told you at Uni, this is the village of the dammed, and she has all the powers. Now do you understand why I did not want to come home?" She was visibly shaken. "Why do you think all the young here move away, or go to Oxendale for nights out?"

"Deads it is wrong, and I am pretty sure it is illegal." I shook my head.

"No Birch, it is all sown up in legal red tape, trust me, Hatty has tried several times to undo it. We do not live by the same rules you have at home in Uppermill."

She stood there just staring with her bright green eyes, her white hair blowing gently in the breeze. I could see how much she struggled to understand it, but that was how it was, and until someone unseated Marjorie, it was never going to change. Birch blinked.

"Well screw them, the store is still open, Chloe, Deb's we are going on a booze run, and then I say we head back home and get pissed, what say you?"

Antonio was very excited, and squealed with delight and danced on the spot.

Forty minutes later we were all home in my garden round the pool, having had Birch be asked to show identification by Mary, who had then allowed the sale of alcohol. With more vodka, gin, and a bottle of tequila, plus three boxes of larger, and mixers, everyone sat and talked about their life in the village.

I noticed a common thread running through each of the stories, which was deep down inside, everyone wanted to simply be themselves, but had to pretend to be something they were not.

It was a profound moment for me, as I suddenly realised, I had grown up feeling all alone, and isolated, and yet sat there with all of them, I could see I had not been alone all along. The problem was we all felt the same, and no one had been brave enough to speak out until I walked down the street with Birch that day.

It was one o'clock when Chloe, Edwina and Antonio hugged us

and jumped in a cab, their faces appeared to have so much more hope than earlier in the night, but it made me feel sad. I sat out with Deb's who was staying over again, and Birch, and stared into my drink, my voice was soft.

"How many others live here with the exact same story, I mean, how many are locked in the prison of having to appear as someone they are not, just for the sake of a frigging village?" Birch gave a sigh.

"There are too many secrets Dead's, too many people hiding the truth, living in fear of what the villagers will say or do to them, this is the most dishonest place I have been to, no one here is real. Look at Lillian and Celia, having to hide, or Antonio unable to be who he truly is, he is gay for Christ's sake, he has no control of that, it is built in, they cannot just deny it for the sake of convenience. All Chloe wants is just to be a normal female, and experiment with fashion, it is hardly the crime of the century, but here it is. This is so bloody wrong guys, they all have a desire to be something, but Madge and her followers have locked them inside who they really are, and I am telling you, change here will not come easily. All we can do is be true to who we really are, and hope it sets an example for others to follow."

Birch was right, but she failed to see how all of it worked. I gave a sigh, and lifted my drink.

"This place is like this, because they do not want it to change, they have bought into the myth of middle England with its pageantry and moral standing. These people think their way is right, and hold on to power, they will never allow modern ideals to be allowed here. All of us are expected to fall in line, just like my mum did, and every generation before us."

Birch flopped back on her lounger, and stared at the stars.

"I cannot live in a cage guys, I cannot be the kind of person all of those people tonight are. I cannot explain it, but my mind is alive and free, and my spirit soars with it. If I had to lie to myself every day, and pretend to be something I am not, I would die inside, and I could never live like that. I will never allow the person I am to be hidden and secret like everyone here does, it would kill me."

"Why do think I came to Manchester Birch? I have been trapped inside for years."

She looked at me with those bright green eyes, there was so much depths to them, and just for second, I thought I saw a tear. Birch reached across the lounger and held my hand.

"I am glad you did." She gave it a soft squeeze, and it meant everything.

"I have a secret."

Birch and me sat up slightly and looked at Deb's, I was a little surprised, I knew her quite well, and yet I was sure I did not know it.

"What is it Deb's, you have never mentioned anything to me before?"

Deb's stood up and looked us both in the eyes as we lay side by side on the loungers, she took a deep breath and composed herself. She was very serious, and it was obviously something very important. Deb's breathed out slowly and moistened her lips, and then she announced in a louder than normal voice.

"I want to shave my vagina; I want it to look like childlike again!"

Birch burst out laughing, and spilled her drink, and I could not help but start to giggle. Deb's smiled and looked a little embarrassed.

"I have been dying to ask you guys, because I am afraid to do it alone, will you guys show me, I am terrified I will cut something off?"

Birch lay back on the lounger and turned to me, as she giggled.

"Hey Deads, does your dad have brush cutter, with that thatch down there, we will be needing one?"

Chapter 15

Delicate Operation.

The thing about Birch, is that her enthusiasm has a habit of bubbling up, like a geyser, when she smells an adventure, and others tend to get swept along with her. When Deb's made her announcement shorty after Anthony, Chloe and Edwina left, we had stripped for comfort, and had relaxed, and all was well.

Unfortunately, the slightly drunken Birch smelt epic adventure, and the tsunami of her enthusiasm swept over us. Sat on the lounger in the dark, having had quite a few beers, it appeared only natural to help our friend, and so caught in the excitement of Birch, I once again got dragged into the bizarre.

Gathering up the empty cans, and glasses, and full of giggles, we headed to the guest house, where Birch took control, and gave Deb's a rundown of the preparations required before shaving.

I followed along listening, agreeing with each piece of advice, as after all, this was something I had done myself many times, and Birch appeared to be competent.

Once in the guest house, and in full preparation, either I was sobering up, or my natural curiosity was starting to wane, as I had begun to understand exactly what Deb's had asked of us, which led to the obvious question, which I have asked myself many times around Birch.

"Christ, are we really going to do this?"

Deb's was in the shower under strict instructions to wash thoroughly, especially down there, Birch was sat on the wooden chair by the table, once again rummaging around in her large oversized bag. I was pacing around experiencing strange feelings of anxiety, and morbid curiosity.

The shower was pounding away in the back ground, when a sudden large wave of panic flooded into me. I crouched down in front of Birch, and whispered frantically, as I was moving towards a panic attack.

"Birch, I am not sure about this, I am not sure I can touch her vagina, she is a really good friend. It is a sacred act to go there, and I cannot say for sure I can do this."

Birch lifted her head out of her bag.

"What Sweetie?" More panic surged into me.

"For god's sake, listen to me, I am having a crisis." She smiled.

"Oh, Sweetie it will be fine, it is not sexual, it will just be like being a doctor."

That did not help, if anything it made me even more anxious.

"Birch! I didn't bloody play doctors and nurses, when I was small with her, and if I am honest, I don't bloody well want to start now. I am nineteen for god's sake, it's creepy as hell." Birch gave sigh.

"Deads Sweetie, calm down, you are over thinking it, look."

She suddenly grabbed my hand and plunged it towards her vagina.

"See it's just a vagina like mine."

I could feel her soft moist flesh, and recoiled back at high speed. The ability to whisper left me.

"Oh my god, you are wet!?" I stepped back in horror.

"Seriously, why the hell are you wet?"

My head was spinning, why was she so turned on, was she enjoying this, did she have some twisted perversion about Deb's vagina? Birch stood up and gripped me by the shoulders, I was staring to breathe rapidly.

"Deads Sweetie, you need to calm down, I am always a little damp down there, I am a free sexual spirit."

She dropped her hand, and before I could even move, she slipped her hand between my thighs, and ran her finger up my labia, one finger entered just for the slightest moment, and an electrifying tingle ran up my whole body like a shock. I sprang back shocked. Why would she do that, and she smiled held up her finger, which glistened.

"See, you are just as wet as I am, Deads Sweetie it's natural."

I shook my head, this was another whole other calamity, why was I wet? Oh my god, am I aroused at the thought of touching Deb's, my world was crashing when the shower suddenly stopped. CRAP!

Birch simply smiled, and grabbed her bag.

"It will be fine Sweetie, look, she has asked this of us, and we are her friends, and the only people she trusts, so come on, we have to do this for her, it is very important to her."

I took a long deep breath. Birch was right, Deb's was shy and innocent, and very inexperienced, and she needed us to guide her, it was the right thing to do.

Birch walked into the bedroom, and from inside the bathroom, Deb's shouted out.

"I won't be a minute; I am just dying my hair." I looked at Birch, as she laid a large towel on the bed.

"Which hair?" She sniggered, and then placed two pairs of scissors on the bedside unit. A random thought popped into my head.

"Birch, what do we do if she cum's?" Her head snapped round quicker than an owl on the hunt, and her face looked terrified.

"You don't think she will do you?"

I couldn't help but smile, there was a tone of horror and shock, mixed in her voice, and finally I knew she understood me completely. I shrugged, and lowered my voice, as Deb's hummed to herself in the bathroom.

"I don't frigging know, I mean she looked really disappointed, when she found out we had not had sex with her, for all I know she might want a threesome. She is a bloody virgin Birch, one finger slip, and her life choices could change forever."

The bathroom door opened, and we both jumped out of our skin, Deb's came in looking a little pink all over, with a huge smile on her face. Birch suddenly looked really nervous. Her green eyes locked on mine, and she whispered.

"Doctors and nurses."

I nodded and swallowed hard; we were really going to do this? Birch came up at my side.

"We will need a bowl for the hair, make it a big one, and line it with plastic or something, it keeps things hygienic."

I nodded, and spun round, to head for the kitchen. Deb's moved to the bed.

"How do you want me?"

In the kitchen my thoughts were 'not horny,' and I was assuming Birch felt the same.

"Lie on the bed, relax and open your legs wide Deb's"

I stopped in my tracks; I really did not want to see that at all. I crouched down, and looked in the cupboard, there was a large pot mixing bowl, that would be fine, I looked round for something to line it with. We had no plastic bags at all, since Norman and Daisy moved into the village, mum had only used cloth bags.

The tin foil sparkled in a holder screwed to the wall, that would do, and so I reached up for it, and took a large pair of yellow rubber gloves off the rack, and grabbed the long shiny tube, and tossed it into the bowl. It was at that point I had an amazing stroke of genius.

Deb's took off her towel and lay on the bed, and then opened her legs wide. Birch suddenly felt a little nervous, out of her bag came a packet of pink safety razors, and a large bottle of talc. I walked in with the bowl, and the tin foil, to begin the operation. Birch turned, and squealed out in abject terror.

"What the fuck Deads, you scared the shit out of me?"

I stood at the bottom of the bed, wearing the bright yellow overly large, rubber gloves, and had a tea towel tied around my mouth like a surgeon would. Deb's lay on the bed with her legs wide apart, looking like a fox had fallen head first into her vagina, and got stuck.

Birch stood there holding her heart, having been shocked by my appearance, but looked like she was saying the last rights for the fox, and it was at that moment, I felt the giggles hit me. I sniggered, and fell to my knees, almost dropping the bowl. Birch took a deep breath.

"I need more frigging alcohol."

She headed back into the living room, and grabbed a bottle of tequila, then walked back into the bedroom, unscrewed the cap, and took a huge swig, and offered the bottle to me, I grabbed it, lifted my tea towel, and took a long swig. The way I saw it, if it erased my memory, that would be a good thing. Birch took a deep breath, and looked at Deb's

"Okay, let's do this, Deads, line the bowl with foil."

Whilst I pulled out lengths of tin foil to cover the inside of the bowl, Birch sat on the bed between Deb's legs and sprinkled talc all over her. Debs lifted her head and looked down.

"What is that for?" Birch looked up at her.

"It will be a dry shave; this will cut down razor rash, and leave you smooth."

I was on the floor lining the bowl, but I had not heard of that method, I regretted looking up. Deb's vagina looked like a ball of dusty wire wool. I tilted my head, or one of those really bad Halloween wigs you buy in the cheap stores. I started to giggle again. Deb's looked down.

"Ooh, it reminds me of frosty grass in the winter." Birch was holding the scissors and started to giggle.

"Deads Sweetie give me a hand." I looked over the bed.

"To do what?"

"I need you to grab her hair and lift it up for me, so I can cut clean."

"Do I have to?" She nodded.

"Either that, or spread her thighs for me, to straighten her vagina."

I knelt up, and grabbed a patch of white dusty hair, with a thick yellow gloved hand. Birch winked at Deb's, and then started to snip.

As the hair came away, I dropped it in the bowl. Birch snipped and I held, and all was going to plan, apart from a few mild out breaks of giggles, and slowly Deb's revealed her true ladyhood to us, as the thatch was pruned away.

Suddenly Birch gave a loud squeal, and jumped back.
"OH MY GOD!"
My heart almost stopped dead, Deb's shot up into a sitting position, and bent over staring at her vagina, and I lifted my hand to see the loose flappy end of my yellow glove missing. Birch was breathing at a very rapid rate, and sweating.

"Oh, please tell me I did not cut it off?"

Deb's lifted her head looking terrified, and looked at Birch.

"Fucking cut what off?"

Her head went straight back down, as she started inspecting her lady parts, when she saw the yellow tip of my glove.

"CHRIST BIRCH, DO NOT BLOODY DO THAT, YOU SCARED THE SHIT OUT OF ME!"

I reached for the tequila, and took a long swig, Deb's grabbed at it, as her breathing rate slowed, and took an equally long swig, then handed it to Birch who was still trying to regulate her heart beat.

After several long minutes of reflection, and with the bowl almost filled with hair, it was time to complete the task. With gloves that were way too big, bar one finger, common sense dictated they were best removed.

Birch was still shaking after her shock, and so we switched places, and Birch handed me the razor, whilst sprinkling yet more talc on the now very visible, if not spikey, vagina of Deb's.

I have done this in the bath to myself a million times, so how hard could it be right? I gripped the razor, and began to shave down across her tummy towards the split. The talc did actually make it tons easier.

It went reasonably smooth, Birch would wipe the razor with a paper towel, and Deb's was revealing more and more pink skin, I was doing fine.

With most of surrounding landscape cut down and scraped off, next came the tricky bit, her labia, which were nice, round, and plump.

The problem was, as I tried to shave, they kept moving about. Now I am aware of this issue, my problem was when I do it to myself, I simply use a finger to hold it still.

Deb's was already breathing a little faster than normal, which was probably fear, hell I was already shaking like a leaf, and so was naturally concerned about the more tricker aspects of shaving her.

Birch understood, and reached over, and with one finger she placed it on the centre of her labia, and pushed it down.

"Ooh!"

Birch snatched her hand back really fast. Her head snapped round towards Deb's.

"Please don't make that noise Deb's it's very unsettling."

"Sorry, it just made me tingle." Birch looked horrified.

"Tingling is not allowed, it is fucked up, so stop it."

"Sorry Birch, I will try."

She replaced her finger, and the operation continued, slowly the hair came away revealing her clean pink lady parts, all be it with a sprinkling of white talc.

Deb's began to breath faster, and faster, and bit down on her lip. It was then that I noticed a sparkling between her labia, mixed in with the clumped up talc. I jumped back off the bed and pointed, as I felt utter horror surge into me.

"WHY IS THAT WET?" Deb's lifted her head up to her chest.

"I am sorry Abby, no one has ever touched me that way before." I dropped the razor.

"Screw that, I am out."

Birch started laughing. After several minutes of calming down, and a couple more shots of tequila, I swapped places with Birch, all the tricky stuff had been done, and so I was more an observer, as Birch worked with skill, and at a high speed, and finished the job off.

We ended up stood at the end of the bed, tilting our heads as we examined our work. Debs decided to rub in more talc, god knows why, because it was starting to look like a freshly dusted pastry. Birch appeared happy, as she turned to me.

"I must admit, I did think it would look more like a fluted cuff, but I think it's quite neat and pretty, what do you think?" I shrugged and tilted my head more.

"I would say salty clam." Birch shook her head.

"Yeah, I get that, it does a little."

Deb's sat up and examined our work, she ran her finger through it to remove the built up talc, Birch shuddered.

"Deb's dear, don't do that here. it's a little messed up, with us stood here watching."

"Sorry, I will do it in the shower, it feels very hot, so I will try to cool it down."

Birch walked round the bedroom and rummaged through her bag.

"Yeah, well water will not solve that, you are probably best off using this."

Out of her bag she lifted a vibrator, I felt a surge run through me.

"Eww! You are not letting her use yours, are you?" She grinned.

"Sweetie remember the cupboard? It's a spare. I think having felt what she did, it is prudent to let her experience the other." Deb's went beetroot.

"Seriously guys I cannot do that to myself, I don't know how." Birch winked.

"Well you cannot miss the target, so just point at it, and shoot."

Deb's headed off to the bathroom, and I felt drunk and exhausted, since knowing Birch, I had done some messed up stuff, but this? This had to be the weirdest night of my life.

It had been a long day, what with the council meeting, all the talking over the way people felt about living in the village, and Deb's.... Yeah, forget that, I am trying to. I finally, and drunkenly, made it into bed with Birch, and a clean shaven Deb's.

In a way, as weird as it had been, she was actually over the moon and happy, although looking at how close and how tight Birch was wrapping around my body, I am sure she is a little wary of being too close to Deb's at the moment. Sleep I hoped would take me, and sure enough it did.

I have no idea what time I woke up Saturday morning, which actually marked a whole week of my return to home, had it really gone that fast? However, I stirred from sleep to screams, cackles and weird high pitched yelps, which turned out to be Birch. Her phone had woken her up, and having listened to the news, she had exploded with jubilation. I opened my eyes to hear her screaming.

"It's coming, it's coming."

I had a crushing headache, as I looked at her stood in the doorway.

"Stop frigging playing with it then."

She stopped and frowned, and then understanding, she burst into her cackle of laugh, and jumped on the bed.

"Deads Sweetie, Petal is being brought back, she has passed her MOT, we have cool wheels."

I love Birch to bits, but cool wheels, is not how I would describe her ride. Rust bucket, sack of shit, death trap, all come to mind first. With Birch on the bed happy and jolly, and hugging me through the duvet, wearing a huge smile, I realised it was time for me to rise.

Having wrestled the barnacle, I call Birch off me, I wandered out into the garden in my knickers, holding a large mug of coffee, I was confronted with a naked Deb's, who was sat on a blanket on the grass with her legs spread wide open, showing off her newly shaven pride and joy.

It was a little too early, so I slipped on my new sunglasses, which had little skulls on the frames, and flopped down on a lounger. I could see through the guest house window, Birch was on the phone again, talking very excitedly.

It was one in the afternoon; I had slept a lot longer than I thought. Birch was waiting for Petal to arrive at around three, so I figured I had two hours to drink lots of coffee, and for the paracetamol to kick in.

I was drifting and relaxed when Birch came out of the guest house, she was so happy and excited, she plopped down next to me, on the lounger at my side.

"Deads you do know what this means don't you? We won't be stuck here; we can go anywhere we want without being stuck in the village. I need to do a few things to Petal, and then we can go mobile." I smiled, keeping my eyes shut behind my glasses.

"That is really nice Birch, I must admit, it be will nice if we can go into Oxendale, I wouldn't mind doing some shopping and stuff. The shops here are fine for the residents and things you need in an emergency, I wouldn't mind looking at some clothes shops, and dropping some things off at the charity shop. I have been thinking, I want to go through my wardrobe, and get rid of a load of things, having wheels will make life for us a lot easier."

"Yeah, I must admit, if I am really honest, I wouldn't mind getting out of the village, this place is getting to me a bit. It would be nice to walk and talk and shop without looking over our shoulders, or noticing how we are being watched all the time.

I think I realised last night in the hall, how much Marjorie controls everything, and everyone. Talking with Edwina and Chloe, and especially Anthony, I felt so sad for them, I cannot pretend to know how that feels, I mean Anthony is gay, it is not his fault, he did not choose it, and yet he is not allowed to say it out loud. I mean Jesus Deads, it is his sexuality for Christ's sake, he has no say over who he is attracted to, or how he feels inside, that is nature, not a deliberate choice."

She was right, and I thought about Birch's little stunt with me, I have thought about it a lot. I have never been attracted to women, but as Birch kissed me and made her way to between my legs, the truth was… I was really turned on, and yeah crazy as it sounds, I was disappointed when she got out of the bed and told me it was joke.

Was it just a Birch thing? I was not really sure, all I knew was if she had done it, I would not have stopped her and enjoyed it.

In the eyes of this village that is wrong, but I feel so close to her, so connected, I really do love her. She has been the rock beneath me for a year, and we have grown closer and closer, and I could not deny, if she wanted it, which I know she does not, I would have a full on sexual relationship with her.

I can do that, I think in many ways the village would expect it, and not be surprised if I did, but for poor Anthony, that is not possible, and the difference between us is, I have stood up and stood out, and for that I am hated.

"I have been thinking Birch, Anthony is forced to live his camp image, here in his home place, his flamboyance is expected, it is part of his life as a stylist, but to the locals that sit in his chair as he works his craft on them, it is like he is playing a role. The sad thing is he isn't, that is who he is, but relationship wise, he can never take it any further. He must be really lonely inside." Deb's sat up.

"Edwina was saying last night, they have talked a lot in the last two years. Apparently when he gets down, he goes for walks along the canal, which is how she got to know him better because she does too. One day she asked him if he was lonely because he could not publicly have a boyfriend, she said he freaked completely out, and told her never to mention it again. I guess he thought she would tell everyone, because let's be honest, as long as he is not publicly gay, his business is safe, but if he does anything and people find out, he will lose everything. I think that is really horrible and wrong." Birch gave a nod.

"That makes sense, I can see why those two found each other, they have a lot in common. They both have the same secret so it makes sense." Deb's gasped.

"Edwina is gay, how do you know?" Birch shrugged.

"What you don't see it? Deb's it is so obvious, she may as well have it written on her forehead." Deb's looked really shocked, I lifted my glasses and looked at Birch.

"Do you like, have some sort of built in gay detector? I must admit I never saw it last night; she came across as just being an ordinary girl. I saw and heard nothing that would imply she is that way inclined." Birch shrugged.

"Well she could go both ways, I just know that by the way she looked at the girls in the meeting when she was sat with her parents, it made it pretty clear to me, she was more inclined to go that way." Deb's stood up and walked over to the loungers.

"I think it is odd, we have grown up here, and yet somehow we have never questioned anything. I have lived here since mum got married, and I have just accepted always that this is how it is, but this last week, I have sat a lot and thought about it. If you live here, the rich cannot marry the poor, you can only dye your hair approved colours, your make up must conform to their ideals, you cannot wear alternative fashions, you cannot be gay or lesbian, you cannot be drunk in the town if your female. None of these things are against the law, they are accepted aspects of life anywhere else, only not here, and those are the things I know of, so I have to wonder, what else is unacceptable in this village?"

Birch lay back and looked at the blue sky.

"Look at this way Deb's, there is one thing that they hate more than anything, and they will do everything to prevent you from having it, and that my friend, is simply the freedom to choose to be who you want to be."

I nodded and my glasses slipped back on my eyes.

"Let's be honest Birch, that is what they saw when we arrived, and walked through the village, and that is why they hate us." Deb's gave a sigh.

"That's wrong guys." Birch looked at the sky, and felt her mind soar.

"It is Deb's, but who is going to tell Marjorie that? If you do, you will find she already knows, she does not want to change it, because it was always her plan to begin with, her motivation is complete control, and she aims to have it, even over us."

Chapter 16

Small Changes.

With the delivery of Petal, which happened around 3:45pm, Birch became as crazy as a bumble bee on crack. Mr Wilks got Petal off the trailer and handed over the keys, it had cost her £375.00 and he offered her back the change, but she was high on happiness, she gave him a huge kiss on the cheek, and told him to buy everyone who worked on Petal, a drink with it.

You cannot obtain a car and not drive, and so we made a hurried picnic, and headed up Waterside Lane towards Sutton's Farm and beyond, and yes, Birch drives exactly as she is on foot, she is a psychopath.

She tuned the engine on, I clicked in the seat belt, and then was pinned to the seat, with a jolt, as she took off at speed. Apparently, she goes to a club with her dad and drives these things, but from what I could hear, as we rumbled up the lane, with the windows open, and a loud engine, she mainly drives off road, and therein lies the problem, we were on the road.

We passed Suttons, and carried on towards the summit of the long heathland, where we parked up. With our basket of food, we walked to the edge of the hill, and looked out across the landscape and Wotton Dursley. With the three of us sat on a blanket, surrounded by food and cold drinks, we left the alcohol at home, we enjoyed the remoteness of the place. and especially the space.

It was good to be far away from Marjorie, and the problems we faced in the village, and just have space to breathe. Running wild, laughing, and spending a few hours completely free did us wonders.

As we raced up the road past Sutton's, my mum was sat at the desk in the study, catching up on some of the paperwork for the parish council, when the phone went off. She put the phone on speaker, so she could continue to work, but very soon sat back and listened.

"Hello Felicity, I thought you would be sat in the office, which is why I am ringing now. How are you and the girls doing?"

"We are fine Edwin, Abby is much better and more relaxed, now she has settled in at home, she is still in the guest house with Birch. I thought I would leave her, seeing as they are having such a good time. As for myself, I am doing fine, I have actually had a lot of time with the girls, and I have enjoyed it, I never realised how much I have missed her since she has been away."

"Good, I am glad you two are getting on better, you know, I am not the monster you think I am; it is important you two have some time together. How have the villagers been with her?"

"They hate her, what did you think, they would just accept her? Norman and Daisy have been here for five years, and they still treat them with derision. Abby is seen as a threat to them, you know what they can be like?" She heard him sigh on the phone.

"I want to do something; I just don't know what."

"You can talk to Peter Saxon for one thing, Abby went into the shop on Wednesday, and she has not said anything, but I could see how hurt she was when she came out. Abby has always loved those two, especially Mary, and I do not know what Mary said or did, but whatever it was it really upset her. I was at the meeting Friday, and I could hardly talk to her I feel so upset. You and Peter are good friends, so talk to him, she has not changed you know, she is still our Abigail, she just has darker hair, she is still as polite and respectful as she was, but she is hurting, and you need to help."

"I will ring him this evening, and see what I can do. What about transferring University, are you still considering that? To be honest Felicity, I cannot say I am over joyed with her appearance, because I am not completely, I can live with it, just. But I have had a few evenings talking with other conference members, and they have families too. I have seen pictures, and frankly I was surprised at the wide range of hair styles and colours their children have. I suppose it made me realise she could have looked worse. I listened carefully to what you said before I left, and yes, I took it all in, and I do not think we should separate her from this Birch girl. I won't say I agree with everything the girl does, but I admire her spunk, she stands up for what is right, and that is what I have always tried to teach Abigail, so I think for now, we should leave her as is."

Felicity understood this was not easy for him, she knew him well enough to know that this was an olive branch, and the first he had offered in a long time.

"I am happy to hear that Edwin, because to be honest, I do not think we could separate them if we tried. The Edwin I used to know would have said the same. I aim to leave her as she is, to find her own path, after all isn't that what we had to do? I will be absolutely frank Edwin, I have looked at myself through Abby's eyes these last few days, and I do not like what I have seen. We used to be like her, but this bloody village got under our skin, and before we knew it, we had changed. I have agreed to things I never should have, and I feel pretty bloody guilty about it."

"Yes, I know what you mean, I too have been thinking a lot down here, and I am ashamed to admit it, but I have played my part in it too, the problem is, how do we get out of it, do we quit the council?"

"No, we change it, I am going to run against Marjorie in the November elections again, I almost beat her last time, and I am going to give it another shot. I think change needs to happen in Wotton, and if you want my opinion, I think we should try and make that happen."

"I am happy to hear you said we. You know you will have my full backing if you do. Look Felicity, I did listen, I really did, I want change too, it has been on my mind since I left. I have decided to take a little more time, Gordons in Exeter has been after a visit from Graham or myself for a while, so Graham is heading back to London tonight, and I am going to go on to Exeter, and sort them out and take a couple of days. I have too much going on my head, and I need to straighten it out. I rang to ask if you will be alright with that, if you want me home, I will come straight back."

"Will you be alone?"

"For Pete's sake Felicity, I am really trying here, yes, I will be alone, if you want to check, Angela will be back in the office and answering the phone on Monday. I am sure you know how to find out all about me from her. I promise we will talk when I come back, and I have everything straight in my head."

"Alright Edwin, go see this firm and sort them out, and take whatever time you have to, Abby and Birch will be fine, I shall watch over them. When you are ready come home, we will be here, but I am serious Edwin, we cannot carry on as things are, sweeping changes need to be made. It sounds ridiculous, but all I want is for you to be the man you were, I married you for a reason you know? I think you have forgotten that. Think about that while you are in Exeter."

"Alright Felicity, I will do, I have to go and sort things out with Graham, I will ring you from Exeter alright?"

"Alright, drive safely Edwin, and I will talk soon." She gave a long sigh as the call ended, and rested in the chair.

"This is your last chance Edwin, please don't mess this one up, Abby cannot handle much more."

Delphine Chappuis, was the business partner of Anthony. She had trained him straight out of college, with the dream of one day owing her own place. Her real name was Daphne Chapel, and she was from Oxendale. She worked as a mobile hairdresser, and she worked long hard hours, in order to achieve her dream.

Anthony had the same dream, and rich parents, and so at age forty, she had joined in partnership with him, and they opened the salon in Wotton. The names changed, and the business boomed, mainly because it was a long drive to Oxendale, and so with a site in the village, and a fresh new look, and some fake elegant props, Delphine and Antonio entered the life of the rich.

It was normal every day after the shop closed, for Delphine to walk her dogs along the canal, and so tonight, Anthony decided to take a leap of faith, and meet her. He waited by the old rundown wheel house, and as she approached, he made out like he too had been for a walk. Once established, he walked along with her, as her poodles ran around on a long leashes.

"I wanted to talk to you alone, away from everyone." She understood.

"I saw you with Abigail and her friend last night, I cannot say I did not expect this." He was nervous, and his ticks made him twitch more.

"I have always liked her, she was nice to me in school, and I feel sorry for what has happened to her, I know what it's like to be bullied." Delphine gave a sigh.

"You certainly do, I understand, to be honest I think her hair is wonderful, and the fringe is absolutely right for her. Didn't I always say a good fringe would frame her face perfectly? You see I was right."

He stopped and stood in front of her, it was clear he was really nervous. He fidgeted and twitched, and she felt sorry for him.

"Oh, Anthony whatever is it that has got you so worked up, won't you tell me? I mean look at you, jumping about all over the place, if I had my scissors with me, I would put them in your hand, because I know when you pick a pair up, all those ticks disappear. You are a born stylist of that there is no doubt." He jerked and fidgeted.

"I have not always been honest; I see that now. I spent until late talking with Abigail and her friends, and I saw how they face everything, and they are honest about themselves." He looked her straight in the eyes.

"You gave me a chance, and you trained me, and I owe everything to you, and I also see you as my best friend, I do Delphine, I wouldn't have made it this far without you." She smiled.

"Anthony whatever it is just say it, stop putting yourself through this, we are partners, you can say anything you wish to me." His eyes filled with tears.

"I need you know, that I am not who they think I am, I am sorry, but I am gay, and I am afraid you will hate me for it."

The tears flooded into his eyes. Delphine stood there and gave a small chuckle, she pulled him into a hug, and he burst into tears.

"Oh Anthony, why are you torturing yourself like this, do you not think I don't know that? I have known your mum for years, I watched you grow up. Oh, Anthony dear, I have been in this business my whole life, I am forty years old, did you honestly think I did not know?" She released him and looked at him.

"Stop being silly, and torturing yourself, you are not telling me anything I did not know when you first started training." He pulled out a silk handkerchief and wiped his face.

"Why didn't you say something?"

She smiled, and held him gently by his shoulders, the two dogs pulled on the leads round her wrists, as they sniffed around the pathway.

"It's not my place really is it now? Yes, I am your business partner, but you are allowed a private life. What you do or who you see in private is not my concern, as long as we are both on time, and the salon is open, that is all I worry about. You are the best I trained, and you have a great skill with those scissors, and as long as we are there side by side, I am happy. Looking at this face though, it is clear you are unhappy." He shook his head.

"I am not really, but I hate not being able to be completely me." She looked at him closely.

"Anthony, you can be you, but you also cannot forget where we work, we work in Wotton, and they are not like us, they have old ideas and old ways. You know what they are like? Look at the things we hear about Abby and her friend all day in the salon. They are not as kind as they pretend, and I will not deny, when it comes to you, I worry about that."

"They have done nothing wrong; Abby just dyed her hair, and has better fashion sense now. I am a stylist, all the girls in the village should look like her, because that is what girls her age look like now. I want to do that kind of work, I spent two years in college learning it, we should be doing that." Delphine agreed.

"You are not wrong Anthony, and yes we could double the business, and bring another stylist in if we could do that, but we do not live in Oxendale anymore, we work here, and it is different. Look, the dogs are getting restless, why don't you come back to my house, and we will sit with a cup of tea, and let us take a look at how we can make a slow change. We have a lot of posters in the back room, maybe we should put one or two of those up, and see what people say. You never know, someone might ask, how about we do that?" He flicked his long fringe back, and gave a sniffle.

"Thanks, you are the best, you know that?"

They walked slowly back, talking about what they could do, and how they could make some small changes. Together they sat in Delphine's parlour and looked at their ideas. It would not be easy, but if they took it slow, who knows what they could influence, after all the one thing they did know about the women of Wotton, is they would do almost anything to appear to have the best hair in the village.

We spent a glorious afternoon and evening, lay in the grass under the sun, with our eyes closed, laughing and talking, it was the best feeling ever, just to be free from everything. I lay there feeling the hot sun beating down on me, and I really did not want to move. I gave a long sigh.

"We will have to go back soon, it's been so wonderful, I wish I could have been naked."

"I have been for ages." I sat up and turned to Birch.

"Why didn't you say something, I didn't know we could sunbathe naked here, how did you know?"

She lay there on the blanket with a big smile on her face, wearing only her bright flower covered sun glasses.

"I didn't know, I just wanted to be, so I was. I did not know if you two wanted to do it, to be honest I was so lost in thought I didn't think to ask."

I felt cheated somehow, but again knowing Birch, I really do not know why I was surprised. It was a sad event packing up and walking back to the car, it was a terrifying event driving home. It was mainly downhill, and even with new brakes, I still worried, because Birch rarely used them.

Deb's hung on in the back for dear life, as the Land Rover bumped and jostled, on the old rough road, I leaned over the partition to talk to her, I did it mainly to look at her, that way I did not have to look out of the windscreen. It somehow felt better not knowing what hair pin bend was coming up, I had my feet pressed against the sides of the footwell to stabilise me.

Don't drink and drive is a good message, unless you are a passenger with Birch, then drink tons before you drive, it will calm your nerves, and if you die, you will be too pissed to notice.

We made it home alive, whatever angels we had watching over us, I thanked, as I staggered out of the passenger door with wobbly legs, to keypad the gates. Birch drove in, and Deb's opened the gates at the side of the garage, so Birch could drive though into the back.

I knew mum would need to get her car out of the garage, and dad was expected home today, so he would park outside. I also thought he would freak out when he saw a rusty old Land Rover on the drive, so to avoid conflict, I did my best to ensure it was hidden.

Deb's followed me into the guest house, where I poured two very large Southern C's neat, and downed mine in one. My knees were still wobbling, and my hands trembling, so I grabbed two beers and took one out to Birch. She was walking round Petal admiring her lovingly, she looked up as I approached, and her eyes sparkled with delight.

"That was fucking awesome."

It was one way describe it, the fact my whole life had passed before my eyes on route, convinced me that the word used to describe our safe return home was probably, Miracle.

I left Birch to crawl all over her new car, and Deb's and myself headed to the lawn, to relax, and allow the alcohol to quell our nervous systems. I peeled off the layers and stretched out, next to Deb's, she looked at me.

"You can drive, and I can drive, why don't we take it in turns, that way we can reduce the odds of dying young considerably?"

It was a bloody good suggestion, the problem was, looking at Birch fawning over her new car, was how do we sell her the idea?

I needed to think, it had to appear like it would be an adventure, if I could pull that off, we had a really good chance of surviving the summer.

Chapter 17

Cleaning Up Crew.

On Saturday, boxes started arriving. From the moment Birch had acquired Petal, she had been planning and ordering online. So as we sat on the grass after eating, she excitedly opened boxes, to reveal, new padded and very flowery looking seat covers, a radio with an MP3 player, a lock for the gears and steering wheel, and yards of fabric and tassels, of every colour known to nature.

The last box was filled with assorted cans, of paint, chrome cleaner, glue, and car polish, for just about everything. It felt like Christmas, and with each box, she talked more and more, in a fast, bubbly, excited fashion. Birch had planned out our entire week, and it was going to be the week of the rebirth of Petal.

We sat on the patio as it went dark, ripping up boxes, and burning them in the chimera, as we talked and drank, and just enjoyed the excitement of Birch. By one o'clock, the fire was out, we were once again drunk, and the three of us collapsed into bed. Sunday was a little overcast as I got up, mum was out, and the bells were ringing. We were out of bread, so I decided to head up to the house to find food.

Deb's came out of the bedroom, as I came out of the kitchen, rubbing her eyes, her normally long wavy brown hair, was matted and all over the place. It was nice to see she was wearing knickers again, and had stopped proudly displaying her pink childlike pussy to all of us.

"What you doing?" She yawned, and blinked her eyes.

"I am going to the house; we are out of bread." She nodded.

"Okay, I will come too."

Together we headed up to the house, and ended up sat in the kitchen drinking coffee, and eating toast at the counter. I was on my third cup of coffee, and was starting to feel somewhat alive again, when I heard the familiar sound of the guest house door bang, Deb's put down her cup.

"Birch is up, wait for it?" I sniggered.

She soon appeared looking irate, wearing her long black robes, which were wide open exposing her naked self. She stood in the doorway, her hair all over the place, her eyes half open, and wearing a look of utter annoyance. I smiled.

"Morning." Her glare was intense, even through her half open eyes.

"ARE THESE DOORS AIRTIGHT?" I shrugged, and looked at Deb's, she shrugged.

"It's your house!" I looked back at Birch.

"I think so?" She turned and grabbed the handle.

"GOOD!!"

She pulled, and the door slammed shut with a deafening bang, that shook the frame.

"Fucking bell twats... One of these days, I am going to climb that fucking tower, and steal his fucking bell, or drop it on him."

She walked across the kitchen towards us, stopped between us, and kissed Deb's on the cheek, and then she turned and kissed me on the cheek.

"Morning Sweetie." She headed for the kettle.

Birch discovered bacon in the fridge, and so breakfast went from toast, to sandwiches, as we all sat at the counter stuffing our faces, and slowly coming back to life. Deb's had to leave and show her face at home, she had missed church for the second week running, and looked a little apprehensive. I looked at her as she dressed

"Will you be alright?" She nodded.

"I told dad last week, I have missed it for a year being at Uni, so it's not like I have been a regular face there much." She looked up, as she pulled her jeans on. "It's just mum, you know what it was like for her here when she first came, she likes to keep up appearances, it keeps the gossips quiet."

I understood, so ten minutes later I waved her goodbye, and returned to the garden, where the Land Rover passenger door was wide open, and Birch's legs were waving around in the air out of it. I looked in to see what she was up to.

Birch was lay on her back, with her right hand up behind the console, where different coloured wires were waving around.

"What the hell are you doing?" Her muffled voice came out from within the footwell.

"Grab my legs will you, it will stabilise me, this stupid bloody wire will not go through the hole, and I keep falling out." I grabbed a leg in each hand, and stood there holding her, I looked down between her legs.

"You need a shave." I sniggered and then realised I was between her legs, holding on in each hand.

"Hey Birch, if I had a strap on, I could make you my bitch." I giggled as she twisted.

"Deads Sweetie, if you had a strap on, I would let you. God knows a cock about now would really help. I am impressed that you actually got laid in this hell hole of sexual repression before Uni." She twisted.

"Thank god for that, I got the bitch through." She wiggled and sat up, I was still holding her legs, she smiled and her face dropped.

"Sweetie are you alright, did I say something wrong?"

I was stood there between her thighs, still holding her legs, and inside I felt my stomach twisting and churning. I wanted to forget that night ever happened. She looked at me with those intense green eyes, and I dropped her legs, I was going to leave, but she grabbed my hands and pulled me close.

"Why won't you talk about it?"

She let go of my hands and grabbed my face, she was so close, her eyes appeared so much bigger, and so filled with love, but I couldn't, I wanted to, but it was buried too deep, I looked down.

"I want to, I really do, but not yet." She pulled me into a hug.

"Alright Sweetie, I am here when you are ready."

I felt like a hypocrite, I had spent a week here watching people admit their deepest fears, and reveal who they were, and yet here I was, exactly the same hiding my secret, I was no better than the rest of them, especially considering I had Birch. I felt her hand in mine.

"Come on, see what I have been doing."

She walked me round to the back of the Land Rover and opened the door. Inside she had laid the fabric on the plastic covered long side seats, and covered the floor in a thick piece of foam.

"See... I asked Mr Wilks to fit the floor out, so it will not only be water proof when I have covered it in the rubber sheet, it will be like a mattress, we can sleep in it...Well when I have put up the tie back curtains we can. I have to staple the fabric to the seats, but they too will be great for sitting, and also, they will be great for lying on and looking at the stars. I am putting the sound system in, so we will have tunes, I want to mount a speaker up there." She pointed.

"I need some good floor mats for the front, and I am going to cover the dash in something colourful, and then all we have to do is decorate it, and pretty a few things up, and she will be dazzling."

I was impressed, she had really planned it out, although I still felt there was one problem.

"What about the outside, it still looks like shit." She chuckled.

"For now, but wait till I am finished, she will look happy and full of love, which is why I bought her, because this will be yours and mine to escape in whenever we want, and it just so happens that we can also screw in the back." She winked. As with all things Birch, she had thought of everything.

Birch returned to work on her wiring, I felt uneasy, so I walked back the garden and left her too it, and went back to the guest house. I lay on the bed and closed my eyes, I remembered that night, I remembered James, it was as vivid in my mind as it had ever been.

I remembered how we had snuck in to the farm storage shed in the field behind the Church, and how he had arranged the hay bales. We had kissed and he undid my blouse, I never intended to go that far, but I really liked him, and we had been dating for two months. I will never forget when he took off his shirt, and I undid his pants, even now I still get turned on thinking about it.

We were naked before I knew it, and my school uniform was on the top of the bales, just where he had thrown it, the memory of him kissing my boobs, and the electric sensations, as he went lower, I thought I was so in love with him, and I wanted him to be my first.

I gasped on the bed, just remembering that moment he entered me, and rolled over on my side, I had my hand in my jeans, what the hell was I doing? I could not stop as my hand flowed with the stroke of the memory of him. Oh God it was the most freeing and amazing thing I had ever known. I was out of it, and on cloud nine, my whole body tingling as I looked up at James sliding back and forward in front of me, it was glorious, and then my heart almost stopped.

"Who was that?"

I sprang up off the bed, my heart racing, and I looked round, I was still in the bedroom. My heart was pounding and I was sweating, I felt jittery and weak, and my hand was still down inside the front of my jeans, and I was soaking wet down there. I caught my breath and pulled my hand out, was I dreaming or just remembering, I really did not know?

When I came out of the house, mum and Hatty were back from church, and inspecting Petal, as Birch proudly went through her plans all over again. I walked up towards them, and mum smiled, I slid in at her side, and she slipped her hand round my waist.

"Are you alright Abby?" I nodded.

"Tired and I feel grubby, I was thinking of having a bath." She smiled.

"Long soak might do you good, relax and unwind a bit." I smiled and nodded.

"Yeah, I was thinking that too." She leaned over and kissed my head.

"You go and soak, we are going to hear the plan of the century, as Birch tries to convince us of how she is going to make this vehicle look in any way respectable, before your father comes home." I chuckled.

"You cannot deny, the girl has spirit." I turned, and then thought of something.

"I thought dad would be home last night?" She shook her head.

"He has a contract to deal with in Exeter, he will be a few more days yet." She smiled.

I left them to Birch, and her fanciful dreams to restore her bucket of rust, and headed indoors to run a bath. I turned on the taps, and headed to my room and stripped, as I looked in my wardrobe at what I had on the rails.

Just like at Uni, the washing was piling up, and I needed fresh clean clothes, the problem was that pretty much all of this was not really what I wanted to wear anymore. I went through it, tossing things I would never wear again on the bed, and when I was finally done, there was not that much left.

"I need to go clothes shopping... Shit the bath!"

I high tailed it out of the bedroom and down the hall, and came skidding into the room just in time, the water was already reaching the overflow.

I dumped in a bath bomb, and watched it fizz, and then gently slipped into the roasting hot, deep water, and slid right down until my chin was level with it, and it felt fantastic.

With my head on a folded flannel, and my eyes closed, I felt like the water was washing everything away, and I wanted it to.

I have no idea how long I was there, I just relaxed, and was half in and half out of reality, as my mind floated restfully on the water. It was warm and cosy and felt safe, and it was all I needed right now, as I drifted into nothingness. Like most things in my life of late, I was dragged into reality at an alarming speed.

"BANG!"

I jumped and slipped in the water, and went under, as I came out of my dream state, by thrashing around wildly, trying to breathe like fish, and failing badly. My head came back above the water, and I gasped in a huge breath of life saving oxygen, to expel the copious amounts of Texas Dewberry flavoured water out of my lungs. I sat with the water sploshing around, my hair stuck to my tits, coughing my lungs up as my heart raced. I turned to the bright faced, and happy eyes of Deb's who suddenly looked sad.

"I am sorry, did I frighten you?" I coughed and breathed in.

"Hell no... I was already drowning when you got here. What the hell Deb's?" She gave an apologetic smile and sat on the toilet, Birch came in.

"I am sorry Abby, I got a little excited, because I got these off my dad, and I wanted to show you them as soon as possible. I looked at her holding a bunch of what looked like tickets in her hand. Her chest swelled up with happiness.

"These are tickets to the Oxendale Festival next weekend. I have a camping and parking pass, as well as five tickets." Birch looked impressed.

"Great I am filthy…. Shove up."

She pulled off her long top, and straddled over the side of the bath, and as I moved forward, she slid in behind me.

"Come on I will wash your back… Oh this is heaven, wow your bath is really big."

I looked at Deb's. "So, tell me, what is this festival about?"

She beamed with delight, I felt the sponge rub up and down my back. Her eyes were sparkling like Petal's headlights.

"It's a concert, well a festival. Two days of live music, booze and good vibes."

I felt Birch's hands slide round, and she started to fondle my boobs, she moved close and kissed my shoulder.

"You know what else will be there my dark little beastie?"

I slid her hands down off my boobs and regretted it, as Birch went exploring.

"No, what?" I jumped as she slid in between my legs.

"Pack it in Birch." She kissed my shoulder closer to my neck, and I felt all funny and shivered.

"Cock… Lots and lots of cock, and boy do I need one."

I tried slapping her hand, but it just splashed the water, and she started to giggle. Deb's was still oozing excitement.

"Yeah, cock is good and all that, not that I would know, but guess what is even better?" Birch turned and frowned.

"Oh, you poor misguided little flower, Deb's dearest, there is nothing better than cock."

"Well for me there is… Battered Taco are headlining." Birch sniggered.

"I will be happy if mine gets battered." I looked at Deb's.

"Who the hell are Battered Taco?" I tried to turn back, and look at Birch who was still sniggering.

"Have you ever heard of them?"

"Guys seriously, you have never heard of Battered Taco?" Birch sniggered.

"I have seen a few after Friday nights at Uni, Deads being one of them." Even I had to laugh. Deb's was not put off.

"They are a really good rock band, they are like beefed up bluesy rock, they play a lot of Whitesnake stuff, they are really good, and the guitarist Jimmy, is hot as hell, god I get wet thinking of him."

Birch leaned over my shoulder, as she hunted for the soap.

"Deads, it's two days away from here, in a tent, with booze and men, and that is all the info I need. Here lean back and I will wash your hair, then you can do mine."

Twenty minutes later, I was sat on my bed in a towel, as Birch dried my hair with the dryer.

"I know we have a tent, it's a good size one, I think it is in the garage, we have a lot of camping stuff, but none of it has been used for ages." Birch clicked off the dryer.

"If we work hard this week, Petal will be ready, so we have no problems with transport, and we can get loads of booze in, these places cost a fortune, so the more we take the better." Deb's was still very excited, she looked at me.

"We will have two spare tickets, I did think of Edwina and Chloe, do you think they would come?"

I had no issue with it, but the sleeping arrangements could be tight, we would probably need another tent.

"I think you should ask them, but where would they sleep, the tent won't hold all of us, and that permit is for one tent?" Birch leaned over.

"They could use them as day passes, or buy another tent pass, or stay in a local hotel." Deb's nodded.

"Great idea, I will ask them."

The rest of the day was spent planning, we headed into the garage and unpacked the tent, it was a good size, and had enough room for the three of us plus supplies. The sleeping bags smelt a bit musty, but mum told me she would wash them. We sat in the garden and listed the provisions we would need. Deb's mum was heading to the supermarket on Tuesday, so Deb's took the list and promised to collect everything for us.

That evening, as we ate at the garden table with mum and Hatty, Deb's phone pinged. She looked up excitedly.

"The girls are in, they have got a friend with a tent, and they got a pass for camping online, so we are good to go."

I cannot deny, I was starting to get really excited; I had only seen one band live, and that was when I was at Birch's. Looking at the line up online, there were loads of different bands on. As the night progressed, we sat drinking and laughing. Around midnight

Deb's went home, and we crashed into bed and snuggled up.

Monday came, and my second week home started, and it was going to be a busy week. Petal needed a much needed face lift, and so Birch and I set to. The first job was to kit out the back, and armed with a shot gun stapler, I worked on the seats, as Birched worked on the floor mat. Next came curtains, and cleaning, and the days became filled with laughing drinking and working hard.

The days slipped past, Deb's arrived with supplies, Chole and Edwina turned up with Anthony, who was a little disappointed, but with a fully booked salon, it was out of the question, so he understood. I promised to send him pictures all weekend so he could feel a part of it.

We polished chrome, glued on fabric, and hung little gems and ornaments all over the place, to which Anthony would give his expert opinion, and it was all thumbs up. Wednesday was roof cleaning day, and we climbed up on the white roof, armed with scrubbing brushes, and hot soapy water.

It was another hot sunny day, and clothing was pointless. On our hands and knees, we scrubbed off algae and bird shit, but by the time we finished it was gleaming. Deb's polished all the windows, Edwina did the chrome frames, and Chloe scrubbed the wheels, and I had to admit Petal was looking pretty good, it was just a shame that the paint job was camouflaged in green and pale blue.

As always Birch had a plan. She sat on a stool at the back of Petal, it had a new replacement door which was grey, and she wanted to sketch a picture on the back. She had ordered some decals online, and one of them was custom made. It was bright purple letters reading, 'all girls together,' but she wanted something else below it. My mum came up behind her as she tried to sketch in light pencil.

"So, what are you up to now?"

Birch scratched her head, she pointed to the transfer laid out on the floor.

"I want that at the top of the door, but it needs something else, I was thinking of doing us girls, but I am not that good, so I am sat here wondering what else I can do?" Mum looked at the door.

"I tell you what, you get on with the rest and leave this bit to me,

I would like to be a part of making Petal look elegant." Birch was excited.

"Really? Flick you are a life saver, I know what I want for the rest, if you could help, I would be so happy."

Birch took over the rest of the Petal's paint job, as my mum disappeared, and then came out with her paint box and a stool. She sat at the back, and went straight to work, Hatty sat smiling as Birch moved round to the side.

Birch's idea was that she could not repaint the whole Land Rover just yet, but it was a design of patched RAF combat colours, so her idea was to outline each coloured shape in other colours. She shook her cans, and got ready to paint, as she lifted her can ready Hatty raised an objection.

"Good God girl, not like that!"

She walked over and took the can out of Birch's hand.

"Do it like this, that way it will not bleed and run, and you will get a more accurate line, see?" She sprayed the line, and followed the shape in bright yellow, and it looked amazing. She nudged Birch out of the way.

"Here let me do it, I have a better trained hand."

Our project had been hijacked, as Hatty and my mum took over, and we sat on the grass eating crisps and drinking beer, and by seven pm, the paint was dry, mum had almost finished, and we were almost ready to show the new look Petal to the world. All we had to do was apply all the transfers, and she would be done.

We walked round to the back to see mum's work and I gasped. On the door she had painted the five girls faces, and they were stunning, she looked up and smiled.

"Not my best work, but given the time, I think it's a pass." Hatty walked up.

"Let me be the judge of that."

I felt a strange feeling inside me, I actually wanted to cry. Mum stood up and I saw my face, with my red tipped hair, next to Birch with her lovely birch bark hair, and Deb's, Chloe and Edwina. It was just a stunning likeness. I looked at Birch who actually had tears in her eyes, she grabbed my mum and wrapped her arms round.

"It's perfect Flick... Just perfect."

She was right, it stood for everything this summer was becoming. Hatty went inside and grabbed her camera, and we all stood at the back of Petal, either side of the painted door, and she took a picture. She tilted the camera down to check it out on the screen at the back.

"Not one for social media, too much nudity, but I will message it you as a keep sake of the moment, this is an event that should be recorded."

She was right, it was hot and sticky and most of the work was done after a long week. Chloe and Edwina, sadly had to leave, as work called, but I sent them a picture I took on my camera of the finished artwork. Once we cleaned everywhere up, Birch is really messy, those of us who were wearing the few garments we were, stripped off and dived in the pool to cool off.

Friday was chaos, we had washing to do, provisions and tents to pack, and Birch had to add the finishing transfers now all the paint was dry. I headed into the house with tons of washing, whilst Birch and Deb's applied the long flowery and scrolling ribbons that decorated the sides of Petal.

Mum came out of the house with two long silk scarves, and climbed up on the bonnet, and tired them to the long ariel, and the job was done, the transformation of Petal was outstanding. Even I was impressed. Birch beamed with delight.

"Isn't she beautiful.... Guys I am telling you, I will never forget this, it has been the happiest week of my life, you are all amazing, and I love you all for this...Thanks."

The tyre had been attached back on the bonnet, and Hatty did the honours.

"I name this vehicle Petal."

She poured half her beer over the wheel, and we all yelled, screamed, and applauded, it was such a happy moment, and I am so glad I filmed it on my phone.

Washing done, dried, and sorted, food and tents packed, Chloe's friend had delivered theirs to us, Petal was set and ready to go on the drive. And after a night of celebration, we all crashed into bed early, setting the alarms on our phones. Tomorrow the adventure would begin, and in our hearts, all of us one way or another were looking forward to Battered Taco.

Chapter 18

Festival Festivities.

7:00 am Saturday morning was supposed to be the most exciting moment of the week, I had a headache, as did Deb's, and Birch was grunting, and walking naked round the house looking for a sock.

To say it was difficult to get motivated, was an understatement, Deb's kept looking at her watch, actually she was squinting, opening her eyes fully was just too painful for her. She checked her watch again, and I looked at the bedroom, where Birch was trying to put her sock on with her eyes closed, and I was starting to panic.

"BIRCH PLEASE!"

The moment I yelled, all of us regretted it, Deb's had her hands to her head, and looked at me almost mystified.

"Why would you do that?"

I regretted it too, but I know Birch, and didn't I manage to control her when the vicar came? I turned back to beg her to please get dressed, and she stood there wearing short denim shorts, a blue vest, and sunglasses.

"Hi Sweetie." I had to look twice.

"How the hell did you…. You know what, forget it, you look…. Actually, pretty amazing."

With travel mugs of coffee, and paracetamol, we made it to Petal with time to spare. Deb's jumped into the back as mum hugged Birch, and then me, and together we came through the gates, I held out my hand.

"Why don't I drive?" She frowned.

"I want to drive." I shrugged.

"Do you know the way?"

I could see Deb's nervously watching through the window. Birch thought about it, which looked painful considering her headache, she handed me the keys. Deb's punched the air. I jumped in the driver's seat, and put the keys in.

"Are we ready girls?"

The response was groans, so I turned the key and we were off. Petal was a bit more basic than I am used to, and it had been a year since I had driven, but all in all, I was really enjoying it, as we headed on to Manor Road.

The silk scarves were flying, and Birch plugged in the USB stick to the mp3 player, and the speakers roared into life.

Birch was instantly awake and started to jig in the seat, Deb's who was not recovering as fast, decided to lie on the floor, and wish she had died in the night. I turned onto the main street, and Birch suddenly jumped.

"Gum.... Deads I need gum."

We were driving along the green, as the village came to life for a new day, and I indicated and pulled up, I pointed across the street.

"Shop.... Go buy, and hurry."

Marjorie was in the Tea Rooms, having her first tea of the morning, scowling out of the window.

"What on earth is that monstrosity?"

She watched as the Land Rover blasting music stopped, the door opened, and Birch jumped out, she recoiled with horror.

"Oh my god, that monstrosity belongs to them, could they possibly drop any lower than they already have. Is there no end to that woman's vile and disgusting behaviour?"

Birch came running back out of the shop, and Marjorie sneered.

"Look she is barely wearing clothes, that common hussy is beyond words."

Birch jumped in with a beaming smile, and six packs of gum, I put the car in gear, and we were off again, turning right on to Station Road, and straight down to the restaurant, where Chloe watched from behind the door.

I pulled up, and Birch jumped out, and ran round to the back, in what had been rehearsed by us over the week.

On the signal, Chloe ran out and jumped in the back, I was impressed, she had very short white shorts on, tied with a bright tie dyed scarf, A pink very loose fitting, cropped vest with no bra, and a pair of suede light brown boots, and a circlet of braded flowers in her hair, and her makeup changed her complete appearance. I had to admit, she looked completely different to how I had always seen her.

Once in, Edwina came out, in a short cream pixie skirt, and a very tight green vest, which made her boobs look much bigger than I thought they were. She had on knee high brown boots, and a matching floppy hat, her long dark brown hair was down, instead of tied up as normal, and like her sister she was unrecognisable.

She jumped in, Birch shut the door, and came giggling round to the passenger door, and jumped in.

"Hit it my dark little beastie." I screeched off from the curb, and everyone fell about in the back.

We drove down Station Road, and round Pilkington's, and up the back roads towards Oxendale and the festival. Birch was bending over leaning over the partition behind the seat, talking to Chloe and Edwina.

"You guys look so cool, why didn't you say you were Festies?" Edwina looked a little confused, Birch sniggered.

"You know.... Boho Chic, meets hipster?" Suddenly Edwina smiled, and looked at Chloe.

"This is going to be so cool; we can be us for two days straight." I laughed as Birch said.

"Welcome to the club sisters."

The event was not that far, and we bobbed along what was almost an empty country lane, I had figured everyone was going to use the main Oxendale roads, so I hoped to get in early and ahead of the crowds.

From somewhere behind me, there was the highest pitched scream I have ever heard. I jumped in the seat, and looked in the mirror, before I could work out what was going on, Deb's screamed again.

"SPIDER!"

Birch, who had been leaning over the partition behind me, suddenly crashed backwards, and fell against the dash, then disappeared into the footwell, her legs pointing upwards.

Debs was half way over the partition squealing like a pig, and came sprawling down straight into Birch. I stamped on the breaks, and the motion thrust Deb's right into Birch's vaginal region.

Edwina and Chloe squealed, and were hurled into the provisions and tents. I hit the hazard lights, and got out, feeling shaken and panicked.

"What the hell, it's a tiny little frigging thing, Deb's I could have crashed?"

I opened the door, as Chloe looked up from between the sleeping bags laughing.

"You guys are fucking awesome!" Birch was laughing.

"Deb's baby, I love you too, but sex using you whole head is just wrong, you won't fit in."

Edwina started laughing, as I leaned in with a smile, and grabbed Deb's by her short's waist band, I pulled, and she came out looking red. She looked at me.

"Why does Birch's vagina smell so sweet?" I looked at her with disbelief.

"What... Deb's we almost crashed over a frigging spider, why is Birch's vagina scent even relevant?" She shuddered violently.

"It was big."

"Huh?"

"The spider, it was huge." I shook my head, and reached in for Birch, Chloe was still laughing hysterically. I grabbed Birch by the leg and pulled, she popped out with a smile.

"Hi Sweetie." She looked at Deb's.

"A dab here and a dab there, and it stays sweet and tasty for days." She handed Deb's a small bottle. Behind us a car honked its horn, Deb's showed me the bottle.

"Does it really work?" The car honked again.

"I don't frigging know, just get in the back."

I led Deb's round the back, where Edwina was holding the spider in question by its leg, she showed it the annoyed driver behind us with a smile, he did not appear that impressed. Deb's stepped back and shuddered.

"Ergh!"

I had no time for this, as I opened the door, she threw it out, the guy in the car behind us was looking angry, I smiled. Deb's got in and, I ran round to the front, and jumped back in, Birch bounced up and down on her seat.

"Are we there yet mum?" She leaned back and started to laugh with her cackling laugh, I put Petal in gear, and we were off again.

There was a long line into the festival, and the going was slow. Birch sat on the spare wheel in the sun, joined by Chloe and Edwina, and bottles of beer. The windows were open, and the music was playing, Deb's sat in the passenger seat with her boots off, and her feet on the dash, drinking her beer. I had the short straw; I was behind the wheel.

It took over an hour to get in, and then we finally drove onto the camp ground, and parked up. We had three hours before the first band, on the huge stage that loomed in the massive field next to ours. Music was playing through the huge speakers as a DJ stood in a small booth at the side of the stage.

It felt wild and exciting as the bass thumped across the area, and I could not help smiling. Birch dragged out the tent bags.

"Hey does anyone know how to actually put up a tent?"

We all looked at each other, the answer was a unanimous.

"Nope!"

The following hour taught me that basically, a tent is a cloth like bag, which is deliberately designed to be annoying, frustrating, and is more stress inducing than the sound of Bev footsteps in the hallway.

We fought and struggled with it, and at one point, as I held up the tent cover, and Chloe slid the pole into place, Birch leaned over, looked in and commented.

"Chloe dear, if you push any harder, Deb's is going to lose her virginity."

Our aid came in the form of two guys named Ryan and Jake, and within minutes, both our tents were up, and Birch was assuring them, that our thanks would be shown later, and she handed them a beer each.

With the tents up, and our sleeping bags in place, we were ready to start the weekend. The first act was a famous DJ I had never heard of, mixing tunes, so we opted for comfort, and stayed by the tents with our booze stash, and pulled out the cushions, and the tartan blanket, from the back of Petal, and sat back to watch the thousands of bright happy people around us.

The vibe in the air was fun and music, and we soon got into the groove to enjoy our day. Deb's, Chloe and Edwina started dancing, with their drinks in their hands, and all around others by their tents joined in, as we laughed and jigged, with bright happy smiling faces.

Birch dug around in her bag and lifted out a glasses case, I looked at her puzzled.

"I didn't know you wore glasses?" She smiled and opened the case.

"Oh. Deads Sweetie, these are not glass's, but they do let me see the world better."

She lifted out a spliff, and gave a wild grin. Deb's pointed and looked shocked.

"Is that drugs?" Birch lit it and took a long pull, she held it in, and then in a high pitched tone, she responded.

"Yes... You want some?" She blew a long stream of smoke back out, Deb's eyes almost popped out of her head. In a shot she was down at Birch's side.

"Give me some."

Now I was shocked, never in my wildest dreams, did I think I would sit in a field watching Deb's smoke a spliff, what was happening, was my little shy and innocent, virginal, friend, finally becoming a woman?

Several shots and few totes each later, we were ready to party, and off to the main field for the music.

The place was packed. In front of us, the huge stage loomed up, and music blasted, it was loud and wild, and the ground vibrated with each heavy bass thump. As drummers pounded and guitarist wailed, on their instruments, I thought the pub band were good, but this was levels above it, and it was as wild as I have ever known possible.

The people all around us were smiling and cheering, dancing and singing. Three girls were even dancing topless. I have never seen so many happy faces in one spot, the electric vibe in the air was intoxicating.

We danced, screamed, and yelled, and laughed, it was incredible as the music blasted out over our heads. I screamed myself hoarse, and it was the most fun I have had since getting to Wotton. I was gyrating with Chloe as we laughed, when Birch grabbed my arm, and yelled in my ear.

"I will see you at camp." I saw the tall figure of Jake with her, and she winked, I gave her a nod and smiled.

Birch ended up in Jake's tent, she lay back on the sleeping bags, as she unbuttoned her jean shorts, before she could do anything, he pulled them off, and reached for her top, she beat him to it, and it was off in a shot.

"Finally, some action."

She sat up, and grabbed his jeans as he struggled to pull the top over his head in the confined space, she was ready to go, and was wasting no time. His pants came down and out popped his equipment, and it was more than satisfactory, she smiled.

"Oh, thank the gods, I am going to enjoy this."

Finally, after a struggle he was naked, and he moved towards her with his more than ready beast, Birch pushed him back.

"Whoa hold on soldier, you want to go paddling in this stream, then wear your wellies." He frowned.

"I left them in the outhouse at the farm." Birch gave a sigh.

"I meant condom; you have a condom, right?" He looked upset; she gave a gasp.

"Oh shit... Good job I came prepared."

She slid her bag over and rooted around it, and then with a smile, she pulled a hand full out, and tore one open. With the look of a wild wolf approaching a kill, she grabbed his manhood and slid it on, then with a gasp, she lay back with a smile, and opened her legs wide.

Jake leaned over and started to kiss her boobs, she put her chin on her chest and looked at him.

"What ya doing?" He looked up.

"Huh?"

"Jake you are stupid, but sweet, and you have a weapon worthy of any police man's belt, you can do all that later, but I have a desperate need. I have not had a cock in me in weeks, so please, skip the starters, and let's get straight to the main course, okay?"

He nodded, grabbed her legs, lifted them up to his ears, and in he went, Birch lay back with a happy sigh.

"Finally!"

Jake started slow, and Birch moaned in pleasure, and then

suddenly he went at it hell for leather, he pounded at great speed, and her head started to slide up the tent. Birch looked up at him and screamed.

"Whoa…. Whoa… Christ Jake, if you screw any faster it will ignite, this is not scout camp, we are not lighting a frigging camp fire, slow the hell down, I want to enjoy this." He grunted looking frustrated, and slowed his pace, Birch smiled.

"Oh my god that is better." She bit her lip, and arched her back.

It was getting late, and Deb's was getting more and more excited, the final act of the day was about to appear for the first of a two day stint, and as the lights on stage lit up, the announcement came.

"Rock it out there bitches, for Battered Taco!"

I still smile when I hear it, the stage and Deb's exploded at the same time, she screamed and wailed, and I was exhausted, but as Deb's hung round my neck singing every word, and dancing, I could not help but feel so energised.

Chloe, and Deb's grabbed my hands, and we danced like maniacs, I was having the time of my life. Wow I thought the gig in the pub was good, but this was beyond belief, and the hour and twenty minutes passed before we knew it.

Long after the band left the stage, we hung around, mainly because we were exhausted, and out of breath, and there were just so many people there.

We walked slowly up the field, Deb's was talking at high speed, and looked like she was on a permanent sugar rush, and Chloe and myself could not really get a word in, so we just walked side by side and listened and smiled.

It took an hour to get back to the tent, where Birch sat with a group of guys talking, Chloe looked round.

"Where is my sister?" Bitch gave a smile.

"She is engaging her hormones in your tent." Chloe smiled and grabbed a beer, then sat down next to a guy called Kent.

"Hi."

Deb's was stood motionless, as Birch stood up and introduced her friend.

"Deb's this is…"

"Jimmy Blazer!"

She stared at him with adoration. Birch came over and stood at my side, as I looked at the guy in top hat with goggles attached, in a silk shirt, and with a long brown coat on. I looked at Birch.

"How the f...?" I ran out of words, she smiled.

"That guy Jake, he is a mate of his, so I showed him a picture of Deb's and told him she wanted to screw him, and here he is." I was stunned.

"Birch you are full of surprises." She shrugged.

"You want surprises come here."

She walked over to the tent opposite. and put her finger to her lips. She gently unzipped the fly sheet, and I bent down to look inside through the gap she made. My eyes almost popped out of my head, there inside, Edwina sat straddled over a big guy, her hips thrusting back and forth, as she leaned back and moaned.

"Oh Gawd!"

I looked at Birch, who winked and pulled out her phone, and slipped it through the flap.

"That's the drummer... Looks like Edwina can go both ways; I never saw that one."

I had to chuckle. A few minutes later Edwina started to get noisy, and Birch pulled her phone back, and gently slid up the zip.

The recording was saving on her phone, we tip toed away, and back to our tent, I looked round the camp site.

"Where is Deb's?" A moan came from the tent and I looked at it, I looked at Birch, and pointed.

"She is in the tent." She shrugged.

"I did tell him she just gets wet thinking about him." I started to giggle.

"My god you are amazing."

I cannot deny, I was a little bit shocked, Deb's was becoming a completely different person, she had shown a side of her that was brave, bold, and very daring, and I could see how much she had changed since school.

We sat down to eat, and hit the good stuff, out came the gin and vodka, and as we sat there all happily drinking, in the background came the sounds of true love.

"Oh god... Oh god.... Ooh god.... Oh my god...... ARRRRRRR...

OH JIMMY!" Birch smiled.

"Looks like Deb's has finally joined the ranks of us young women."

We spread another blanket out next to Petal, and with cushions piled against the back wheel, Birch and I settled down to watch the camp through the semi darkness, as with all things Birch, there was plenty of alcohol.

I was happy and relaxed leaning against her, when two figures came out of the darkness. Chloe staggered up and looked at them.

"Oh bollocks!" She flopped down at my side; I heard the voice long before I realised who it was.

"Hi Abigail, I saw the car and thought I would come over."

My heart froze, what the hell was Nigel doing here?

"This is my friend Eric." I looked up. and even though it was quite dark, he looked familiar.

"I know you right?" He crouched down and smiled.

"Yeah, I was in your school, I was in the year above you." I nodded; I had thought so. Birch looked up at him.

"Shame about your company, but sit down and have a drink." He smiled and Birch handed him a bottle of beer.

"The drink is made by the devil; I never partake of it." Birch sighed, as she looked up at Nigel.

"Isn't it past your bed time or something? You know Nigel, we have all partaken of the devils brew today, and we bloody loved it, and just to be clear, red wine is alcohol, how was communion last Sunday?" He looked upset; Birch lifted her bottle.

"Cheers." She took a long swig. I looked at Eric.

"Your friend does not appear to be as much fun as expected?" He looked embarrassed and leaned forward and whispered.

"He had the tickets; it is the only reason I am with him." Birch started laughing, and saluted him with her drink. Nigel stood there shuffling his feet.

"It is getting late Eric; we should go to sleep." He turned and looked back at him.

"You go on Nigel; I will catch up in a few minutes." He shuffled around a bit.

"Okay then... See you in a bit.... Night Abigail." I raised my glass.

Eric was really relived, he sat with us and had a few drinks, poor lad had been bored to death all night. We all sat around drinking and talking, and Edwina appeared wearing a large black silk shirt, she plopped down next to Chloe, she was exhausted.

"That drummer is an animal, we have done it three times, he has stamina like I have never known, he like flops, and then pops back up, he is having a little rest, I told him I needed a drink, and will be back in a bit." Birch sniggered. Edwina looked at Chloe.

"I need a bloody break; you want to go a few rounds?" Birch gagged, and sprayed her drink all over Eric, and she turned to Edwina.

"Are you okay with your sister screwing him too?" She gave a sigh.

"He is a drummer, it's dark, and she could use the action, it's not like we will ever see him again, is it?"

It was a good point; I could not find a single argument to fault it. She looked at her sister, and put a pack of condoms in her hand.

"Go in naked, he likes it when you are top, and use these."

Chloe winked at me, and got up. She slid off her top, dropped her shorts, and walked naked through the dark to their tent, Eric looked more than surprised, Birch just smiled.

"We really are, all girls together."

I leaned back and giggled, he had no idea. The zip of our tent finally came down, and Debs popped her head out wearing Jimmy's top hat. She slipped out, and came over with a huge smile on her face, and sat next to Birch.

"I did it guys, I did it with Jimmy." She giggled like a little girl. Birch handed her a cup full of gin.

"Trust me, we heard, the whole bloody camp heard, welcome to womanhood, and finally knowing you are straight."

Deb's took a drink, and I smiled at her; she was beaming with happiness. Jimmy appeared shortly after tucking his shirt in, he looked round the camp.

"Has Zac gone?" Birch pointed her drink back towards the tent behind us.

"Still busy." He nodded and knelt down, and kissed Deb's very passionately.

"I gotta go Doll, but call me yeah?"

Deb's nodded with great enthusiasm, it was kind of nice to see, she was so happy. I looked at Eric, I remembered him now, he was captain of the football team at school.

"Eric why have you not hooked up with a girl?" He gave a laugh.

"I tried three times, but I had Nigel." Birch flinched.

"Ouch!" He nodded and looked disappointed.

"He is the kiss of death to fun, he rang me up and told me he had tickets, I came thinking I could ditch him in the crowd, but he is like a fucking homing pigeon, you cannot get away from him."

I sniggered, I knew that feeling I grew up in the village with him, I looked at him.

"You want to get your own back?" He smiled and nodded, I got up off the floor.

"Come with me."

I grabbed his arm and yanked him up, and then led him over to the tent, he looked really surprised. I stooped down, and walked in, and then slipped off my top, he was on his knees in the door. I looked him right in the eyes.

"I am really, really horny, pretty drunk, I am going back to Manchester, so you are not my boyfriend, this is a onetime deal only, because I really need to screw, are you in or out?"

He crawled in and started pulling off his shirt.

"Christ Abby, I have always wanted to do this, I just never thought you would." I slipped off my shorts.

"It's your lucky night then." I threw him a condom.

Before I knew it, he was all over me, kissing me slowly across my breasts, and my whole body was on fire, I had an ache inside, and I needed it vanquishing. To be honest, I did not really care it was Eric, horrible as it sounds, it could have been anyone, but all day I had felt it growing, and having watched everyone else do it, I wanted it too, actually scratch that, I really needed it.

He moved down to my hips kissing and licking, and I wanted to explode, the need was growing more and more, it had felt like forever since I had last been with a man, and the urgency inside me was driving me wild.

He reached between my legs and started to lick, and my body exploded. I lifted my hips, wanting to pound up into his face, and then the first wave coursed through me like a raging fire, and out of my mouth came a gasping little scream, as my body exploded. My legs were trembling out of control, I was cumming like crazy, my god he was good, and he was not even inside me yet.

He slid up and started to kiss me, we locked together gasping for air, I could taste myself on his lips, and it just turned me on more, and then as he broke free, I felt it, and my whole body trembled, he was in me, and it felt great. He looked down at me.

"I got to tell you Abby, I won't mange three in one night." I gasped as he thrust into me.

"Once is enough, just take it slow and make it last, I really need this." He nodded.

"Sorry coming through, it's an urgent sexual emergency."

Birch crawled in, followed by Ryan the guy who helped us put up the tent.

"Sorry, Edwina passed out in the back of Petal." She looked at me and winked.

"For Christ's sake Birch, I am shagging here!" She smiled.

"Yep... And you are doing dammed fine job, I am proud of you." She looked at Eric.

"Don't frigging stop, the girl needs this."

Neither of us had realised he had stopped, and suddenly he started again. I was too far gone to care. Birch stripped in seconds, and had Ryan stripped just as quick, and soon both of us were at it, side by side writhing in ecstasy.

Eric was losing his pace and I twisted, he fell over, and I rolled him over, and climbed on top, and this was even better I was in control, and working at my own pace. Ryan was pounding away in Birch, and the tent was filled with moans and groans. Birch swung him round and sat on top of him, we were facing each other as we screwed the guys. I smiled.

"You know this is really messed up right?" She lifted her hand and we high fived, she gave an hysterical laugh.

"I have always wanted to do that."

I could feel another orgasm building and I focused, was it weird that watching Birch shag, was getting me even more turned on? My hips moved faster and faster, his hands came up to my boobs and he started to play with my nipples, I ground down as hard as I could, and my breath started coming in faster rapid bursts. It was building… I pushed harder and faster, I needed this so badly, and then…

"OOOOOH!"

I leaned back and my body jerked, my head exploded, and a wave of tingles and joy came crashing over me, he bucked up sending another spasm into me, and I just shook, as he grunted.

I jerked several times, and then flopped forward on top of him, and gasped for air. Somewhere to the side of me, I heard Birch as she went into noisy orgasm, but I just lay on top of Eric, as he folded his arms around me, it was enough, the beast was sated.

We lay together for quite some time just holding each other, Birch was out cold, and Ryan had gone. I rolled off him, and drifted in that sacred space, of sexual fulfilment, unaware of time. It was a while before I realised someone was moving, when I sat up. Eric was pulling on his pants.

"Hell Abby, I wish you were back here for good." I smiled.

"As I said Eric, this was a onetime deal only." He looked disappointed.

"Remember, when you see Nigel, tell him what happened, it should be enough to shake him off for a while, as he goes off and cries," He laughed.

"It does seem sort of cruel." I looked at him.

"If it helps, he asked me out hundreds of times, and I have always said no. I told him I would not date him if he was the last man alive, but he just won't quit." He crawled up the sleeping bag and leaned in to kiss me.

"I guess this is bye then, thanks, take care of yourself Abby." I nodded.

"You too."

Eric walked into the darkness, and a very drunken but happy Deb's came crawling in, she smiled at me, her top hat decorated with a large pair of flying goggles slightly to one side of her head.

"I absolutely love festivals." She passed out, and slammed into the floor, her top hat spun across the tent floor, and hit the bags.

I woke up before the other two, still naked. I grabbed my long top and slipped it on, and crawled out of the tent, and walked to Petal, where Edwina lay passed out. She was still wearing the black silk shirt, and her red swollen and neatly groomed vagina on full view. I chuckled as I pulled out the stove, water and the box with supplies in it, and headed round to the blanket, on the floor, where we had left it, it was a little damp, but I set up for coffee.

It was still pretty chilly as I lit the gas stove, and put a pan onto boil, and it was not long before I sat back, feeling the new sun on my face, as I sipped my coffee, and my body started to warm.

It was shortly afterwards, Chloe appeared, she was still naked, her clothes were where she had dropped them. She shivered as I made her a coffee. She sat down next to me and leaned in to get warm.

"You had a good time?" She smiled.

"Yeah, I really have, thanks Abby, we will always be so grateful to Birch and you." I smiled, and put my arm round her and she snuggled in, and shivered.

Slowly the group came alive, sounds from the back of Petal, announced a hangover, and an exhausted looking Edwina appeared, I put the pan back on to boil. Next came a groggy but happily smiling Deb's in her top hat, she sat close to me, and radiated joy.

"I loved last night, thanks."

"It was all Birch, not me."

"Yeah, but you were here if I needed you, that helped."

With Chloe and Deb's on either side, I was warming up fast, and I breathed in and relaxed, enjoying the peace. Not far away, the countryside woke up to Sunday, and like every Sunday, what was fast becoming a ritual, began. It started in our tent.

"YOU CANNOT FUCKING BE SERIOUS!?"

The tent flaps burst apart, and an irate looking Birch, stepped out fully naked, and looked right round the whole horizon.

"Is there no end to their taunting? We are sinners' you twats, leave us the fuck alone." She looked down at me.

"Fucking bell twats, they are like a frigging virus, it's a bloody liberty that's what it is, have they no sanctity for that sacred ritual of the after effects of sex and Alcohol?"

Somewhere in one of the tents close by, a voice shouted out.

"WILL YOU JUST SHUT THE FUCK UP?" Birch pointed in the direction of the voice.

"See.... See.... It's a bloody liberty that's what it is, even they are pissed off with them." I shook my head, and laughed.

"Birch... I think they are telling you to shut up?" She frowned.

"Oh.... Right... Yeah, I get that, obviously he is not going to church today.... Frigging part timer." She plopped down in front of us all and smiled.

"Morning Sweetie's."

The second day of the festival, was to a degree a repeat performance for Birch and Deb's. Jimmy returned before his performance and disappeared with Deb's back to his caravan.

Birch went for a few long walks with a friend, and Chloe, Edwina and myself danced and sang ourselves silly. By 10pm we were packed up, and finally out on the road, after waiting for hours to get off the site. I saw Eric alone as he left the site, and he blew me a kiss and waved, and I drove back towards Wotton Dursley, Deb's talked constantly about her time with Jimmy.

She happened to mention that during sex, he put his goggles on her breasts, to frame her nipples, which grew so big, they touched the glass, and Birch found that hilarious, and suddenly Deb's had the nick name of 'Goggles'.

Chloe and Edwina, have proven to be wilder than I had ever thought, and I had seen another side to both of them. I think the last day did us good, we had bonded over our experiences, and our stories of the previous night's activities. By the time we pulled up outside the restaurant, I was sad to see them go. We all sat in Petal, as they thanked us again and again, they had been free to be them, and the change in them was really noticeable, especially when they jumped out, but instead of running indoors quickly, they stood on the pavement and waved us off.

I drove onto Waterside Lane feeling happy, Birch jumped out, and key padded us in, and as I pulled in, there was dad's BMW on the drive. I drove round it slowly as the gates closed, and pulled up by the back gate through to the guest house. Birch unhitched the gate and swung it open, and I drove in, and pulled up, and turned the engine off.

It had been an amazing weekend for all of us, but for me, the thing I loved the most, was no one pointed, no one whispered, and no one really knew me. I had been free to be me, and do as I please, and that was the best feeling ever.

Chapter 19

Sobering Theories.

I really remember very little of Monday. I felt tired and exhausted, and just slept right through the whole day. Whilst I was out cold, Birch woke at some point in the afternoon, as did Deb's, and together they unloaded Petal, and packed everything away. Chloe and Edwina, dropped by to yet again to say thanks, and they picked up their friends' tent, and for all that time, I had been flat out in bed. Deb's had gone back home to show off her new hat, and fill her parents in on all the fun, well most of it, somethings remained an 'all girls together' subject only.

I finally woke up on Tuesday morning, feeling fresh and alive, and came out of the bedroom to the sound of rain, after a long hot spell, in the night it had thundered, and today was overcast and wet. Birch looked up and smiled as I came into the room.
"Feeling better Sweetie?"
I gave a big stretch and wandered to the kitchen to make coffee. Birch spoke as I made my drink.
"You must have had a good time, you are probably not aware, but it is Tuesday." I leaned round the door to look at her.
"Seriously?" She gave a chuckle.
"Eric was better than I thought." She gave a snigger.
I came back in with my coffee, and sat crossed legged on the floor with her, as always Birch had no use of clothing indoors, but who am I to call her, I was only wearing panties. I felt calm and relaxed and she smiled.
"It has been hard since you came home, you have faced a lot of stressful situations, I think letting go and living a little has helped. You certainly worked out your aggression on Eric, poor lad, I am surprised you did not snap it off."
My memory of it was different, but it was also more internal, more about how I felt, and how it was feeling at the time, I looked

at Birch, she sat watching with her bright green eyes, her long hair hanging down.

"Was I really that bad? I don't remember a huge amount, I just had a need inside me, and I had to get it out." She gave a gentle nod as if understanding.

"As I said, it's been stressful, and you needed an outlet, but you were pretty aggressive, if I am honest, it is why I got on top, watching it turned me on even more. It was pretty dam hot to watch it, I thought at the time, there is the real dark little beastie, that is Deads." I smiled. She sat back with her arms on the floor behind her.

"So.... Will you be seeing him again?" I shook my head.

"No.... There is no point getting involved, I mean he is a nice guy and all that, but what is the point when I will be gone in four to five weeks?" She shrugged.

"I don't know, a local who screws is not a bad friend to have, no one said you had to be serious Deads, I am sure he will be back if you ask." I shook my head.

"I deliberately did not get his number, I told him it was a onetime thing." She smiled.

"It's probably a good job I got it then, if you change your mind, let me know."

I had to chuckle; there she was thinking ahead of me again. I lifted my cup and took a swig.

"You are one to talk, what about Kev, wasn't he supposed to be a onetime thing, and yet here you are trying to tell me to hook again with Eric." She winked.

"Kev and me understand each other, I was telling Deb's yesterday, because she asked how I could sleep with those guys when he was my boyfriend. I know he is on the road, and just like Deb's, there are girls out there who will want to sleep with him, just because he is in the band. I am twenty years old; he is twenty one, I will not be settling any time soon, and neither will he. He has the right to live a free life being exactly the guy he is, and groupies are part of the life he lives. I am free too, and I live true to me, and yes, I was horny as hell, I mean it's been a while, I have a high sex drive, so I saw my chances and took them, you did the same I may add. Eric was not looking to sleep with you, he was just looking for friendly people to get away from that bloody Nigel. I hate to say it my dark little beastie, but that was all you, the guy looked shit scared when you dragged him up."

"Was I that scary.... Don't Birch, you are making me feel guilty?" She leaned forward and clasped my hand.

"Deads you were you. Look you are a sexual being, and you have needs, and you saw your opportunity, and took it. The way I saw it, he cannot have been that scared, because once he was done, he stayed. I saw the way he held you close and talked quietly to you, and the way he gently lifted the hair out of your eyes. If you ask me, I think he secretly wanted that to happen, I mean let's be honest, Ryan pissed off as soon as he was done."

I understood what she was saying, it did make sense, but this was still all new to me, even after a year, I had nineteen years of oppression inside me, and I found it hard letting go like she did, I had to ask, and hoped she would not hate me.

"Didn't you feel used?" She laughed.

"Was Ryan or Jake using me? Probably, but I needed to get laid, so was I using them? It all depended on me Deads. I could have said no, I just didn't, the way I see it, is if two consenting adults want to screw each other, why shouldn't they? Let me tell you something my mum told me that might help. If I stay with Kev for the rest of my life, he will probably give me a good life, because actually he really is a nice guy. The facts are though, there is no one man who can completely satisfy a woman one hundred percent. honestly, it's true, and by the same chalk, no matter how much I wanted to, I could never fully satisfy Kev the same. We are all born sexual, and at times we look at others, because it is nature, it is natural to want choice, it is in our DNA. I think one of the reasons marriage's fail, is because they tie their lives to what I call enforced monogamy."

I had read that in one of her papers, and understood it, she smiled as she spoke, and her eyes twinkled.

"For some people that is enough, just the one person for life, but for others it is not. It does not mean that they do not love who they are with, in most cases they do, very deeply, but they have a need that cannot be sated by their partner, and it may surprise you to know it is not always sexual. The world has socially defined rules, that say we must all have a one true love, and be faithful forever, it is enforced monogamy. I will never float with that, it is not right for me, and actually it is not right for Kev. Sex is not the most important part of our relationship, and if it continues, it never will be."

I understood, but my mind was on my mum and dad, I could not see them like that, and I have always thought I would have that life like theirs at some point in the future.

"I am not sure how I feel about that Birch." She smiled at me.

"Well, that is for you to find out, and at some point in your life, you will know. It is right for me Deads, and it is how I have chosen to map out my life, you will have to choose at some point how you map out yours, and actually if you think about it, that is why living here has been so hard on you." I did not understand.

"How is it hard on me?"

"I am the one thing they are not; I am honest about it, and do not lie about it, I love sex, and I will never apologise for it. That lot out there, gossiping and pointing the finger at us, not one of them has a pure mind or life. I bet if we uncovered the truth of this place, you would find adultery, sexual deviance, criminal behaviour, gender discrimination, domestic abuse, gender doubt, and a whole bag of other assorted attributes of humanity. I am telling you Deads, the one thing you will find without any shadow of a doubt, is envy on mass. All those two faced twats out there, have something to hide, and they look at you, and they look at me, and they hate us because we are not hiding it like they are. Once you fully understand and come to terms with that Sweetie, then you will not feel the guilt and stress you do. Don't hide it, wear it with pride and never apologise." Birch took my cup, and stood up.

"More coffee Sweetie?"

My head felt it had been completely blown. She had hit the nail right on the head, they did not like our in your face attitude. I thought of Mary and the way she looked at me in the shop. I had always loved her, out of everyone in the village she was special to me, and just knowing, even though she had not said a word, I had seen it more in her eyes and her expression than anything else, and I had tried to hide it, but the truth was I was heartbroken.

Some naive part of me honestly thought she would accept me no matter what, but I was wrong, and that led me to another thought. If Birch was right, what were Peter and Mary hiding? I turned and looked at Birch as she was making new coffees.

"How can you be so sure about these people, I mean Birch you have only been here two weeks, I have been here all my life, and I know nothing about them?" She smiled as she poured the water from the kettle into the cups.

"Deads, it is just simple deduction, do you think Manchester is any different? It's not you know; all you have to do is pay attention and watch? My dad would bore you with a long lecture about the behavioural pattens of human's, and what he would basically say is if you watch the behaviour of a person, it will tell you a story without them saying a word. I am sure you have heard of actions speak louder than words, well that is true, watch and look for a pattern, and the truth will reveal itself. I watch carefully and take note, that is the only difference between us."

I was intrigued, and thought I would test the theory.

"Alright then, what have you noticed about Peter and Mary?" She came in and sat down and handed me my coffee.

"You mean the post office lady and her husband?" I nodded, she sat back against the comfy chair, and sipped her coffee.

"They are going away for three weeks in September, and again in late December, the shop poster shows when they have cover for holidays. When I went for chewing gum, one of the customers was talking about the South of France, and wished them good luck. Mary has a sunburned cleavage, and really tanned hands, and yet they work long hours inside most days, so where did the tan come from? The odds are that whilst they are in the shop, they would have no time to sit out, so they get a good tan when they are away." I frowned.

"So, they sunbathe on holiday, that is hardly a shock." She agreed.

"Yes, that is true, but when she was on the little stepping stool, stretched up to the shelf, to lift a box, her loose top rode up, and she is brown all the way up her entire back. Taking into account her age, and that on holiday, she may wear a short sleeve top or shirt, by that standard her back should not be tanned all the way up, because it remains covered, so why is it tanned my dark little beastie, you tell me?"

"I am amazed you noticed so much; I didn't even notice she has a tan."

"And that is how they hide, they are in plain sight, in full view of everyone, but those people around them are not as observant as you may think, most people never see what is right in front of them. Mary sees your hair and judges you; she forms an assumption about who you are. You have seen Mary who appears conservative, and formed and assumption of who she is, and the crazy thing is, both of you are wrong."

"How... How are we both wrong?" She shrugged.

"She thinks you are a total slut, and you think she is a moral and an upstanding conservative. You are not a slut, which is a word I hate, and Mary is far less conservative and a lot more liberal than you think." I was starting to get confused.

"Birch you are not making sense, why is Mary liberal?" Birch grinned.

"She is just like me.... Naturist?" I gasped.

"Shut the hell up...... No way, Mary naked in public... Actually, Peter too, yuk!" She laughed.

"Obviously I have no proof, but the evidence is pretty strong, I mean to be honest Deads, I have, as you can see, no issue with it, but Marjorie? Oh, hell can you imagine what she would say if she found out, it's no different from Lillian and Celia, their fear is the same fear. It is shame that keeps them in her web. It is like the guy at the Craft Shop, he always has red eyes, and the other day he had a large delivery of vermiculite." I frowned, not really understanding.

"What the hell is that?"

"Well, it is not something a craft shop would sell, and not in those quantities. It is a special type of rock used in hydroponics, which is the most effective way of growing Cannabis. His red eyes, and the number of bags he had delivered, told me grower, and in some quantity. You see, you have a secret weed grower in the village, all you have to do is watch, it is right there in front of you."

My head was mashed, I had not seen anything at all to even suggest that could happen in the village. I must admit, she really made a great deal of sense, and I was really curious.

"So, what else do you know about the people round here?" She gave a very sly smile.

"I just have theories, I want to wait until I have more proof, but trust me, you will be the first to know when I can prove anything, although one thing I think I have right, is Nigel. When I called him a stalker, I was not joking. Twice I have seen him with a camera with a long lens on it in the village, so keep it in mind, I think it was not a coincidence he showed up at the festival. Be careful Deads, before Saturday night I was not so sure, but now, I think I am right, he is a creepy little weasel. It would not surprise me if he does not have a computer filled with pictures of you. He probably whacks off to them every night, so don't turn your back on him, I think he has been watching for a very long time."

I understood her, I cannot deny, he had pestered me for a long time, and I thought back to Eric's words, 'he is like a fucking homing pigeon, you cannot get away from him' it had been at that moment when I had decided I was going to sleep with him, before that I had thought because he was Nigel's friend, I could not really trust him.

Call it intuition, but the sound of his voice, and the way he looked when he said it, told me, I would be safe with him. It was bizarre to even think it, but I had to ask.

"I actually believe you are right, but you know what, it is impossible to prove it Birch." I shuddered just thinking about it.

"I hate it, oh god, just the thought freaks me out, but even if he does.... You know.... That!" A cold tingle ran down my spine and my whole body shuddered. "It is not illegal to pleasure yourself in your own home."

I felt sick just thinking about it, Birch looked at me giggled.

"You are right, there really is nothing we can do about it, unless of course we catch him in the act, and film it." I wrinkled my face and shuddered.

"I am not as twisted as you Birch, I really do not want to see that, those pictures do not belong in anyone's mind. It may only be a small point, and honestly you amaze me, but I got to ask, honestly, how the hell are you going to do that?" She chuckled.

"I am working on it, and I need to hurry, because I will be doing it on August tenth, so I have only five days to do it." I frowned.

"Five days, why so little time?"

She reached back on to the small unit, and grabbed a sheet of paper, and handed it to me. I took it and looked at it, it was the dates sheet from the parish council meeting, I still did not understand, I looked up at her.

"How does this answer the question?" She smiled.

"How do you like your burgers?"

"Huh?"

"Look again." I read through the dates.

"Oh shit, we missed the play on Saturday night." I read down the list and suddenly I saw it, and I looked at Birch who winked.

"Barbeque at the Vicarage, holy shit Birch, the whole bloody village will be there." She smiled.

"I do not know about you, but when my mum throws them, the one thing my dad hates the most, is loads of people tramping all over the house, but of course if you are Marjorie, and you are house proud, you will love showing off how well you live to everyone, her whole house will be open to roam, and I aim to thoroughly roam it with you."

I felt a pang run through me, I will not deny, I thought she was insane, but there again I have always sort of known that. What scared me was Birch wanted to put me in the house of a woman who wanted to destroy me, who I may also add, would be surrounded by all the people she had convinced I was another Hatty. I admired her confidence, because as I sat there looking at her, I think mine made a dash for the door. Birch leaned over and pulled me into a hug.

"I love you Sweetie, no one will hurt you while I am there, I promise. I will not leave your side, and don't forget, we won't be alone, we will be all girls together." I relaxed a little, she had such a great way of making me feel safe.

"I love you too Birch, but I cannot deny, I really am frightened of her, and I really do not want to step in her house. If the girls are with us, it will help, I think the festival really made a difference to us, so I will trust all of you, but please listen, we must be careful, you have not seen her in real action, she is as scary as fuck."

Birch leaned back. "I have been watching her, trust me I do not underestimate her at all." She sprang up off the floor.

"I got to call mum, she is in London doing some public relations thing for her books, I am hoping she has some free time to come over, and see us. I would love her to meet your mum and Hatty, she would totally get Hatty, it would be cool to see her too."

She sat at the table and logged in to her computer, I went to refill my cup, I looked back as I filled the kettle.

"You know Birch, you are very sharp and alert today, did I miss something whilst I was asleep?" She frowned and then understood.

"I have not had a drink since the festival, I thought I needed to detox a little, plus it's not much fun when you're not doing it with me, so I waited for you to wake up."

I giggled as I put the kettle on to boil, she really was so unpredictable at times, just when I thought I had her pegged, she did a complete about turn. I watched her as her mum came into view on the laptop, and saw the smile on her face, I loved to watch her when she was happy, her eyes just exploded with life and joy.

Marjorie Wallace sat in her living room with her son and husband, she was on the best Chesterfield furniture, and surrounded by antique tables and bureaus. Her carpets were the best quality Wilton, and everything in the room was neat, orderly, and had its place. She sat back in her armchair, and looked at Nigel.

"Well don't think I did not warn you. I told you when your father bought those tickets, you would be entering a den of sin, are you surprised to find they were all fornicating out of wedlock? That is what her type does, they are the same as that Harriet whore, although it is good to know they have been joined by two more. I was not aware of the Pemberton girl's involvement with them. The Wheeler girl is a problem, her mother is trash, but her step father will need to be handled carefully."

Nigel looked unhappy, and was pouting, Marjorie looked at him with utter disgust.

"You need to get over her, she may have been a viable option at one time, but her true colours have shown now, and she is nothing more than a tramp. I don't want you moping about here over her, now pull yourself together." He snivelled.

"I love her, I always have, and I don't care, I want her and her only." Marjorie looked at husband.

"Do you understand now, I mean look at him Milton, it is pitiful. I told you he would grow up like that snivelling mother of yours." He closed his paper and folded it neatly, he sprayed as he spoke.

"The boy likes her, let him have her, I mean a boy needs to sow his oats, let her school him, and we can arrange a marriage to someone more fitting of the family." She appeared impressed, and looked at Nigel.

"Well your father has actually had a good idea, he does occasionally. So, if you want her, then take her, just do it quietly and do not humiliate us, but I mean it, when you have had what you want, dump her. We will find you a wife more fitting of your station, I am I clear Nigel?" He appeared to cheer up.

"I promise, but I want more than Eric, I want her at least ten times, and then if I have to, I will do as you want." He sniggered and smiled. Marjorie got up.

"I have things to arrange and Marion will be here shortly, and I want to see what she has found out. I have no trust of those two whores, and I have no intention of being fooled again. I also want to know what she has on the Pemberton girls. I have an idea of how I can separate that Birch bitch and Abigail, and if I can cut out those Pemberton's at the same time, things here will run a hell of a lot better."

Birch sat cross legged on the floor smiling.

"Okay mum I love you too, please try and come over if you can, I know what Katie is like, so if it is not possible, we can still talk on here. Abby sends her love." She blew a kiss, and her mother blew one back.

"I love you Jemi love, watch over Abby, and give her my love too." The call ended and Birch looked up.

"Mum sends her love."

She looked round and started to sniff, she stood up and sniffed the air, she walked to the door and opened it, the rain was still beating down into the lawn. Birch sniffed and then looked back at me stood in the bedroom doorway.

"I smell cake." I had a sudden feeling of inner dread.

"Oh, hell it has started, I had hoped we would have a little longer." Birch looked at me like I was crazy.

"What has started, do I need to worry?" I gave a chuckle.

"No, it's mum, she is baking, actually she will be baking for weeks, the cake competition is coming up, and she will be practicing for the perfect sponge cake." Birch appeared really happy,

"Ooh, how many will she make?" The poor girl had no idea of the hell that was to come.

"It will be at least three cakes a day for weeks, and in between there will be jams, and endless flower arranging, she will drive you crazy." As I said, she is not all there, she exploded with joy.

"I frigging love cake, and I want to make jam with your mum.... Ooh do you think she will let me make blueberry and mango? Oh god I hope so, Deads Sweetie, this is my idea of heaven, I love baking, and I once did a course on ikebana, we should get all the girls round, after all, we are all up against Marjorie." I shook my head.

"Jesus Birch, I am getting a drink, I prefer you drunk, you're starting to sound like a Stepford Wife, are you joining me?" Birch gave an almighty shudder.

"Oh, screw that... Pour me the biggest you have got."

Chapter 20

Shops and Breakdown.

I was starting to feel that I had met my match, every time a cake was baked, Birch went even more bonkers than normal, her love of cake even overcame her love of alcohol, and by Thursday I had reached my limit, she was permanently like a meerkat, constantly sitting up and sniffing the air.

I was down to my last ace, as I got out of bed, and Birch lay sprawled out fast asleep, and after I had made coffee and toast, before my mum started her next cake baking marathon. I placed a coffee at the side of the bed with a plate of toast, and whispered the only words that I knew would unlock her. I knelt down at the side of the bed, level with her face, and took a deep breath, and prayed for success.

"Birch…. Birch…. Clothes shopping." Her eyes snapped open, I smiled.

"Morning my pretty, Petal is lonely and needs the company of a car park with other cars, and we need to leave her to chat, whilst we exercise the power of a golden card."

She sat bolt upright.

"I'm in."

Oh my god it worked perfectly, I retreated to the living space, and allowed her a moment to drink and eat toast. I sat in the only comfy chair, and lifted my cup, ready to have a quick intake of caffeine.

Birch walked into the room fully dressed with her bag. The coffee had not even wet my lips, as I stared at her. She tapped her foot.

"Well come on then Sweetie, we have an image to mould."

"Huh…. How the fuck…?"

I got out of the chair and walked to the door of the bedroom, the cup was empty and the toast was gone, and she was dressed. My head spun, as I turned to ask how and pointed at the room.

"How The... Did you... Forget it.... Let's go shop." She jigged on the spot with excitement.

Two phone calls later, a half dressed Deb's, and two tired waitresses', and we were driving at high speed towards Oxendale, hoping we would live. Oxendale is the centre for all of the surrounding villages and towns. It is the only place you will find a shopping centre with shops that actually sell clothes from the modern world, not the bland post war conservative sacks they sell in the village.

Shopping with Birch is a spiritual experience, this girl knows it all, take Chloe for instance, boho chic desire. Birch walked down the line hardly looking, simply grabbing at items off the rail, and passing them back, and absolutely everything looked amazing on her.

Edwina in Birch's eyes was gothic boho chic, with a side of hipster, and again she was spot on, man she is on a level I will never attain.

We walked through GGB, and she was inspiring, she knew it all, biker goth, rainbow goth, Lolita goth, grunge goth and traditional goth, and she simply walked through it, and mixed and matched, and I had the perfect image I had dreamed of. This girl is without doubt, the ultimate guru of clothes shopping.

I felt I should kneel on the floor, pray, and give thanks to the gift of this goddess of the clothes rails.

We walked miles, stared in amazement, giggled with excitement, gasped in awe in the mirror, and lustfully slavered over shoes. After three hours of exhausting shopping, we headed back to Petal with masses of bags, and filled her to the brim. I was happy and excited, I had a whole new wardrobe, which meant even if I wanted to, I could not possibly return to the old Abigail Watson.

Hope was in the air, and I was walking on cloud nine, I just could not wait to get home, and try it all on, especially the thigh high leather boots, which had laces all up the side.

As we hurled through the rain, with the wipers running on high speed, towards Wotton, Choe had become impatient, and had took off her top, and was trying on new crop tops. The fact that she constantly had her tits out, while we drove through streets filled with people, showed just how far she had come.

Birch was in high spirits and laughing, which actually was a huge concern, she is not known for focusing a great deal, and so distracting her whilst driving was not the best thing.

Alive and still intact, we dropped off Chloe and Edwina, and cruised into Waterside Lane with fits of the giggles, unaware that my mum had a visitor at the house. With Petal parked up and safe on her spot in the garden in front of the guest house, and loaded with bags, we crashed in through the kitchen door in fits of giggles to the smell of freshly baked cake. I pulled off my coat, grabbed the bag with my boots in, and excitedly turned to Birch and Deb's.

"Come on I want to show mum."

We fell through the kitchen door, and giggled all the way down the hall, and as I turned past the stairs, and entered the living room my heart turned to ice, and I froze. Still giggling Birch bumped into me followed by Deb's. Seeing us, my mum stood up.

"Abigail darling.... Martin has come to talk to you, he has been asked by Marjorie, if you would reconsider taking part in the choir evening?" I dropped the bags!

I stared at him just stood there, where he had risen from his seat, that fake smile and boyish grin, as smooth and polished as ever. As he stepped forward to speak, and I felt something inside me break, and I started to lose control, as all the bad feelings came racing back.

"Abigail it is so nice to see you again, you really are the best you know, I have always wanted you back. I simply will never accept no for an answer, you know how much I want you?"

My head exploded, I was rapidly losing control, and I felt trapped, my heart was pounding, and my insides were twisting and turning. It was hard to breathe, and I did not know what to do. I honestly thought I was going to vomit, and panicked as I looked at my mum, I cannot explain what happened to me, I just exploded.

"WHY IS HE HERE?" It really did come from nowhere, before I knew, it was out, she looked shocked,

"Abi.... Gail!"

"I DON'T WANT HIM HERE, THIS IS MY PLACE, HE HAS NO

RIGHT!"

She recoiled in shock, I felt the tears burning into my eyes, they were coming, but he would never see them again. I promised myself, never again, I stared at him with hate.

"YOU DO NOT BELONG HERE, I WANT YOU GONE, DO YOU HEAR ME, I WANT YOU GONE FOREVER!"

It was too much, I could not take it, I was going to vomit and needed to leave. I twisted round and slammed into Birch, she tried to throw her arms round me, but I pushed her away, and I ran. I ran like I ran to Manchester, my world became the same blur as that night, so I ran, and I ran, and I just kept running, and this time I was not going to stop.

I headed for the door, the gates were too slow and I vomited, and gasped as my heart broke with pain.

Birch looked at Martin Hinkley the Choir Master in shock, her words were more to herself than him.

"Oh god, I knew it."

She turned to follow me as the front door slammed, and screamed

"DEADLY WAIT!"

Deb's was lost for words, as Martin turned to Felicity, looking completely unshaken.

"How strange, has she always been this highly strung? I must admit, I have never seen anything like this in my life. Are you sure these people she associates with are good for her?"

It angered Deb's, she knew Abigail, and if she was this angry, there was something wrong, she stared at him with hate.

"What the hell did you do to her?"

Outside, Birch looked left and right, there was no sign of her.

"Oh, Deads where did you go?"

The rain was pouring down, as she looked left and right again in hope. She pulled out her phone and dialled, and then held it to her ear as she ran down Waterside Lane towards Manor Road.

"Pick up, pick up, oh please Deads pick up." It went to voice mail.

"Deads Sweetie, I am coming, but I don't know where you are, please Sweetie, don't run away, wait for me I am coming."

Martin Hinkley stood in the living room, and looked at Deb's.

"It is rude to assume young girl, why am I responsible for Abigail's outbursts? She is obviously confused or mixed up; I have no idea at all why she would react in such a rude manner. As is clearly obvious by the language used by her so called friends, I fear I am not wrong." He turned to face Felicity. "I will excuse myself Felicity, I fear my presence infuriates this insubordinate child."

Felicity was struggling to know what to make of it all, Deb's was not as slow.

"I am not a girl, I am woman, and yes I do think you better leave, you have done enough for today."

He pointed at her, and her hazel eyes burned with defiance. "What?"

He shook his finger at her, and then barged past her, bumping her with his shoulder. Deb's stayed resolute.

"Yeah, get out, you have done enough damage today."

Felicity had tears in her eyes, never in her life had she seen Abigail act like that, it had shocked her to the core, and she did not know what to do. Deb's came forward, and looked her in the eyes.

"It's okay Mrs Watson, she will be fine, Birch will get to her." Felicity swallowed hard.

"My daughter needs me; I need to get Hatty." She grabbed the phone and dialled.

Birch was on the main street at the end of Manor Road, when Martin sped past in his car. She saw him and glared at him, but he was driving too fast to notice. Birch looked left and right, the rain streaking into her eyes and down her face.

"Think Jemi, think, that is what mum always said, what do I know about Deads?"

She dialled again, as she looked all around for any trace of her.

"She would not run to the village; she would avoid it. She is afraid and lonely, and she is scared, come on Jemi think, you have known her for a year, what else has she told you? Think for fuck sake, she needs you."

The phone again went to voice mail, Birch was starting to panic, as her mind raced at high speed through every conversation they had shared, and then it hit her.

"She has a safe place, she would run to get away, not to get fit, yes she told me that. There is a path that runs from the back garden to the canal. THE CANAL!"

Birch was soaking wet, as the rain pelted down, her pale top was ringing wet, and had become transparent, her long skirt was stuck to her legs, and her pumps were filled with water, she was shivering, and not even aware of it. Seeing the bridge Deads had told her about down the road, she turned, and ran for all she was worth towards it.

Her mind was racing, 'the back of her house is that way, so find her place of safety, I have to go right and down that path.' She hit the cobbled steps down to the tow path at speed, and raced down onto the sandy path, her eyes were scanning everything as she ran.

She knew the houses were large and ran back some distance, so wherever this place was, it had to be much further along the path. To her right the trees were rising upwards, she knew that they became a woodland behind her house, so she ran for her life, in hope of seeing something, anything that would give her a clue, she needed to find her, she needed her safe, she just needed to hold her.

Hatty was out, Felicity was out, and Debs was out, as they checked up and down the street, hoping she would be close by. There was no sign of Abby or Birch at all, they could be anywhere, there was just no way of knowing. Deb's brought her phone to her ear.

"Where are you Birch?"

Birch was sprinting at high speed, gasping for air, watching the bank rise steeper, trying to work out just where the back garden of number six would lead out on the canal. Her soaked feet slapped and splashed on the floor, her long wet hair, glued to the sides of her face, as she panted, with her exertion.

Her phone rang and she skidded to a halt, gasping for breath, and lifted it up to her ear, feeling hope, and without looking, answered it.

"Deads Sweetie is that you?"

"Birch where are you, have you found her?"

Her hope crashed inside her. She continued to hurry as she spoke, going as fast as she could, her eyes following the bank and the lines of trees above her.

"Deb's I am on the canal, I am looking for her safe spot, do you know where it is?"

"No… I didn't know she had one." Deb's started to cry. "Birch I am heading towards Suttons, you have to find her Birch, we have to find her, she needs us."

Birch slid to a halt next to a derelict building, gasping for air.

"I know Deb's…. I am looking…. Keep looking too…. We have to find her; she really needs us right now."

Deb's wiped the tears from her eyes that had mixed with the rain, and gave a sniffle.

"I won't give up on her, and you must not too, keep looking Birch, we need to find her."

"I know Sweetie, call me if you see her."

She ended the phone call, and looked round; her chest was on fire, as she tried to breathe, her legs were screaming for rest. The old collapsed building was slightly up the bank, she scanned the area, with her hand shielding her eyes from the rain, it was once a pretty big building. Through the trees she saw and old semi broken stone arch way. She gasped in more air.

"Well, you do not get more gothic than arches, and if I was a vampire, that is where I would hide in the daylight, I think Bram would highly approve of it."

The corner below the arch was my safe spot. It was hard to get to, and out of sight of the back gate, and the canal path. Dad never found me here, I was always safe, this is where I read the book I had taken in secret. I knew it was mum's, and she would be angry, but she loved it so much, and I wanted to know why.

This is where Bram showed me the truth of freedom, the way to escape, a way to overcome the world around me. This is the place I first met a vampire, and like him, this was where I would hide from those who wanted to destroy me.

I sat shivering and soaking wet, all those memories that I had hidden for so long flooded into my mind. I didn't want to see them, I had finally been free of them, they were no longer in my dreams, no longer in my head, and he had to come back and brought them all with him.

He had no right, it was my place, my home, he did not belong, I didn't want him there, I wanted to forget. I tried, I tried so hard, why... Why.... Why did he have to ruin it, I was finally happy with Birch?

"Birch.... Birch I need you. Birch where are you, I need you... I really need you.... Where are you my Birch?" Warmth surrounded me, what was this?

Birch scrambled and slipped, tearing her skirt, and she clawed her way up the steep incline between the trees. She had heard something, it could be nothing, it was hard to hear with the rain pounding into her ears.

Brambles tugged at her hair, yanking her head back, her feet slipped and slid on the mud, she clawed at anything she could to get purchase, and she fought through the undergrowth, and finally as she clawed through the mud, she saw her, and her heart almost exploded with relief.

Abby was crouched down in the corner, under the broken archway, saying the word 'Birch' over and over. Sheer force of willpower dragged her free of the tangled mess that pulled at her, as her skirt tore more. She half staggered, half slipped towards her, and fell on her knees in front of her, gasping for air. Birch pulled out her phone and hit speed dial.

"Deb's.... I.... Found .... Her." I felt her, she was there, I felt her arms, and reached out, Birch pulled me close.

"It's okay Sweetie I am here." The tears were coming again, I don't want to cry, I have cried too many times because of him.

"I don't want to cry Birch."

I looked up and my heart broke as I saw her, those beautiful green eyes were sparkling, she was crying. Birch was crying and I didn't know what to do, she never cries, she is my light, she is my laughter.

I reached up my hand and looked at her, as I tried to wipe the tears away, and saw the cuts on her chin, then my eyes became blurred, I could not bear seeing her that way.

"Please don't cry Birch, I am sorry, I am so sorry." Birch lifted her hand, and wiped away my tears.

"Deads, I am so sorry, I knew… I knew and I did nothing, I wanted to, I really wanted to, and I should have done something, you needed me, and I failed you, and I am so sorry."

I couldn't bear it, and my heart broke, and the tears I was trying so hard to hold back flooded out of me to match with her sobs, her arms closed in tighter, as I buried my face in her neck, and just wailed in pain.

"This is good, tears are good Deads, let them out, you have held onto them too long."

My emotions were all over the place, I could not think, I did not want to think, I just wanted Birch to hold me. I wanted to stay there, safe and warm, she has always been there, always looked out for me. I trusted her, she would not let me down like they have, Birch was all I wanted. I felt her pull me back, and I looked up at her, she was so beautiful.

"Deads, you cannot keep on like this, you know that right? Sweetie you need to talk about it, you need to tell me what he did."

I shook my head, I didn't want to, I didn't want her to see me like he did, but out of everyone she was the only one I could tell. What do I do? It is like it is happening all over again, I did tell last time but it was pointless. I looked at the floor, I was ashamed of myself, after all I had done to get past it, I was right back where I started. I heard Birch's phone ring and I looked up; her eyes never left me.

"Hatty she is fine, I am with her, please just give me some time, and I will bring her back, please Hatty just trust me. I will do for her, what you would for Flick."

The call ended but her face did not move, her hand dropped with her phone, she gave a small smile.

"I am here Sweetie, now talk to me."

It took a while, and I told her the story of James and me, and how we made love in the old shed behind the church, and how I had thought someone was watching. It was really hard, but she was the only one I could tell, I trusted her. I was shivering and shaking, and I could not control it, I looked at her ashamed of who I was.

"You gave your virginity to your boyfriend, so how does this involve your choir master Deads?" I looked down.

"I think he was the one that saw us, I didn't know, I left James and went straight to choir practice, and everything was normal, I was really happy, I loved James, so it was not wrong, right?" She nodded.

"There is nothing wrong in what you did Deads, it is normal for most girls. So, what happened at choir practice?"

Oh god, am I really going to tell her, she will hate me I know it? I could feel my heart pounding, and I had anger swirling around inside me.

"Everything was fine, but.... Birch please don't hate me, but I let James cum inside me, I thought he had used a condom, but he hadn't, my panties were full of it, and they were cold, wet and sticky. I did not know it came back out, but it was dripping, I just wanted to clean myself before I went home." I gasped, and felt panicked "Birch I am sorry, I didn't know, I honestly didn't know."

"Did he catch you cleaning yourself?"

I nodded, I really did not want to say any more, she was being so calm and kind, she was Birch, the girl that had sat for hours talking to me at university, was I really going to do this?

"I was in the back room, everyone had gone home, I was putting the hymn books away. I saw the tissues on the table, so I grabbed a few, and pulled my panties down a little, so I could wipe them inside, I didn't even hear him."

Oh god I did not want to go there again, I felt the terror rise up inside me and I started to cry again.

"He slammed me down into the table, and pinned me there, he was hurting me Birch, he hurt my neck he was pushing so hard."

Birch closed her eyes, and I saw the tears run down her cheeks, it was too much for me, and my eyes were getting so blurred again, her voice was so calm, but I wasn't, I could feel the storm inside me growing again.

"Deads Sweetie, you know I love you, so please, you have to tell me. Did he rape you?"

I stood up quickly, and pushed my back into the wall, Birch fell backwards on to the floor as I stared at her, feeling terrified, was I really going to say the words again.

"HE TRIED TO, BUT I WOULD NOT LET HIM!"

I was shaking, shaking so hard it made Birch look like she was shaking too. I could feel my back banging on the wall, those horrible tears were there again, but I had done it, I told her.

"Birch it was him, he had watched me with James, and he came in to the store room and called me a slut, he asked me how much I liked it, and told me James was no good at it, and he was going to show me how it was really done. That is when he grabbed my panties, and tried to pull them off. He was hurting me Birch, he was so strong, my face was pressed so hard into the table, and it was hurting. I told him no and he had to stop, but he laughed at me, he said I was no longer a baby and he was going to prove it. Birch he hurt me so much, and I was so scared of him, I am so sorry, I am so very sorry Birch."

I could see my tears hitting the floor at her feet, she just sat there almost on her back watching me, she was crying too, and I hated it.

"My panties were round my ankles, and I heard him, he was breathing fast and saying horrible things, I heard his zipper, and I panicked. I panicked Birch, I started to cry and beg him not to, he just laughed, and then I felt it, it was on my bare bum, and he guided it down towards where James had put it."

Those shakes from that day came back, I could not stop them, as my body violently began to bang on the wall, I wanted to be sick, and I was losing control again, my lips trembled, and I took a deep breath and gasped in air as I clenched my fists.

Birch sat on the floor crying, she was shaking as violently as I was, I could see the horror in her eyes, and I wanted to stop. I wanted to run away again, but deep inside I knew... I knew I had to say the words and tell her, she was here, she had kept her promise, and now I had to keep mine.

"My hands were on the table, and I have no idea how, but I grabbed the table and pulled, and as his thing came near to where it should go, I could feel it, and I screamed, 'No' as loud as I could. The table fell backwards, and I hit him as I fell with it, and rolled on the floor. I was so terrified Birch, I was so afraid, I got up to run and tripped over my panties. I was so scared Birch; I was so scared. They came off, so I ran, and he screamed at me.

I looked back at the door, and he was on the floor with his pants round his legs. I was terrified because he was holding my panties up and shouting 'cum filled panties with your name in them slut.' I didn't wait, I just ran. I could hear him screaming 'I will show everyone, what will they say Abigail? Your cum filled panties, you slut."

Birch got up off the floor, and came close to me, she pulled me into a hug, and just held me, and it felt good. I had told her, there had been so many times I wanted to, and I almost had. I finally had done it, and she just held me close, and it felt good, the calmness started to wash all over me.

"Sweetie, this cannot stay a secret, you know that don't you? Everyone is worried about you, and out looking, they are going to ask questions, you have to tell them."

I felt the anger explode up inside me, and pushed her back hard, and shook my head.

"ONLY YOU CAN KNOW, I CANNOT TELL THEM." She sighed.

"Deads they are going to ask, you really screamed at him, they will ask whether you told me or not? Can you not see, this should not be hidden, people should know what he is like?" I shook my head.

"NO!"

"Sweetie you do not understand."

The anger came flowing up again, and before I could stop it, I pushed her away with all my might. Birch staggered backwards almost falling into the trees.

"BUT I DO UNDERSTAND.... I TOLD HIM, AND HE DID NOTHING.... DO YOU UNDERSTAND NOW?" She looked shocked; her eyes were wide.

"Wait... What... Who?"

I was the only one who understood, that was the frigging point. They are not like her people, these people are different, she had not been here long enough to know them properly.

I tried to breathe in and calm down, I wanted Birch to really understand all of it, she was the only living soul I knew would. She was silent, too shocked to speak, I nodded, finally, I think she was starting to see it as I did. I bent over to breathe, and lifted my head to look at her, as the air flowed in calming me down.

"Birch I told my dad, but Hinkley was too clever for me. I ran here to hide for a while, he rang my dad, and told him he had caught me masturbating in church. When I got home my dad went mental and hit me, I told him it was a lie, and he had tried to rape me. He just would not believe me over Hinkley. Don't you see, he was the choir master in the church, I was just a stupid sixteen year old, they all stick together, the truth is meaningless with them?"

Birch stood there soaked through to the skin, with tears in her eyes, and shook her head slowly.

"I cannot accept that Deads.... I just cannot, it goes against everything I am. The truth is the truth, and it must be heard, we have to make sure people see him for what he is."

I gave a sigh, and fell back against the wall. She still did not understand, was I wasting my time?

"Birch he rang me two days later, he gloated, because he knew, he knew he had got away with it. He had saved my panties, he has them Birch, they are 'kept safe' as he put it, and I knew there was nothing I could do. It was no longer about me anymore, it was about them, and their way of doing things. Birch don't you see, telling everyone, will completely destroy my family. I know what that is like, I saw what they did to Ellen Wheeler. I had to just shut up and live with it, and I have done, I have kept my mouth shut, for three years, no one knows." Birch gave a sigh.

"This is so wrong Deads, you have to speak out, you have to show them all what he is like."

"How? Telling my parents is pointless, if we tell Hatty, who will believe her? They have pretty much got the whole village believing she is a whore and a liar. Birch I know you want to help; I love you for it, but can you now see where you are, and what kind of people are around us? I did not lie; this is the bloody village of the dammed. You are missing the facts, look at his wife Julia for god's sake, she is twenty two with a kid who is almost two. You just don't get it Birch, who do you think his wife is?"

I love her to bits, but I could see the shock in her eyes.

"Birch, Julia was my replacement when I left the choir, it's frigging obvious isn't it, he did it to her, and she let him, and she got pregnant, and he had to marry her. Everyone knows he is not happy, it was done to save face, he covered it up, like they all do."

Birch appeared to come back to life, and I could see she fully understood it all. She looked at me with her bright green eyes, and I knew that at least now I could stop hiding. I had finally been honest with her, and she knew my secret. I was no longer one of those shits in the village, and that was so important to me. Now I could finally let go and move on. I walked over and took her hand.

"Come on, you are drenched, let's go home, there is nothing we can do about it. That was three years ago, and this is today."

Birch pulled back on my hand and I turned to look at her.

"I am not sure how or even when, but I will find a way, and he will pay for what he did to you, I promise you Deads, he will fucking pay."

I really loved her for that, but I had already tried. That was who Martin Hinkley was, that was his skill, he can do anything, and he will not get caught, he has probably been doing it for years.

I took Birch the easy way back along the path I had worn out as a girl, which took us right to the back gate. Before I opened it, I looked at her.

"This is just between us Birch; you cannot tell them anything of this once we are inside. I mean it, you I trust, them not so much, so for now please promise me you will say nothing of this to Deb's or the others." Her face was resolute.

"I want to talk to my mum Deads, I have no secrets with her, if I ask, she will say nothing, but apart from my mum, I promise, no one will hear it from me." I nodded.

"Okay then... It's a deal."

Going back in was horrible, mum and everyone made a huge fuss, I felt like a ball being passed, and hugged to everyone. It was not what I wanted, I just wanted to be alone. Birch was a star, she made up excuses, and took me upstairs to run a bath, both of us were soaked to the skin. All I wanted to do was lie in the tub and forget, just like I had back then.

She sat me on the side of the bath as it filled with water. And slowly undressed me, and when it had filled, I got in, and she told me to relax, and she would be back in a bit. I slid down until my chin touched the water, closed my eyes and relaxed, god what a bloody horrible day.

Felicity was stood at the bottom of the stairs, when Birch came down. She took her hand, and walked her into the kitchen, where Deb's and Hatty sat waiting. Birch was covered in mud, soaking wet, and had several long scratches on her arms and chin. She stood in the centre of the kitchen, and looked at Felicity.

"Flick, I know the whole story, but Abby wants to keep it private for now, so I want to ask you something very important."

Felicity looked upset and panicked, Hatty watched carefully from the counter.

"Felicity do you trust me?" She looked lost.

"How do you mean; I do not really understand?" Birch gave a nod.

"I am simply asking you, when it comes to Abby do you trust me?" Hatty spoke up.

"I do, and if I do, Flick will." It was enough for Birch.

"Abby needs a little time, and I will help her with that, but I promise you, I will make sure you all know what happened soon, will that be alright with you? Flick I know she is your daughter, trust me when I tell you, there is a good reason for all this."

Felicity gave a nod, it was clear she was not fully happy, but she understood, she looked Birch right in the eye.

"If you want me to trust you, just answer one question for me, because I need the answer today, I need it now Birch, and if you want me to trust you, show it, and answer me honestly, even if it means breaking your word to Abby." Birch agreed.

"I think I can do that, or at least if I can I will."

Felicity looked very uncomfortable, she was trembling, as her bright eyes, locked on Birch's.

"Did he rape her?" Birch stood fast.

"No Flick, he did not rape her." She closed her eyes and started to cry.

"Thank God for that." Hatty came round and pulled Flick into her arms, she gave a nod at Birch.

A few moments later, Birch walked out in to the garden, and down to the guest house. As soon as she was inside, she closed the door and leaned on it, let out a long flowing breath, and closed her eyes. She lifted her phone to her ear, and hit speed dial, it rang on the other end.

"Jemi darling what a nice surprise."

Tears flowed into her eyes and she gave a huge sob, and she slid down the closed door to the floor.

"Mum... Mum, I really need you; I think I am in over my head, and I don't know what to do. Mum it's Abby... Oh Mum, I really need you, please help me?"

"Alright Jemi, I am coming, now tell me what has happened?"

Chapter 21

Veronica.

I lay back in the bath and felt her behind me, her arms were round my waist, and I felt calm and relaxed. Only Birch could do this, only she had the power to talk, and also be silent.

Debbie had gone home, she was soaked to the skin, she left a message for Birch to call her, and let her know how Abby was. Felicity stood at the door as the rain poured down, leaning on the frame as she smoked a cigarette, behind her on the floor, was the pile of bags and coats. She blew out her smoke, and watched as it floated up between the rain drops.

"Am I that shitty a mother? Something horrible has happened, and she would rather talk to her friend than me, what does that say…. She is as fucked up as me?"

Hatty sat at the counter sipping a scotch, her hair was wet and flat, her clothing still damp.

"You are being way too hard on yourself, have you forgotten how you never went home to cry, you always came to me? Flick she is like you in so many ways, I think you need to have a little faith, you know, I think you should have realised by now, you are not her Flick, you never could be."

She turned and looked across the room at her.

"I hated her, she was a witch, I have done everything I could to be everything she was not, and yet here I am, fucking everything up. Hatty she hardly looked me in the eye, all she wanted was to get out of here and away from me." Hatty gave a long sigh.

"It was not like that and you know it. We have no idea what happened between her and him, all we know is she left the choir for a reason, and Edwin was very hard on her for it. Things between you two have not been the same since…. Look give her time, trust in Birch as you did in me, that girl is twenty, with the skills of fifty year old, and if you ask me, I think at some point you will find Birch comes to you." She scoffed.

"Oh really, how do you know Hatty, for all you know I will never find out what caused this?" Hatty put her glass down a little harder than she expected, and Flick jumped.

"It is what I would fucking do Flick, that is how I know."

Felicity turned to her, and Hatty looked at her with heart broken eyes.

"You still cannot see it, or even admit it can you? The bond we have, the love, the secrets, for fuck's sake Flick open your eyes, they are exactly the same as us. Maybe she did run away to Manchester to escape, but has it for one second dawned on you that it was because there was no one here to match me to you?" Felicity blinked.

"How do you mean, that makes no sense?" Hatty shook her head.

"It makes a hell of a lot more sense than you think. Look living here in this hell hole, with your mother, who let's be honest was a hell of a lot worse than Madge is now, you had me. I was there for you always, it is how we both survived, we had each other Flick. Abby had no one, it has never been about you, I mean that robot you married has never helped much, but she is just like you. She felt as you did, it was never you, it was those fucking fascists that drove her from Wotton. My god, open your fucking eyes for once, Abby needed to find her Hatty, and she found her in Manchester."

The water was almost cold when we got out, but I was feeling better, Birch was like my mum when I was a child, she rubbed me down, and wrapped me in a towel. Her face was in front of mine, her hair was lank and wet, hanging like rats' tails, her eyes were slightly dull, and filled with concern, and she was trying her hardest to appear normal, and failing miserably.

"I will be alright Birch." She looked at me, and I could see the tears in the corners of her eyes.

"Really.... I am not feeling too sure at the moment, and it is scaring me?" I tried to smile.

"I just feel really tired." She nodded and swallowed hard.

"You will, it has been the worst of days and that will take it out of you. Come on then, I will dry your hair, and then missy, it is off to bed with you."

She smiled, and it was a little more like the Birch I knew, but I was not daft, she was wearing her bravest face for me, and I did appreciate it. Birch took my hand and slowly led me down stairs. If I am honest, this is the part I was dreading, we headed to the kitchen and I was hoping we had got away with it, but as we came through the door there was my mum with Hatty.

She turned and saw me. mum started to move but Hatty grabbed her wrist, and held her back, for that I was thankful. I tried to breathe and pluck up some remaining shred of courage, I could see the look of pain and fear on her face, and I hated it.

"Mum?" She swallowed and breathed in.

"Abigail.... Abby I just...."

"I am really tired mum.... Can we talk later?" She breathed out and bit her lip, she nodded.

"Alright Abby, if that is what you want, yes.... I am here when you are ready." I tried again to smile, but I knew it had failed.

"Thanks Mum."

Birch took the lead and tried to lift up the bags, Hatty got up.

"Leave those, I will drop them in shortly for you."

I saw Birch nod, and then she pulled me to the door. Ten minutes later, I sat on the bed with a hot coffee, whilst Birch sat behind me drying my hair. I felt like I was coming to life again, I was alone with just her, and that was what I wanted. I finished my coffee, and Birch took the cup out of my hand, she placed it on the dresser.

"Come on you, into bed with you."

She pulled back the duvet and I slid over, and she pulled it back over me. She knelt on the floor at my side and smiled.

"You are safe now, just sleep, at the moment that is the best thing for you." I nodded and smiled.

"Thanks Birch." Her eyes sparkled with tears.

"It is okay, you have no need to thank me, I told you, it's us girls together." She pulled the duvet up a little more.

"I will be in the other room, just shout, and I will be here, okay?" I nodded

I lay in bed looking at the wall, I felt completely wiped out, I really do not remember that much, my eyes flickered and I heard voices.

"Thanks... Yeah she is fine, I put her in bed, it is better she has a good sleep."

"What about you? Birch I know what it is like taking care of them, I have done it for years, and it's not always easy?"

"I am alright Hatty, I think an early night for me will be good too, it has been a long day."

"Get some sleep you look exhausted, look do not worry about Flick, you did the right thing, I will handle her."

"Thanks, Hatty."

"Get some sleep."

"I will." I remembered nothing after that.

The evening had worn on, and it was 8;30pm, and Felicity was starting to lose her patience, as Edwin walked round the kitchen in circles.

"For the love of god, how many times do I have to say it, she does not want to talk to us, do you not think I don't want her here in my arms? For god's sake Edwin, just accept it and bloody well move on." He looked at her and held out his arms.

"How can I.... I want to know what the hell went on between them? You know, I know you think I am a shitty father, but for Pete's sake Felicity, I am trying my bloody hardest here. Do you think I want her like that? She is all we have, and whether you see it or not, I bloody well love her, and I want to be there." Felicity gave a sigh and lowered her tone.

"I know.... I am sorry, I feel the same, it is so frustrating." He smirked.

"Well now you know how I feel every time you run off to Harriet.... It's this.... And it is bloody well horrible. I just didn't expect to have both of you do it to me."

The doorbell rang, and Felicity lifted her hand to her face and rubbed her forehead.

"Oh, who the hell is that, please tell me this is not all over the village, I do not think I can take much more?" She walked down the hallway, and opened the large solid wooden door.

Out on the step was woman with long blonde hair, she looked early to mid forties. She looked like some kind of professional, in her white blouse and dark blue cropped trousers, she had a collarless grey woollen coat draped over her shoulders, and was holding a large leather designer hand bag in her right hand. She smiled, and she looked vaguely familiar.

"Mrs Watson.... Abigail's mother?" Felicity nodded, her mind raced, was she a police officer?

"Yes, that is me." The visitor smiled again, and swapped her bag to the other hand.

"Hi I am Jemima's mother." She corrected herself.

"Sorry, my bad, you will know me better as Birch's mum, I am Veronica.... Veronica Dixon."

The sudden realisation hit her, and her expression changed from confusion to instant Wotton hospitality.

"Oh, I am so sorry I had no idea you were coming, what a very pleasant surprise.... Please.... Please come on in, Edwin we have a visitor."

Veronica stepped inside as Felicity moved back.

"I am sorry it is a little late, I was in London, and Jemi called, so I tried to get over, but well you know the traffic, it's horrendous at this time. I assume she mentioned nothing about this, typical of her really, I should have guessed."

Edwin appeared with a large professional smile.

"Mrs Dixon what a wonderful surprise, it is so nice to finally meet, we have heard so much about you. I am Edwin, Abigail's father, and I see you have met Felicity." She smiled as she shook his hand.

"Very nice to meet you, and yes, I have heard wonderful things from Jemi about both of you. Will and I, are so grateful for you letting her stay here, it really is very generous of you both, I fear those two are like peas in a pod." He smiled, and waved a hand towards the living room.

"Would you like to come through, is there anything at all we can get you?" Veronica looked at Felicity, who had just closed the door.

"I know it is somewhat rude, but could I take a rain check? I miss her, and would really love to see her." Felicity smiled.

"Of course, how silly of us, it is to be expected, I completely understand, as a mother we can only settle once we know they are fine." Veronica smiled.

"I know she is grown up and full of wonderful dreams and ideals, but to me she will always be my precious little girl." Felicity gave a big smile.

"She really is a delightful girl, please follow me, and I will take you to her."

Veronica gave a sigh of relief, and followed as Felicity took her through the kitchen to the patio doors. Veronica tried to chat.

"I do hope she has behaved for you whilst she has been staying here, she can be a little wild at times, I worry about it?" Felicity was in full flow.

"No... Not at all, she had been delightful to have around, she is such a happy child, and so cheerful all the time. We find she brightens each day." Felicity opened the door.

"She is in the guest house, if you give me a moment, I will get you an umbrella. Veronica waved her hand.

"No need to worry, it is not far, never forget where I am from, we are more than used to rain up north." Felicity smiled, and Edwin who had followed through grinning like an idiot, gave a fake laugh.

I was lost somewhere in my mind, I was warm and snug, and somewhere there was soft breathing, and I was focused on it, just lying in the darkness and listening. It made me feel calm and at peace. Something moved behind me, and I heard another voice, it was soft and caring.

"Jemi... Jemi sweetheart, wake up."

I heard soft moans and my body shook softly. Something behind me jerked, and my body felt lighter and cooler, there was rapid movement, and then everything appeared to move at high speed, and I opened my eyes.

"MUM!"

Birch was wrapped around her mother, who was sat on the bed, one glance, and she had burst into tears, and was sobbing bitterly.

"Oh, mum it has all gone wrong, she is hurt so badly, and I don't know how to help her, please you have to help me, I want to help her."

There was a mass of blonde hair, some black patched and some not, it was hard to see where they started and finished.

"Hey this is not like you.... Shush now I am here. I am here for both of you."

Veronica's face appeared from within the mass of hair, and she looked at me, and saw I was awake and watching them, I smiled and she winked. Birch was weeping bitterly into her mother's shoulder as her mum whispered soft words and held her tight.

I sat up, and Veronica slid a hand away from Birch and held it out, I slid mine out of the covers and took it in mine, she gave it a squeeze.

"I am here for both of you... How about you both get dressed, and I think we should sit and start sorting this mess out, would that be okay?"

I smiled, and gave her a nod. Birch sobbed into her mum's shoulder.

"It is why I called you."

Veronica gave a smile, and loosened her grip on Birch, she pulled her back a little, and leaned into her, just as Birch has done with me so many times. She stroked the hair from Birch's face, and looked her in the eyes.

"No more tears, okay? I am here, and will do what I can to help." Birch gave a sniffle and nodded, as she wiped her nose on the back of her hand.

"Thanks Mum."

Birch grabbed her long black robe, and jumped out of bed, I looked at what was on the floor. I saw a pair of jeans, and black T shirt, so I leaned on the bed, and reached down, and grabbed them. Birch went straight to the kitchen; I heard her mother.

"I am not sure if you have eaten, but I asked the cook at the Hunters to whip up some fries and a burger for you. They are still quite warm, so you had better get them now." I walked out of the bedroom and rubbed my eyes, as she placed a large brown bag on the table. I heard Birch from the kitchen as she filled the kettle.

"The Hunter's?"

"Hmm, I have booked a room there."

She came into the room and sat on the floor in front of her mum, who was sat in the comfortable chair. Birch looked back and smiled, and patted the floor at her side. I walked over and sat down, she pulled her arm round me, and leaned in for a half hug.

Veronica passed over the bag, and Birch opened it, and started to unwrap the food, as the smell wafted out and hit me, I suddenly felt starving.

We sat on the floor for almost an hour. Birch had filled in her mum most of the details, but Veronica wanted far more details, and she asked a lot of questions, and I answered them honestly.

I felt strange, I had found it so hard to tell Birch, I had done everything I could to avoid it, and yet sat on the floor, drinking coffee, and eating a burger and fries, the words came so much easier to me. Like her daughter, Veronica took note of everything, and I could see where Birch had got it all from.

Veronica sat back in the chair and gave everything some thought, she looked at me with the same piercing green eyes Birch had.

"Abby.... The way I see it is this, yes, this man is now married, and so it could be likely that you and this Julia, were his only victims. As you have told me, there has been nothing to show he has done it again, as you have not heard anything about another attack. So.... Let me say this, it is only today that some people have found out about you, and I would speculate, that there could be others just like you."

I had already though of that several times in the last three years. She leaned forward in her chair.

"I really understand your fear of shame. I think that trying to protect your family is a noble quality, but I would ask this, if another girl is molested by him, is that the right price to pay for your silence? Will their families thank you for it? It is an uncomfortable point, but one you have to consider." I felt my stomach twist, her voice softened.

"Abby you are highly intelligent, and you have certainly read enough books to know how the world works. Jemi, you are talented and very good, I know you have to a degree been trained by myself, but you still lack the one thing I cannot teach you, and that is experience, which will only come with maturity and time. Therefore, as unpopular as it may appear, I think it would be better to talk to your mother about this Abby." I shook my head.

"I cannot do that, I told my dad and he took their side, don't you see that?" She smiled.

"I do Abby, but I think you have made a big mistake, one neither of you have noticed." Birch frowned.

"We have.... What?" I looked at Birch and she turned to me.

"Do you know?" I shrugged; I had no clue at all. Veronica leaned back to think a second.

"I would say it is safe to say that Felicity knows nothing at all about this, actually I am completely sure she knows nothing." Birch gasped.

"How can you be so sure, I won't deny I considered it, but there can be no way Abby's dad would keep quiet about that?" She smiled.

"Are you so sure Jemi.... Look at the facts, just focus on what you know, come on, I taught you better than this. Switch off your feelings for Abby, and take a back seat, and take a very long look, the answer is there, it is staring you right in the face."

Birch moved her head from side to side, I could see her trying to focus her thoughts, and she looked distressed.

"I do not see the proof." She looked at her mum. "What am I missing?"

"Jemi, you are too involved, you are a wonderful friend, but you are not her therapist. The only way you can sit with another and walk into empathy, is to push down your emotions, walk into none judgement and look with fresh eyes, only then can you walk in the shoes of another. It is basic counselling, and you know that." Birch looked deflated and put her head down.

Veronica looked at me and I swallowed hard, hell if she was that tough with her daughter, what the hell was I going to get?

"Abby.... She is your mother, seriously if she had any idea, he would never have entered this house, on that you can trust me. Three years ago, just the slightest suspicion, and she would have gone after him with a vengeance. Regardless of what this village thought. She would have come to your aid, and attacked him, again on that there is no doubt." She looked at Birch.

"Jemi.... Would a mother who knows, honestly ask if he raped her?"

Birch lifted her head, and stared at her mother; her voice was almost a whisper.

"Oh my god he covered it up, he told no one, not even his wife. How could he do that mum, she is his daughter?" She nodded.

"I think it is clear, he puts reputation far higher on the scale than domestic issues, this is not uncommon Jemi. Remember how it looks on the outside, is more important than how it is on the inside. If you ask me, and from what you have told me to date, I think that is the philosophy of the whole village." She looked at me again.

"Abby she is your mum. I know things have been strained and you two have only just started to communicate again, but as a mum myself, I can assure you, if you hide something this big from her, you will undo everything you have done since you came home. Can I suggest you allow me to tell her, and for now, because this will be shock for her, we withhold the fact you told your father, just let her know the basics? If you really want to get closer to her, give her this, and talk to her when she asks, trust me, you will thank me later." I nodded, it made me really nervous, but she did make a lot of sense.

"Okay Veronica." She smiled.

"Alright, I have Katie working late again, so I am going to steal your mother now, and do this all over again. I will be here tomorrow, so I would suggest, relax, have a drink and talk to each other. I have never seen you two so quiet with each other. I will however be quite clear to your mother that nothing should be done until she has spoken with you first. Would that be satisfactory?" I smiled.

"Yeah, that will be great Veronica." She winked.

"One more thing."

"Yeah what?"

"What the fuck Deadly, why are you calling me Veronica? I am sure I have informed you that is my mother.... It's Roni!" Birch sniggered.

"Busted!!! I giggled.

"Sorry Roni.... Shut up Jemi!"

Veronica walked in through the kitchen door, and Felicity sat at the counter with a gin, and looked up hopefully.

"Is she alright?" She gave a sniffle, and it was obvious she had been crying.

"Felicity, have you eaten?" She shook her head.

"No."

"Okay good, because my assistant has booked a table at what she says is a highly recommended restaurant, so grab your coat, we need to talk. I will let you in on everything that has happened." She looked surprised.

"But Abby said she did not want me to know."

"Felicity, that was then, trust me, this is what I do for a living, and we need to talk privately, where is your husband?"

She put down her glass, and got up from the counter.

"He will, as always, be in his study."

They walked down the hall and Felicity leaned in through the study door.

"I am just nipping out with Veronica, I will back in a while." He motioned an okay.

As they came out of the door the gates opened and Veronica turned.

"By the way, call me Roni, everyone does, it is a little less formal." She nodded and smiled.

"I am Flick."

Roni was in the bright yellow Porsche, it was actually William's, but she loved to borrow it for long drives. They got in and set off, and as Roni set the sat nav, she began to tell Flick the story told her by Abby, minus the fact that she told her father.

We sat on the bed with drinks, leaning against the headboard, Birch was holding my hand, and had not let go of it all evening. Her phone pinged and she picked it up and read the message.

"It's Deb's, she is really worried about you, she got just as drenched as we did, and she has not really had a chance to see you are fine." I understood.

"Tell her it is okay; she will text all night if she does not see me, let her know to use the side gate." Birch gave a chuckle.

"She is on her way, why do get the feeling she already had her coat and shoes on, and was waiting?" I smiled.

"That is who she is, she is like Hermione crossed with a rock groupie." Birch sniggered.

It did not take long for the sound of footsteps to arrive at a fast pace outside, and then the door clicked and banged.

"Abby.... Birch?"

"In here."

Deb's appeared in the doorway as I lifted my glass to drink, and before I could take a sip, she was in the doorway looking....

"Holy shit!" Birch gave a wave.

"Hi Gog...!"

Deb's stood in the doorway wearing a collarless cream shirt, brown leather braces that were connected to dark red corduroy shorts, and knee length leather riding boots, and an under bust Basque. She had a long brown heavy coat, and her hat with goggles on top of her head. I turned to Birch.

"Did you order a dominatrix?"

Deb's stepped a little closer, she was in full steampunk gear, and actually she looked amazing, her hair was tied slightly to one side, she had a monocle, and brown eyeliner. She opened her arms and nervously asked.

"What do you think?" Birch looked at me, and we were lost for words, she winked and turned back to Deb's

"Goggles Sweetie, I think I am wet." Deb's smiled.

"Really?" She looked at me.

"I wanted to cheer you up, but all I could think of was showing you my whole collection. I got the coat today, to finish it off. I do have a whip and a brass telescope as well, but I thought maybe leave that for another time." I nodded feeling a little lost for words.

"I think you look amazing Deb's; I really do." She gave me a huge smile and came over to the bed, sat down and took my hand in hers.

"Are you alright now, I was really scared for you?" I nodded

"Yeah, I am, I am also drunk and you are not... Grab a glass."

The meal was emotional, set back in a quiet corner. Roni was relaxed and gentle in each line she used, very aware of the impact she was having on Flick. The conversation was open and honest, as Roni went through the whole series of events from start to finish.

They finished their main and waited for dessert, and sat back finishing the wine. Flick was calmer and feeling more relaxed, and by the time the bill was paid and they were walking down the street, there was a far less formal and more relaxed atmosphere between them. Flick pulled out a cigarette and lit one up, and offered one Roni. She smiled.

"I shouldn't really, but what the hell, I have one occasionally."

She took it and stood still as Flick clicked her lighter, and Roni leaned in to light it.

"I think she is very like you, it is strange Roni, but I feel that sense of calm she has in you too." Roni smiled as they walked on side by side talking.

"I think she has it stronger than I do, my grandmother was the same, Jemi in the midst of complete chaos, which I will add she caused, will have this aura of complete calm in her own madness around her, she is an amazing child, she has been a joy to raise." Flick gave a nod.

"She is a very amazing woman, I cannot deny I have grown very fond her, and I understand what you mean, she just has that knack of turning everything inside out and upside down, and yet if I am honest, she makes utter sense. I admire her, Abby idolises her." Roni smiled

"Abby has a brilliant mind; I was very taken with her when she stayed. I loved the way she looked at things, it is like she has the eye of an artisan. She would make one hell of a therapist, or a teacher, but I actually think that she will have a future as a writer. If she puts that eye to good use, and turns it into words, she will have a bright future indeed." Flick smiled.

"You know I did not know she had lost her virginity; I have always imagined that one day she would come to me, and we would talk about it. I feel I have lost something important between us, I had hoped this summer I would be able to reconnect with her. I feel I have missed out on something important, and I have made mistakes, I was against her going to Manchester, it caused so many arguments between us, but when she stuck to her guns and went, I missed her terribly. I was so very lonely, I know this may sound crazy, but I would rather she was cross with me but in the house, than four hundred miles away." Roni took a deep breath and took in the night air.

"All is not lost Flick, she suffered a trauma and it held her closed in, but I think that now she has finally opened up, things will get better between you two. As I said, let her take the lead in this matter and let her guide you, if you respect her thoughts and wishes, even if you do not agree, it will ultimately pay off, because what she needs more than anything at the moment, is for her to find her own path. I think Jemi is part of that, I know my daughter, and she deeply cares about Abby, and Jemi has an odd way of pointing out the obvious, which will help Abby find her direction. I think you worry too much, and look at this way, if Abby had not gone to Manchester, how would those two of found each other?" She smiled and nodded her head.

"Those two are friends for life, I think there is no doubt about that."

They reached the car and it flashed and beeped. As Flick went to open the door, Roni looked over the roof.

"Would you like to know what my daughter told me a few days back, I think it may cheer you up, but you must not breathe a word, if I tell you?" Flick was curious.

"Go on." Roni smiled.

"Jemi has always wanted to enter into practice at my side, for as long as I can remember that has been her goal. A few days ago, she told me, that when she qualifies, she wants to open up a southern office for me. Jemi wants to build a brand new practice in Wotton. I thought that was a rather wonderful idea." Flick started to laugh.

"Seriously, Wotton, has she any idea of the ripple that will cause?" Roni winked.

"I think my daughter knows exactly what she is doing, and if you ask me, just from the little I have heard, I do not think she will be short of clients."

She gave a chuckle, opened the door and got in, Flick followed, it was a very amusing thought.

On the drive back, Roni glanced at Flick.

"So, what is the deal with Edwin and you?" Flick sat back and gave a long sigh.

"I think I have aged too much for his eye, he spends more time away from the house or locked in his study to even notice I am there these days." Roni nodded.

"It is not unusual Flick, sometimes in long marriages, life dulls the shine of who we once were, work, kids, and commitment can be the death of many feelings. I get a sense a good roll around in the hay would do you a world of good." Flick chuckled.

"It has been so long; I am not sure I remember what to do." She looked at Roni.

"What about you and your husband, I think you called him Will?" Roni gave a smile.

"We had a bad patch a good few years ago, it is crazy, we are both in the game and yet even we failed to see we were drifting. I suspected there was someone else, I was never sure." Flick leaned forward in her seat; she was interested.

"How did you cope with it?" She shrugged.

"I figured if he wanted another, I would show him I am equally as viable, so I bought the sexiest underwear I could find, and I mean, we are talking red and very slutty, and then I took him to a swingers club." Flick gasped in shock.

"Holy shit... What you actually did it with someone else in front of him? My god, Edwin would kill me." Roni laughed.

"Well, it was nothing that severe, but after thirty minutes of men hitting on me right in front of him, and I am telling you Flick, those guys were not shy, and very specific about what they wanted to do to me. He took me into another room, and we had the most amazing sex we had ever had. You could say I opened his eyes again to who I was." Flick gasped.

She could not even imagine doing that, she had nowhere as near as much courage.

"I take it that it worked?" She nodded.

"Oh yes... He saw the light that night. The thing is Flick, he has not forgotten who you are, he married you, he has just lost sight of you, and I will add also himself. Most affairs that start are actually accidents, another woman treats them like we used to before all the kids and bills and worries of life. In a way it makes them remember something from their past, the sex happens usually by mistake. Trust me after years of therapy, with men and women, I have found it never began with sex in mind, and I have never worked with a cheating spouse yet, that did not truly love their partner. If you want my advice, show him that the girl you were is still there, you may find he remembers who he once was." She gave it some thought.

"I would like that; the problem is how do I find me again?"

"You are already on that journey Flick, just keep watching Abby.

When I get lost and insecure, I watch Jemi, and she shows me the way back. I probably should not say this but I did hear something about your friend. Didn't she have sex in the pool with Edwin's brother, and he was outraged by it?" Flick gave a giggle.

"Yes... Hatty is as wild as she ever was, he was very upset about it." Roni nodded; the village was in sight at the other end of the road.

"Maybe he was jealous, and maybe you should get him in the pool, whip off his shorts and give him a dammed good seeing to, I think he may like that." Flick went beetroot.

"Good grief... I am not sure I could do that." Roni laughed.

"Well if you really want to know, throw a young lad in, and then send Jemi in after him, I am quite sure my uninhibited daughter will show you how it is done." She started to laugh, and Flick began to giggle.

"You have a very twisted side Roni; I can see where Birch gets it from."

The car pulled up outside the house, and Roni smiled.

"Home safe, remember, let Abby guide you, and trust me, it will all work out."

Chapter 22

Observation's and Conversations.

When I woke up, it was like everything was back to normal, Birch was naked with her head between my small boobs, Deb's was naked, snuggled into Birch's back, with her hand on her ass, and I was naked, and feeling a huge amount of pressure on my bladder, and I really needed to pee.

The thing about Birch, is she is actually a very thin and toned girl. She looks perfect, her skin is flawless, and as white as alabaster, even though she hardly wears clothes, and is always out in the sun.

Her waist is thin, and she looks like you could lift her with one hand. All this is well and good, but when you are lay on your back, not wearing clothes, and she is sprawled across you, and you really need to pee, pushing Petal up a hill with one finger, is easier than getting her to move.

I heard Deb's make a soft moan, I felt hope, as long as she was not dreaming of Jimmy again, she was waking, which would lighten the load. She opened her eyes, yes... Score!

"Deb's.... Deb's Birch is on me, and I need to pee." She yawned and looked at me.

"Yeah, good luck with that, I almost peed in my sleeping bag at the festival, if it had not been for a fly crawling on her nose, I would have had a lot of explaining to do with your mother when we got back."

"Deb's I am going to pee, please do something." She looked at me like I was an idiot. I looked down.

"Your hand is on her ass, can't you rub it or something, I don't know, slide a finger down, if she gets horny, she will wake up." Deb's freaked.

"What.... No frigging way.... Abby I am straight now.... I got Jimmy, why would I finger Birch?"

I could feel my bladder screaming at me, and desperation was setting in.

"Deb's please I am about to pee, any second now, it is going to be all over the bed." Deb's looked nervous.

"Is it really that bad?" I nodded the best I could.

"Deb's I am begging you; I cannot hold it much longer. OH GOD THERE IS LEAKAGE!!"

She panicked, and looked at me with a determined look in her eye.

"I will just for you."

She started to rub Birch's ass, and then closed her eyes, and swallowed hard.

"Okay I am going in."

She held her breath, and I watched her slowly side her hand towards the gap. I honestly could not believe she was doing it. Suddenly Birch started to giggle, and rolled over scaring the crap out of Deb's, I groaned.

"Birch!! You ruined it." She smiled at Deb's

"Sorry Sweetie, I cannot sleep with you, I have no spare hats." Both of us burst out laughing, and she looked at us with shock.

"I almost bloody fingered her for you Abby... You bitch's." Birch pulled her close, and kissed her cheek.

"I love you Gogs." She turned to me.

"Honestly Sweetie, I never thought she would go for it, the shoes are yours."

Deb's gasped, and slid off the bed, she stood there with her hands on her hips.

"What the hell! I almost became a lesbian again, because you had a bet on shoes?"

I needed a pee, so I ran to the toilet, I left Birch to explain.

"Gogs, when we were unpacking, we found these boots." She bent down and pulled out a pair of boots from under the bed, Deb's gasped.

"Oh my, they are really gorgeous." Birch nodded.

"None of us bought them, so no one owns them, and we could not decide, so after a long talk, we had to come up with something that would prove the greater mind, and Deads beat me, although...." She smiled sweetly. "I am flattered you wanted to... Well you know... Play."

Deb's stepped back from the bed. Birch winked.

"I have never gone that way, but to be honest, I liked the way you touched me, you have very soft hands, are you free for an hour?"

I was sat on the toilet, when I heard a high pitched squeal in the bedroom, Deb's came flying out of the bedroom looking flustered, and Birch let out a huge cackle of a laugh. She looked at me.

"How do you sleep with her? you know she is a pervert right?" I couldn't help but giggle.

The previous day had been terrible, and as Birch and I sat on the bed the night before, we both agreed we needed to let go of some steam. So, in traditional all girls together style, that meant laughter, and shenanigans. Step one was a prank, and who could be better than our sweet little Goggles, and so when we discovered the shoes, we decided a prank to determine the winner, or owner.

It had stopped raining, and even though the lawn was a little soggy, the loungers were dry, so a full scale coffee and toast on the lounger's party began for breakfast. The three of us lay naked in the sun, covered in toast crumbs, and I felt relaxed and calm, and normality felt like it was going to return.

Okay I was trying my hardest not to think of it, just like before, I chose for today to ignore it, so I could have a break, and put the bad feelings I felt behind me.

It was nice to just relax and giggle, with the endless jokes from Birch and Goggles.

The back patio doors opened and Roni and mum came out, and down the garden, Birch sat up, and her mum kissed her.

"Mum, this is Goggles."

Roni smiled, Deb's looked a little embarrassed, after all she was naked, she had no idea how relaxed Roni was. She smiled.

"Goggles, that is a really unusual name, knowing my daughter I am a little confused, how did you earn it?" My mum nodded.

"I must admit, when you came back from the festival, I noticed, and have wondered myself." Deb's looked at me with a please save me expression.

"Yeah Gogs, tell them."

She went beetroot, and stumbled on her words, I leaned

forward and saw Birch trying to fight back her giggles. I was not aware that breasts could blush, but Deb's do.

"Well... Er, you see... The thing is!" Inspiration hit, and she smiled a big smile, and turned her head showing her pony tail.

"I have goggle bobbles." She smiled with pride. Birch gave a nod of recognition. Roni looked at 'Goggles.'

"I hate to be rude Goggles, but could I have a coffee please, I need to talk with Jemi, Abby, and her mum alone for a minute." Deb's smiled, she understood, and was glad to have a chance to hide, until she was a little less flushed.

"It's not rude Roni, you are helping her, I will go make all of us a coffee."

Deb's left with a smile, and Roni sat down.

My mum sat on the lounger next to me and took my hand, Roni looked at me.

"Abby, I thought deeply about what you told me yesterday, especially about staying quiet. I phoned Will today, and he spoke to his law professor colleague about this. What this man did to you was wrong, but when I looked at the facts, and have considered every option, I have to say, there is one fact that makes me understand that actually, if you were to report him, you would find it impossible to get an evidence based conviction. The fact is, it will simply come down to your word against his, and I think it is honest to say, he will paint you as black as black, and no matter if it is lies, there are some who will believe him, and neither Flick or myself want to see you endure that in court, you have suffered enough."

I did feel relived, I was worried my mum would not buy into it, but was happy she had, she squeezed my hand and I turned to her, she smiled.

"We will have to find another way, and we will if we put our heads together." Birch looked at her mum.

"Why no conviction, Deads could win the jury over?" Roni nodded.

"Yes, she could, but at what cost? Jemi sweetheart, the only way it could possibly stick is with solid evidence to prove he did it, and there is none." Birch frowned.

"He has a pair of her panties, wouldn't a search turn them up, and provide proof he was there, which will add weight to Deads case?" She nodded.

"At first, I thought that, but we both missed the obvious that your dad didn't, those panties have semen stains, which proves she had sex, but a DNA test would not match with Martin, because it belongs to James. That could damage Abby, just think about how that would look, she had sex with one man, and Martin could paint that to look like she tried to seduce him, and then backed out, and I think the way his mind works, that is what he would do." Birch understood.

"I see that now, yeah, you are right."

Deb's came out of the guest house with a tray filled with coffees, Birch frowned and looked at me.

"We have a tray?" I shrugged.

Deb's smiled, as she placed it on the floor and started to distribute the drinks.

"It was on the side next to the fridge against the wall." Birch looked stunned.

"That is a tray? I thought it was a mirror, I use it to do my hair when Deads is hogging the bathroom. I used the chopping board when the bell twat came." I looked at Deb's.

"Me too."

For the next hour the fun continued, as we all talked and laughed, and it felt nice, to not be the one everyone was talking about. It was so nice seeing mum light hearted, and I was delighted to see her and Roni getting on so well. I remembered thinking when I was in Uppermill, how it would be so nice to have this at home, and yet here I was just sat watching and enjoying. It was time to leave, and Roni hugged Flick.

"Thank you again for talking, and for having to put up with my daughter." Flick gave a smile.

"I must say I am sorry your stay has to be so short; it has been lovely to meet you, and get to know you a little, you will always be welcome, and as for your daughter, it is a pleasure to have her with us."

Deb's offered a hand, and Roni took it and leaned in close to whisper.

"I know the real reason you are called Goggles, Jemi told me." She went beetroot as Roni stepped back.

"I added it to my online references, under Steam Punk kinks, well done you, few have found new kinks, I have not already listed. Although I have to ask, did they work, you know your nipples, did they look bigger?" Deb's gasped with shock as she went bright purple. She swallowed hard.

"I am not sure; it was Jimmy looking." Roni gave a giggle.

"Well done.... I am impressed, thank Jimmy when you next see him."

I walked with Roni and Birch to the hall door, she turned and hugged me tight.

"Take care of yourself and my daughter, you did the right thing telling her, it has lightened the load already I see. Have fun Abby, be you and be proud, and never mind what they think, never forget, if they call you, it says far more about them, than it ever will you." She kissed my cheek.

Birch walked her mum to the car, and she grabbed her mum and squeezed her tight.

"Thanks, I have no idea what I would have done without you." Roni smiled.

"Jemi, you only made one mistake, I saw that the moment I walked in."

"I did... What did I do wrong?" Roni held her tight.

"Jemi you are her friend, not her therapist, do not think you can counsel everyone. She needs a friend more than a therapist at the moment, so just be that, use your insight by all means, but do not lose sight of the line between the two." Birch understood, and her mum moved back, and walked round to the driver's side of the car.

"Here."

She pulled something out of her pocket and tossed it over the roof, Birch caught it and looked at the memory stick in her hands.

"What is this?" She smiled.

"Access to my private server, it is an online interview I did with a member of a very private and exclusive club five years ago. I used it when I wrote the kink section on golden showers, I am sure that even though that man's face is hidden, you may recognise him or his voice. He made a big mistake and named his partner, which is why it never went online on the web site. I think it might help you two a little. Call it an act of revenge from a parent to a hostile village." Birch smiled.

"How juicy is it?"

"You cannot show that anyone Jemi, but you know how powerful dropping a hint can be."

She understood. "I will see you in September mum, drive carefully, and give my love to dad."

"Take care of her Jemi, I love you."

"Love you too mum."

Roni drove off and Birch watched her leave. I stood in the hall behind the front door, peering round it.

"BIRCH... For god's sake, what the hell are you doing, didn't you hear me calling?"

She turned and frowned.

"What?" She walked through the gates.

"Birch you're stood on the road in broad daylight, and you are naked." I waved her to hurry, and she looked down and then back at me and shrugged.

"So what?"

I gave an exasperated gasp; she was never going to fully understand the workings of this village. She had a handicap, she was Birch, and I was not sure they would ever get used to it.

In the vicarage, Marjorie gasped into her phone, as Mrs Perkins, reported what she was seeing out on the road.

"SHE IS WHAT?" Never in all her life had she heard anything so shocking.

"That hussy has no shame at all, I cannot believe I would say it, but.... She is worse than Harriet Barker."

Mrs Perkins was sat fanning herself on the bed. She was so overcome with shock, she had to phone Marjorie immediately.

"I was quite overcome Marjorie, I have never seen anything like it in my life, she was stood there bold as brass, without a stich on, and not a care in the world. I must say it Marjorie, and I know it is unchristian, but I am starting to wonder why Felicity Watson was ever considered for the council. I have no idea what she is up it to in that house, but I am certain it is immoral."

"I am starting to see that Gwenda, I feel changes are coming to the council, you mark my words, by November things are going to change."

The day had grown hot, and Deb's and Birch were in the pool, mum was sat at my side on the other lounger. We had drinks, and were relaxed, and everything felt a little more normalised. Mum turned onto her side to look at me, she slipped her sun glasses into her hair.

"I am sorry I was not there for you; I should have been, it is not right you had to do that all alone."

"Mum you were in a meeting at the time, I could hardly have run to you there now, could I?"

"You could have come to me, I would have stood by you, I hope you know that?"

"Mum it's done, it cannot be undone, and as Roni said, without proof, it would have been hard to prove anything. You know I hate to bring it up, but you could have told me about dad and you and lot sooner." She looked away.

"That is not fair Abby, that is very private, I wanted to keep you out of it until something was settled." I turned on the lounger and sat up.

"Mum, Martin Hinckley was going to rape me, that was very private for me too, I was so ashamed I did not want to share that either, so it looks like we are both as bad as each other doesn't it?"

"You are getting way too smart for your own good, no matter what I say you have a comeback, can't you see I was trying to protect you?" I gave a sigh, I understood that.

"It is called growing up. Why do you think I wanted to go to Manchester? Mum, I was being smothered and forced to be something I wasn't, no matter what I said, you dictated the terms of my life. I am not a child any more, I am a university student with my own ideas and my own mind, and it is time you understood, I have a say in my own life now. I am tired of us fighting, it gets neither of us anywhere, and I hate it, don't you?" She looked upset and sat up.

"Of course I am, I don't want all this falling out, I have always wanted us to be close. Abby you are my daughter and I love you, and yet for the last few years I have felt I was losing you. Nothing is as important to me than you."

"Not now.... But back then that was not true, was it? All that mattered was what people think and people say. Dress like this Abigail, act like that Abigail, we use full names in this house, nick names are common. I am sorry mum but what the villager's thought was more important than I was, and that is the reason I left, because I did not want to be like them. I just wanted to be me, and thanks to Birch I am." She teared up.

"Was I really that awful? Oh Abby, that is not what I intended. I just wanted you to fit in, and stay under their radar, they can be so cruel at times, and I did not want that for you. I thought I was helping you." She was crying and I felt bad now.

"Mum you taught me how to behave in public, believe it or not, I have not forgotten. Look all I am saying is, let's stop fighting, I understand you will not always agree with my choices, but I am old enough now to do that. If you try to fight me, I will walk away, because I know I can now, and I really do not want that. If you disagree, tell me, don't yell it, just talk and say why, and let me respond to it. You do that with Hatty, when you get pissed off with her you tell her, but you don't lecture her, you talk, all I am saying is do that with me too." She nodded.

"I am sorry Abby, and yes I have to let go, I know it, but it is not easy you know, wait until you have children, you will see how hard it is. I will never stop worrying about you, not ever." I smiled.

"I can live with that mum; I would expect nothing less."

She leaned forward and pulled me into a hug, and I wrapped my arms around her. Birch and Deb's were at the side of the pool, their faces resting on their hands, as they watched from the edge of the pool. Birch moved her eyes to look at Deb's.

"Do you think they will kiss... I hope so?"

I noticed them in the corner of my eye, they were both grinning like idiots, mum gave a titter as she saw them.

"What did you say about being grown up?" Birch smiled and blew her a kiss.

It was Friday night, and due to extended modernisation

work, Pemberton's was closed. An anonymous complaint to the Oxendale council, had deemed the kitchen door was a health hazard. Twice an employee had clashed with a customer, and so Mr Pemberton had to bring in a builder over the weekend to remodel the doorway.

The good news was, Chloe and Edwina were free for the night, and so was Anthony, and after a hurried exchange of texts, a plan was formed.

Times were set, and it was decided by a massive majority, that a night out in Oxendale was required. Everyone had new clothes, and was just dying to wear them.

Edwina had a friend called Caroline, who had heard all about us, and she lived alone in a two bedroom flat. So, plans were set, to drive to Caroline's, get changed, and then head out on foot, and then return to her place to crash for the night.

Sadly, Chloe had yet another choir practice as the big performance night was only five days away, and the Parish Council was in full swing with its summer program.

They had sold so many tickets, that the event had been moved to the larger church hall, and would no longer be held in the church, although rehearsals for now would.

We looked at the times, and reworked everything. Chole should be finished for around 6:30pm, which fitted in with collecting Anthony from work. Edwina arranged to meet us at the salon with her clothes in her bag, and once we had grabbed Chloe, it was off to Caroline's.

Deb's offered to drive, because as she explained, Birch liked a drink, and Deb's admitted she got drunk quicker than rest of us, so she would wait until we hit the pubs. Understanding she could have alcohol, Birch was happy to hand over the keys. All we had to do was shower and shave, and then get dressed, and we were already in party spirit, by the time Birch entered the shower armed with safety razors.

Six fifteen came, and we hugged mum, dad was not home yet, and we pulled Petal onto the road, and Birch and myself jumped in the back, as we had decided that Anthony could have the front passenger seat. We set off with the music pumping a wild Battered Taco album, and headed for Church Rise, and

Delphine's and Antonio's Salon.

We pulled up with beers in hand, where Anthony dressed immaculately in a green fitted suit, was just doing the last finishing up for the day with Delphine. Birch and myself were larking about as normal. As I showed Birch the vicarage where the following day there was to be a fundraising barbeque, Nigel came out of the church with a load of others, and recognised the car. He stood in the road waving outside the vicarage, until Birch nudged me.

"Hey stalker alert."

I gave a long sigh, and moved to the front, and leaned over the partition into the cab, and waved through the windscreen.

"Hi Stalker, get syphilis and die." Deb's got the giggles.

Birch sat in the back making strange faces, and waving using only half her arm.

"Hi Abby, I want you to be my sex slave." We all started to giggle. "Be my lover Abby please, it won't take a minute." Deb's put her head down and started laughing.

"Birch pack it in, he is still there and can see me."

Birch leaned over between the seats, and looked out of the windscreen.

"Look Abby, I used my genetics to make my dick bigger, and it fell off, can we be lesbians now?"

Deb's was almost under the steering wheel, she was laughing so hard. I slid down in the back out of sight as I fought off the laughter. Birch watched him stood there waving like a robot.

"We waved, what does he want, why doesn't he just go home?" She shuddered. "Fuck he creeps me out."

Anthony finally came out and Delphine smiled.

"Take care of him girls, don't lead him astray, I need him in work for a two o'clock appointment tomorrow." Anthony hugged her.

"Now you are sure about this, you will be fine opening up on your own?" She gave him a big smile.

"Will you just go, and have a great time, go on, go and enjoy yourself for once."

He opened the door and got in. Nigel was still waving, I looked at my watch.

"Where are they?"

Edwina came running across the green with a bag on her shoulder, she came round the back to the open door.

"Sorry guys, I got held up by dad, but hey, I am here, so let's hit it, give me a beer I really need one." Birch looked at Edwina.

"Where is Chloe, is she not coming?" Edwina looked round.

"That's odd, she texted me ten minutes ago to tell me practice was over, and she was heading here." I felt a cold tickle run down my back.

"Is she still in the church?" Deb's shook her head.

"No, they all came out with Nigel, they left but he didn't." I felt the goose bumps run up my arms, as Birch looked at me with a really serious face.

"Deads.... Hinkley." I shook my head and felt a huge wave of fear crash over me. Edwina was staring at us both.

"What?" I was up and heading for the door.

"Not Chole, if he so much as..." Birch was right behind me, as I hit the road running. Edwina looked at Deb's.

"What is happening?" She shrugged.

I felt a massive panic inside me as I rushed towards Nigel, I could only think of one thing.

"Nigel where is Chloe?" He looked puzzled, and then pointed to the church.

"She stayed back to put the books away Abigail."

I ran past him, and in through the gates, and I ran as fast as my legs would carry me, up the pathway towards the church doors. I could hear Birch behind me, and my head raced with jumbled thoughts, as I kept saying 'not Chloe, please not Chloe,' over and over in my head.

The doors to the church entrance were open, and I hurtled in through them to the inner door, and my heart froze as I heard her yell out.

"GET OFF ME, YOU'RE HURTING ME!"

I grabbed the door handle and felt a sudden yank back, I staggered, as I heard Birch in my ear.

"Do not rush in, we need to be quiet as mice, or we won't catch him."

If I am honest at that point I didn't care, I looked at Birch, and she raised a finger to her lips, and then slowly pushed the door open.

"Deads, you lead the way, you know where they are."

"Martin stop, you are hurting me!" I took a deep breath, as I realised what Birch had in mind.

"Okay Birch we do this your way, just let's make it quick."

Chapter 23

Blue Lights.

It had been a long time since I had been in St Augustine's. I have always loved the church; it is a beautiful building. I feel churches are undervalued, there is such beauty inside them. I have seen buildings admired and praised for their architecture in London, but they were just concrete, steel and glass, I never understood how something so cold and dead could be loved.

Inside this church I had always felt safe, there is a warmth to it, almost as if it is living, every hand carved piece of stone, every intricately joined timber. This had been bult by hand, and there was still sweat that had soaked into the stone, from the foreheads of those who built them. I have never had any doubt why I love gothic novels and buildings; it was here in this church I first fell in love with them.

My heart was beating in my ears, it was much darker with the lights out, and the statues took on a more ethereal appearance. I walked as quietly as I could, almost tip toeing on the exposed stone, which had no carpet. I looked to the Lady Altar, where to one side, was the door that led behind the organ, and the large store room and pointed. Birch was at my side; I could hear her breathing heavier than normal from running.

"GET OFF ME, YOU ARE HURTING ME!"

My heart skipped several beats, Birch pulled out her phone, I looked at her confused, how could she make a call at a time like this?

Inside the store room, Chloe was pinned up against the wall, her arm up her back, Martin leaned into her ear, holding her wrist with his left hand, as his right went exploring.

"I heard all about you at the festival, Nigel was very specific. You did not know he was there, quietly sat in the dark watching, did you? Oh, I know all about little sluts like you, walking around naked, flaunting her body, screwing strangers in the dark, you think you are so special, but you are not, you are just a whore to fuck."

His hand slid under her short skirt, and on to her bum cheeks, slowly he moved it, as his breathing started to increase.

"You think you can flaunt it and not expect a man to take the bait? I have watched you for a long time, batting your eyes and smiling, did you honestly think I had not noticed you toying with me?" Chloe tried to wriggle, he pulled up her arm.

"OW!! Martin you are hurting me, you don't have to do this, you need to stop, it is wrong."

He pushed her harder into the wall, and she screwed up her face, as his right hand slipped into her underwear and pushed downwards. Chloe felt her knickers slip, and she tried to wriggle to get free. He pushed harder, and she squealed in pain, and started to cry.

"Please.... Please Martin don't do this, I am sorry, I did not mean to flirt, please... Please you must let me go, my friends are waiting, they will come looking.... Please Martin don't do this, I am begging you."

Her knickers were round her knees, and she was starting to shake violently, his breathing was even faster, as he held her pinned tight, and moved his hand to his pants. Chole heard the zipper, and he leaned right into her ear.

"Your friends will not come, you can scream and yell little slut, no one will hear you, do you think that slut will try and come here? Yes, I know who your friends are, I know what they do. Nigel saw everything, he has always been watching. You are alone, and you will give me what you promised."

The sound of his belt buckle hit the stone floor, and Chloe who was breathing faster, gritted her teeth. She gave out a whimper, as she felt his hand moving behind her.

"No... Oh God no.... Martin please, we can talk, but don't do this." Her tears streaked down her face.

I swallowed hard and was shaking like a leaf, as I walked as fast as I could, I could hear her, and just wanted to scream. Birch had the lead, and was walking towards the door with her phone camera app open and ready. We reached the door and my heart was pounding like a hammer. Birch hit the red record button, and pushed on the door. It gave a slight squeak, and as it opened, I saw the room again for the first time since that night. The table was still there, with the same cloth, absolutely nothing had changed, it was like my moment in there, had always existed.

Birch turned to me, her eyes filled with hate, and handed me the camera. I understood, I was almost paralysed with fear, and memories I never wanted came flooding back into my thoughts, and with them, the tears streamed onto my cheeks.

Seeing Chloe, it all came back, and I started to fall apart. Birch marched across the room, where Martin had his back to us, his pants round his ankles and was stroking himself ready to act. Chloe was shaking as much as I did, and crying, and I was helpless, incapable of anything, stood in the doorway holding Birch's phone, as it recorded the horror that was in my eyes.

Martin shifted his hips back, and made to thrust.
"This is what sluts get in this choir." Chloe shook violently
"PLEEEEEEASE NO!"

And then she was free!

I stood trembling in the doorway, and something rushed past me. I saw Birch grab his collar with a yell of hate.
"DON'T YOU FUCKING TOUCH HER, YOU FILTHY FUCKING ANIMAL!"
He came jerking back in shock, and his arms flailed out to the side, Chole slipped down the wall, and Martin swung round with the force of a screaming Birch, and came face to face with a terrifying Edwina, her eyes glaring with fire, and her teeth gritted.
"THAT IS MY LITTLE SISTER, YOU WANKER!"
Her knee came up at high speed. CRUNCH!!
I flinched... The air ran out of his mouth, and he collapsed to the floor with a squeal, and groaned, Birch let go of his collar, and he dropped like sack of potatoes. He lay moaning in pain on the floor, as Birch who was gasping for air, put her foot on him, and looked at me with glaring green eyes, she was terrifying.
"You wanna kick?"

She looked down at him, and then I saw something I never thought I would see, she was trembling, and started to cry.

Holding his testicles, and sweating with the intense pain, all he could do was stare, unable to speak, and Birch stood over him, tears in her eyes, and a look of utter disgust on her face, and she was angrier than I have ever seen her.

"Just look at you, you call me, all of you do, you call me, and put me down, but look at you. Just fucking look at you, with your pious manner and posh clothing, pretending to be the most respectable man in the village. Look at you now, a pathetic little pervert, who has to rape young girls for kicks, you make me sick. I may not look proper in your eyes, but I am ten thousand times more decent than you."

She pulled back her leg and then kicked, her leg swung with might, and her foot slammed into him hard, he lurched, and groaned on the floor, in pain.

"That one's for Abby."

Edwina had Chloe in her arms, and stood her up, Birch turned and walked over.

"It is okay Sweetie you are safe; you are one of us remember, all girls together?"

Birch crouched down, and took hold of her knickers, and slipped them slowly up. She saw me shaking and smiled. Deb's had arrived, and I had not even noticed. She looked at me with a frightened look on her face.

"I called the police." She burst into tears, and pulled me close and hugged me.

"I am so sorry Abby, I never knew."

She had worked it out, and Birch's comment had pretty much given the game away. Anthony stood there looking horrified. Birch came over and slipped the phone out of my hand, and stopped the recording, it started to save the footage. She looked at me and winked.

"Let's see him try to talk his way out of this."

Martin groaned on the floor his pants still round his ankles, curled in a ball in agony. Chloe came out with Edwina, and looked at me, I felt relived and heart broken, all I could do was pull her close and hug her as hard as I could.

"Are you alright?" Her arms came round me.

"I am so glad you came looking, I am alright, pretty shaken, but I am alright, thanks Abby."

Footsteps came down the church path, and the doors bust open, my mum came through at high speed looking terrified.

"ABIGAIL!"

I turned to see her, and smiled, Deb's looked guilty, as she dried her eyes.

"I forgot, I called you mum too."

Mum ran up the aisle, and came over to me, and dragged me into her arms, and almost squeezed the life out of me. She let go and turned to Chloe, she did not hesitate and pulled her into a hug, and saw Martin on the floor, his pants round his ankles, writhing in pain, as he held his genitals.

"You poor girl are you alright?" Chloe smiled.

"I am fine Mrs W."

She stared at Martin with hatred, released Chloe, and made to go for him, through the doorway.

"Why you filthy, disgusting, I will...!" Birch snatched the back of cardigan, and pulled her back.

"Flick, leave him, the police are on their way, trust me he got a good one from all of us."

Blue flashing lights are a rare thing in Wotton Dursley, and so naturally when they came hurtling round the green, with sirens, and up to the Church, everyone came out. Talk began, and who better to gossip, than Anthony and Delphine. Once the police arrived, shortly followed by an ambulance, Deb's is thorough to say the least, the doors to the church were off limits to all.

I watched as they carried Martin out, still writhing in agony on the stretcher, I can honestly say I felt nothing. Well apart from, wow, Edwina has a hell of knee, it was like suddenly everything inside of me just left. His eyes caught mine, and I stared at him, it was not gloating, happiness or hate, I was devoid of anything. I noticed Chloe had looked back at him, with same look in her eyes, and so I felt that this must be the reaction of anyone who had endured what we had. Birch leaned in to me.

"Not so sure he will be having any more kids." I honestly did not care.

"He already has one, if I am honest Birch, I feel sorry for his kid, poor devil has that for a father. God Julia is stupid, why tolerate it, why put up with him as a husband, she cannot possibly think it would stop him?" Birch gave a sigh.

"The past is filled with women who either knew nothing, or covered for their abusive husband's, my mum has always talked of how she does not understand why some women stay, and support them. She always said, fear is the most powerful weapon of mankind." Deb's leaned in.

"My mum took a lot before she finally got away from my real dad, even then he still tried to win her back, it was so hard for her, she is the bravest woman I know."

We all sat on the pews waiting to be interviewed. Chloe was wrapped in a blanket, as the paramedics checked her out. Her parents arrived and talked to Edwina, and they sat at the front as we sat patiently at the back. My mum was talking to the vicar, much to the annoyance of Marjorie, who had been held at the gate with Nigel, as Martin Hinkley in handcuffs was placed on a stretcher and taken to the ambulance. Birch leaned back looking round.

"What is that door for?" I looked back, and knew just where she was going with this, and decided to say nothing. Deb's leaned over.

"That is the steps to the bell room, why?"

Deb's and her big mouth, I should have acted quicker, as I saw the sudden sparkle in Birch's eyes. I looked at her and shook my head.

"Nope... Not happening Birch, you will leave them alone." She frowned.

"You are no fun.... All I wanted to..."

"Nope not happening, forget whatever crazy thought you have running around in that brain of yours, the police are already here, and I want no more trouble with them."

She gave a sigh and reached into her bag. Birch pulled out her keys, and then a bottle of beer, she snapped the cap off and sat back.

"Birch what the hell? This is a church." She shrugged.

"It is your church, not mine, I can drink in mine." It was not the point, even Deb's backed me up.

"Birch, don't you think it is a bit disrespectful?" She looked at her.

"Goggles Sweetie, if god made everything, then he also made hops and barley. There are foods on this planet that have to be cooked in order to be edible, well if you cook hops and barley and a few other things you get beer, therefore it is your god's wish that I have this." I looked at Deb's who was thinking about it, she looked at me.

"I want to find a reasonable argument against that, but it sort of makes sense, what do I do?"

I sat back. "It's Birch, just give up, she does that to your head." An officer walked up.

"Abigail Watson and Jemima Dixon?" I nodded to him.

"Could you please come with me to make your statements?" I stood up, Birch leaned over the seat to Deb's, she took a swig of her bottle.

"Here, hold this a minute." She pushed the bottle into her hand, and walked off. Deb's looked terrified. She looked at the statue hanging above the altar of Christ.

"I am so sorry, please don't excommunicate me, she is my friend, it's what she does."

The statements took a while, but finally we were told that we had to leave the church, mum was still busy, and Deb's had to give her statement. Anthony had already done his, and was waiting, texting the news to everyone outside by the doors. We walked out, and I saw the crowd that had gathered just below the vicarage, Marjorie saw me and scowled with hate.

"Oh shit." Birch took my hand.

"Come on, we will wait on this bench for the others." She smiled at Marjorie and lifted her beer in salute, Marjorie was horrified.

"Good God, she was drinking alcohol in the church!" Marion who was at her side shook her head, and tutted.

"What do you expect from a tramp like that?"

I sat back and closed my eyes; I felt a small hand grip mine and I smiled. Deb's said little, she just sat at my side and it was enough. My mind swirled, I was glad it was over, it was finally over, and yet I felt guilty. I had sat in the church, and watched Chloe very carefully as she was questioned, I was the only one in the church who fully understood her, I knew what she was feeling, and I felt that was my fault.

Birch sat down and handed me a beer, she passed one over to Deb's. She shrugged.

"It is only sacrilegious inside; kids have been getting pissed in church yards since beer began." I smiled; I knew it was pointless to argue. Birch sat back and leaned on to me, she patted my leg.

"I know what you are thinking and you are wrong. Deads you had no proof; he would have got away with it. At worst, he would have had to leave here, and then go and do it elsewhere to a girl who had no chance of a friend coming to save her. You saved Chloe tonight, it was you who tipped me off, I was just bored she was late, and I wanted to party. Your face told me the truth, you looked terrified, and because of that, because of you jumping out, I followed, and I knew it was not going to happen again, because of you. I filmed it, he has no hope of getting off, once I upload this with the crime number to their server."

She held up her phone and I saw the thumb nail for the video, she was right, we had the evidence this time. I sat there waiting, feeling the eyes of Marjorie burn into my soul, and drank my beer on the bench, until finally everyone came out. We walked down the path, Birch in the lead, towards the waiting Marjorie, Birch smiled, as Marjorie scowled at her, and directed her comment to Marion.

"I might have known this tramp would be involved." She turned and looked Birch up and down with utter distaste.

"Only you could bring the police here, I know your sort, and the same for your so called companion. Utter trash the pair of you, cavorting naked in the streets and now this." My mum stepped forward.

"NOW YOU JUST WAIT...."

Birch lifted her hand to stop her, and then turned back and faced Marjorie head on.

"I take it you are unaware of the circumstances and so I will go easy?" Her voice rose a little louder.

"I won't tell the village how you employed a rapist, and left him alone with defenceless girls. So, I will not describe how we stopped him with his pants round his ankles, raping Chloe tonight. I won't tell the village how it was your son, who spied on us at the festival, and told your rapist who to attack. But I will tell the village that I stood naked on the road today, and waved my mum goodbye."

Birch lifted her head and looked at the crowed, where Mary and Peter stood watching, she looked them straight in the eyes.

"I am a naturist, yes I am shameless and proud of it, it is not against the law to be naked, it is only illegal if it is lewd, offensive, behaviour, and I do not think waving goodbye to my mum is." She looked at Marjorie.

"Read that bible you preach from, your God's original design was two naked vegetarians living in a garden, shame only began with the snake."

Marjorie looked shocked, and stepped back lost for words, Birch smiled.

"See you at the barbeque, I have plenty of money, and apparently, you need to raise some."

She turned, and walked towards the crowd and Petal. We all stood and smirked, even mum, and then walked past her, following Birch who did not have a care in the world, and was swinging her bottle, heading back to Petal.

The road was filled, as they watched from behind a yellow tape, and we headed for the sidewalk, all around the gossips were chatting, it was big news, a rapist had been caught. A car screeched behind the crowd, and there was a commotion. I just carried on walking, heading for Petal, everyone was staring and I felt really uncomfortable.

Petal was where we left her, mums' car was parked on an angle in front of Petal. I saw Birch grab the door of Petal, and I just wanted to go home.

From the side, the crowds parted roughly, and before I knew what was happening, I was snatched up and squeezed almost to death, I gasped trying to breath, engulfed in the arms of who?

"Abigail… Abigail…. Abigail." I felt shocked, and then heard the sniffle. "Are you alright, you are not harmed, if you are, I will kill him?"

The squeeze got tighter, I was just hanging, my toes just touching the floor, and I heard my dad sniffle into my shoulder.

"I am so sorry." My limp arms went up to him, it was weird as hell, but also nice.

"I am alright dad... Father, I am not hurt." He sobbed again.

"Father, you are squeezing me to death, honest I am fine." He loosened his grip.

Holy shit he had tears in his eyes, I mean he actually was crying. I did not even know it was possible. He looked at me and smiled, I was in utter shock. He gave a sniffle and took my arm, and he walked me over towards the salon out of ear shot. He was trembling, this was all news to me, and I had no idea how to react. He stood in front of me and wiped his eyes, with his hand, and he looked me straight in the eyes. He spoke very quietly.

"I am so sorry Abigail, I know you told your mother nothing, and I am grateful, even if I do not deserve it. I wronged you, and I regret it, I should have listened to you not him. I have no right to be forgiven, and I am not asking that of you, but you must know, no matter what, you will always be my little girl, and I am proud of you."

I felt the tears in my eyes, never in a million years did I think that could happen, and yet it made me so happy. I smiled through my tears.

"I love you dad, I always have. I didn't tell mum the whole story, because of that very point. You are my dad and she is my mum, and it is a big ask, but whatever went wrong, try harder, find a way, do this to her, she needs it far more than I do, but I am glad you did it." He wiped his eyes and gave me a nod.

"I will try, I promise." I smiled and handed him my beer; he looked a little awkward.

"Better not, I already got a speeding ticket tonight, let's not add drunk driving to it." I gave a chuckle.

"See you at home, my friends are waiting, we will probably come back as it's too late to go out now." He gave me a nod.

"That's fine, just hide the jeep."

Some things will never change, but I liked that. I giggled, as I turned and saw my mum stood by Petal, I walked up and saw the happiness in her eyes.

"It's up to you two now, I have done my bit."

The Pemberton's had not been very comfortable with the idea at first, but Chloe had convinced them she was fine, and she was, she is much stronger than me, well she had been at school. She had dealt with creeps and weirdos a lot, even as a waitress, she had always had to deal with those who thought they could touch.

Once over the initial shock, and surrounded by us, she calmed down, and found her smile. We climbed into Petal, and Deb's started her up, reversed down the road a little, some idiot in a BMW had skidded to a halt, and blocked the road. Deb's turned Petal around, and we were taking the party to the garden. It was still light, we had a few hours, and we aimed to fill them with frolics and fun, because as Birch pointed out, that is what Friday's nights are for when you are student, it is Uni rules you know?

We headed out on to Manor Road, and then Waterside Lane, Birch was deep in thought, she looked up at me.

"What Sweetie?" I knew her so well; she was up to something.

"Whatever it is, don't do it." She tried to look innocent.

"I was being good, honestly I am not always plotting." Deb's shouted from inside the cab.

"Yes, you are." She giggled.

"Alright if you really want to know I will tell you.... All I was thinking is.... Do you think those bell things, have detachable ringers?"

She was priceless, and we all sat back laughing, as the gates opened, and Petal rolled onto the driveway, and through the gates to the back.

Chapter 24

Twisted Truth's.

The events of the previous evening had created havoc for Marjorie. Her plans had turned to chaos, as every one of the villagers was talking, but not about the Watson girl and her friend, but about her.

There was a lot of gossip, especially around her son Nigel, as Birch had made it quite clear, it had been Nigel who had tipped off Martin on who to target. Marion, was in complete melt down, it was 9am, and at 4pm a barbeque had been planned, and Marion was convinced the event should be postponed.

Marjorie was incensed at the suggestion, as in the back of her mind, the words of that white haired whore, echoed. 'I have plenty of money, and apparently you need to raise some.' Just the idea that she was richer than her, was just too much to bare.

"I want that event, and I am having that event, and I will look that whore in the eye, and not bat an eyelid, no one in this village is going to stop me."

Marion had never seen her so angry, even Harriet had never pushed her this far. Marjorie paced around her office.

"I have never backed down in my life. Yes, it may not look good, that Hinkley has ruined everything with his perversion, but this house of cards will not topple with one bad Joker, I still hold all the aces." Marion looked at her with adoration.

"You are so right Marjorie, we shall gather the council, and do this, and it will be the best fund raiser we have ever held." Marjorie swelled up with pride.

"You can count on it!" The phone rang, and she picked it up.

"Celia, what is it?"

Marion watched as her temple twitched, and on the other end of the phone, Celia was trying to choose her words careful.

"Marjorie I really am sorry, but Patrick Johnson's Agent has cancelled, apparently the news of Martin reached him first thing this morning, and he has decided that considering his profession as a life coach, and force for positivity, he will be compromised if he attends the seminar at the Summer Fete."

It was just too much for her, and she felt her anger rising, her tone changed to sweetness, which was not a good sign.

"Celia darling, it is unfortunate, but these things are sent to try us, we will just need to find another life coach, to talk." Celia was not convinced.

"Marjorie, that is not such an easy task, these people are booked up months in advance, we may have to cancel."

"I have never cancelled anything in my life, so get on your phone, and find me another guest speaker. DO YOU HEAR ME?"

Celia held the phone away from her ear.

"I shall do my best."

"Do better!"

She slammed down the phone, and Marion jumped. Celia looked at Lillian, and looked panicked.

"Oh, Lillian dearest, we are in really big trouble; we have fourteen days to pull off a miracle."

The guest house was at its fullest, Anthony was asleep in the chair, Chole and Edwina were sprawled together on the living room floor, and Deb's, Birch, and myself were in the bed. We had returned home, sat in the house, and talked until late into the night drinking.

I filled everyone in on my experience, and talked of how guilty I felt. Chloe understood, she had always thought that his attention to Julia was a little too creepy, which is why she had made the decision to quit the choir after the choir evening.

Birch was angrier at herself, because she was the one that suspected Nigel, but had no idea the information he gathered was being shared, and she took note, that Marjorie was pulling far more strings than even she thought.

It was agreed that the only way to gain acceptance, was to show Marjorie for what she was, which was in fact, a woman who used her money and influence, to control and direct public opinion her way. Our objective was clear, we had to find a way to shift public opinion, and expose her, as we had Martin Hinkley, the only question was how?

The night after that became a bonding session of drunken hugs, which ended up with them all passing out, well actually Deb's and Anthony went first, Chloe came second, closely followed by Edwina, and finally Birch and myself staggered to bed together, only for me to pass out on the end of the bed, and Birch had as always, taken care of me and climbed in beside me.

I woke up earlier than normal, it was 10:30, and after finding a baggy t shirt, I stepped over the bodies, and headed for the kitchen to make a coffee. It was warm, but not as sunny as it had been, so armed with a coffee I wandered outside, making a mental note that chilli was off the menu, Birch had outdone herself, and so I left the door open.

Mum and Hatty were sat at the garden table, smoking, so I wandered up, I had seen Hatty in the crowd last night, and assumed that as dad was back in work, she came round to get the full details, I was right.

Mum had the cordless phone on the table, which was not a good sign, and I assumed that this morning the village would be rife with gossip, and I was not wrong. I sat at the table and Hatty winked.

"How are you and Chloe?" I sat with my legs up on the seat, holding my cup in both hands as I sipped it.

"We are fine, we all talked a lot last night." She smiled.

"Glad to hear it." I yawned, and looked at mum.

"Is the gossip bad, or did we survive?" She gave a sigh and reached for another cigarette.

"It depends who you ask, Chloe was seen as a victim, but Madge has been to work, and there are quite a few who are leaning towards Madge, and her bleeding heart sob story, she has been taken advantage of by Martin, and she feels utterly betrayed. It appears the fund raiser has not been cancelled, and will still go ahead, I would imagine she will use it to play victim, and garner sympathy from the village. I am sorry Abby, but Birch and yourself have not had a popularity boost, even though it was you two who were the real heroes of last night."

It was not unexpected, Birch had predicted it last night, none of us were expecting welcome wagons. Hatty lifted her cup, and looked at us both, she thought for a moment.

"If there is one thing I know about this place after a life time of living here, it is that there is a very big difference between what is said publicly, and what is said privately. I think you may underestimate that Flick, you did at last year's election, from what I saw, these girls scored points last night, and when Birch faced out Madge, a lot of people noticed it. You have been aligned with Birch; it may yet work in your favour Flick." Mum was uncertain.

"Private thoughts are one thing, but if people do not speak out, her grip will only get tighter." I did not understand things the way Hatty did, but the solution appeared clear to me.

"Go into stealth mode, and start your campaign now, to be honest mum, it is a postal vote, so do the work now, after all the vote is anonymous, use it to your advantage." Hatty nodded, and mum sat back in her chair, and took a puff of her cigarette.

"You are aware she is already attacking all of us?" Hatty shrugged and smiled.

"Listen to your daughter, and very quietly attack back, you already have your first piece of ammo, she employed Martin, so use it, ask why he was never vetted, and left unsupervised with young females?"

The phone went off, and mum answered it, it was Angela from the bakery. Mum walked into the kitchen to grab her notes for the event, I looked at Hatty.

"Will you be coming today; I know you don't normally do these things?" Hatty looked through the glass doors at mum.

"Yeah, I think I am going to hang around your mum today, just to make sure she is alright, well I will until you dad gets back, he has gone to the office, and will be back for the event." I was glad to hear Hatty had her back.

By the time I walked back to the guest house, Chloe was up and cooking bacon and eggs. Edwina was still asleep on the floor, Anthony was stirring, Deb's was helping Chloe, and Birch was sat in bed sniffing the air.

"Sweetie, I smell bacon, mmm, I love bacon."

It took a while to eat, organise, and get dressed, Anthony who had hung his suit up in our room, took a quick shower and dressed, and the transformation from simply Anthony who we knew, to flamboyant Antonio was complete with the addition of hair gel, and ten times the time it took me to do my hair. He gave twirl and clipped his scissor pouch to his belt.

"So, darlings what do you think, I am not the most stylish of the styled, I mean honestly who would not want my genius creations, to adorn themselves with?" We all chuckled, but I felt a little sad.

I really liked Anthony, I liked him when he dropped the drama, and was simply himself, he appeared more relaxed with less ticks. Antonio was simply an act, but it was one he had to perform every day, just to be tolerated, and it got to me a little, because under the flamboyance, drama, and arrogance, was a really kind, caring decent person, and I was glad that I had been given the chance to see that.

He left us to go to work, and Chloe and Edwina took over the table, and laid out their makeup, I was stunned at how much they had. My makeup consisted of a small cloth bag, they had a roll of tools, a stack of shadows, powders, and eye pencils, lipsticks and mascara, it was to say the least, impressive.

Chloe had decided she was coming out, she was not going to hide anymore, and Edwina was with her, and so out came their clothes, for their night out, and they were determined there was to be no more hiding, to which Birch highly approved.

At three thirty, we left the house on foot, and made our way towards the village, I was in a black lace top, with skin tight ripped and frayed black jeans and boots. Birch was in a tie dyed matching low cut flowing top and full circle skirt, with a shawl round her hips, Chloe had on tiny cut off jeans, adorned with lace, a loose flowing baggy cream crop top, and a lace thigh length coat, Edwina was similar, but had a black skull t shirt, and both wore ankle boots and a black cowboy style hat. Deb's had gone full steam punk, with Jimmy's hat, and we looked pretty amazing, and everything Marjorie hated, so yes, we looked to her like whores.

On the road between the church and the vicarage, large gazebos had been set up, under which a team of chef's were cooking, over huge coal filled grills. Birch was stunned.

"I thought this was a barbecue, not a bloody industrial food kitchen?" I sniggered.

"This is Marjorie's event; did you honestly expect the vicar tossing burgers on his back yard grill?"

Lillian and Celia had closed the Tea Rooms, and were busy running an outdoor hot drinks tent, the girls from the Hunter's Arms, had a beer tent, and somewhere in the vast garden around the vicarage, a brass band was playing, and everywhere you looked there were collection tins for donations.

Members of the council were busy organising, Celia was glued to her phone, as she had to watch poor Lillian struggle. Celia was looking very stressed stood to one side by the vicarage wall. The line of frustrated people was growing.

Birch took the lead, and she suddenly slipped behind the counter next to Lillian's side.

"What do you need Sweetie?" Lillian looked exhausted, and the event had only just begun.

"Oh, Birch you are an angel, I need eight coffees."

She wasted no time and grabbed the paper cups, and reached for the large tin, and started to spoon out the coffee. Chole seeing what was happening followed suit, and slipped in, behind Birch, to top up an empty water boiler. She turned, and started laying out cups as Birch or Lillian required them, and shortly the panic was quelled, and the operation began to flow.

I grabbed the collection tin, and walked down the line of waiting customers, and the first collections of the day began, albeit grudgingly, it was me smiling with the tin after all.

Birch looked at Celia, who she quickly understood was trying to book a celebrity, she leaned into Lillian.

"Celia is very stressed is everything alright?" Lillian was very flustered.

"Our guest speaker has cancelled after the terrible goings on last night." She turned to Chloe. "Oh, you poor dear, and yet here you are with your brave beautiful face, helping the village, you are simply the bravest girl I know, bless your sweet heart."

She pushed three cups across the table to a customer, and then looked at Birch.

"Marjorie is insistent we book a new speaker, she has no idea how impossible that is at short notice, poor Celia darling is under so much pressure, it is simply breaking my heart to watch her."

Birch understood, and she slid four hot cups of coffee filled by Chloe, towards a waiting gent and winked, he smiled, and the woman scowling at his side, gave him a sharp dig in the ribs.

Birch slipped back, grabbed Lillian by the hips and squeezed past her.

"Excuse me Lilly." Lillian's eyes lit up and she smiled, as Birch deliberately rubbed her way past. She moved towards the edge of the stand and Celia.

Celia ended yet another call looking harassed, Birch walked up and held up a blue business card in front of her, Celia frowned.

"What is that?" Birch gave a smile.

"How would you like to book, one this country's top selling authors, and motivational speakers for your event?" Celia gave a sigh.

"Bless you Birch darling, but as I am starting to find out, it is impossible with such short notice." She shook her head.

"Not if you are on the inside, it isn't. I happen to know for sure, this author has no bookings until October, and they are free, and all you have to do is follow my instructions to the letter." Celia's eyes opened wide.

"Are you serious, what do we have to do?" Birch leaned in close to Celia.

"Make absolutely sure no one finds out my last name." She frowned.

"I am not sure I understand?"

"I will give you this card, it is for a red haired, lesbian called Katie O'Reilly, and she is so hot, oh my god I get wet thinking about her." Celia's eyes opened wider, and she swallowed hard, her voice was almost a whisper.

"Oh... Oh really?" Birch winked.

"She is my mum's agent, do you have a pen, if you do, write this down?"

Celia was very flustered, and she fumbled in her hand bag.

"I have one here, I am sure." She produced a pen.

"I have one, now what do I do?" Birch gave a sly smile, and wet her lips seductively.

"Tomorrow afternoon phone this number, tell her who you are, and that Jemima Dixon has told you to call her, and book Dr Veronica Gemma Dixon, to give a motivational speech here, at your event, and to wave the fee. Tell her, if she books it, I will pay her by fulfilling my promise to her, on the first Saturday I am back at university." Celia wrote it all down word for word.

"Got it." She swallowed hard.

"And this woman is a red headed hot lesbian... Oh dear.... I know I should not ask, but what have you promised?" Birch gave a sexy grin.

"All I can I can say is it involves nudity, aromatic oils and sweating, oh you have no idea how sweaty I will get, she drives a hard deal, and it will be delightfully naughty." Celia gasped, and went beetroot.

"Oh my.... Oh, my indeed." Her breathing increased, and she swallowed hard.

"You would do that for me?" Birch winked.

"I am always extra nice to my friends Celia, I thought you knew that? Now go and help Lillian, and relax, and enjoy your day." Birch turned, and faced me with a smile.

"Where next Sweetie?" I looked at Chloe, she smiled.

"I will catch up in a bit, I want help get the line down, you know, do my bit?" I gave a nod.

"See you in a bit then."

As we walked away, towards the burger stands, I looked at Birch.

"What did you just do, have you promised yourself to a lesbian?" Birch giggled.

"Katie is ace, we used to do spar days together, you know the full works, sauna, spar, massage, but with Uni, I have not been free enough. I promised her one soon, because she is driving me nuts about it, do you want to join us, it's loads of fun, we always end up in a bar after."

"So it's not sexual?" She shook her head.

"Only in Katie's mind, but she knows it won't happen." I became wary.

"If I come, I am not going to be fed to her, am I?" Birch started to laugh.

"Oh Sweetie, you are my dark little beastie, your vagina is safe in my care." We headed into the beer tent.

Birch as always, was very attentive to everything, we walked round the stands, and bought some burgers, and sat eating them on the gate to the show field. There appeared to be far more people than normal, I had not been for a few years, but it was clear it had really grown in the last few years. It helped the clouds had cleared a little, and it was getting warm. As we sat there, she nodded to the butcher.

"Who is that?" I looked up.

"It's Phillip Morrison the butcher why?" She pointed to a woman stood close to him, over by the burger stand.

"What about her?" I saw Amanda the florist.

"She is the Florist why?" Birch chewed on her burger.

"Screwing each other." I shook my head.

"No, I don't think so, Phillip is happily married with kids, they live at the top of Manor Road, nice family, his wife is really pretty." Birch swallowed and took a sip of her beer.

"So why is he stroking her ass when no one is looking? She is not objecting; I would say she is enjoying it. I am telling you Deads, he has consensual knowledge of her body, watch, he is definitely doing her."

I could not believe it, Birch had to be wrong, Phillip was a really decent and well respected member of the village, his reputation was concrete. I watched, and then I saw it, she leaned in, and I saw his hand slide over, and he gently rubbed her bum, he went a little lower and she giggled. I could not believe my eyes.

"Holy shit Birch!" She smiled.

"Told you.... Body language and behaviour, says much more than words."

I was stunned as he did it again. I tried not to stare, but I could not help it, I could not believe it, they were so open, and obvious, and yet no one else appeared to be picking up on it, it made me think about what Birch had told me, about hiding in plain sight.

We had been in one spot for too long, and people were starting to notice, the disapproving looks were coming at us from all angles. I slipped off the gate, almost spilling my beer.

"Let's move, the vultures are circling."

Birch had been itching all day to get inside the vicarage, I had been trying to avoid it. In all honesty, as much as I loved her, when it came to Marjorie, I did not trust her one bit. Her house was open to all today, I have seen it too many times in my life, but I knew I could only keep Birch away for so long. She was convinced they had some deep devious secrets, and to be honest, looking at the vicar and Marjorie, I was very sceptical.

The house was big, it was clear the church was affluent in these parts, it was again Edwardian, and stylish. The whole place was filled with antique furniture, portraits of people no one had any idea about, large pots and stylish ornaments.

It was tastefully decorated with a floral theme to match the endless wooden panelling. which appeared to line every wall. Compared to most of the people in the village, this was as rich as you could get. Birch looked round.

"God it's like a museum, people do actually live here, don't they?"

She looked round the large extravagant and tasteful living room.

"There is absolutely nothing in here that is remotely personal. She has that mutant of a son, why are there no pictures of him, come to think of it, where aren't there any family pictures at all, it's creepy Deads?"

I must admit, I had never noticed before, but now she had mentioned it. I could see she was right, we wandered out and down the hall towards the back, all the doors to the rooms were open, except one, and yes you guessed it, Birch wanted to know why.

I was already uncomfortable, this as far as I was concerned, was enemy territory, and my guard was well and truly up, I grabbed her sleeve.

"Please Birch, just leave it, we could get in a lot of trouble?"

She had that twinkle in her eyes, and I dreaded knowing what was going on in that over active brain of hers. I heard the catch click, oh bugger, she was going to go in, my heart rate increased, and I felt scared.

"Birch no... Please behave." She winked.

"Sorry I don't speak Marion English."

The door quietly opened, and as was becoming normal in my home village around her, that powerful sense of dread swept over me. She stepped in, grabbed my hand and yanked, I jerked forward with a yelp, and it was too late. I was inside the vicar's study, and she had slipped the door closed behind me. I stood there looking round at the walls of bookcases. Birch was up to no good.

In the centre of the room there was huge mahogany desk filled with papers. In the centre was a laptop, Birch went straight over to it, and grinned from ear to ear, she looked over it at me.

"Who leaves a laptop open. and logged in?"

"Honestly I don't care.... Birch we need to get out of here... If she finds us in here, we will be toast."

It was too late; she was already clicking with the mouse. I felt my heart in my throat.

"Bingo!" She looked up and gave a huge smile.

"You want to know about someone, look at their search history, and oh baby, I think we just won the lottery." She looked very excited. "Oh vicar, you naughty... Naughty boy!"

Okay she had won, I was intrigued and walked over.

"What have you found...? Holy Shit!"

Birch clicked open a link, and suddenly the sounds of thrashing and whipping came out of the computer on a low volume. I stared at the image of a woman in high heels and a mask, whipping a man who was tied to a medieval looking device. She lifted her arm, and then let go with the whip, I cringed as it stroked up his back leaving a thick red line, the camera panned back and I gasped.

"Why the hell does he have a hard on?" Birch chuckled.

"He likes it." I was horrified.

"Why the hell would he, she is whipping the shit out of him?" The whip cracked again, I cringed.

"Look at the frigging blood." She nodded.

"Deads people like this, it is normal for some people, this is what turns them on." I shook my head.

"Not me... I hate pain." She shrugged.

"It is far more normal than you would think, and actually, a lot of surveys have proven that marriages in the BDSM community, are actually more loving and stronger than many average vanilla marriages. I am telling you Deads, you would be surprised what turns people on."

"Christ Birch, I don't know how you can be so calm, our vicar is a pervert." She giggled.

"No Sweetie, I am the pervert, this is kink, and there is a difference... Oh Praise the lord, what have we here?"

Watching the video had horrified me, and suddenly I found I had a new emotion, sheer screwed up living terror! I looked at the screen, I stepped back and pointed in alarm, as my heart rate went into overdrive.

"WHAT THE FUCKING HELL IS THAT!?! Birch looked at me innocently.

"It's the vicar Sweetie, why?"

Words failed me, I stepped away from the screen not able to comprehend what I was seeing.

"No...No... No... No.... I cannot have that picture in my brain."

I shook my head, as I stepped away more from the image of what I think was a man, dressed in all shiny rubber, with a hood like mask. I had no idea what it was, all I knew was it had a mouth hole, nothing else, and there was something fucking massive sticking out of his bum. It was too much, and I could not handle it, my limit had been reached, I had only one question.

"Birch, how the hell is that the vicar?"

She was so calm about all this, and I could not understand how, my heart was hamming in my chest, she looked up from the screen.

"Well firstly it is in his private pictures folder, and secondly, look at the teeth."

Holy shit it was him, there was no doubt, my brain had collapsed. I was sweating like crazy, my heart was racing, and I wanted to look away, but I was glued to it with morbid curiosity, and could not move.

Birch reached into her bag and pulled something out. It was a memory stick, she plugged it in. My heart jumped again, and I flooded with panic.

"What the hell are you doing?" She gave me a huge smile.

"I am grabbing a copy."

I shook my head, hoping to shake some form of understanding

into my already malfunctioning brain. My voice came out as I felt... Confused, disgusted, in shock.

"Why.... Why Birch.... Why would you want to...? Whoa you are more screwed up than even I thought."

She closed down the picture, and pulled out the stick, and dropped it in her bag.

"Okay we have seen enough; I have what I need."

I am not sure 'seen enough' could fully explain how I felt, I wanted to run away and bleach my eye balls. If everyone made a list of things that should not be seen, I knew without doubt, I would win hands down. I was nineteen, and would carry that image in my brain for the rest of my life, death about now, felt like a merciful release from what would be a tortured life.

We slipped out of the door, and back into the hall, and I knew, I would never ever be able to look him in the eye again. I felt weak, my body was simply no longer strong, that picture had sucked the life force out of me. I grabbed Birch by the hand.

"I know the force is strong with you, but I think I am not cut out to be your jedi, I am too innocent to walk your path master." Birch gave a cackle.

"Training has always been hard my young apprentice, stay the course, and you shall arise a knight." She put her arm round me, as we walked towards the garden.

Out in the garden, on the vast lawn, all the villagers were surrounding Marjorie, as she laid on the woes of the previous night's events, and just as Hatty and mum had said, she was milking it for everything, including fake tears. Birch was once again in her bag looking for something. Her phone started beeping, and she pulled it out, and read the message, she smiled.

"Come on, we are needed."

She grabbed my hand and pulled, I spun on the spot, as Birch almost dragged me back into the house.

"Birch!... What the hell, I thought we were going to walk round the garden?"

She walked really fast, not letting go of me, we walked back up the hall, turned and headed up the elaborate wooden stairs. I was dragged along trying to keep my balance.

"Birch slow down, what the hell is going on?"

"You will see."

We turned right at the top of the stairs, and walked into the upstairs corridors, lower down, a door opened and Deb's peeped out, she gave a wave and disappeared, Birch moved towards the door and let go of me. She turned straight into the room, and I followed.

"Why is Deb's up here?"

I entered the room; it was Nigel's room. Against the wall was a large flatscreen connected to his computer, and on the screen was thousands of thumbnail pictures, and every one of them, was of me.

I felt my breath catch in my throat, and my stomach twisted, especially when I saw pictures of my bedroom window, where I was naked drying my hair, it felt worse than what Martin had done.

The tears welled in my eyes, and I swallowed hard, I had no idea why this hurt so much, it just did, and I felt wretched and I wanted to be sick. Birch looked at Edwina sat in the chair.

"Okay she has seen it, go to work." She turned to me, and pulled me into her arms.

"I am sorry Sweetie, but you had to see that."

I loved her for it, and I hated her at the same time. Deb's came in close.

"Birch asked us to check this out, he has been spying on not just you but all of us, he has pictures of all of us, even at the festival."

A black box opened in the centre of the screen, and Edwina started typing at high speed.

"Not for much longer, the next time that little fungus opens this folder, he will be in for the shock of his life, I am adding a live stream, so it should make for good viewing."

Lines and lines of words, symbols, and numbers, were appearing in the box, I had no understanding of it, but it appeared Edwina did. I wiped my tears and leaned in to her.

"What does all this mean?"

She was typing at high speed, watching the screen carefully.

"This is a bomb, it is a special kind of bomb, but when that little troll opens his picture files, he will have the shock of his life, as each picture deletes itself one after the other, he won't be able to stop it, and as he watch's, he will be live on camera for everyone to see. This time everyone else will be the voyeur, and he will be the one being watched." I got the basics of what she was doing.

"How will everyone be watching?" She smiled as she typed.

"I did three years at college writing code; I also dated a few hackers there. I built the community website and the forum connected to it. I just linked his live feed to every phone on its mailing list on that site, and they will get a live feed straight into their phones of our little Nigel, watching his perverted life be destroyed."

I felt a surge of emotion well up in me, and a lot of uncertainty.

"Are we doing the right thing here, two wrongs don't make it right?"

She typed in the line, and then stopped and looked at me, and smiled.

"You want the honours? Abby, you more than any have the right to activate it, just press that button and everything he has on you will go forever, and we are done."

I looked down at the keyboard, and the enter button, she smiled.

"You have more right than any of us, he has years worth of pictures of you, so press it."

I reached over, and my finger hovered for a moment, was this right or wrong, I was so unsure, I closed my eyes, and hit the button. I gave a small gasp, and opened them, and saw the screen.

The black box disappeared and a few others popped up, and then disappeared, his computer made a grumbling sort of noise as somewhere in the background, a hidden process was activated, Edwina clicked off the monitor.

"Okay we are done here." She got up, and patted my back, and looked at Birch.

"You were right about the password, I got in first time, no need to hack it. Okay let's go before we are noticed." I looked at Birch. She smiled.

"A-b-i-g-a-i-l, he really is fucked up."

I shuddered, and felt a cold tingle run down my spine. Edwina slipped her arm round me.

"I have added a little insurance, I will be watching him, and if he tries to upload anything else, I will see it and I will stop him, you have no need to worry Abby, we have your back." I nodded.

"Thanks."

We slipped quietly out of Nigel's room, back into the hall, Deb's pointed out each door.

"Bathroom, toilet, guest room, the vicar's room, another guest room." I looked at her.

"Do they not sleep together?" She shook her head, Birch giggled

"Would you? Can you imagine waking up to those teeth, showing through a black gimp suit, Christ that would give you the willies?" Deb's looked confused; I shook my head.

"Whatever you do, never ask what you are thinking, all I can say is, you never want to see it, and I have not the ability to put into words, what should never be seen, and I want to be a writer." She looked really worried.

"Okay, I won't ask."

"Trust me, you have been spared a fate worse than death, you chose wisely."

We reached the top of the stairs, and Deb's pointed down the other side of the hallway.

"Her bedroom and office are that way." I turned to go down the stairs, and I knew it, I just bloody well knew it.

"Ooh Guys!"

"Birch No."

"But Deads." I turned on the top step.

"NO!... I don't care what bat shit crazy idea you have bouncing around inside your head, I don't, I just want to get out here alive." She looked even more excited.

"Come on Deads it will be cool, all I wanted to do was masturbate on her bed, and film it to show her. It will be hilarious. I mean let's be honest, it will be the only sex that bed has seen this decade?" I shook my head.

"Birch I have a tolerance level for your messed up, twisted shit, but after that picture, I am way beyond my level. I am not filming you frapping on Marjorie's duvet, forget it." I started to walk down the stairs; I was leaving. She came down to my side.

"It's okay you know; I wasn't going to let them watch, just you?" I glanced at her, and she smiled.

"What can I say, I feel safe with you Sweetie?" I did not trust her at all, and glanced at her, she grinned.

"I just wanted to know if it would turn you on?"

"You are so well past screwed up; you have no idea how much I worry about you at times?" She leaned in.

"I know Sweetie."

I finally achieved my goal of the day, and successfully got Birch out of Marjorie's home without incident. We walked up the garden path, where mum was stood by the gate. She looked exhausted, for her it had been a very long day, taking donations and promoting the summer events list to as many visitors as possible.

"You look tired mum." She smiled.

"My feet are killing me; I wish I had worn different shoes."

"How long have you got left?" She gave a sigh.

"Few more hours yet, your dad will be here soon to help, he is on his way back now."

"We are heading down to the green, but if you need help, text us, we don't mind you know? I mean, we know they hate us, but these funds keep the village looking good, and we all want that too, so just let us know."

Hatty came moving quickly up the path towards us.

"Watch out the Fascist is patrolling."

"Harriet Barker! What are you up to?" Marjorie came strolling up the path.

"I was admiring your antique furniture Madge, you know, just making sure it was real." She scowled.

"You are always up to no good, what were you taking pictures of?"

I felt I nudge on my hand, and looked down, Hatty had her back to me, and was holding a memory card in her hand out towards me. I took it, and slipped it into my pocket.

"Just taking pictures for the parish magazine, and recording the event as I always do. You know, you should be more gracious Madge. I am doing my bit to help the village, even a whore like me can be useful."

She took a deep breath, and was just about to speak when Birch stepped in between them.

"I almost forgot, the money you raise keeps this village beautiful, and I actually think all of you have done a wonderful job protecting such a quaint and picturesque village."

She lifted a large bunch on twenty pounds notes out of her bag.

"As promised, a donation, keep up the good work. I fucked shit loads of men to make that much, I won't deny, I am a little worn out, but as Hatty said, even us whores have our uses."

She smiled as Marjorie's eyes opened wide, and I can honestly say I have no idea if it was the money, or the fact that Birch had told her to her face, she had fucked men to get it? What I can say is, both Mum and me stared and the floor as our shoulders shook with laughter, seeing Marjorie lost for words was priceless.

Chapter 25

Birthday Treat.

I was glad to be out of the vicarage, and glad to be away from Marjorie. Having seen all the pictures, and how many pictures were of me, which Nigel had taken over the years, felt like just another violation of my life here. My insides felt unsettled and mixed up.

I had heard Martin talking to Chloe last night, as I had approached the door, telling her how Nigel had showed him them, and I realised that the persecution that I had felt since coming home, had been going on for long before I returned. I was starting to understand that Nigel had played a much bigger role, in what had happened to me when I was sixteen.

I was starting to wonder, if it even was Martin, I had seen at the door that night as James had sex with me, and if was it actually Nigel who had shown Martin the pictures of James with me?

It looked to me like it would have made no difference if I had dyed my hair or not. I had been watched since long before I went to Uni, those pictures proved it, and I was starting to wish that I had never come home at all.

It was still early, so we gathered as a group on the green, surrounded by others, who were sitting eating burgers or just chilling out. We filled Chloe and Anthony in on all that had happened, it was Deb's who spotted the obvious.

"Where is Nigel anyway? I was sure he would have been in his room."

It was a question I could not answer, it had been strange that he had not appeared in his usual creepy way. Birch leaned back on the grass.

"Who cares, he is boring, I am hot and sticky, I need a pool and alcohol."

I was not going to argue, we were in full view, and no matter where we were or what we did, our every move was watched. It was decided that home and the pool would be a much better plan, and I just wanted to be as far away from the eyes of the villagers as I could be, which at the moment was home.

By the time we arrived home, the sun was at its highest, and it was roasting hot, just the walk home on the hot concrete was enough. In the house Birch was first to the pool, off came her clothes and in she went. Normally I would have gone straight in, but I felt a little strange, I looked at Anthony.

"Is this okay for you?" He gave a chuckle.

"Abby darling, you really have nothing I would care for, I do not have the level of confidence you have, but please, go have fun, just being here, being accepted is my joy."

I understood him completely. I had felt that way at Birch's house to begin with, especially with Bev there, and it had taken me a week to feel fully part of them, Anthony was still adjusting, he needed time, just to get use to the feeling of being accepted.

Feeling better about it, I jumped in with everyone else, while Anthony slipped off his jacket, neatly folded it, and placed it on the back of a lounger, and then relaxed with a beer. Our afternoon slipped by laughing and joking, and loving being cool in the water.

I was messing about with Birch, and Deb's when three loud beeps rang out over the noise of laughter, Edwina stopped at the side of the pool.

"Show time girls, hurry."

She pulled herself out of the pool, and dripping wet she grabbed her phone and opened it, we were all watching, she looked up.

"He just switched on, and is logging in, hurry up."

It was a mad dash, and sprint to the loungers, Birch ran straight to the guest house. I sat down on the lounger dripping all over the place, I swiped up the screen, and tapped the link to the site. Birch came to the door of the guest house.

"I have the laptop on, come on hurry."

Edwina gave a commentary from her phone as we all hurriedly headed into the guest house, and sat down on the floor in front of the table, where Birch had the laptop facing the room, Edwina watched her phone.

"Well I think we know now where he was today. He is going to upload new pictures, as soon as they enter that folder, and he tries to open one, the link will be activated." I suddenly felt very nervous, I turned to Birch.

"Is this right, are we doing the right thing?" She smiled.

"You saw what he has been doing, and soon my dear dark little beastie, you will see why, and understand why I worked with Edwina to set this up." Edwina looked up from her phone.

"There is an upload starting, it looks like he has quite a few new pictures, so we will now know where he was watching from today, he was certainly taking a lot more of us than I expected, get ready."

The link on the screen activated, and the full screen opened revealing a split screen, on one side was Nigel's desktop, and on the other was white noise, as the camera activated. The picture of Nigel at his desk appeared, and all us jumped back with a shriek.

"EWWW!" Deb's physically slid back two feet.

"Oh God.... Oh god.... Why would he?"

I froze, just understanding why he had taken all those pictures, made me feel sick, and my stomach twisted. Birch was all smiles, Chloe had her face in a pillow hiding, and Edwina was laughing. Anthony was caught between interest and revulsion, I was there with him, and Birch, well she is pretty twisted, and was enjoying the show with a smile.

Nigel was completely naked, in full view of everyone, and completely unaware. He had a bottle of lotion, and placed it on the desk, he lifted a towel to wipe his hand, and then grabbed his mouse with one hand, and his other, which was below the desk, started to stroke something, it did not take much to work out what. Chloe looked with horror on her face.

"Ew.... Is he doing what I think he is?" Birch smiled.

"Oh yes he is, he is showing the village to real truth of who he is."

On the screen the desktop side filled with the box revealing all the thumb nails of me. He went straight to one of the bedroom pictures of me naked, and clicked it. His stroke got faster, as it opened, and as he stared at it, his face in some ugly contorted, focused form of lust, he gasped out.

"Oh Abigail.... Oh Abigail... Abigail.... Abigail. His voice went higher, "ABIGAIL!!!!

I felt sick, and ashamed, and I went cold, it was not just creepy, it was vile, and perverse, and disgusting. My stomach churned. Edwina got excited.

"Here goes."

A pirate flag suddenly appeared on the desk top screen, and Nigel who was starting to stroke even faster suddenly frowned. The flag disappeared to show thumb nails popping and removing themselves from the file. He let go of himself, and stared with horror at the screen.

"NO!" He leaned in close to his monitor, his face contorting.

"No... No... No!" He grabbed his mouse, and started clicking frantically.

"Stop... Stop...No!" Nigel then tried hitting his keyboard keys.

"No, no stop, what is going on? Oh no, stop!"

He started banging the keyboard with his flat lotion covered palms, as he become more and more worked up. Tears appeared in his eyes as desperation set in, but there was nothing he could do, I watched as pictures of me taken for years just vanished, and Nigel started to whimper in desperation. He stood up to grab the screen.

"WHOA!!!"

This time everyone jumped back, as his aroused member came straight in to view, filling most of the screen. Anthony leaned forward.

"Oh, you poor darling." Birch leaned in to look closer, I stared at her.

"Jesus Birch do you need to look at it that closely, it has filled most of the screen?" She shook her head.

"No, I am regretting eating too many hot dogs today." Nigel sat down in his chair holding his head, and started to cry.

"Why is this happening?"

I felt a pang in my chest, but seeing him wanking to my pictures sickened me, and just knowing by looking at the pictures, he had been doing this for years, made me want to retch. So many emotions were flowing around inside me, I was unsure of what I was really feeling, the only thing I was sure of, was it hurt deep down inside me.

The oddest thing about the experience was no one was laughing, I was not really watching Nigel, I could not take my eyes off the screen, as I watched the photo file slowly empty, picture after picture of me just disappeared, and I felt relieved.

It also hurt, because the whole village had this live stream going to their phones, and everyone could see every aspect of my life for years, because Nigel had documented all of it. Somewhere off screen came a screaming voice.

"NIGEL!!" He jumped in his seat, and looked at the door with a terrified look. The voice got even louder.

"WHAT THE HELL ARE YOU DOING? THE WHOLE BLOODY VILLAGE CAN SEE YOU!" He stood up and yelled.

"NO DON'T COME IN!" He whole tiny erect member was in full view, and I shuddered, and felt sick.

The sound of the door exploding open, crashed in the background. Birch gave a squeal of delight, as Nigel jumped back, and grabbed his now falling manhood with both hands, to be honest one hand would have done it. Marjorie was off camera but was irate.

"TURN IT OFF, FOR GOD'S SAKE, TURN IT OFF, IT IS BROADCASTING TO THE WHOLE VILLAGE."

Nigel suddenly understood, and turned back to the screen with a shriek, and reached out for the camera, exposing himself again, but it was too late, it had been seen everywhere around Wotton, the screen went black as Marjorie's last words were cut short.

"YOU BLOODY STUPID, USELESS, IDI...."

It was now the giggling began; Deb's stood up.

"He deserved that, for what he did." She looked at me, and I could see the anger in her eyes.

"What he did Abby was disgusting, I am glad everyone knows."

The weird thing was, I wasn't, yet again, I had been the focus of yet another village scandal, it would be my name once again linked to another round of gossiping, and I knew exactly how that would end. Marjorie would target and blame me for everything. I looked at Edwina.

"She will know it was us." She gave a shrug.

"She cannot prove it, his computer was not hacked, I used his password, so all his computer shows is that he logged in, and he ran the code. His keyboard is well used, and he had lotion on his hands, it will be impossible to get clear finger prints to prove I touched it, and also, it is you and Birch, she will accuse, not me, so even if they did get anything, all it would prove is it was not you two."

Birch slid up at the side of me, and patted my leg.

"You will be fine, the whole village now knows he has stalked you, and what he has been doing with your pictures. There is not a woman who saw that, who will not see you as anything other than a victim, Marjorie will be the one who has to explain things." I felt sick.

"I need a drink, and some air."

I walked out of the guest house, and sat at the edge of the pool with my legs in the water, and sipped my drink. It was still really hot outside, and had been stifling with us all sat together inside. Chloe appeared, and sat at my side, she said nothing just slipped her arm around my shoulder, and pulled me towards her.

"I don't know how I feel Chloe, my stomach is twisting and churning, and I do not know if it is anger, or regret." She squeezed my shoulder.

"Give it time, and you will know."

My emotions had been on a roller coaster since arriving home, everything had been so clear in Manchester, I knew who I was, I had a sense of purpose, and even though life with Birch was crazy, I had felt an inner peace I had never known.

"I regret coming home Chloe; it has been nothing but hell since I walked down the street. All of them looking at me all the time, gossiping, and saying things about me that are not true, it has been so hard. He had pictures of me naked in my bedroom Chloe, he found a way to take pictures of me when I thought I was safe, and now everyone has seen them."

I felt my eyes burning, and saw the first two splashes hit the water and ripple, and there was no holding back. Chloe pulled me closer, as I cried. As my shoulders shook, she just held me, and her voice was soft, and reflective.

"Abby, when we were at school, I saw you as an enemy, especially after you punched me in the face. That first night when you came in to the restaurant, I was rude because I was jealous, and to be honest I got what I deserved. When I stood in front of you, Debbie and Birch on the green I was so scared, you have no idea, because the truth was, I thought you were the bravest person I had ever met, and I regretted the things I had done in the past. When I apologised, you could have told me to piss off, and I would have done, because I deserved it, but you didn't do that, and it still amazes me now. We made friends, and the last two weeks has been the best time of my life in this shitty village. Last night Martin would have raped me, I tried to fight him, but he was too strong. Before you all got there, I felt him put his dick on my bum, and slide down towards my hole, I gritted my teeth and waited for him to fuck me, because I knew there was nothing else I could do, I felt sick to my stomach."

Chloe took a deep breath, as if just thinking about it made her sick again.

"Today I wore clothes in this village I have only ever dared to wear in Oxendale. I helped run a tea stand with two ladies I have never even spoken to, and found out they were really sweet. Tonight, I am sat naked with my feet in a pool at your side, these are things I could only dream about two weeks ago. All the people saw was a side boob, your waist was below the window, hell you could put that on Insta, and it would not get taken down. Honestly who cares, I would walk through the fete naked with you at my side, because all we have done wrong is we just want to be us, and left alone to be it. If you have to be angry, be angry at Marjorie, because ultimately, she is behind all of this, and she will never understand the freedom, or happiness we have had together, and she hates us for it."

I gave a sniffle and wiped my nose on my hand.

"I am not really dealing with any of this very well am I?" She squeezed me softly.

"You are doing the best you can, and that is all that counts." I nodded.

"Thanks Chloe... You missed out, screwed a drummer in the dark." I chuckled, she giggled.

"You want to hear something weird?"

"Go on." She gave another little chuckle.

"When we got back, because it had been so dark, I had to look up what he looked like online, and he is defo not my type, oh god Abby, he was as ugly as hell, but my god his dick was awesome."

I couldn't help but giggle, Birch had been sat silently behind me, and I did not even know, she leaned forward and put her arms around me, I looked down at her delicate chains and bangles on her wrists, and lifted my hand to hold hers.

"Deads Sweetie, everyone now knows what kind of a person he is, and never forget your greatest power in this village."
I squeezed her hand, but if I was honest, I felt useless and powerless.

"What power do I have?"

"You have a mum and dad on the church council for starters, and you also just happen to have made friends with a very sweet boy, who hates injustice and works right in the heart of the gossip network. Nigel showed those images to a rapist, he was a friend of Martin, and because of that, Martin chose you and Chloe to attack, and so tonight we showed Nigel the power and danger of sharing images, and he will learn from it."

The patio doors opened and mum came out on to the patio.

"Abigail… Birch, can I see you a minute?" I felt the dread in my heart as I turned to her, she had called me Abigail.

"Give me a minute mum, I need to get dry." I grabbed a towel and dried my legs, Edwina tossed me a baggy top, Birch pulled on her long top, and we both walked up to the house, mum was inside standing by the counter. We walked in, and approached her, she said nothing, just pulled me into her arms and held me. It felt nice, I had expected an explosion. Mum looked at Birch.

"How involved were you?"

"It was all me Flick, Abby did not know about it. When I found out Edwina had done code at college, I asked her if we could get into the computer to delete the images he has been taking. I heard Martin telling Chloe he had seen the ones from the festival, that was when I knew Nigel was taking them, and sharing them with him, and I assumed Nigel was using them for his solo sex motivation. Edwina told me she could write some code to stop it, if she could get access to his computer, so the barbeque was our best chance. It was all me, I kept Abby distracted, and Edwina took care of the computer. The live stream was a last minute idea she had, because Marjorie had the council close her dad's restaurant, and force him to remodel it." She nodded.

"Thanks for being honest, and thankyou Birch for showing the village the truth, I really wish it had not been my daughter, but I think people needed to know." I looked at her.

"You are not angry with us?" She looked down.

"I am very angry, but as Edwin said, you were an innocent victim in all this, and my anger should be placed where it is deserved, at Marjorie's door, and he is right." Birch sat down.

"Marjorie knew about the pictures Flick, he showed them his mother, that is why she hit out at Chloe and Edwina, the pictures from the festival showed us all together having fun." Mum let go and lifted the bottle on the counter, she poured out three glasses. I took the glass.

"What has dad done?" She lifted her glass.

"He is on the phone, he rang Marjorie and threatened to press charges, and now he is talking to the other members of the council, he is very upset. I told him I wanted to talk to you two first before we acted." Birch took a swig of her drink.

"It cannot be traced Flick. This was done on Nigel's own computer, we worked out his password and logged in, it was not an outside hack, nothing on his computer shows it was done by anyone connected to Abby. It is why Edwina did it that way, if they try, it will look like he made a mistake and broadcast himself by accident, Abby is completely safe."

"Good... You will be pleased to know, Hatty was in hysterics when she rang me, she told me it was the best present she has even been given."

Mum chuckled and took a drink. I realised it was her birthday and had forgotten, I felt a bit guilty. The door behind opened and my dad walked in.

"Abigail... Are you alright?"

He walked right up to me and pulled me into my second hug in years. I relaxed and looked up at him, he looked tired and worried.

"I am fine dad, honestly I really am." He let go and swallowed.

"That little shit will suffer, I can assure you, I won't rest until...."

"Dad stop!"

He looked taken aback, and stumbled into silence, I took a breath.

"He has been punished, he was caught live on stream playing with himself to pictures he took in the village, do you not think that is enough?" Birch took sip of her drink.

"He also has a really tiny penis; I mean, my god; I think my finger is fatter and longer."

She held up her hand, and wiggled her little finger as she stared at it.

"Not sure any girl who saw that will want him, I mean, wow, talk about a needle dick!"

Mum gave a snort and giggled, I looked up and my dad was smiling looking at her, she looked round the room and shrugged.

"What....?"

I think that was the first time I heard my dad laugh in years. He just cracked up, as she smiled at him, and I stood back and watched in amazement. He roared out a huge belly laugh, and just exploded. I was stunned, but could not help starting to laugh with him. The phone started to ring and he took a deep breath in to compose himself, and chuckling, he lifted the phone to his ear.

"Peter, yes, I know, shocking, we are outraged..."

He turned, and left the room as he headed for his study, mum leaned over and kissed Birch on the cheek.

"You really are a most wonderful girl."

We returned to the garden, swam a few more laps of the pool to cool off, and then it was decided that seeing as it was Hatty's Birthday, we should go see her and celebrate.

After a mad scramble to get into our own clothes, we grabbed some booze and bags of crisps, and headed round to Manor Road, and knocked on her door.

Hatty's house had stayed pretty much the same as it had when her mum lived there, surprisingly she was a really neat person, considering she walked round the village in old clothes and covered in paint. She had a large desk in the corner, and a state of the art computer, she did a lot of sales from her website, using it.

The one thing I loved the most was her pictures, all her walls had framed art, but none of it was hers, all of it was from students she had taught over the years, but apart from that, it was just a very ordinary house.

The part of her house I loved the most was her studio, which she had built at the end of her long garden. It was as wide as the garden, and built from brick, and the whole of the front, had glass doors that could be slid right back, letting in the air and the light.

She was delighted to see us, as we wished her happy birthday, and like all visits to Hatty's, we ended up in her studio, which was far less orderly, but was just awesome. It was a huge room, that had a bed covered with all types of fabrics, a wall and large spotlights, for taking pictures, large shelved units, filled with thinners and brush cleaners, and several easels.

There were stools and old chairs dotted all over the place, on which she would pose models, and the floors were covered with pots of paint, and old rugs. The spare spaces had finished works on canvas, which were stood up in deep rows from the wall. It was an artist's paradise, and one Chloe loved the moment she walked in.

One easel stood alone in front of a stool, with a large canvass on it, covered in a sheet, that was her current project, and even though we were curious, it was clear, no one could see it until till done. We sat on chairs, stools, the bed, whatever was available and we all talked.

"What you did was taking a big risk, but I think it was worth it, it is about time that family got pulled down a peg or two. What you did right, was you inadvertently created a stale mate." Birch frowned.

"How?" Hatty smiled, and swept her hair from her face.

"Nigel has broken the law, he has taken pictures through a window without consent, and used them for sexual purposes, he has also shared those images, and that is illegal. You young lady, hacked his computer, and sent out an illegal sexual broadcast, which is again illegal. Both parties broke the law, but neither party can press charges, without admitting their own crime, it's a stale mate." It made sense.

"Does mum know this because dad is pretty mad?" Hatty gave a nod and smiled.

"They are both aware, I actually spoke on the phone with him about it, and staggeringly enough, we were cordial and polite with each other, that is why I am drinking, after that I needed several to clean out my mouth." I giggled with the others, I had to ask.

"So how have we come out in all of this, has it made us look bad?" Hatty shrugged.

"At the moment you are about sixty percent in favour, a lot of people are appalled at what he has done, most women say you

were violated, and the men who have daughters are fuming."
Birch looked at her for guidance.

"So, what now?" She took a drink.

"Martin and now Nigel, have put her on the back foot, so she
will go in defence mode as she tries to regain the initiative, so
watch your backs, her kind side towards you will be gone. When
it comes to all of you, she has a long arm, and will apply a lot of
pressure, so be wary. Abby stop hiding, it has been noted your
appearances are few and far between in the village, it is time you
took a more visible roll. The summer stage is set, and it is now
that campaigning begins for November. You need to be out there
showing the village she is not the only option, and that your mum
is a more open minded candidate. I told her all this last year, but
this year she has all of you, so start talking about Flick, and show
people they have a champion, because there are a lot of secrets
in this village, and that is the strangle hold Marjorie has on
everyone."

Chloe looked at her, none of us understood the village politics
like Hatty did.

"If they are secret, how do we know who to talk to?" Hatty
smiled.

"The events of Martin created a good distraction, because
Marjorie had an open house, and was too busy with that prissy
little stooge Marion, it is why I went. I got into her office, and
picked the lock on her filing cabinet, and oh boy did I get a
surprise." I dug in my pocket.

"That reminds me, this is yours." I pulled out the memory card
and handed it over to her, she smiled.

"Have you looked at it?" I was surprised, and shook my head.

"No... I thought it was private, so I have been holding on to it
until I saw you again." She winked.

"This is the key to helping your mum win, Marjorie has two
secrets, one of them shows she is using people's secrets to keep
them in line, which is why they fear her, and are compliant."
Birch leaned in with great interest.

"Who is she blackmailing?" Hatty smiled.

"Peter and Mary, Colin and Angela, Lillian and Celia, she knows
about Jeremy and me, but she cannot use that, as I will admit it.
She also has proof that Derek is dealing dodgy antiques. She has

a file on you Birch, but it is empty, apart from you being naked in the street, and you have already admitted that. There were more, but I found something else, but for now, I want to sit on that, it will be useful soon." Birch sat back and thought for a minute.

"Okay Peter and Mary, the post office, right? They are naturists. Lillian and Celia is pretty obvious, I mean how people do not know they are lesbians astounds me?" Chloe's head snapped round.

"THEY ARE LESBIANS?" I giggled.

"What you didn't know?" She shook her head.

"I just thought they were really kind, they were all over me complimenting me, telling me I was pretty, it was nice. Birch you should have warned me before leaving me alone with them." She shrugged.

"You were safe enough, they are really sweet, I like them a lot. I do think they are looking for a third to join in though." She winked at Chloe.

"Fuck that, I am not even a first." We all chuckled, as Chloe looked a little panicked. Birch continued.

"Didn't know about the antiques dealer, and who are Colin and Angela?" Hatty lifted her glass.

"They run the bakery; they are swingers." We all gasped, Chloe sat back in the old chair.

"Holy fuck the whole village are deviants, I feel sort of boring for being just straight." Birch smiled.

"Not that boring, you did screw possibly the ugliest drummer that has every graced a stage." She shuddered.

"Don't remind me, I will always regret looking him up on line." Edwina laughed.

"I saw him in the twilight, but I was not that interested in his face so a sat on it, and you cannot deny, he had a good dick?" Hatty gave a gasp.

"You let your sister fuck your guy, holy shit!?" Chloe nodded.

"The bitch never told me how ugly he was, I thought she was being nice, she just let me screw him, so I could not hold it against her." I had to laugh, as Edwina laughed at her sister. Hatty clapped her hands together.

"Okay I could not get more, but we know she is using people's private lives as a weapon, so what do you have?" Birch had that twinkle in her eyes.

"Well, the guy at the craft shop is growing weed, the butcher is boning the florist, and as for the vicar?" I shook my head in despair.

"Please Birch, I already want to tear my eyes out and burn them, do not afflict the people I love with such torture." Birch chuckled as she slipped out her phone, I turned to Deb's.

"If your soul is pure, do not look it will destroy it, and send it to hell."

I should not have said anything, Deb's just became even more curious. She slid forward in her seat as Birch located the picture on her phone and opened it up, and showed it to Hatty, she almost fell off her stool.

"Jesus Christ, Birch, what the hell is that?"

I looked at Deb's as Chloe craned her neck to catch a glimpse.

"If it makes Hatty do that, are you really sure you want to see it? Be warned Deb's, your soul like mine will be stained forever."

Birch turned the phone round and showed her, she fell off her chair, and pointed.

"WHAT THE FRIGGING HELL IS THAT STICKING OUT OF HIS ASS?" Birch swung it round to look at it, and Chloe recoiled away.

"Holy fuck!" Birch smiled.

"Yep, pretty much." Hatty sniggered.

"You are sure that is the vicar?" She spun the phone round for Hatty to take another look.

"Look at the teeth, there is no doubt. I would love to know whose legs those are, I did wonder if they are Marjorie's." Hatty examined the picture closely.

"I am not certain, I wish it was, I mean ramming a dildo that big up a man's ass, I think would be sort of her thing." We all shuddered at the thought, I felt my legs go weak just thinking about it. Hatty chuckled.

"I know about the weed; I have bought some of it."

I was shocked, Hatty smoked weed, this village was starting to look a hell of a lot more different than I had always pictured it.

The night continued, and we looked at some of Hatty's paintings, and as we admired them, and appreciated them, especially some of the nudes she had painted. Hatty asked if any of us would model for her.

What followed was a nude shoot, as clothes came off, and she set up her camera, and all of us posed. Anthony stripped down to his boxers, and as Hatty arranged him for the shoot, she told him.

"Good god Anthony, looking at your junk though those, you have more than enough for any guy, trust me, any way this is art, the rules don't apply." And with that, down came his shorts.

He was startled and shocked, and I walked over naked and stood at his side, and slipped my arm around him. Hatty gave a grin, and started to shoot as I smiled, and played around making him laugh, and before long Birch joined us, and the three of us posed with big smiles.

It felt odd being naked next to a guy, and being photographed, it was really liberating, and great fun. The poses were not rude or sexual, more classical in style, and by the end of the night Anthony was posing alone, as Hatty smiled at him.

"Wow you look amazing, it is so hard to get male models, I do hope you will do this again, I have a million ideas for great paintings?"

I think it did him a world of good, because the confidence we all saw, was not that of the fake Antonio, it was the real Anthony, and it was nice to see it.

The night had to come to an end, it was late when we hugged her goodbye, and wished her happy birthday for the millionth time, and all went our separate ways. As we left, she told all of us it had been her best birthday for years.

Later on, Birch and me lay in the dark in bed, she snuggled into me and relaxed.

"Deads I am sorry if I hurt you, I was trying to help you, did I go too far, because I know I can at times?"

I stroked her hair as she lay on my shoulder.

"No... It is fine, I think I had to see it to really understand it, he went too far Birch, not you, the way I saw it was you were standing up and fighting back, and I am grateful, but I also think I need to stand up for myself as well, it is not right you feel you have to do it."

"I made you cry, I hate that."

"No, he made me cry, it was never you." She kissed my shoulder.

"Good.... Night Sweetie, I love you."

"I love you too Birch."

Chapter 26

Community Service.

Nigel disappeared, and was nowhere to be seen, rumour had it, he had gone to stay with a relative in Cornwall. Marjorie also took a leave of absence, my mum had been involved in bringing six other choirs together for the choir evening, and so she took the lead role in the Parish Council, and covered for Marjorie. I kept a low profile at home, which involved lying in bed playing tons of music, and reading books with Birch.

Deb's did occasional volunteer days at the care home, and had asked us a couple of times if we wanted to join her, and so on Wednesday morning, joined by Chloe and Edwina, we jumped in Petal, and drove up to Wotton Dursley Hall. The old manor house, which had been converted into a home for the local elderly.

The Manor is a large estate that was accessed via the large gates on Manor Road, it was set in very large grounds of many acres, and was covered in large fully matured trees, hundreds of years old. My dad had actually taken me as a girl to see the cedar, and firs, and the many different types of pine, it had several massive old oak trees, and its crowning glory was a very old Elm, which had survived the outbreak of Dutch Elm disease.

The house itself was a listed building of immense size, it had over one hundred rooms, but alas the last real owner, Brigadier, Sir Albert Rupert Bagshot, had found the running costs far too high, and sold it to a chain of care homes, and retired to live in the Bahamas. I thought it was nice for the elderly, but it also made me feel sad, as I had seen it with my dad, with its elegant day rooms and an amazing library, and all of that was now gone, and the house was separated, into single rooms for each patient.

The doors to the main entrance however, were still very

impressive, as we drove up to them, where we were met by Ellen, Deb's mum, and given special tabards in bright orange to wear.

All of us trooped into the day room, where there was a wide selection of elderly ladies and gents, and we began our day talking to the patients and helping out with toilet visits and making brews.

My first impression as I watched half a dozen old ladies and gents with their walking frames, wandering around the furniture, trying to avoid each other, was it was rather like a senior citizen version of Pac Man.

They all muttered to themselves, or smiled at me, and it was good fun, especially for Birch, who had taken a strong liking to a lady sat in the comfy seated area in front of a large flat screen TV.

I was wiping down tables after breakfast, which was as messy as watching Birch cook, when she came up to me with a big smile.

"Oh wow, Deads, there is this old lady with grey hair, and she is awesome, I want to be like her when I go as bonkers as she is." I looked at her as I wiped.

"And you think you are not already because of what exactly?" She giggled.

"She is as cool as hell; I call her Granny Death." I looked at her, and lowered my voice.

"Birch for god's sake, you cannot call her that, you will offend her, you know, considering her age, why would you do that?" She turned and pointed.

"Look at her, she is just like the woman in the Darko movie." I had to admit she was not that wrong; she had a drawn face and long white hair.

"I think you should find out her name, it is more humane you know, treat them with dignity?" Birch nodded and looked back at her.

"Come on and meet her, she is lovely."

I followed Birch across the room towards what looked like a really sweet and cute old lady, sat in her chair. I crouched down and looked at her, she glared at me, and it was a little unnerving, so I smiled to show her I was friendly.

"Hi, my name is Abby, what is your name?" She scowled at me.

"Fuck off slut!" I blinked, and looked back at Birch, who was smiling, like she had won the lottery, I looked back at her.

"Excuse me, what did you say?"

"What, are you fucking deaf? Slutty whore, go on, piss off!"

I stood up, and backed off, feeling a little more than intimidated. Birch looked at me with a huge excited smile.

"She is great isn't she, I frigging love her to bits."

It was my own fault really, I should have known better than to trust Birch, and yes, add some black patches to her hair, and I was looking at what would probably be Birch in another fifty years' time. I could see why she liked her so much, I thought to myself as I walked back to the table, if she farts like thunder, they are a perfect match.

It took a while, but Birch finally found out she was called May, and her and May spent a good few hours walking round, as May insulted everyone she met, much to Birch's endless amusement.

There was a loud screech from the other side of the room, and we all turned, Chloe was stepping back, away from a grinning old man, she looked at us.

"Dirty old bugger just pinched my ass."

Several other old guys were looking at him with pride in their eyes, and grinning like idiots, Deb's looked at me.

"That one is Graham, stay out of arms reach at all times from that one."

I nodded feeling I had to be very wary, he sat laughing as Chloe rubbed where he had pinched her.

It was not long before Birch found another favourite, called Jessica. During lunch time as she worked with me, round the table handing out the meals, Ellen was dishing up from the meal trolley, Jessica looked up at Birch and smiled.

"Are you an angel as well?" It touched Birch's heart, and she gave Jessica a sweet smile.

"Oh Jessica, what a lovely thing to say, but no Sweetie, I am no angel at all." Jessica gave a big smile.

"That's good when Gabrielle comes to bed me again, he won't dump me for your bony ass then." Birch's face instantly lit up, and she laughed, and looked at me.

"I frigging love this place, it's awesome."

I just shook my head, and carried on serving. Edwina came up the corridor looking worn out, she walked in and came over to me.

"Do not go in the second toilet for at least an hour, there is guy in there called Burt, and he has a dick like a marrow, and he is just stood there stroking away. I had no idea what to do, so I just turned around and walked out. Hell Abby, he was bigger than the drummer, it made my eyes leak just looking at it. I am going to let him finish, I do not have the heart to stop him, he is so proud of that monster, and if I am honest, I would be too if I was a bloke."

After dinner, which was exhausting, we all grabbed wheelchairs, and armed with older ladies, we took them out in the grounds for a walk, well it was more of a push really. Dorothy was allowed a cigarette which Ellen gave us, and once outside she lit up, as Deb's pushed her along.

It was hot in the home, and even though it was a nice day and quite warm, being out felt cooler and fresher, and everyone appeared to enjoy it. Birch took May, who spent the whole time swearing at everyone, much to the amusement of Birch.

I drew the short straw, and got Jessica, who was convinced I was born of the antichrist, and spent the whole time telling me no angel would ever bed me, because I was a seed of hell, and would be burned at the stake when the day of reckoning came. I couldn't help but think that she reminded me a great deal of Marjorie.

The hours after dinner were a nightmare, everyone needed the toilet, so we spent over an hour helping old ladies on and off, and it was really hard work, and as Chloe pointed out, which I was at the time, trying my hardest to unsee what I had seen, and forget.

"Oh My God, I never want my vagina to look like that, and why is it hanging near her knees?"

She stepped back away, a look of complete terror on her face, she looked at me, her face white as a sheet.

"Did you know they can do that?"

Our shift was to end at 2:30, and by two I was exhausted and ready to go home, there was a moment of calm, and Ellen handed me a cup of coffee. I sat at the table I had wiped down a thousand times, and flopped back into my seat.

"Whatever they pay you Ellen, it's not enough." She smiled.

"You get used to it, the days fly by, and no matter what happens, you cope. They are a sweet bunch when you get to know them." I smiled at the look on her face.

"Deb's has your kindness and compassion; I really can see where she gets it from." I lifted my cup and took a swig.

"The people of the village should appreciate you more, what you do here is really hard work, and these are their relatives." She gave a nod.

"I cannot argue with you Abby, but you fail to see the real reason all these people are here." I frowned unsure of what she meant.

"The real reason, I thought all these people were sick, or not capable of living alone?" She took a sip of her drink, and watched me.

"Some of them are ill, many are now sliding into dementia related illnesses, but a lot of them were quite capable when they came here. Abby, you have more in common with these people than you realise, because most of them are here for two reasons, the first is they are all rich, and have greedy relatives who want to asset strip them. The second reason, which I think is the most important, is they had become an embarrassment in the village."

It hit me hard, as I looked round the room, Ellen saw me looking at them, and she leaned forward onto the table.

"You and I have a lot in common with these people Abby."

Hearing Ellen say it out loud really impacted on me, I shook my head and smiled.

"You should never feel like an embarrassment Ellen, you are such a kind and caring person. It is not us; it is them in the village, they have a sickness and are blind. Look at Deb's she is a wonderful girl, and honestly, going through what I have done these last few weeks, I would not have got through it without her, she really is amazing and she is so clever. I mean, the stuff she is doing at Uni, that even goes beyond Birch and me, I have to tell you Ellen, I really admire Deb's." She smiled.

"I am proud of her, and I love how Bradley idolises her, he spoils her too much, and I do tell him not to, but yes, she is a good kid, like you as well Abby, but life here is not like in Oxendale, we can never for one moment let our guards down." I understood her.

"They are wrong Ellen; they are blind and corrupt. Mr Wheeler is one of the good guys, I am glad Deb's and you have him, I remember how hard it was for Deb's at school, I am glad things got better for her." She put her cup down on the table.

"Bradley is tolerated because he is richer than all of them, it is the only reason they leave him alone. I won't deny I hate it, but he really is a good man Abby, and the daft thing is, he does not even care about the money. He gets more joy sitting in the country having a picnic with Debbie and me, than he does selling property. He is not like them, and he stands up to them, I really love him for that."

Edwina appeared looking terrified, she looked round the room, and spotted me an Ellen.

"I need help, I think Rosie exploded, and Chloe is trapped!" Ellen gave a titter and went to get up, I nodded at her.

"Have your coffee, I will help her, you still have a few good hours to go, we will be done here soon." Ellen laughed as I moved away, she looked back.

"Are you sure, if it's Rosie, you are probably biting off more than you can chew?" I waved back to her.

"No problems we can deal with it, there is three of us."

She chuckled as I left the room, and walked towards the toilet. As we approached the door, Edwina grabbed my arm looking panicked.

"Look Abby, I know she is my sister, but if you cannot get her out, abandon her to death by starvation or asphyxiation, be smart and save yourself."

I frowned, as I pushed the door open, Edwina stayed outside, I looked back at her.

"Are you not helping?" She shook her head, and put her hands to her mouth.

"Piss off, let her die, there is no frigging way I am going back in there." She leaned back on the wall, and took deep long breaths.

I went through the door and turned the corner, and stopped sharply, as the smell hit me, and caught my breath. Rosie was a big lady, it looked like she had been sat on the toilet, and had decided to get up, and walked out mid movement.

Chloe was sat on the sink in the corner with her legs up in the air looking desperate, as Rosie stood there crapping all over the floor. Chloe had her hands on her mouth, and retched violently, the smell was disgusting. She pulled her hand away from her mouth, as she saw me and screamed.

"SHE IS LIKE A FUCKING SHIT FOUNTAIN, ABBY, PLEASE TELL HER TO FUCKING STOP, BEFORE WE ALL FUCKING DROWN IN SHIT!"

I felt my stomach churn and I retched. I stepped back trying to breathe, it was everywhere, and it just kept coming. I could not get my head around it; the whole of the floor was swimming in her shit, my mind went into melt down, how could this happen? I looked at Chloe retching her heart out, I was starting to unravel and panic.

"Chloe, I don't know what to do, it is not her fault, she does not understand!" She pulled her hand off her mouth.

"CALL THE FUCKING FIRE DEPARTMENT, OR EVEN BETTER, GET THE FUCKING MOUNTAIN RESCUE, BEFORE SHE KILLS ALL OF US!"

I felt panicked, I had never been faced with anything like this in my life. I took deep breaths through my mouth, using my nose was out of the question, as the stench was the worst thing I had ever known. I felt utterly useless, and my brain raced to find a solution.

"Chloe just jump across it!" She looked stunned; her eyes opened wide in disbelief.

"Who the fuck do you think I am, Eddie the fucking Eagle? Abby these trainers cost me ninety quid, and they are brand new. There is no fucking way I will walk down there until that lot is gone.

Rosie gave a loud whining sound from her rear, and another load came splattering down, I jumped back, and felt the heave in my stomach, Chloe retched again, I was out of ideas. I had never dealt with anything like this, I could not handle it, and felt utter panic, I needed help, I turned to the door, and she screamed even louder.

"ABBY, PLEASE, DON'T FUCKING LEAVE ME TO DIE WITH HER!"

I came out of there a lot quicker than I went in, I slammed against the wall next Edwina, gasping in fresher air. Well, I say fresher, it was warm and stale, but was not saturated with that stink.

"I cannot handle this, I love Chloe, but you are right, it's better her than us." Edwina nodded rapidly, still holding her hands to her mouth.

"Yep, sacrifice the one to save the few, I am still young and aim to live."

"What's up guys?"

I turned to look, sensing hope in my utter desperation. Deb's and Birch were walking up the corridor towards us, I pointed at the toilet door.

"No words can describe what lies beyond that door, Chloe is in there, and she will probably die and haunt it like Myrtle for eternity. She was lucky, she got fucked over by a big ass snake, Chole will die by shit fountain." Birch looked at the door, and Deb's smiled.

"Is it Rosie, has she done it again?" I gave a rapid nod, still trying to keep my stomach from emptying, Edwina looked stunned.

"Again...? What! this is a regular occurrence? Holy shit, how many staff have died in there, at the hands of Rosie, and her explosive shit fountain?"

Deb's went in followed by Birch. A few seconds later the door swung open and Birch reappeared looking really excited.

"Guys come look, it looks just like a map of Africa." I stared at her with disbelief.

"I feel sorry for you Birch, you are like May, really fucked up, and you don't even know it." Edwina retched.

"Birch! for god's sake, close that bloody door!"

It took until almost three for Birch and Deb's to clean up enough for Chloe to come down off the sink. I cannot deny, they were our heroes. Ellen took Rosie for a shower, and we handed in our orange tabards, and finally walked into the heat of the day, and felt cooler, and relived it was over.

It was an important lesson for me. I really felt for Rosie, she was completely out of it, and had no idea of what she was doing. Just the thought of crapping myself in public terrified me, and yet she did not bat an eyelid. God is that what life comes to, stuck in a toilet covered in shit, and not even able to understand how awful that is?

I left the care home thinking life was a bitch. I really felt sorry for those poor residents, they had all lived full lives, with love and fun, and people they cared for, and yet most of them were no longer aware of it, and it felt cruel.

I realised how important now was, and this summer had been a really tough one, but at the end of the day, it was all irrelevant. I can see that to live life and enjoy it, is all that is important, and for those who are so blind they cannot see it, and call people like my friends and me, for what? Dressing differently, or changing our hair colour, I feel really sorry for them.

The residents of Wotton Dursley, were no different from those in the care home, they had forgotten how to live, and probably all the dreams that they had when they were younger. I had no intention of being like that, I wanted to live every second like it was my last, and I wanted to embrace every moment of life I could, especially with Birch.

She was so at home in the madness of each day, just like she was with May or Jessica, to her it was not insanity, it was living a new experience. It was real, another different moment, and as I sat in the back of Petal, looking at the freed Chloe inspecting her trainers, I realised that hiding at home was wrong, because that is what the people of the village were already doing, they were hiding from each other, and hiding from themselves.

We dropped Chloe and Edwina off, and headed home, Chloe was the in the choir and doing tonight's solo, so she had to get ready, and then we headed back to the house.

Birch rolled into Petal's parking spot, and we jumped out, and I walked to shut the gates. I turned round to see the distinguished looking figure of my Uncle Jeremy, talking with Birch, I gave a sigh, was there no level he would not stoop to?

I crossed the drive, and walked down to him, he had been sitting on the loungers, and seeing Birch, he had naturally pounced. He noticed me as I approached, and smiled.

"Abigail darling so nice to see you."

"Cut the crap Uncle Jerry, she is off limits." He rolled his eyes.

"Really Abigail, I was just being polite." Birch looked at him.

"No, you were hitting on me, but I am aware you are married, and I was seeing just how far you would go. I am sorry Jerry, but in this case, your reputation arrived long before you did." He looked offended.

"I see I have no secrets here." I agreed.

"Not in this house, I was there remember? You know, when you took advantage of Hatty, and then used her to piss my dad off, and get her banned from here, so you could keep shagging her behind your wife's back?"

He was understandably pissed off with me, but I was not about to lie.

"I can see Manchester has rubbed off on you far more than your family have realised?" Birch took offence.

"Whoa old dude, you bloody well wait a moment, so what are you saying, I am good enough to screw, because what, I am from Manchester, and that is all I am fit for?" He stumbled for words.

"I would not have put it that way, but..." Birch had heard enough.

"Screw you!"

She pushed, and he went falling backward into the pool with a squeal, he surfaced, spluttering, Birch leaned over the edge to look at him.

"I may be from Manchester, but you will never be good enough to screw me old man, so let's just have that particular record set straight, you prick."

I was not even aware that my mum stood watching, and I only realised once she started clapping, and laughing. Birch grabbed my hand, and dragged me to the guest house, she appeared to be really angry. She paced up the room and turned, and paced back again, she stopped, looked at me, and then paced more. I did not know what to do, I just looked at her not understanding, I had never seen her this way before, and it really worried me, finally she turned to face me and her green eyes shone like I have never ever seen them before. It was her anger.

"Let me be clear.... If I ever sleep with someone in this family.... It will be you... I want to, I really do... But I am not there yet, and it could take some time. Your uncle is a real prick, do you know that?"

She actually looked embarrassed, and she looked at the floor.

"You really have changed my life Abby, you have no idea how important you have become, I am a total screw up with sex on the brain, but being here and living with you, it has been the best time of my life, and I love you so much, I just…. Well, if I am honest, I am not sure I can go down on you like Bev would, I almost did, and I have thought about it, but I am not ready, if I ever will be that is."

What the hell do you say to that? I just held up my hands.

"My pussy is sweet, or so I have been told." Her face broke into a huge smile.

"I figured it was, which is why I call you Sweetie." She smiled, and I had to laugh.

"Birch you are getting a little carried away here, I love our friendship the way it is, you don't have to do more you know? Just relax and have fun like we always have. Honestly Birch, I am not in a rush to have sex with any woman, but again if I did, it would be you; I have told you that. Look one night we will get pissed as rats and do it, so I am not going to worry about it until the morning after." She gave a sigh.

"Just as long as you know I would never have slept with him; he is a bit bloody creepy don't you think?"

I suddenly realised what was going on her crazy head, she had thought I was angry at her, because she thought I had really thought she was going to sleep with my uncle, could she really not see I was trying to protect her, and get her out of a tight spot? I understood her more than any, but I knew I still had a long way to go.

Another thought came into my head, as the strange events of the day collided in my thoughts, I looked at her.

"Is this because of today? Birch not everyone ends up like that, we don't all forget, some of us keep everything in our thoughts until the day we leave."

Her green eyes stared at me, as she stood frozen in front of me, she licked her lips and slightly shook her head, her voice was quiet.

"Deads, what if I am May? I know the psychology behind what she has, it could happen to me, and I don't want to live like that, I don't ever want to forget a single moment of the joy we have had.

Deads it scared me, it really scared me to today, because I don't want to be like that, like Rosie, covered in her own shit, and not even knowing."

I gave a sigh, and walked over, and pulled her into my arms, and suddenly there was the serious side of Birch.

"Oh Birch, you can be so silly at times. Birch if you end up like that, I will be there with you, and if I end up like that, I know you will be there too, so why worry about it, no crazy will part us, hell it was crazy that brought us together. We will be together no matter what." She squeezed me hard, and held on for a few minutes.

"Just as long as you are with me, I can cope with anything Deads, just as long as you are there, that is all I care about."

She can be so childlike at times, I patted her back.

"Okay let's eat and then get ready, we have the dullest choir concert ever to attend, and show our support for my mum, I thought I would do a stir fry, what do you think?"

We decided to take Petal, and park outside the salon. We drove to the church, turned Petal around, and parked front facing down the street, in order to make a fast get away, if one was required.

The three of us jumped out, and met up with Anthony and Edwina outside. As always Marion was on the door, she looked at us like we were dirt, and I smiled as I passed her and entered.

The place was far more crowded than I expected, and with the loss of Martin, a new piano player was required, and thanks to Hatty, a very able candidate was found, in the shape of Louise Banks, the music teacher from the high school at Oxendale.

We sat at the back like last time, and watched as the room filled up, unlike last time a lot more people appeared to nod to us, had our standing in the community improved? I was not sure. I was more surprised when Peter Saxon came up to me and offered his best wishes.

"Abigail, I have known you since the day you were born, and like many, I have watched you grow up, I cannot deny, recently, there have been some changes no one expected, and I am not sure how I feel about that. Mary and myself have always liked you, you have always been polite and respectful, and so we want you to know, we think that what Nigel did was despicable and disgusting, and we felt genuinely sorry to see you were targeted in such a depraved way. We hope you know, that we hope you will make a good recovery, and not allow it to dampen your time home?"

I could not ask for more, and I smiled my best smile.

"I am very grateful to you and your wife, Mr Saxon, it has been a big shock, but I have my family and friends around me to help." He looked at Birch and she smiled.

"Cape D'Agde or Almeria? We did Almeria three years ago, wonderful place, especially the beaches, I have heard contrasting stories of Cap D'Agde, I wondered if you knew it?" He looked a little rattled.

"Stick to Almeria, it's probably safer for you." She smiled. He looked back at me. "Take good care of yourself Abigail."

He walked back towards his wife who was nervously watching, he sat down and they spoke, Mary looked back a few times.

The event was about to start and my mum walked on stage, and took a deep breath and began her address into the mic.

"Good evening everyone, and on behalf of the Parish Council, I would like to say a big thank you for attending tonight. We have a few changes to the bill, firstly, our Council Chair Person who would normally take this role, has been called away to attend to some pressing business, and so I have stepped in for her. Birch leaned over.

"Pressing as in squeezing the chopped up remains of Nigel into an old burial spot at the back of the church." Deb's sniggered.

"I am Felicity Watson, and Vice Chair. Recent events have meant that our long standing pianist My Hinkley, has been detained on other business, and so we have brought in a very accomplished pianist, in Mrs Louise Banks, head of music at Oxendale High. Please show your appreciation for her cover at short notice. Birch gave a chuckle.

"He has been detained alright; he is in HMP, don't ruddy well pick the soap in the shower up." I had to giggle. Deb's looked at her.

"Isn't that just a myth though, and not really a thing?" Birch looked at her.

"What the hell Goggles, of course it's a thing, if you bend over for the soap in prison, you end up impaled, just like the vicar." She shuddered and looked paler.

"You promised me that would never be mentioned again." Birch giggled, I sniggered and leaned forward in my seat.

"I did warn you Debs." She shuddered and held her palms up.

"Don't, just don't, it makes my legs feel wobbly just thinking about it." Birch sniggered again.

"You know that is probably why he was on his hands and knees; he lost his ability to stand." Edwina leaned forward and looked at me.

"Or he was praying for someone to pull it out."

We all sat on the back row trying to laugh quietly, even Deb's started to giggle. Deb's looked quite serious.

"I couldn't go to church on Sunday because I am afraid to look at him, mum was not too pleased, and when she asked me why, I did not know what to say. She thought it was because of Chloe, and I went along with it." Birch grinned at her.

"So, you didn't tell her it was because the last time you saw him, he had three feet of dildo sticking out of his ass?" Edwina stamped the floor, and bent over to hide her laughter, Deb's gasped with shock.

"Hell no... Jesus Birch, how would you even tell someone that?" She shrugged.

"Not sure, you can hardly say, hey mum, I saw the vicar today, and guess what he had sticking out of his ass? I see your point Goggles."

"Please stop Birch, I think I am going to pee myself." Edwina got up and headed for the ladies at a fast pace.

All the visiting Choirs gave their presentations, Saint Augustine's came last, if I am honest, it sounded beautiful, but I did feel it would have sounded so much better in a church, as the acoustics were perfect for singing. Chloe stepped forward for the lead, and she was really good, it was strange in a way, because that had been my part for several years. Birch leaned in.

"Do you miss it?" I shook my head.

"Not as much as I thought I would, I think it is a shame Chloe is quitting, she is better than I was, she really does have a beautiful voice."

"It is hard to believe not four hours ago, such a beautiful voice was hurling more than colourful language at us, for not saving her from the shit swamp quick enough. Hell, she called Rosie, but for a moment, I thought she was going to match her in vomit."

When the event ended, we all stayed back to help clean up, the hall had other uses over the summer, and the following day there were yoga classes, and an indoor badminton tournament. We moved the chairs folded them up, and then checked all the windows and doors were closed. Anthony was tired, he had an early day tomorrow, and he walked with Chloe and Edwina towards home.

The three of us waited until mum was safely in her car, and then jumped in Petal. I sat in the back, as Birch pulled away from the curb, and there stood at her gate, was Marjorie, wearing her familiar scowl of hatred, watching as always. I stared at her all the way down the road, it sounds odd, but I just felt this was not over, something inside told me she would come back and fight harder, and she would not stop until she utterly destroyed me.

Chapter 27

Unexpected Surprises.

No one ever really notices how much work goes into a Village Fete. Almost overnight, our kitchen went from a normal family kitchen, to an operations room. In the dining area, the family table had its drop leaves lifted, and locked into place, and paperwork began to appear from every direction.

The study was just as bad, as cardboard boxes appeared in long rows on the floor, stuffed with yet more. This was my mum's side of organising, apparently every other council member had the same.

The church hall was still in use, and so for now, every house was a hive of activity, and on Monday August 19th, each operation would be assigned a set of tables, and the whole lot would be moved to the hall, and the big push for the fete would begin.

Before that, there was plenty to do, we had cakes to bake, jam to create, and flowers to arrange. Mum set up in the garage, on a long table she covered in plastic, and all of us attended late Saturday afternoon, for a lesson in the composition of a good arrangement.

Birch was very excited about it; her experience of flower arranging had been a few ikebana lessons, years ago, which taught her little, and as she so delicately put it.

"Cut the base of the stems off, half fill the vase with lemonade, and then dump the bastards in."

Mum could see how that would work, but assured Birch, she could help her improve and be 'a tad better.'

Our first lesson was choosing a container, and we had plenty to use, mum had a huge box filled with jugs, glasses, vases, and other water containing items, and we all had a good root around, to find something that would suit.

Birch was delighted to find a pot boot, Anthony grabbed and artistic vase, Deb's and old milk jug, Chloe a flowery vase, Edwina a metal measuring jug, and I was very happy with an old metal lamp, into which mum had fitted a black plastic tube.

Mum explained the concept of balance, and the uses of foliage, and a lot of other things that made no sense to me, and Chloe looked blankly at her and asked.

"So basically, we just piss about with them, until we think they look good?" I looked at mum and nodded, that I understood.

Mum's exasperated gasp, pretty much was her surrender, and so she let us lose with buckets of flowers, until we all stood back eyeing our efforts, feeling we had created something as important as a Rembrandt.

Anthony was pretty good, his arrangement looked really impressive, Birch's had a wild somewhat raggedy look, but it was far better than mine, and she named it "Boho Heart," and we all agreed, it was perfect.

We had a week to improve, as the final arrangements would be made on Friday, morning, and displayed on Saturday for judging. With our first attempt over, we headed for the kitchen and drinks

Dad was home working at the dining table organising, and he had booked from Wednesday off, as he would be overseeing the erecting of the tents, and marking out all the pitches for the traders and amusements. He had a huge plan laid out on the table, double checking each stand or stall carefully with his list of those who had booked.

We all sat at the counter, where mum handed out cold bottles of beer to us, she even had one herself. We sat there laughing when the phone rang for the millionth time that day, mum answered, and then looked at us, she handed the phone to Birch.

"It's for you." Birch frowned and took the phone.

"Hey Bitch, you owe me a sauna, I just finalised a deal with some posh bird called Celia, your mum will be there to give a talk. I am not sure on what, she will choose probably today, but she wants you to video call her at six. I want you naked and steaming, on the first Saturday you are back, it is now an official deal, back out at your peril Bitch." Birch giggled.

"No worries, I will be bringing a friend, and she is hot as hell, I think safety in numbers around you is advisable." Katie gave a chuckle.

"If she is not eye candy, I am spanking you good in the steam room."

"If you are coming down you will meet her, she is called Deadly, and you won't be disappointed."

I turned to look at her a little concerned, what was she getting me into now? Judging by my mum's face, she was thinking the same. The call ended and Birch smiled.

"You have your special guest speaker Flick, and she will be free, no charge, but there is one slight condition, no one must know she is my mum. She is Dr Veronica Gemma Dixon, and I am just Birch, will that be okay?"

Flick looked at Edwin who had looked up from his plans, and turned and smiled.

"We owe you a huge thanks, the special guest speaker is such an important aspect of the event, not having booked anyone would be a real dampener to the event. I really am all of a flutter, and I have no idea how to thank you." Birch smiled.

"Thank Abby, she is the one who told me how bad it would look, which is why I got Katie on the job, but be warned, she draws a big crowd. Make sure you have every seat you have out, my mum will fill them, especially at only £5 a ticket, she normally charges £125." She turned to me, and winked.

"The publicity wagon will be here Wednesday to boost advertising; Katie is already on the phone letting people know, and updating the web site. Oh, just so you know, we are having a spar day with her when we get back to Manchester, so guard your vagina."

"What?"

Deb's looked equally as startled; Birch giggled. Anthony, Chloe and Edwina, did not have a clue of what we talking about, and just went on Deb's reaction. Deb's looked at me.

"Will you be alright? You know Birch, it bothers me that we have to guard our vaginas whenever we meet your friends." Birch gave a snigger, my mum looked alarmed.

"She is prettier than Bev, but way more ferocious." Deb's stared at me, and swallowed hard.

"Oh hell, not again!"

Chinese takeout was ordered curtesy of dad, and delivered, and we all sat out on the patio, and tucked in to an early meal, as my parents had plans for the concert at the hall tonight. We had done another few day's of no drinking, mainly because we had been so busy helping out.

We frolicked in the evening sun, whilst Birch talked on her laptop in the guest house, mum and dad returned to their tasks. It was our first free night, as we had been so busy since the choir event.

It was a pretty warm evening as we moved pool side, and relaxed with full stomachs on the loungers, and talked of life, the fete, jams and cakes. Deb's was the first to strip and jump in the pool, and suddenly over the next hour one by they jumped in, and splashed around having fun. I gave Anthony a nudge.

"Just do it, it is obvious you want to." He looked back at the house.

"Your parents are here Abby, what will your dad think?"

"Seriously Anthony, he has given up trying to get anyone here wearing clothes, they will also be heading out shortly for the bands concert at the hall. If you are bothered, keep your boxers on, come on."

I slipped off my shorts, pulled my top over my head and dived in. A few minutes later still in his boxers, Anthony joined us to great applause.

My dad looked out of the glass door.

"Are you fine with that, I mean he is a boy after all?" My mum gave a titter.

"Edwin, you have met him and spoken to him, they are safer with him than anyone else."

Suddenly realising, he looked back at the pool, where he watched as Edwina dived in, grabbed Anthony's shorts and pulled them off.

"Oh, I had not realised, he is like that, oh dear, I always thought it was an act.... It's not, do the villagers know?" Mum came to his side.

"Probably not, and maybe it is better that way, he is a really nice boy. I like him, and he has talent for flower arranging that is pretty dammed good. I am quite looking forward to seeing what the judges say."

Edwin watched from the kitchen, as we all fooled around and

laughed, Birch having finished talking to her mum, came running naked out of the guest house, and dived in, he smiled.

"You know Felicity, Birch does have a knack of pulling together all the lost sheep. I think it is a shame Marjorie cannot see that." She smiled at the counter, and opened two beers.

"Here, take a break, you deserve it, and then we better get ready, and hope tonight goes off well, everyone is looking to us at the moment, with Marjorie out of the frame."

As it grew cooler, we grabbed our clothes, and took the fun into the guest house. Birch plugged into her laptop, as I grabbed mine. The music went on, and the glasses were refilled, and we crashed out all over the floor laughing and joking, where I filled in the blanks behind guarding my vagina from Bev. I sat there laughing.

"Honestly, I really thought I was going to be raped, and Birch just says ever so casually. Lie back on the bed and take your pants off, and I was like, fuck you Birch, let her have yours, mine is a man only zone."

They all burst out laughing, and suddenly Birch raised her arm and waved, we all quietened down and she looked at me.

"I had completely forgotten about this, my mum gave me this link, because she thought I should watch this video interview she did, and I know it is important, but I am missing something. I have a listened to this guy who is talking about doing water sports."

Birch unplugged her head phones, and turned up the volume, and we all sat quiet, and listened as the guy talked about the golden rain. I suddenly realised what the video was about. I am not sure Deb's got it, but Edwina was on it immediately, she leaned back closer to the table to listen better.

The guy droned on and on about the joy, Deb's was lost. Birch was staring at the screen, focused on every word, but nothing, and then suddenly I heard it.

"People will never understand the intimacy of it, I have never felt closer to Marion than I do having done this."

I thought my head was going to exploded, I stood up really fast.

"HOLY SHIT!" Everyone jumped, and turned to look at me, Birch was all eyes.

"What?" I stared at her trying to understand this correctly.

"Birch he said Marion." She shrugged

"So what?" And then like a bolt of lightning it hit her, and she stared at me.

"No fucking way.... That prude of a little miss perfect? No, we must be wrong, I mean Christ Deads, we are talking Marion for god's sake, she does not even show her vagina to the toilet, let alone piss on someone." Deb's gasped.

"Whoa hang on.... Who pissed on who, that's gross?" Edwina patted her leg.

"Keep up girl, they are talking about Marion and her water sports." She nodded.

"I thought it was sailing and yachting, not pissing Edwina, who the hell does that?"

Chloe smiled and winked at her, and was very casual.

"What have you never pissed on a guy Deb's?" She looked horrified.

"Oh my god no.... Holy shit, have you?"

The look on Deb's face was one of absolute shock, she slowly moved away from Chloe, although I have to admit, I was also really interested in knowing. Chloe giggled.

"No... But I would if he asked me, but if he tried any of that shit with me, I would cut his hose off."

I have had a lot of strange moments in my life to date, but stood in a small confined room, with four other naked girls, and a naked guy, talking about golden showers, has to be the weirdest to date, and yet it was happening.

Birch skipped the video back and put her headphones in, and listened again very closely, I watched her eyes as they moved to the words and she understood. It was strange, she was quiet and as still as a rock, with just her eyes moving, sat by the window and framed in the last light of the day, and I cannot deny, with her patchy long white hair, and her perfect body, she looked stunning.

It is weird, Chloe and Edwina have amazing bodies and are both pretty, I can see that, and it does not bother me at all, Deb's is my best friend in the village and it's the same, but when it comes to Birch, I cannot deny, I am super attracted to her, and it makes no sense to me at all. How can I only be attracted to one woman, and not others? I do not think I will ever fully understand me.

Anthony got up to go to the loo, he stepped over the others, and entered the bathroom, Chloe nudged Deb's.

"Now is your chance, go ask him." We all started laughing, she shuddered.

"Screw you, Chloe."

Birch sat back, and took her head phones off.

"This makes no sense, let's just say the woman is Marion, which is highly unlikely, then the guy she does it to must be from round here, so this so called Derek, has to be a local, but who?"

She swung the laptop round, and we all looked at the darkened figure on the screen. I leaned forward to get a close look at the face that had been shaded to hide his identity, it was impossible to tell who it was.

Chole and Edwina knelt up and looked to no avail, Anthony returned from the toilet, and just glanced, and he tutted.

"Well, I mean, that hair no matter how dark it is just jump's out of the picture doesn't it? I mean look at it, there is no hiding that. I have been trying to get the thing tamed for years, but he won't let me near it with the scissors. I told him I did, you will look ten years younger when I have finished, but no, he knows best, and his wife cuts it.... Cuts it, really, I would say it's more butchered, I wouldn't be surprised if she used a scythe."

Everyone in the room was staring at him, he looked at us and swallowed.

"Am I rambling again?" I shook my head.

"No.... Anthony, do you know who that is?" He gave me a strange look.

"I just told you.... Didn't I?" I shook my head again. He gave a smile.

"OOPs! As I was saying, that mop is not at all hard to miss. I have no idea who this Derek is, but that there with that uncreative monstrosity for a haircut, well that is Ronald isn't it, you cannot miss that rough flick by his left ear. Honestly, Abby darling, I want to chase him down the street, and cut it off, it infuriates me."

My brain went into turmoil as I looked up at Birch, who was staring at the picture.

"You mean the gardener guy who cuts the grass?" Anthony gave a nod.

"None other, it's him, it's so obvious."

I was trying to process all of this, but my brain refused to let me. Chloe, Deb's and Edwina knelt up, and Birch turned the screen round to them. Edwina screwed up her eyes.

"I am pretty pissed, but I do think Anthony has a point, Abby, pull the village website up, and let me compare."

I dragged my laptop across the floor, opened another window, and typed the address, the site came up, and I clicked the tab for the village maintenance, and there he was pushing his mower. Anthony pointed to his left ear.

"See... ooh it's infuriating."

I lifted my laptop and placed it at the side of Birch's, and there it was, a perfect match to the shape of the guy called Derek on her screen.

"Holy shit, it is Ronald." Chloe chuckled.

"Dirty old Ronald, he is getting pissed on by Marion, whoa that is the most fucked up thing I have ever heard of in this village."

Wasn't it just, but I was still having a hard time dealing with it, I mean we are talking about Marion, the woman who uses words like Potty Mouth? I shook my head.

"There must be another Marion around here, there is no way it can be the Marion we know." Deb's shook her head.

"Ron is about fifty isn't he, and Marion in her mid thirties, he is so rough, and scruffy, he smells of oil. Marion is all prim and proper, it must be someone else, they are complete opposites." Birch sat back on the wooden chair.

"Weirder things have happened Deb's, it is that which makes me fascinated by it, you just never know who is up to what. Behind closed doors Marion could be a completely different person. Let's be honest, if it is her doing it to him, that is a very powerful thing, especially for someone who is completely dominated by Marjorie. I think it makes far more sense than you realise. Don't forget who put me onto this, my mum can walk down a street and point people out, and tell you what they get up to, she has like a sixth sense about sexual deviance." Edwina sat back down.

"That's me screwed then... Remind me to stay indoors if your mother visits."

For the rest of the night, we sat and relaxed, and shared stories of growing up, Birch was distracted, and not her usual fun self, she had her head phones on, sat at the table and was typing, I wandered over and looked at her laptop. She was writing at high speed, something I have seen her do a thousand times. She looked up and took her head phones off, I smiled.

"What are you doing?" She looked at the word document open on her computer.

"I am writing mum's talk for the event, she asked me earlier what would be the best subject for this place, and when I told her, she asked if I would like to write the first draft, and she would add to it." I was impressed.

"Wow Birch does she let you do that; I think it's awesome?" She gave a nod.

"I started doing it with her a few years ago, she thinks it will help when I join her practice. I have to work to her standard for three years before she will allow me in as a partner. To be honest Deads, it sounds impressive, but it is a lot of work, and mum sets a high bar, I need to learn a lot more before I can stand next to her."

Once again, I saw yet another side to Birch, she never failed to shock and surprise me. I mean, I know about her work at Uni, I have watched her for a year, she studies like no one I have ever known, if I am honest, she has been my biggest influence. Just watching her in my earlier term, I felt driven to work as hard as her, which is probably why I have done so well. Yes, she can be wild and crazy, and often appears flaky, but I know when she gets her head down to it, she drives herself hard to achieve the best.

Seeing her write for her mum, who is an internationally renowned authority in her field, just blew me away. I know her mum, I have spoken to her mum, hell I lived with them, and I guess I saw her mum as something bigger. Just watching Birch, as she typed at high speed, and knowing it was all from memory, I suddenly realised, they were the same, and I have no idea why, but it blew my mind.

I left her to work, and I settled back on the floor with Chloe and Edwina, and had a few more drinks, it felt good, as I looked round at the people who were naked, and relaxed. Each of them had added to the fun, they had each brought a special something to the group, and in such a short space of time, they had become so special to me.

These were the friends I should have had known growing up, well Deb's was, but the others I had known of, yet never bothered to talk to them. Admittedly I was shy and afraid, but I regretted the fact I had not approached them sooner, could my life have been better or different, I really was not sure?

I came out of my thoughts as Chloe nudged me, Deb's was smiling at me, I jerked back to reality.

"Sorry, what.... I was drifting?" Deb's looked at me.

"Chloe was telling us she wants to have her hair done, but not at the salon, she is going to go and see Anthony after work to do it at his place, she just said she would never have had the guts, if it had not been for you." I turned to her and she smiled, and leaned over and kissed my cheek.

"You are pretty inspiring you know that don't you? I mean look at us Abby, we are all naked, pissed and happy. Hell, look at Anthony he has his junk out, and is happy about it. None of us would have ever have done this, if it was not for you." It was too much.

"Yeah, you would, like everything it takes time, but eventually you would have." Anthony shook his head.

"You are wrong Abby, you are the reason I can say the words I have always been afraid of; I have lived my life ashamed of what I am, and you called me on it, and told me it was nothing to be ashamed of. I told Delphine I am gay, and she embraced me, because you showed me it is wrong to hide who I am, I will always be grateful for that Abby." His sincerity really touched me, and I swallowed a lump in my throat.

"I love you guys, you are all my best friends, but it was Birch who helped me, you should thank her, she was at my side, honestly, I wanted to run back to the station and leave, without her I would never have done it." Birch spoke from the other side of the room.

"I encouraged you to be you Deads, but by being you, it showed everyone else how to be themselves. Let's call it a group effort, and raise a toast to us, Whores of Wotton." Deb's lifted her glass.

"All girls together...Oh no offence Anthony." He giggled.

"Oh, Deb's darling, I would rather be one of you girl whores, than in some alpha male sports team... Although?"

We all started to laugh as he considered the possibility of playing sports with rough hunky men.

"The showers would be fun."

He gave a huge giggle, and we continued to laugh, although it was not long before we all felt the effects of the day's events, and the booze, and soon, beds appeared on the floor, and with Birch and Deb's, I crashed into bed and was gone.

The morning brought a familiar pattern, I woke up and lay still, Birch was as always wrapped around me holding my boob, with her leg over me. I wondered as I lay there, how strange it would be to wake up in a single bed in Uni without her. It was approaching that time, and the bells struck. Birch sat bolt upright, in one swift movement.

"Fucking Bell Twats."

I lay still trying to ignore it.

"Pool" The bed moved, and it suddenly felt cold on my back.

"Fucking Bell Twat, I am going to church one Sunday, just so I can hang that bastard with his own bloody rope."

I heard the stomps, and the groans from the others as Birch marched through the sleeping bodies, and then a few moments later the splash. Deb's sat up and yawned, I rolled over and she smiled.

"I am making coffee; do you want some?" I sat up and rubbed my face.

"Yeah, if you don't mind?" She leaned over and kissed my cheek.

"Seeing as you let me sleep here whenever I want. I need a pee first."

She slipped off the bed and wandered out, and I could not help but think how much she had changed in the last few weeks. She was walking round the house naked, in front of Anthony, hell even my mum and dad yesterday.

What had happened to that shy reserved girl, was Birch right, did she need me to show her the way? I was hardly the best guide;

I was still learning. Okay I have had more sex than her, but in most other things, I was not that much different.

She arrived with coffee, and sat on the bed, I looked at her.

"Do you get frustrated?" She sipped her coffee.

"How do you mean?" I thought about it.

"You know… Do you think about sex and want to have more?"

"Well, that night I did it with Jimmy, the first time I was really scared, but the second time, wow that was just amazing. I cannot deny I have thought about it more than you think." I shrugged.

"So, do you want more?"

"I want to, but come on Abby, how can we round here? I mean look at the village, it's hardly crawling with guys, and Jimmy may come back for a couple of days, but let's be honest, he is in a band, there will be others." I sighed.

"I could use another festival; I wouldn't mind hooking up and having some sexy fun."

"So why don't we? Let's take some time out, and see what is out there, we have a busy week ahead of us." Edwina walked in, and yawned.

"If its men you want, there are always parties in summer. I know a few places, where Chloe and me have hung out, and we always get laid. A few groups I know drive out to a lake not far from Oxendale, it is in the middle of nowhere, we party on the lake beach, and then basically we all get laid."

Deb's was really keener than I thought she would be.

"Wow how old are these guys, and is it like an orgy?" Edwina scratched her thigh.

"I wouldn't say orgy, but Chloe has had a few in one night, they tend to be twenty plus. I suppose it is a take it if you want it sort of deal, do you want me to ask around? I will warn you though, only drink your own booze, and take just bottles, keep your thumb in it, you will find some of them use pills, so be aware of it."

I shuddered, I did not like the idea of pills, but I had been to enough parties at Uni to know who to avoid.

"Yeah, it sounds good, I will talk to Birch when the bells stop."

Chapter 28

Katie.

I flopped back on the bed exhausted.

"I am not ready for this Birch; I have never worked as hard in my life." She smiled and sat down on the bed.

"I have enjoyed it, I have been to these things at home, but never helped set one up."

My arms ached, we had spent Sunday after meeting up with mum after church, to help set up the Church Hall, with tables around the edges, in order for all the admins to work together on the final preparations. Yesterday had been spent running all the boxes from here to the hall in Petal, it was bigger than mum or dad's car, and it made more sense. Dad also thought it was good to have the car seen outside the hall, as it showed we were involved at the side of my mum, who was still handling everything. I think that was just an excuse so he did not get his BMW messed up.

Today, Katie had arranged with Birch, to meet her at the Hunters, and show her around, and help with posters for Veronica's talk. It had also been agreed, that all the team would act like they had no idea who Birch was. I thought it was odd that she wanted to distance herself from her own mother, it made no sense to act like strangers at all, I lifted my hand and stroked her hair back.

"Why pretend you are not related to your mum, I really do not understand it, does her fame embarrass you?"

Birch gave a titter and lay back on the bed and looked at me.

"I want her to arrive to a big welcome, and get the full red carpet treatment. If they find out I am her daughter, they will realise they have been stitched up. They will find out when the time is right." Her eyes twinkled.

"What are you two up to, you worry me at times, so knowing

you are working with a more educated version of you, sort of bothers me?" She smiled.

"You really are an inspiration, on Monday I will work with my mum for the first time ever in public, because being here inspired me to write a format my mum has never used, and we hope it will make the people here see some sense." I frowned at her.

"Why does the thought of this bother me, and how do you mean a new format?" She reached over and stroked my fringe away from my eyes.

"Mum has wanted to do a more audience involved routine for a while now, instead of just giving talks, I think I have found a way to involve the audience more in her presentation, she is very excited about it."

The day was really warm, but there was a fine drizzle, I had on my shortest black shorts, which were frayed, so decided to put on my long black thin coat, Birch had one of her dad's old worn denim shirts on, as we walked down the road towards the village centre. There was a hive of activity, the doors to the Church Hall were open, and people were coming and going. Inside the council worked at handing exhibitors passes, and paperwork about their exhibits.

On the green, the local radio was setting up a mobile stage, this would move to the main field on Friday for the event, they would be broadcasting live all tomorrow, and for the whole weekend. Extra stands had appeared outside the shops, there was money to be made, and lots of extra little trinkets would be available throughout the whole event.

This fete had grown to be the biggest and most well known in the area, and the one thing this area had, was a lot of wealthy people, and the villagers had every intention of milking them for every penny they could.

We approached the road as two large tipper trucks, came thundering through the village and turned, to drive up towards the church, Birch watched uncertain as to what they were for. I pointed up towards the church and the large field.

"They are here to tip fresh gravel on the roads through the parking field, if it rains hard, it can be difficult getting off. Derek Sutton will have his backhoe up there spreading it out."

Outside the church hall, a van was parked up with the large words 'K.O. Productions,' on the side, men were coming and going pushing large black boxes on wheels into the wide side double doors, Birch smiled.

"Good she is here, come on."

She grabbed my hand and pulled me across the road, as we made our way into the Hunters Arms, and up the back stairs.

"You will love Katie; she is wild and brilliant."

I must admit I was not sure; on the phone she had sounded like a bit of a predator. It is probably silly of me, but the fact that there appeared to be some form of sexual connotation, linked to her doing this as a favour for Birch, really bothered me. Birch led me down the corridor to room 10, and knocked, inside a very northern voice answered.

"Come in."

Birch grabbed the handle and dragged me in with a squeal. I was dragged inside to see a tall really attractive woman, in her mid thirties, with long flowing bright coppery red hair, and eyes so blue, they were piercing. She was wearing just a pair of very lacy neon yellow ladies' boxers, and as she saw Birch, she gave a squeal of happiness.

My head was still back in my first impression of why say come in, when you are almost nude, what if it had been a member of staff? My mind boggled, as I watched her throw out her arms and Birch ran happily into them.

She pulled Birch close as they both squealed, and then suddenly, she slapped her hands down, and grabbed Birch's butt cheeks really hard and shook them.

"Oh, this butt is wasted on straight men." Birch hung from her neck.

"I have missed you Katie, you old slapper."

Katie smiled a huge smile, and then grabbed her face and kissed her, I was really surprised.

"Come here you wild little nymph, and give me smooches."

All I could do was stand and watch, feeling a slight pang in my stomach. Birch was all smiles and really happy, she slipped her arm round Katie, and looked at me, her eyes were dancing with happiness, and yet I felt a cold shudder run down my spine. Oh crap, was I jealous of Katie?

"Katie, this is Deadly, my best friend in all the world." Katie looked at her, and raised her eyebrows, then tuned to me and smiled.

"So, this is my competition, is it?"

I swallowed hard, not sure of what to do, she walked towards me her big boobs jiggling, and held out her hand.

"Hi I am Katie, I am Jemi's old boss, and her mother's promoter, nice to meet you Deadly."

I was a little wrong footed, she was stunning, I took her hand and she smiled, and then she yanked me into a hug with a chuckle. I was suddenly face planted in soft white breasts, and the smell, oh god, she smelt delicious. Katie kissed my cheek, and whispered.

"You lucky girl, you have a friend for life there, be good to her." She pulled back and smiled, and gave me a knowing nod.

I smiled back, but I cannot deny, she made me feel nervous. Katie turned to Birch who was at the table by the window, pouring out a drink.

"You did not tell me she was so cute Jemi, I can see why you have been hiding her, she is scrumptious."

Birch came over and handed us glasses, I took mine feeling a little out of place, is it weird I feel I do not belong here? Katie headed to the bed and sat down.

"Okay business, why the pretence, and what have I brought your mum into? Her stay here is my responsibility, is she safe here, you know what weirdo's follow her round?"

Birch moved to the bed and sat down next to her, I sat in the only chair in the room in front of them, silently watching.

"Mum should be safe from anyone here, any weirdo's that turn up will be from out of town as normal. I want to stay separated from mum because here no one knows who I am, apart from a few trusted people." Katie gave a nod, she looked up at me and winked.

"How does this involve you Deadly, I assume you are connected somehow to this new format?" I shook my head.

"I am as in the dark as you, Birch has been working on this privately with her mum." She gave me a nod, and looked at Birch.

"Why have you got such a beautiful friend, and you are not

screwing her? God girl, stop playing the straight card and admit the truth." Birch giggled.

"In your dreams bitch." Katie chuckled.

"Okay so why all the tech, we only have it because we used it in London?" Birch nodded, looked at me and then looked back to Katie.

"Mum will fill you in on everything, this is a brand new format, it is like nothing she has ever done before, and we want to trial it here, before taking it out on the road, sort of a practice run if you must. Katie, I have been working on this for a long time, just work with us on it." She patted Birch on the leg.

"Okay kid, this is your party, I will play along.... I take it this means you are not coming back, and are going to join her in practice?" Birch smiled.

"I loved our year on the road, but as you know, this has always been my dream, she has offered me a partnership, and once I have served my time, I am taking her up on it." Katie nodded and got up.

"To be honest kid I don't blame you... So how does this scrumptious little gem work into all this, or shouldn't I ask?" Birch looked at me smiled.

"I am going to set up mum's second practice in Wotton, so I can be close, and there is a lot of possible clients with cash here, so it's the best place for me to be... But that is a secret as well for now, so keep it quiet."

I was stunned, I stared at her and then just blurted it out.

"YOU ARE?" She smiled.

"Yes Sweetie, you can write or work here, and we will still see each other every day. We can buy a house and live outrageously, and be the talk of the village, after all, someone has to succeed Hatty." She winked, and then raised her eyebrows.

I could not believe it, I will not deny, I knew she had taken a gap year to work, but I had thought a great deal recently about what would happen when Uni was over, I had even considered living up north, it never dawned on me she would want the same as me. Katie pulled a long face.

"I have an hour free; you girls wouldn't want a threesome by any chance, just watching you two is turning me on?"

I had to giggle, wow she was so straight out with it, Birch

winked at me whilst smiling.

"We are fine Katie; we have posters to hand out." She got up off the bed, and poured another drink and sighed

"Back to the dildo for me then, okay you two go to work, I have an itch, and Tony is going to play." Birch sniggered.

"Tony is the only guy she ever slept with, she had a cast of him specially made whilst we were in Italy, she whips it out when women are scarce." I could not help but giggle, Katie winked at me.

"He was so good I almost went straight."

Katie gave me a hug, and slipped her hands down over my bum and gave it a soft tweak, and sighed.

"I am so jealous Jemi."

We left the room agreeing that from now until the night of the show, we would act like we did not know her, which apart from that visit I didn't really. We made our way towards the church hall and mum. Whilst Birch filled me in on her gap year travelling Europe with a group of fiction authors, doing promotional events.

"It was hard work, but it was a riot, we had loads of fun, and I got to see loads of great places, although it took it's toll, I was hardly sober."

We arrived in the busy church hall, and grabbed a big armful of printed posters, which had Veronica's face on, and made our way towards the shops.

In the Tea Rooms, Birch made sure they had told no one about it being her mum, and handed them two posters, one for the window and one for the wall. Lillian was delighted. I headed for the Post Office/Village Shop; Mary appeared surprised to see me.

"Abigail!" I smiled.

"Hello Mrs Saxon, I am helping mum prepare for the guest speaker, and handing out posters, would you mind placing one in the window." I held one up.

"Well absolutely Abigail, I hear she has quite a following, and we may get double the normal crowd." I nodded.

"I have heard she is very popular, mum said it is amazing we could get her, so fingers crossed we will have big influx of funds." Mary came round the counter with her tape.

"Indeed, every penny will count, we need to keep this village in peak condition."

Her whole manner was completely different since the last time we spoke, she was more the Mary I knew. She looked at me as she took the poster off me.

"You know your mum is doing a wonderful job taking on all Madge's tasks as well, it has not been unnoticed by the residents." I gave a nod as I watched her.

"She has always worked for what is best Mrs Saxon, she is very open minded, and listens to the needs of those living here, although I do worry, she works too hard."

"She has indeed, but we see how dedicated she is, no doubt she will be rewarded for it one day... There how does that look?" I smiled feeling more relaxed.

"Wonderful, thanks for all your support as well, you and your husband work equally as hard." Mary gave me a smile, and she looked round to see if the shop was empty.

"Abigail, can I ask you something personal, will that be alright?" I suddenly felt nervous.

"I suppose so, how personal?" She looked round again.

"Your friend, you know, the white haired girl.... She told Madge she was a Naturist, is that right?"

I felt relived, for a moment I had thought she was going to ask if I was still a virgin. I nodded and smiled.

"Yes, she is, she is called Birch, we spend a lot of time naked, it is good for the body you know, and is wonderful for the mind and inner happiness, why is that a problem?" She looked really surprised.

"You too.... Are you two not embarrassed people know about it?" I shook my head.

"Not at all, mum and dad are fine with it, and I have a nice body, she has a gorgeous body, and we are both happy with how we look. I am not ashamed or embarrassed at all. I understand not everyone gets it Mrs Saxon, but as Hatty always says to me, what others say about me, says more about them, than it ever will me. We are all born naked, why would anyone be ashamed by that? We look the same, just the proportions are a little different, that's all." She raised her eyebrows.

"I think you have a very positive attitude, Abigail; I must admit,

I admire your confidence." I winked and lowered my voice.

"You would be surprised just how many of us there are in this village, it's not just Birch and me, there are others, they just keep quiet about it, but I will say this, we have not been alone on our naked days." She gasped.

"Really... I would never haver have guessed?" I winked again.

"That is our secret, okay?" She smiled and looked pleased with herself, I know how she loved the inside gossip.

I made my way out of the shop with a smile, Birch was coming out of the bakery, and I walked down to gift shop, she stopped.

"You do this one, I am dying to meet the naughty florist." We parted again, and entered the shops.

That night we collapsed onto the bed together exhausted, with aching feet. We had done every shop in the area, even the train station, and my legs were killing me.

"I need a bath, I am going to the house to run one, are you joining me?" Birch started to chuckle, I frowned.

"What?"

"Is there anything we have not done together? By the way... Yes, I will be joining you." She turned and smiled at me.

"There is one thing we have not done together Birch... Sex.... Why does Katie think we should have sex?" She threw her towel at me.

"I will tell you in the bath."

We ran up to the house wrapped in towels, it was still raining, and headed for the bathroom, I turned on the taps as Birch sat on the toilet lid, I sat on the edge of the bath, she gave a sigh.

"Okay this is what happened. As you know we spent a year on the road, she was my boss, and Katie, as you have seen is as flirty as hell. She was always telling me how she wanted to bed me, and I turned her down. We had screwed our way across Europe, I got the guys and she got the girls. One night after two weeks solid with no breaks or time off, we arrived at hotel in a village outside the main town in Italy. She had been sleeping with one of the crew, who just decided to leave, as she had fiancée, and Katie was pissed off at her."

I leaned back and threw a bath bomb in the water, and watched as it fizzed, and the bubbles flooded up to the surface of the water.

"When we got the hotel, we were the only females, and they had suffered a fire a few weeks earlier, and so there was a shortage of two single rooms, they offered us the double. I thought it would be fine, and it was, until we had loads to drink. We had both showered, and were wrapped in towels like this, I climbed into bed drunk as a skunk, complaining at the lack of men, and she got in at my side. Everything was fine, until she rolled over, and started to kiss my nipples."

I suddenly started to feel hot, I felt the heat creep up my body, and I could feel I was getting wet, holy shit, this story was turning me on!

"To be honest Deads, I got really turned on, I mean hell she is good, if you know what I mean? I had been horny all day, and there had not been any time for any action, so she hit me at my most primed. I thought about it, and I was enjoying it, so I thought should I let her. Anyway, she started going south, kissing me, and I was so turned on and started to squirm on the bed. The problem was, when she reached between my legs, I snapped them shut. I cannot explain it, I just didn't want her to go there, and it freaked me out." I gasped.

"Holy shit, how did she react?"

"I was scared to death, because she was my boss, but she was really cool about it, and told me it was fine, and that I wasn't ready yet, but to tell her when I was. I tuned on my side, I was angry with myself for not going through with it, because I was really turned on and had been all day, and I needed to get some relief. The next thing I know, she cuddled me and then slipped a dildo between my legs, she told me it would feel like a man and take care of me, and she slipped it in, and for want of a better word, she banged me with that, and I came like crazy, and it did make me feel really good."

I could feel the heat in my face.

"Jesus Birch." She smiled.

"She was fine the next day, it was like nothing had happened. I asked her if we were okay, and she laughed, she told me she would never let something like a rubber dick come between us, and we have been great friends ever since. Go figure, because I was fine with that, I love her to bits, I have just never wanted to sleep with her."

I gave a long, staggered, breath, not at all certain of what to make of it all.

"Wow that was a hell of a story." She giggled.

"The crazy thing was, the guy the employee was engaged to was Tony, she screwed him and took a cast of his penis to remember him by, and to piss off the girl who left our staff down on a big job. I am telling you Deads, Katie is the craziest person I know."

The bath was ready and we slipped into the hot water, she sat behind me. I closed my eyes.

"I am ashamed to say it Birch, but I got really turned on listening to you talk about it." I was leant back against her, and she slipped her arms round me.

"Yeah, remembering it is quite the turn on, but as I said, I cannot do that with her. I am not sure if I ever will, but if I do, it will not be with Katie." I relaxed and gave a sigh.

"Sexuality is such a mine field, isn't it?" She chuckled.

"Not really... I think when something is right and feels good, it is right for you, you care too much about what others will say. Let go of that and face yourself, the answers are inside you, all you have to do is be honest with yourself. I think everyone wants to screw something, it is just choosing what and how that people worry about, and really, they shouldn't. it is actually what I like the most about Katie, she does not hold back and says what is on her mind. She really wants you in her bed, I could tell, she was also really serious about the threesome."

I jumped forward feeling really surprised. and turned to look at her.

"Seriously, I thought she was joking?" Birch shook her head, and then started at me.

"Oh shit... Did you want to do it?" I gasped.

"Hell no!" She smiled and shrugged.

"Just checking, because if you had, I would have joined in with you." She started to laugh.

"You are too easy to wind up."

"Fuck you Birch." She giggled.

"Turn back, and I will wash your hair.... Pass me the shampoo."

I leaned back my head, as she rubbed her fingers into my scalp, the aroma of the shampoo filling my nose, and I relaxed with my head filled with her story of Katie.

"You know, it is strange, if you think about it, does it really make a difference who does what?"

She ran her fingers down through my hair, checking for knots.

"How do you mean?"

"Well you know… It's like when Eric went down on me at the festival, it was amazing and I ended up having a huge climax, but you know what, I am not sure I would have been any different if it was a girl. I really need to be stimulated, I was so frustrated, if a girl had done it, I am not sure I would have cared. I needed that climax, it was all that mattered to me." Birch reached for the shower head and started to rinse my hair.

"I have thought about that too. I know a bisexual guy in Huddersfeild, and he has said it is not that much different for him. He told me, the feeling is pretty much the same, it is just he feels differently about each person who does it. I remember thinking about it a lot at the time."

I sat forward and turned to look at her.

"What you mean like the perception?" She nodded, and then turned me back round to finish my hair.

"Yeah, think about it Deads, if you are receiving it, it cannot be that different, so I suppose it is in the giving that we see the difference. Maybe it is just that we are indoctrinated into the stereo typical roles of life from childhood, which is why it is perceived as wrong. Maybe the world does need to be re-educated to be more fluid. A mouth is a mouth, and a vagina is a vagina, it is the same effect no matter who it is doing it." It made some sense.

"Maybe everyone is really meant to be Bi?" She chuckled.

"Now that is why I am doing sexual psychology. There are a lot of anthropologists who think the same way, I mean they have been studying the bonobo, which is our closest living primate, and they are definitely Bi. It really makes you think, doesn't it?"

"If I am honest, all I can say is I like the way sex makes me feel. I know there are a lot of people who will see that as wrong, but I do not really worry about that. I used Eric, because I really needed a man, I am not sure if I was right or wrong about that. He told me he had always wanted to sleep with me, and he wanted to date me, so I suppose we both got what we wanted to a degree?"

"Okay you are done."

Birch pushed me forward, got up, she straddled over me, and then slipped down in front of me, and handed me the shampoo. She leaned back and I poured some out into my hand and started to massage it into her hair.

"To be honest Deads, I do not really worry about it. I am honest and up front, I tell them it is just sex, and the way I see it, they can stay or go. If they go, I will find someone else. Madge thinks that makes me a slut, but you know what, I have never had a guy walk out, so what does that make the men?"

It was a good point, and strangely enough, I had never until that very moment, even considered it.

Chapter 29

Working Week.

The week was just getting harder, and Wednesday was chaos, Deb's joined us to bake cakes, make Jam, and practice flower arranging again. Chloe and Edwina had the restaurant kitchen, and their mother to guide them, as she was a qualified pâtissier.

My mum was out on the site with dad on his first day off, organising the tents, and pitches. The kitchen looked like a bomb had hit it, and cleaning up took ten times longer than the actual baking, but eventually we finally collapsed in the guest house and had a very strong vodka.

I collapsed into bed early, and woke up around eight, with Birch as always curled tight around me. Having finally wrestled my way out of her grip, I sat by the window and had coffee, it was looking a lot brighter, and at least the rain had stopped. Birch's phone was flashing, she had messages, but she was not awake yet, and I thought I should leave her a little longer.

I heard Deb's groan and walked back into the bedroom, she was on top of the duvet, legs wide open, seriously after the shaving incident, I felt I had seen that way too many times, although I did note it was becoming quite prickly and would possibly need attending to soon, and that as far I as I was concerned, was her job now.

I looked at the floor, which was how I picked my wardrobe each day, my clothes were scattered and mixed up with Deb's and Birch's. I thought as I surveyed what was strewn around, my gran would probably have a fit if she saw this. Deb's opened her eyes and smiled, suddenly realising how she was laying, she snapped her legs closed, I giggled.

"That thing needs a razor if you want to stay smooth."

She looked down and stroked her fingers through the fuzz.

"Yeah, I suppose so, I have meant to do it, just not had time." I pointed behind me.

"There are razors in the shower if you need some." She looked me, and I read her thoughts.

"No, you pervert, shave it yourself." She giggled.

"It felt nice when you did it." I glanced at her watching me.

"That is what worries me about you, I am not sure about you any more, I think you swing both ways."

"Do you really think so, I won't deny I have asked myself hundreds of times?" I turned round to face her.

"Does it matter Deb's? I don't think there is anything wrong with liking people, I mean look at Edwina, she is happy and open about it. If you are, then you are, stop over thinking it." She smiled and looked at Birch and then back at me.

"You should listen to yourself Abby, you might learn something." I frowned.

Back in the house the doorbell rang. Felicity was getting ready for yet another day on site, she pushed the gate button without thinking, and walked to the door, opened it and stepped back with a horrified gasp.

"Good god!"

The bright happy face of Bev stood there with her violet turfed hair, tattoos, and facial piercings, and her obvious heavily tattooed size, which was decked out in tight jeans and a vest, with no bra.

"Hi is Jemi here... I am Bev by the way?" Felicity looked horrified.

The gates were open and Roni walked through, she came smiling up to the door.

"Hello again Flick, we are down for a few days, but I wanted to see Jemi first. This is Bev by the way."

She came up to the door as they both stepped in.

"I take it Jemi is still in bed?"

Felicity gave a nod still staring in horror at Bev, Roni pointed through the house.

"Go through Bev, out through the doors and down to the guest house." Bev nodded, and walked off; Roni turned to Felicity.

"See how much worse it could have been for Abby, if you ask me you got off lucky, her mother is still mortified, and she has looked like that for four years." Felicity shut the door.

"I am not ruddy well surprised Roni, my god if Abby came home looking like that, I would have to kill her or me, I not am sure which, but one of us would have to go." Roni gave a titter.

"How are things, you seem calmer, and yet more stressed?" Felicity smiled.

"I am a lot better, Abby and myself have found middle ground, and I am very pleased about that. This event is hard work though, it does take its toll, but we are nearly there. I am so grateful you will be speaking, you really got us out of a bind." Roni smiled.

"Don't thank me, this one has been arranged and organised by Jemi."

I was about to make us a coffee, when I heard the patio door bang. What I heard next froze my heart, it was like history repeating itself.

"Are you there Jemi?" I stepped back from the door, back into the bedroom.

"HOLY SHIT WHAT IS SHE DOING HERE!?" Deb's jumped.

"What is it?"

I felt panicked, she would know by now the clap had cleared up, I turned to Deb's

"Guard your vagina." The voice came again but louder.

"You up Jemi?" Deb's heard it and turned instantly white. She looked at me as I panicked.

"It's her, isn't it? Oh shit.... I am the weakest; she will rape me first.... Please Abby I just decided, I am not gay, I don't want those teeth down there."

I was trying to think, but my brain was racing, we were all naked in the same bed, talk about giving her a calling card to jump in. I looked at Deb's who was visibly falling apart and had crossed her legs.

"Shit... Shit.... We need Birch, shake her, and wake her the hell up."

I ran round the bed as Deb's grabbed her, and shook her with a strength I did not know she possessed. I fell to the floor at the side of Birch, as Debs was desperately shaking the shit out of her.

"Birch.... Birch... Birch for god's sake wake up, Bev is here."

The magic words were spoken, her eyes snapped wide open, and she sat up at high speed.

"Guard your vagina." I looked at her.

"WE FUCKING KNOW THAT, WHY THE HELL IS SHE HERE?"

Birch looked round at Deb's who as white as sheet and trembling in fear.

"VD won't work this time, and you are the weakest."

Deb's looked terrified, as the door to the guest house opened, it was too late she was in. I crawled back into bed, and tried to hide behind Birch.

"Jemi are you in here?"

"In here Bev." Deb's head snapped round at high speed.

"What the hell Birch? Go out there!"

The huge frame of Bev walked in, and Deb's gave a high pitched squeal, and slid down under the duvet. I smiled and gave a weak wave.

"Hi Bev, what the hell are you doing here?" She smiled a huge smile.

"Jemi, three girls together... Wow, you greedy bitch. Hey Deadly, and who was that other sweet looking slice of meat I just saw?"

Panicked mumbles came from under the duvet. I grinned at Bev.

"That's Deb's she is a little shy."

Birch slid off the bed, and reached for her long black robe, Bev stepped back to watch, and I realised, I was suddenly exposed and my full nudity was on display.

"Oh, very nice girls, is your friend equally as shapely?"

I lifted the duvet to hide a little. Birch pulled her robe on and gave Bev a hug.

"Bev Sweetie, how the hell did you get here? I will put the kettle on."

She walked through to the living room, and Bev followed. I gave a gasp and flopped back on the pillows; my heart was racing. The duvet moved, and I could just see Deb's face staring at me.

"Is it okay if I just pee the bed, because I really need one, but I am too afraid to go out there?" I smiled.

"She looks scary as hell, but really is very sweet, hurry and get dressed, and we will go out."

Ten minutes later after a bone crushing hug, whilst Deb's sat on the loo, pissing more than she ever had, which I put down to fear induced, I sat on the floor with a coffee, as Bev sat at the table, and she explained how her mum was looking after the cats, so she could travel down with Roni and Will, for the event, as she was to be part of the crew, as a member of the security detail.

Roni came down to the house and hugged Birch, and feeling safer with more women around, Deb's finally made it out of the toilet. Roni smiled and she pulled me into a hug.

"Abby my dear, you are looking so relaxed, I am so pleased to see that. I hear you have both been talking, that is good to know. I was worried when I left here last time." She gave Deb's a hug.

"So nice to see you again Goggles, you are a little pale dear are you okay?" She smiled and gave a nod.

"I am fine Roni, had a bit of a scare, but all good now thanks." Roni understood, and turned to Birch.

"I want to head into the village and get a look at the venue, so I am going to jump in with Flick. We have decided to stay a little longer, so we will be here until Wednesday morning, we have booked in at the Hunters, we arrived later than planned last night, so I have let your dad sleep in, it was a long drive, and he was so tired." Birch's eyes lit up.

"Dad is here too, why didn't you let me know? Oh, cool he can meet Petal, he is so going to love her." Roni smiled.

"I did send you a message earlier. I saw Petal coming in, I see you have applied your own unique stamp to her, she does look like a good one, he will be thrilled with her." Birch beamed with delight.

You see this is something that stumps me, and I have to ask, is this a northern thing? Petal has been painted, I get that, she looks a thousand times better than she did, but I saw her before the face lift, and she is a piece of crap. I mean she was literally rotting when Birch got her, I still do not understand why anyone would not just buy a better car. When you think of what she spent, she could have got a really decent second hand, people carrier, and covered that in daisies. I do not think it will ever make sense to me, and yes, I know, it's Birch, and I probably will get used to it.

Roni left, and whilst Bev and Birch did a quick catch up, I sat with another coffee, outside on the loungers with Deb's. She lay back and gave a long sigh.

"Jesus Abby, I have never been so scared in my life. I mean I am not being horrible, but she walked in, and I was not at all prepared to see her. I jest not, when I tell you, I was so scared, I felt my vagina try to turn round, and creep back up inside me. I mean, I have seen girls at Uni with piercings, but nine... Holy shit Abby, although I cannot wait until she has to get something out of your mums' fridge, I bet all the magnets jump off, and stick to her face." I must admit, I had to laugh at her, it was good to see the colour returning to her cheeks.

When we were all ready, we walked into the village, I noticed how whatever side Bev was on, Debs was on the extreme opposite, I looked at Bev.

"I am not sure this village is ready for you Bev." She gave a chuckle.

"Yeah, I have had some funny looks, you know, it must have been like that when the first cave men saw fire, they kind of looked at it, and then shit themselves, that is sort of how it has been for me."

"Oh, I know that look, Birch and me still get them."

We visited the church hall, where Katie was in control on the stage, and men were setting up the equipment. I stood back and watched. All round the room, there were tables filled with paperwork, and villagers were coming and going as they checked on their entries. Outside large vehicles were arriving for the main field, they would be transformed into fair rides for the weekend.

Birch stood in the middle of the room, and watched with a keen eye, as the scaffold for the lights, and projection screen, was put into place, and I realised this must have been what she had done with Katie on tour. Katie had a head set on, and was walking round with Roni, going over everything, and I was intrigued. Mum came up at my side.

"It is a lot of work for one night." I nodded.

"Roni is even bigger than even I thought, I looked her up last night online, she is one of the highest paid guest speakers on the circuit. Her online videos have millions of views, and her books have been translated into ten different languages, she is huge."

"Well if she can draw a bigger crowd, than the washed up B list celebrities, Marjorie has brought in for our previous events, I will be happy."

I watched her face, I could see the pressure, this was not just a fete, this was the start of her campaign to unseat Marjorie.

"Is Marjorie going to appear any time soon?" Mum gave a sigh.

"She is already out, apparently she is at the Tea Rooms, no doubt she has seen Bev, I am hoping that will keep her happy for a little while, I am sure she will have to come up with a few new words now, after all Abby, compared to Bev, you look pretty normal." She giggled.

Marjorie had seen Bev; she had been watching from her favourite window seat.

"GOOD GOD, WHAT ON EARTH IS THAT?"

She pointed out of the window, with a look of horror glued to her face. Lillian bent down to peer through the curtains.

"I believe she is a lesbian, she arrived last night at the Hunters. Apparently, she is part of Dr Dixon's security detail, that is what Amie Bosworth told me. The girl certainly looks capable, with all those tattoos and muscles, I think she has a rough charm, don't you?" Marjorie stared at her in shock.

"Have you lost your mind, look at her, in what way or form is that even remotely female, she looks like a painted primate?" Celia leaned in for a look.

"Times are changing Marjorie, it is like the cultural revolution all over again, at some point we will have no choice, but to accept that things are not as they were. Today is all about technology, LGBT, and our innermost thoughts. You can be anything you want to be these days, and the young have really embraced it, I think I envy them, they have freedoms we have never been given."

Marjorie stared at them both looking out of the window.

"Well, it won't bloody happen on my watch." Celia turned and looked at her.

"We have to embrace change Madge if we want this village to last, if we stay the same, it will die." She stood up.

"This is fiddlesticks, I will never accept the likes of that walking round this village, it is bad enough that whore brought that other one here with her. We do not need the likes of that poverty stricken Manchester trash here, I will never allow it.... Not ever!"

Marjorie stormed out of the Tea Room, and Lillian and Celia watched Bev. Celia turned to Lillian.

"Is it wrong that I want her to sleep with us?" Lillian gave a titter.

"Oh my, what a thought... Should we ask Birch, or should we invite her for tea?"

Celia gave a small titter and nudged Lillian.

"Are you thinking what I am for afters?" Lillian gave a very excited giggle, and blushed.

By the time we got home, my dad was flat out in bed, mum told us Peter had taken over, and all that was left to do, was to direct the traders as they arrived towards their pitches. The tents were up and the site was ready, and we had to prepare our final exhibits.

Mum had two identical cakes side by side, she cut thin slices from one of them, and gave Birch, Debs, and me a taste. I could not deny it was wonderful.

"Mum it's as good as it has always been." She sighed.

"Yes, but that is the problem isn't it, I have never got past second with it." Birch swallowed.

"It is better than mine." Deb's nodded.

"Mine too." Mum gave another sigh.

"I have done the best cake ever, but I doubt it is good enough." Birch gave a smile.

"I know what it needs... It needs a little Birch magic, wait here."

She disappeared down to the guest house, and few minutes later she came running back. She slipped in through the door, and held up a small plastic bag of purple crystals, my mum freaked completely out.

"I AM NOT PUTTING DRUGS ON MY CAKE!"

"Huh!"

Birch looked confused, she looked at the bag in her hand, and then realised, and smiled.

"It's not drugs Flick, it's sugar, a very special sugar." She gave a big sigh of relief.

"Thank god for that, I thought it was crack." I stared at her in utter disbelief.

"Hang on a minute, it is okay for her to have a bag of drugs, as long as they are not on your cake?" Deb's giggled, mum shook her head.

"I didn't mean it like that Abby."

"But you did think it was crack?" She looked embarrassed.

"Well, I don't know do I? All you young ones, are up to all sorts of things these days?"

"Mum I dyed my hair, changed my clothes, and discovered the joy of being a naturist, and none of that was crack induced, I can assure you. I have told you; we don't do drugs."

"Well, the occasional spliff, but it's nothing untoward." I looked at Birch, and she smiled.

"Hi Sweetie."

Birch took the mortar and pedestal, and ground a few tea spoons of the lightly plum flavoured sugar into a powder, she then sprinkled it thinly on top of the sponge cake that had been cut, and took another slice, and handed it to mum.

She took a bite and her eyes rolled right back into her head. I cannot deny I was a little bothered seeing that. I thought, I hope she is not going to cum, I have done and seen a lot of weird shit in this last year, but seeing my mum cum, was something I never ever want to see.

"Oh my god that is sensational, all the flavours just explode in your mouth." Birch smiled.

"Right do as I did, and sprinkle some on the cake you are exhibiting, if that does not clinch it, you never will Flick."

The day was finally over, and we all crashed into bed exhausted, we did not even have a drink.

Friday arrived, and we were woken early by mum, who was still raving about her cake, and so made us a full English breakfast in bed. Dad was already on site, Edwina, Chloe, and Anthony texted that they were on their way, as we had to get our flower arrangements done, and leave them in the cool garage, with the fan on, to stay fresh. As part of the organising team, we did not have the luxury of being able to make them last minute.

The day was to be busy, we had the church hall to clear, and seats to set up, and then we would be on site, helping guide traders, and exhibitors alike, to their allotted spots. I must have a walked hundreds of miles, just showing people around, wearing a bright yellow vest that had 'Steward' in big letters on the back.

We were split into pairs, Birch got Chloe, Edwina paired with Deb's, Anthony was paired with a tall stocky guy called Brent, and I ended up with Molly, who was related to Marion. She hated me the second she saw me, which was alright, because I absolutely detested her.

I had to spend the day listening to her spout on about traditional values, and the right way to do everything, I just wanted to scream at her 'Oh yeah, you aunt pisses on the gardener,' just to shut her the hell up, and I came so close.

We were given a forty minute break, and I went looking for the others, I found them all outside what would be the rest tent over the weekend. The tent was basically an escape for a break, where hay bales, horse feed and various spare props were stored. I looked at them all stood outside eating, I looked at Birch.

"Why are you not all inside out of the sun?" She gave me a wink.

"Go look."

I slipped in through the flap, and all appeared well, and then I heard a soft moan. I craned my neck to see round the hay bales, and saw Chloe leaning on a bale. I smiled and walked up to her, as she put her head down and gave another long sensual moan, and that was when I suddenly realised.

Chloe was bent over leaning on the bale, her skirt was up, and her draws down, and behind her pumping like a traction engine was Doug, middle son of Mr Pilkington the local farmer, and land owner of the site. Chloe gave another long moan.

"Oh God... OH!"

And that was my invitation to exit, I turned sharply and walked briskly to the flap, and came out. Birch smiled.

"See Sweetie, that is why we are out here." I stared at her.

"And you could not have just told me, it was because Chloe was screwing in there?" Birch shrugged.

"She did say, she did not mind us watching, Deb's thought it best we wait here, until she is done." Inside the tent she screamed.

"OH GOD!!" Birch smiled.

"That is probably around now."

It was one o'clock and I finished at three, but I had just about taken enough from Molly. Yet again she was banging on about morals, and the traditional ways of living, and how things looked, and I could not possibly stomach another moment of the bitch.

We were on our way back to the gate yet again, I walked in between the horticultural and the craft tents, and as she followed me in, banging on and on, I just turned and stared at her with hate.

"Do you ever shut the hell up?"

She gasped with shock, and I was having none of it.

"You know what Molly; I don't give a shit what your aunt thinks. I don't, honestly, I just don't give a flying fuck... Not one.... All I have heard since I have returned, is the same hypocritical bullshit, you, your aunt, and Marjorie spew out, and not one of you is honest, not one of you. You all slag me off for dying my hair, you know what, fine! It's different, I get it, and it is not traditional, well has it ever entered that tiny indoctrinated mind of yours, that maybe, just maybe, I don't actually give a shit about tradition? I like being a rebel, because it makes me feel good. Honestly if the devil was to come out of the floor, I would screw him in front of you, just to prove it, so do me favour, shut the fuck up, or piss off, and leave me in peace. Good I am glad we cleared that up."

I turned and walked away, she stared at me.

"The Devil will come forth, and drag you into the bowls of hell Abigail Watson, and he will devour you flesh." I looked back and smiled.

"Well, at least it is good to know, at least one of us will be getting laid." She almost fainted.

At nine pm, having worked our asses off all day, we all stood back, and admired our final flower creations, all set up in our allotted squares, on the long white table. Every exhibitor had a number, mine was 37, we were not allowed names, so we could not be identified. My creation had been entitled. 'Light the way.'

Birch had named hers, 'Boho Delight.' Anthony had out done himself with, 'Inspired by Venus.' Deb's looked great, 'Friendship' Chloe made us all giggle, it was her best by far, and she labelled it 'Dope.'

Edwina did pretty good too, I really liked it, but I was certain she would get marked down, as this year, Marjorie was not showing, as she was one of the judges. She had named hers. 'It's a Birch thing.'

Our cakes were displayed, our jams on show, so all we could do was walk back to Petal, and head home for a well earned rest. I had not seen Molly since, which was a great relief. All I wanted to do was get home, lie on the hard floor to ease my back, and chill out.

Tomorrow we were free to do as we pleased, and I was really looking forward to it. This last week had almost killed me, but I felt happy. I had been seen to be there, and helping as I always did, and despite some dismissive looks, most people had appeared to have appreciated it.

Deb's was out cold, and so I crashed out leaving Birch once again working on her laptop, and did not even feel her when she slipped in besides me.

Chapter 30

The Village Fete.

I was still sore after the week, but as I sat in bed on Saturday morning, I felt happy. We had dropped Chloe, Anthony and Edwina off at his place last night, as he was going to sort out their hair, and then the girls were going to crash at his house.

I got a text from Chloe, which was why I am awake, she told me he gave up his double bed for her and Edwina, and he slept on his sofa. I had to smile, he was such a decent guy, and a real gentleman in every sense of the word. She included some pictures and I was blown away.

"Wow he is good, look at that." Deb's leaned over while Birch still snored.

"Wow that looks insane!"

She was right, her hair was done in all pastel colours, it started pink at the top, fading to lilac, then pale blue, and then green, and a very pale yellow at the tips, it was mind blowing. Edwina added a video clip, and at first her hair looked normal, and then she turned and flicked her hair, and it exploded with holographic colours, it was wild. Deb's gasped.

"I so want that done for Uni."

Anthony was far more talented than he realised, but there again, this was the kind of thing that he had told Delphine he wanted to add to the salon, and to be honest, both Deb's and I thought he should.

It is not an easy task waking Birch up, every time you shake her, she farts, so it becomes a challenge, to see if you can wake her, before she gases you out, and you flee the room retching. Today we failed, and both of us stood outside naked, and gasping for fresh air.

I was about to suggest going to the house for coffee, when I noticed a familiar shade of purple in the kitchen with mum.

"Holy shit, guard your vagina." Deb's disappeared faster than an apparating wizard.

I headed indoors quick. Debs was crawling on all fours, at high speed, when I heard the patio doors bang.

"Deb's what the hell are you doing?" Her head popped up from under the bed looking panicked.

"I have lost my knickers." She sounded both terrified and desperate.

I lifted a clean pair off my case, and flicked them at her with my toe. She grabbed them, fell on her back, shot her legs up in the air, and pulled them on, in one fast, swift, movement. Bouncing up on her feet, she grabbed Birch's t shirt, and dragged it over her head, and gasped with relief. She heard the door to the living room open.

"Deads, Birch are you there?" Birch shot up in the bed.

"Guard your vaginas." I sniggered dressed in pants and a shirt.

"But you are the only one naked Birch." She looked down.

"Oh crap." We walked out of the bedroom all smiles.

"Hey Bev, you want a coffee?"

It took over an hour to sort Birch out, but the weird thing was, she dressed slow, in cool clothes, sprayed her armpits and vagina with deodorant, and then sat at the table like a ghost, and applied her eye liner. She turned, looked at me, and blinked, with those dark gothic, surrounded green eyes and seductively blinked again.

"What do you think Sweetie?" And she was wide awake, and weirdly enough, I was wet.

We all met at the salon, and dressed to kill, as we walked towards the church, and the big gates at the end of the road, that was the entrance to the site of the Fete. It was 10:30 and judging was still in progress, and mum and dad like all the other stewards of the day, were walking around with radio's guiding people, and giving out advice. The car park was filling up fast, as the PA system sounded loud across the field, announcing the next class for the horse judging.

Bev took a great liking to Anthony, she hugged him tight, which almost crushed him.

"I got your back bro, have no fear."

It was sort of cute, he was a like a little doll, compared to her, but she could be as a fierce as a Rottweiler, and I knew he would come to no harm in her care. My point was proven a little time later when he was suddenly surrounded by four big guys, as they laughed at him.

Bev appeared with a burger, stepped into the ring, handed her burger to Anthony, and sized up the biggest, he sneered at her, and BAM!

She headed butted him, and he went down like a sack of carrots, and lay on the ground out cold, Anthony just gasped with shock. Bev stared at the other three as they looked at their friend on the floor.

"Do we still have a problem?"

The next tallest looked at her, and shook his head.

"Fuck no!"

They turned, and fled, leaving their friend out cold on the floor. Bev took her burger back, and winked at Anthony, he gave a terrified sheepish smile.

The fete was the biggest in the area, and there was a lot to see. Like any local show it had all the veg classes, cooked goods, flower arranging and of course a lot of animal events, with some equestrian, but to top off that, there were craft stalls, clothing stands, food stands, and fair ground rides.

Music blasted from everywhere, and the atmosphere was one of excitement. Kids ran wild through the grounds, laughing and screaming, and we were not much better, a group of misfits, with bottles of beer, and larking around, as we spent money on clothing and candy floss. It was so much fun, and I laughed so much my stomach hurt. Hatty had a tent filled with her art, and I walked in with Birch.

She was so talented, and I was captivated. She painted landscapes, portraits, still life, it was all there, many of which were scenes from the village I knew well. They came in all sizes and prices, and were not cheap, but I thought they were worth every penny. I opened a vinyl book she had which had photographs of all her paintings, and as I flicked through, I stopped, I tuned to Birch.

"Hey you see this picture of a canal, isn't that on your living room wall?" Birch looked at it.

"Yeah, mum bought that online a good few years ago." I was astounded.

"She has Hatty's art?" Birch shrugged.

"She has a few, as soon as she got here, she went round to see her in person. knowing mum, she has probably bought another. You know Hatty is well known Deads, she sells all over the place."

I had never thought of it before, she was Hatty, my mum's best friend. I mean I knew she could paint, but I just did not think of her as a famous artist, she was just so normal, so grounded, I had never realised she made her majority living from online sales, and she was that well known.

We wandered out of the tent, and I looked round. Chloe and Anthony were shooting at targets, I glanced at Birch.

"Where is Bev?" Birch shrugged.

"Does it matter?"

I suppose it didn't, I mean she can take care of herself, but this was Wotton, and she was northern, and some of these little old ladies were brutal.

"I am not that sure Birch, we should just let her wander, she is better close to those who understand the territory?" She nodded.

"Good point, we should go and find her, you check out the rest tent, I will check out the burger stands, you know how she likes burgers?"

I wandered off to go check out the rest tent, and walked slowly up the central avenue of all the show tents, small posts were outside each tent, with signs stating 'Judging in Progress.' I arrived at the tent, and taking into account my last encounter with Chloe, I peeped in through the flap.

All appeared fine, so I slipped in. The place was stacked with hay bales, most of which would be used if it rained, to soak up the puddles. I walked slowly along a wall of stacked straw, and heard a soft strange noise. I have no idea why I whispered. "Bev, are you in here?"

There was another sound, like a 'mmm' sort of noise. I tip toed along to the end of the bales, and peered round, and was surprised to see Edwina. She was lay back on a bale, and she gave a little twitch, then her eyes rolled into the back of her head.

"Oh Gawd!"

I cannot deny I was really intrigued, and moved round just a little more, she gave a huge gasp of air.

"Oh... My ...Gawd!" What the hell was making her gasp that way? I cannot deny I was dying to see who she was with. Suddenly she arched upwards.

"Oh... Oh... Oh... OH GAWD!"

That was it, I was looking, I mean Edwina knew I was there, or at least I think she did, and I really needed to see what could make a woman get that vocal. I slid round the corner of the bale, and took a look between her legs, expecting another drummer like character. You have no idea of the sheer terror I felt, when I saw a patch of bright purple hair going round and round like beans in a grinder.

I walked out of the tent, and straight into Birch, I gasped with relief, and just pushed my head onto her shoulder.

"I found Bev; she is in there.... I am just going to the medics tent." Birch looked alarmed.

"Oh my God, Deads Sweetie, are you feeling ill?" I shook my head,

"I am going to get my eyes disinfected.... Some things cannot be unseen." Birch smiled.

"Oh Sweetie, I get you, it's scary isn't it?" It was thirty minutes later when Edwina appeared picking her teeth.

"That girl should fucking shave." I cringed, and gave a violent shudder.

She staggered slightly, and I gripped her arm. Edwina staggered again, and then stopped and went stiff.

"Oh, god Abby help me, I can't stop cumming, I feel weak all over and.... Oh gawd!" I grabbed her, and held up as she went ridged, and trembled on the spot.

Bev appeared smiling, and gripped Birch by the arm.

"That girl isn't no novice, you lied to me." Birch gave a chuckle.

"Are you displeased with her performance?" Bev gave a gruff laugh.

We spent the day, laughing, staggering, drinking beer from the beer tent, and eating masses of burgers. It was finally time to see how we had done, we walked towards the cooking exhibits, and

I did everything I could to try and soften the blow for Birch, by telling her that Lemon and Marshmallow curd was not really a jam. Anthony agreed wholeheartedly he screwed up his face, and shuddered, Birch was having none of it.

"Oh, Sweetie you have so much to lean, my work on you will never be done." I smiled.

"Is that such a bad thing?" She giggled.

"Not really."

We arrived at the tent and walked in, there were hundreds of jars of jam, all displayed with their little cards with numbers on. We walked down along the line, when Chloe screeched with delight.

"Oh my god I won third."

Her and Edwina started to dance, and twirl their hips, in a strange dance of celebration. We already had the giggles, so it was easy to laugh, Chloe lifted her bright green ribbon with pride. We walked further down the table as we looked at all the other jams, and then as we approached the end, and I saw I had not won, Birch froze on the spot.

Her curd had a bright blue ribbon on it, I was in shock, Birch had come second. I had to concede instant defeat, and admit that curd was in fact a jam. To be honest I am still not that convinced, but the judges of Wotton, felt differently and who am I to argue?

The nice thing was, it meant the world to Birch, she was so stoked, and happy. She lifted the ribbon like it was the greatest prize she had ever won.

"Deads isn't it pretty, I think I will put this in Petal after the show."

It was crazy, she was the most world wise person I knew, and yet looking at her with her ribbon, there was a child like quality, and total innocence to her, she looked so adorable, as she smiled holding her little blue ribbon.

We walked out of that tent with pride, yes, we were misfits, but hell, we had a second and third place under our belts, and we riding that wave right down to the floral tent.

None of us were prepared for what we found, which was a huge red ribbon on Anthony's arrangement, it was like the best thing ever, which was made even better by my third place ribbon.

Anthony burst into tears with joy, we hugged him constantly, as he blathered away wiping his eyes. Birch gave a smile, and I lifted my ribbon and looked at it, it was so silly, but it made me so happy, it was the nicest thing this village had done for me, I guess being a number had its perks. I looked at the gang.

"Guys we have to find out how mum did, I mean, she put so much into it, oh god, I hope she did not come second." Birch understood.

"Mum needs us, let's go."

We marched like an army into the next tent, where mum stood alone staring at her cake. I stopped afraid to approach her, I could feel my stomach twisting into knots, Birch took my arm.

"She is there Deads, if she has done well, we should congratulate her, and if she has won something, then we should hug her, and congratulate her, because look, either way she is alone in an empty tent, she needs us."

She was right, but I had seen her lose to Marjorie so many times, and I could not handle it if she had lost again. Birch almost dragged me towards her. Birch pushed me in the back and I staggered forward. I took a deep breath.

"Mum.... Are you okay?"

She turned and looked at me. I felt my heart crash into the floor, behind me everyone was holding their breath, a single second felt like an eternity. She stared at me, and then lifted her hand, and we all saw she was holding the red ribbon.

I have to say, it was like every birthday I had ever had hit me at once, behind me screams went wild, and almost deafened me, and she smiled a most beautiful smile.

"Abby... I did it.... I actually did it."

I cannot remember when I last hugged my mum so hard, it had been so long I had forgotten what it felt like until I wrapped my arms around her and pulled her so close. Feeling her hug me and have everyone I loved in one space was so wonderful, I broke apart and smiled.

"You did it, you beat her, I am so proud of you."

"Well you know, without the crack, I would probably have lost." Birch leaned in and hugged her.

"Yeah, but you sprinkled it, I am just your dealer, so that means you did it, and you believed in us, which sort makes everything else is irrelevant."

For the rest of our time in the fete, we could not be subdued, I just did not care who stared, or what wise cracks I got, I felt invincible. All of us had given our all to helping set the fete up, baking our cakes, boiling our jam, and arranging our flowers. We were the unlikeliest bunch of misfits, who were expected to fail, and yet we hadn't. Between us as a group we had scored high, and it really lifted all of us, as we walked round in our modern clothing, with our coloured hair, and big smiles.

As we walked out of the gates, we saw a bright smiling Norman with Daisy, regardless of Marjorie's opinion, he had won best in show for his marrow, proving that organic growing was not to be ridiculed. Several other growers were around him, shaking his hand and asking him for tips. For Norman, this was a massive victory, in his fight for greener ways of growing, and he was milking it for everything he could, whilst he had the support, and I did not blame him, he deserved it.

That night round the pool with mum and dad, we had drinks to celebrate, not long after we arrived and poured our first drinks, Bradley and Ellen Wheeler arrived, followed shortly by Roni and Will, and of course Bev. It was a fun filled night as we all sat back, and watched Birch beam with pride, as Bradley and Will inspected Petal.

I still did not get it, Will was so excited, as he ran his hands along the bonnet, talking wildly to Birch. He was in a really nice shirt and jeans, but that did not stop him crawling underneath it with Birch, and they both rambled excitedly, and the only words that made sense, was Birch, who would clap her hands, and smile, and almost shout. "I know right." To her dad repeatedly. Roni just smiled, she was used to it, she looked at my dad, who like me, had no understanding of it at all, and told him.

"Ignore it, it's a Dixon thing."

As the evening wore on, and we got drunker, Birch relaxed on the grass at my side.

"At least with the fete, there will be no fucking bell twat tomorrow, that will be nice." I looked at her and frowned.

"What are you talking about, it's Sunday, there will always be church." She lifted her head off the grass.

"How can there be, all the idiots that go there will be busy, the fete opens at ten, I thought the bell twat started at ten thirty?" I shook my head.

"Birch they arrange cover, actually mum asked me, but I told her I was exhausted and wanted some sleep. They will open up then take a break, so the service can go ahead as planned. Sorry Birch, they will never stop, you are going to have to accept it eventually." She groaned into the grass.

"Country living can be really painful, those twats have too much power."

Roni and Will had to return to the Hunter's, Bradley and Ellen hugged Deb's, and Birch grabbed her bag, as well as her dad, and said she would walk him half the way back to the Hunters.

I was tired, and as everyone left, Deb's and me headed for bed. I stripped and slipped in, the duvet felt cool after a long hot day on my skin, and lay face down in the pillow, and just relaxed. Deb's lay on her side and gave a sigh.

"Did you see Edwina today?"

I had no idea what suddenly brought this on, I lifted my head and looked at her.

"Honestly, seeing Bev go at her like a beaver felling a tree, is not something I want trapped in my head, but it is there forever." She chuckled and then looked seriously at me.

"Can oral really make you cum so much you cannot walk?"

I had no idea, in every case I had been through, the guy always followed through screwing me.

"To be truthful Deb's I just don't know, I mean oral for me has always been a warm up for the big finish, but I have to admit, I have never known anyone cum that much. Why are you even asking? Birch would probably be better to talk to, she has done far freakier things than I have."

"Yeah, I know that, but it just made me wonder, Abby, I trust you, and while we are alone, I want to talk to you." I rolled on to my side, to face her.

"Okay, what are you wondering?" She looked a little nervous.

"Do you think it is wrong to wonder about... You know, sex with a girl?"

I was the last person she should ask; I had been asking myself that all summer. I thought about how I could approach this.

"From what I have read, which is Birch's papers at Uni, it is a normal part of being female. Birch will tell you most women are Bi; they just refuse to act upon it. Some girls do it a few times, weirdly enough it happens a lot at Uni. Some are openly Bi all their life, which I think is Edwina, she is so confident about it all, it is sort of reassuring in a weird way. Deb's is this something you are, or something you want to try, because it is important you know the difference?"

"That is the problem Abby, I am not sure, I sometimes see girls and I get turned on, but then I look at guys and feel the same. I have had sex with a guy, and I liked it so much I want to do it again, I am just not sure about girls." I understood her.

"So, try it and see, I don't know what else to tell you. If you sleep with a girl, then like Jimmy, afterwards you will know."

She started to fidget, and I could see she was looking for the right words.

"Deb's just say what is on your mind." She gave a sigh.

"I don't know how to ask a girl to sleep with me." She had me there, and that was for sure.

"I don't know either... I suppose it is just like guys, I mean you have great boobs and a sexy ass, so if a guy likes you, then you pretty much know it. I suppose if a girl does, then it would be the same, and you would know she was into you, after that then all you have do is kiss her before she leaves, and you will have her in the bag. It is just like guys really, I don't wait for them to hit on me, if want them, I make it known by kissing them." It made sense and she smiled.

"That really helps, thanks, I knew I could talk to you." I smiled.

"I will always be there for you; you do know that don't you?" She smiled.

"So, do you want to try screwing or go to sleep?" She burst out laughing. "Sorry low blow... You are way too into Birch." I looked at her giggling.

"No, I am not, we are close, but it is not like that, we have been roommates for a year." She giggled.

"Yeah Abby, keep telling yourself that, if a girl looked at me the way you do her, I would defo be sleeping with her." I gave a sigh and rolled over.

"You are weird, go to sleep." She giggled, and snuggled into the pillow.

We were both flat out when Birch got back late, she smiled, looking very happy, as she striped, and slid in between us. I vaguely remember her snuggling into me and feeling her warmth, but that was about all.

I woke with a stinking head ache, vodka did that to me, Deb's was up, and like me, she had a pounding head, she looked at me with tired eyes.

"We need to start drinking more water before bed, feeling like this is too much."

I wriggled free of Birch, and sat up right on the edge of the bed. Deb's was walking around naked holding her head.

"I need coffee." She staggered into the kitchen. I yawned.

"What time is it?"

"About ten fifteen I think, if you are tired go back to sleep, we have a free day."

I must admit I wanted to, but I knew from experience that once I was awake, I would not go back to sleep, unlike Birch, who could fall asleep at any time in any place.

She once fell asleep on the bench outside the cathedral in Manchester, we were sat there feeding the birds, and she went, just like that, I have never seen anything like it. I got up and walked into the living room, and headed for the window, it was going to be another really hot day.

Deb's placed a coffee on the table and sat down opposite me, both of us looked like death. It was strange seeing her with her hair down, I was so used to seeing her with it tied back, it was far longer than I realised and it framed her face in a way that completely changed her appearance. Okay it was sticking out all over the place, but it looked good.

"You look different like that; you should wear your hair down more." She smiled.

"My bobble snapped, Anthony told me I should wear it down, he said I have very healthy hair." I agreed.

"It does always look good."

My phone went off, and both our heads almost exploded. Deb's jumped just as hard as I did, and I snatched it up and clicked answer, just to have quiet in the room again.

"Mum, I thought you were at church."

"I am, I am outside. Abigail tell me honestly, was it you?" I was too hung over for riddles.

"What was me mum?"

"Abigail, I raised you not to lie, so if you were involved then tell me honestly." My brain was just too slow this morning.

"Mum it is early, I am hung over, and tired from a week of killing myself, so please tell what the fu… What it is you are on about?" She sighed.

"I hope you are being straight with me Abigail, because someone has gone and filled the bells with spray insulating foam, and they are silent for the first time in fifty years. The vicar is throwing a fit, and says it will take at least a week to remove the foam, and then clean them back up."

It took about a millisecond to work out who would do such a thing.

"Mum talk to Deb's a minute."

I handed my phone to Deb's and headed for the bedroom, I grabbed Birch and shook the living shit out of her, she shot up into the sitting position looking like she had died.

"WAS IT YOU, PLEASE TELL ME YOU ARE NOT THAT BLOODY STUPID?"

I grabbed my skull, it hurt so bad. Birch's eyes were still rolling round in her head.

"Deads what the hell, it's Sunday, I don't get up until that bell twats starts his game, fuck off and let me sleep." She flopped back on the bed.

I was so angry inside at her.

"Why the hell would you fill the bells with foam, you know they would look straight at us?"

She opened one eye, and it moved until she found me staring at her, my head was really hurting and my blood pressure rising.

"Who did what, to what fucking bell?" I gave a sigh of impatience.

"It was you, do not toy with me Birch, this is really serious the vicar is doing his nut over this." I flopped on the bed.

"Birch why…? Things were just starting to improve for me, and now everything is fucked up again?"

She sat up in bed and pulled me into her arms.

"Deads, honestly it was not me, to be completely serious, I am pissed off I never thought of it." I looked at her.

"Honestly Birch… You are not lying about this are you? You have done some mad shit, and I would not put this past you, everyone knows you have spent all Summer complaining about them." She looked hurt, and her voice dropped.

"Sweetie, I love you, how could you even think that? I have never lied to you, and yes, I hate that fucking bell twat, but I know how important home is to you. I would never knowingly hurt you; I cannot believe you think I would do that do."

She looked so sad; I felt a pang deep inside me. Deb's came in and handed me the phone. I took it.

"Mum this was not done by anyone here, I absolutely promise you, it has nothing to do with us." I heard her give a sigh of relief.

"Alright Abby, we will deal with it, I am just glad you were not involved."

The call ended. Birch flopped back in the bed and pulled up the duvet, I felt really guilty, I leaned over.

"I am sorry Birch, but you can understand can't you, no one hates them more than you?" She pulled the duvet even higher, she sounded angry.

"Well obviously bloody not… Now sod off both of you, I want to sleep."

Debs' looked dreadful, she grabbed my hand as I was about to move closer to Birch and apologise.

"Abby, just leave her, let her sleep."

I got off the bed and walked to the door, as I looked back, all I could see was a tuft of white hair with a black patch on it, I gave a sigh and turned, and as I did, I heard a faint sob.

Chapter 31

Sobering Sunday.

Outside the Church, everyone gathered by the doors, and the conversation was rife. The sound of the loud speakers from the fete, blasted across the field, announcing the bull competition, and the talk was hurried and guarded.

Marion and Peter Saxon were in the vicarage dealing with the police, Marjorie had called them immediately, and on the road between the vicarage and church, crowds of people swarmed past, happy, and excited, as they went through the gates to the Village Fete.

Felicity stood with Hatty, as around her there were many conversations, she had heard the name of Abigail mentioned several times in the other groups. It was very clear who the village thought was responsible, and they were making their views known. Felicity gave a sigh and ended the call.

"That was Edwin, he has reorganised the relief staff to cover for a little longer." Hatty nodded, she looked at Felicity.

"Trust her Flick, she is different, she is not stupid, and neither is Birch, if they say they have not done it, they haven't."

"Well it is easy to say isn't it? By the sound of things, she has already been tried and found guilty. Oh, Hatty you know how wild she can get, this is exactly the sort of prank she would pull?" Hatty shook her head.

"I disagree Flick, if Abby says they were not involved, then they are not. For god's sake Flick have some faith in her, this is exactly why she went all the way to Manchester, you always see the bad, never the good. Flick she is like you, not me, don't forget that."

Loud voices came from the church doorway, and Felicity closed her eyes for a second, she had no doubt what was coming, Hatty leaned in.

"Trust her for god's sake."

Roni appeared at the gate, looking worried, Harriet noticed her, patted Felicity's arm, and walked down towards her. Roni looked worried as Hatty approached.

"It is all over the Hunter's. Please tell me this was not one of her pranks?" Hatty smiled.

"No, we spoke to Abby and she says they were not involved." Roni gave a sigh of relief.

"I have tried to phone her, but she is not answering, I assumed she was asleep, what with no bells to wake her, I won't say I did not worry. She has made her opposition to the church more than obvious on many occasions."

Marjorie came out with a group talking loudly, this was her chance to even the score, and she was taking it.

"I do not think there is any doubt, those two tramps have targeted the church since they arrived here, I will make sure the police know everything about them."

Felicity spun round and stared at the powdered pompous face of Margorie, as she stood with a fixed smug smile.

"Like what exactly Marjorie? As far as I can see the only thing that created an offence here is she dyed her hair, and that is not exactly a cause for prosecution these days is it now?" Felicity stared at Marjorie.

"I have spoken with Abigail and she has assured me she has had nothing to do with it." Marjorie scoffed.

"Well excuse me Felicity Watson, but it appeared to me that when your daughter turned up here, even you did not recognise her, so as to your ability to give me any kind of assurances to her conduct and behaviour, is somewhat weak. Let's be honest, everyone here knows who did it, who else would?"

Felicity stared at Marjorie with hate, and felt her blood starting to boil insider her.

"I have no idea who would want to do such a thing, but if I tell you it was not Abigail, then it dammed well wasn't. As for not knowing what my child is up to, I would be very careful Marjorie Wallace, considering it was your child who was taking illegal pictures of a sexual nature of my daughter, and passing them on to a Rapist. A Rapist I may add, who then not only tried to rape her, but also another member of this churches choir. As vice of this council, I for one would like to know who exactly did the background checks on Martin Hinkley, because as far as any of us parents in this parish are aware of, to date no information has been supplied to us. That is something I will be taking up with the villagers when I run for chair.”

Marjorie looked absolutely outraged, and her face turned purple.

“How dare you even suggest I had any knowledge of such things; I was equally outraged by his conduct.” Felicity smirked.

“Who’s, Martin’s or Nigel’s? So where is the report, and the copy of his background check, I am still waiting for it?”

Hatty stood back with all the other villagers, and watched with a faint smile. After all these years, the fire was still there, she had honestly thought the village had tamed her, but finally she saw a little of the Flick she once knew, and she was proud of her. Marjorie struggled for words.

“It has been a very busy time; we have had a lot to do.” Felicity scoffed.

“Don’t you mean Peter, Mary, Lillian, Celia, Edwin and myself have had a lot to do, from what I can see, you have been too busy licking your wounds, and reinflating your pride in the vicarage for the last week. Abigail, and her friends did not do this, she may not look like she used to, but deep inside she is a decent and respectful girl. It would serve you greatly Marjorie, to hold that fork tongue of yours, and remember that. I raised Abigail, and she turned out wonderful, and you are all so blind you cannot see that. Well all of you are wrong, her and Birch are kind loving and decent, and Edwin and myself are very proud of her…… I have an event to run, so if you will excuse me, I will get on with it as I have been doing, and you can go kiss ass, like you always have, I believe the police are waiting for you.”

Felicity turned and marched down the path with her head held up, and Hatty stood with Roni, and watched with smiles as she walked towards them. She reached Hatty and faltered.

“Hatty I think I am going to cry.” Roni looked at her with intense green eyes.

“Don’t you dare Flick, you stood your ground beautifully,

and now walk with pride onto that field, and go serve your community... And Flick.... Thank you for defending Jemi, I appreciate that." Felicity took a deep breath.

"She is a lovely girl, I have become very fond of her indeed, she is a credit to you Roni."

Lillian and Celia came scuttling down the path, with Mary, and as Felicity walked onto the field, they moved in beside her with quiet congratulations. Hatty looked at Roni.

"Do you have a few spare minutes? I have something I want to show you at my place, I think it may be very useful to Birch."

It felt strange sitting out in the garden, with just Deb's. We sat in silence in the sun, and my mind drifted inside myself. I felt guilty, I had hurt her, and I hurt because of that, and I did not know how to deal with it, or confront it. I made Birch cry, yet she had been so strong and so tough, how could I be so foolish, she has never once lied in all the time I have known her, why did I have to go and doubt her?

"I screwed up Deb's." She gave a soft smile, and patted my hand.

"It is allowed you know, just once in a while. It has been a long exhausting week, and we are all tired. Let her sleep, honestly, when she wakes up, you can both talk and you can say what you need to say to her. Abby, we have been here remember? We have had our fall outs in the past, and yet I have always known deep down, I could depend on you if I needed to, and Birch more than any knows that too. You know you are both so close, you really are like lovers, you know. You two understand each other in ways none of us ever will. It is like you have some kind of telepathy between you. I can tell you Abby, I felt a little jealous at first, but watching you two, and being with you both, I have grown to understand it."

I felt so horrible inside, and I just did not know what to do, I felt the tears form in my eyes, and Deb's smiled.

"See how much you care about her? Give her some space, and then when she is rested go talk with her." I nodded and tried to smile.

"I never should have doubted her, she has never once lied to me. I was in the wrong and I should make it up to her." Deb's smiled.

"Tell her that when she wakes up."

Deb's went to make another coffee, and I closed my eyes, and just lay back on the lounger, and felt the heat of the sunlight on my skin. Deb's returned holding her phone.

"I got a message from Edwina, there is a lake party today, whilst all the adults are busy at the fete."

I shielded my eyes from the sun with my hand, and looked up at her.

"You go, I am not in the mood to party." She looked torn, and I sighed.

"Deb's go screw something, you are so desperate it shows. I am staying here, I need to sort things out with Birch, it will be easier to do it alone. If things get sorted, we will meet you alright?" She nodded.

"Just go make up with her and come, I will worry if you are not there." I sat up and picked up the fresh coffee off the floor, my head still hurt.

"Deb's what are you going to do if you have a party at Uni, sit in your dorm because Birch and me are not there? This will be good for you, and let you get out with other friends, you will have Edwina and Chloe with you, so you won't be alone. Look in a matter of just over a week, I will be back in Manchester. This will be a good step for you." She sighed.

"I know, I just hate the thought of you being here all sad on your own, and yes I know we will be going in opposite directions soon. I hate the thought of it, which is why I wanted to make the most of now with you guys."

"Deb's we still have time, I am sure Birch and me, will be able to find some other weird and debauched way, for you to use goggles in sex before we leave. Go have fun, get laid, get drunk, and then tell me all about it." She sighed.

"Okay then, just so you know, I really hate this, you two need to fix it and soon." I laughed.

"We will, give us the space to do it." She nodded.

"Okay Abby. I will get dressed and see you soon. Edwina has borrowed her dad's van, so if you can, come join us."

I watched her walk back to find her clothes, and fifteen minutes later after having a shower, she appeared dressed and said goodbye. I watched her leave, and settled back to wait for Birch.

I closed my eyes and felt the sun again, I was so tired, it had been the most draining week since I had got here. I sunk back into the lounger and drifted, my mind alive, with all the feelings I had swirling around in me.

I didn't know if I was sleeping, drifting or dreaming, but suddenly I was drowning. I snapped awake fighting for breath, and as I breathed in, I breathed in water, my arms flayed out, my legs kicked, and I came coughing and spluttering to the surface, and retched and gasped, as I tried scramble to the side of the pool.

I felt for the edge, and dragged myself towards it, and pulled myself up onto it. I gasped a desperate breath, and coughed out more water, as I choked, my eyes filled with tears, and my heart with panic. I gasped in air, by the mouth full as I regained my composure.

My eyes still had tears in them and were blurred as I looked up and saw the fuzzy shape of Birch standing next to the over turned lounger, and I felt really angry. I looked at her as I breathed in more air.

"WHAT THE HELL WAS THAT FOR, ARE YOU BLOODY NUTS, I ALMOST DROWNED?" She scoffed.

"Oh please, it's the shallow end."

My eyes cleared, she was dressed and stood watching, with a smirk on her face. I felt so mad at her.

"THAT WAS OUT OF ORDER BIRCH, WHY DID YOU DO IT?"

"I screwed up right, it is what I do, screw around with people, and fuck things up for them, that's right, isn't it, ABIGAIL!?" I shook my head.

"You scared the shit out of me Birch." She huffed, and turned away.

"I am going to see my mum, I miss her, and I hate not being able to be with her in this god awful village. I am meeting her outside, and going to Oxendale." My breathing was becoming more regular.

"Birch... Wait a minute, look.... I am really sorry; can we not just talk."

"No!" She started to walk away.

"Birch... Just wait one minute, just don't run away like this." She stopped, turned round, and came marching back across the grass.

"I DON'T RUN, I FACE MY SHIT, OR HAVE YOU EVEN FORGOTTON THAT TOO?"

She stared at me, I had never heard her shout at me before, hell I had never heard her shout. Her eyes glared bright green, and she looked scary.

"You know what Abigail, I have done a lot of shit, I've screwed for fun, got pissed and outrageous, smoked dope, and done a shit ton of pranks, and I have been called, and slagged off for all of it, but never once have I run from anything. I faced it all with a fuck you attitude, like I have here. Everyone one of those arseholes, has had it in for me from as soon as I got here, and I have taken it. I have heard what they say, and I have handled every last bit of it, for no other reason than I did it for you. They can say whatever they want, and it will not even dent me, but there is one thing they will never be able to say, because it is not bloody well true. I may be a slut to them, but I have never lied, not to them or to you, not ever. You more than any should fucking know that Abigail Watson... I need to see my mum, the keys for Petal are on the table, go to the sex party, and let some dumb dick head screw some sense into you.... I will see you later."

She stormed off across the grass, as I clung to the poolside, not knowing what to do. In over a year, she had never once been this angry. I mean, it was Birch, she never got mad, but she was with me, and I had no idea how to deal with that.

I climbed out of the pool and picked up the lounger, I could not believe she had tipped me in. I set it straight and lifted the towel to dry myself, and I suddenly felt very much alone.

Was this how it would have been if Birch was not here, would my whole summer have felt like this? I shivered and wrapped the towel round me and walked back to the house and dropped onto the bed. I felt wretched, how could I have hurt her so easily?

I lay with my head on the pillow, and guilt surged into me, she was right, she had never lied to me once, I should never have doubted her. I pushed my face into the pillow and felt the first huge wave crash over me, and the sob came up from my chest, and before I knew what was happening, I was crying uncontrollably, and I had no way of stopping it.

It was around three in the afternoon, when my phone pinged, and I opened my eyes, I was damp and shivering. I sat up and pulled off the towel, and then slid under the duvet to warm up. I looked at my phone, it was from mum.

It had not taken very long to discover who sabotaged the bells. The CCTV footage from the vicarage showed a guy in a hooded top, leaving the church just after midnight, carrying a bag. Marjorie had recognised him as one of the bell ringers, named Brent Anderson.

The police visited his house, and he still had the bag with the empty foam cans in it. It turned out; he had been seen with Anthony at the fete by the other guys in the ringer's group. They ridiculed him for hanging out with a gay guy, and had thrown him out of the group. It appeared Brent was also gay.

In an act of revenge that night, he had gone to the church, and filled all the bells with insulating foam, he worked for a builder, and they used it at work, so he took some.

Knowing the truth just made everything worse, Birch had been honest, and I had called her on it, and it just made me feel even more wretched, how could I have been so stupid? I pulled the duvet close, and pulled my pillows down, and felt the warmth enter my shivering limbs, all I could do was wait for her, and then tell her how very sorry I was. I drifted back into sleep filled with worry, and wishing she was here holding me.

I have no idea what time it was, but I felt her arm slide round me, and opened my eyes. The bedroom door was closed, but I could hear voices in the living room. I slid my hand up, and pulled her hand round to my boob, she snuggled closer into me. I swallowed hard, my voice was weak and croaky.

"I am sorry... I am so sorry Birch." The tears came again and I sobbed.

"Shush Deads, it is done... No more tears."

She pulled me tight. I gave another massive sob and shook, I didn't want to cry, I was trying not to, but I had felt so lost and alone without her, and it still felt painful.

I rolled over and looked at her, she smiled and lifted her hand to wipe away my tears. Her eyes shone so bright, there was so much love, so much soul in them, as she gazed at me, it just made me feel even worse.

"No more tears now, it is over."

I snorted and sniffed up to clear my nose of its running, and she smiled, I swallowed back the tears.

"It was horrible without you, I felt so alone and afraid. Birch I am so... So sorry, you know that right?" She smiled again, and her eyes sparkled.

"I am sorry too, things have got to me, and I took out on you, that was also wrong, which is why I went to see mum." She wiped my hair from the side of my face.

"No more tears, it is done with, and we still have things to do."

Maybe it was the warmth of her skin, I do not know, it could have just been as simple as her arms around me, but everything suddenly felt safe again, and I slipped my arm around her and snuggled as close as I could. Birch kissed my cheek, and I turned to look at her, she smiled that wonderful smile, and just went with the flow.

I lifted my head, and I kissed her on the lips. She responded, and kissed me back, and I felt electric run through me. How could I hide it much longer, my body felt alive, but I knew somewhere deep inside, she did not feel the same. I pulled away and smiled.

"Don't leave me again, it is so horrible without you."

She was inches away, and her eyes were so close and sparkling. She smiled.

"I won't... I promise... We have guests, and stories of rampaging lust to hear, you should get up."

That night we spent another night sat on the floor drinking and laughing, as Chloe, Edwina and Deb's told their sordid tales of their sexually deviant exploits, which involved Chloe having a picture taken by Deb's of her enjoying a spit roast, I felt a little shocked seeing it.

Deb's was way wilder than I thought, she had sex with two guys, and she was very happy about it as she swapped notes with Birch, on the finer points of each man compared to Jimmy. Edwina just smiled and kept her secrets, which in a way I admired. Anthony gave us the full story of Brent, and he even blushed a little, as he had arranged to meet him in Oxendale.

He had got into a lot of trouble, but has offered to clean all the bells, and so no charges were pressed against him. He looked at all of us.

"I think it sucks, they threw him off the bells because he is gay, it is wrong."

The night ended as it always did, we passed out in bed drunk. Well, they did, I was not as tired, and as I lay in the dark with Birch curled around me, all I could think of was I did it, I finally kissed her, and she did not slap my face.

Monday brought me to back reality. It was a bank holiday, and was mad busy, people flocked to the fete, and all of us were on steward duty. I spent the day with Birch, Molly was nowhere to be seen thank god, and we walked around with radios, directing people, and pointing places out, and showing people where the final animal contests were.

By two o'clock I was already exhausted. My mum had an energy like I had never known, she was filled with confidence and authority, as she directed everyone to their duties.

Her showdown with Marjorie, and being proven right, had done her the world of good, although on the few occasions we ran into Marjorie, her air of superiority appeared less dented to me. She still swaggered around like she owned the place, and tuned her nose up, and said rude things under her breath whenever she saw Birch and I.

At three we had hall duty, and I was pleased, to get off the field out of the heat, and into the cooler conditions. When we arrived, we had chair duty, and got stuck in, and added as many extra chairs as we had, to fill in all the spaces. Mum was expecting a big crowd, the celebrity speakers usually pulled in around a thousand visitors, mum expected at least double that.

The stage was filled with metal scaffold and lights, and a huge white screen. Katie was on hand talking into her head set, as the final tests were being undertaken. Lights flicked on and off, the large screen came to life with test images, and all the microphones were tested.

I was surprised to see cameras, Katie was going to film it for a video, which would be put on the website, but the thing that caught my attention more, was a large section at the front, which had been roped off with thick red rope, slid through golden posts. Birch explained it to me.

"This is the VIP section, if you look all the seats have names on them, and my mum has a plan of it. She will know exactly who is in front of her, look you have one here. When people arrive, they will be escorted to these seats, and treated like first class customers. They will get the closest view of today's events." I was a little suspicious.

"Why are these locals extra special, and why are my mum and dad here?" She gave me a cheeky smile.

"This is my production, to be honest, the most frustrating part of all this has been not being able to talk to mum and dad, and not being able to be fully involved. I have had to leave it all in Katie's hands, but I would have preferred to have been here setting it up."

I walked up the steps to the stage, and looked out at all the seats, it made my stomach twist.

"Christ your mum is brave, I would be terrified having to face so many and talk." Birch giggled.

"It can be scary, but like everything, you get used to it."

The place suddenly felt ten times bigger than I had ever remembered it.

"Will you do stuff like this one day Birch?" She stood at my side.

"If I work with mum, then probably yes, I have always thought I would." I gave a long flow of air through my lips.

"You are a hell of a lot braver than I am." She chuckled.

"If you become a famous writer, you never know, you might end up on a stage like this too."

"Yeah, screw that, I will just bang out videos, it's less scary." Katie walked out onto the stage, talking into her head set.

"Right Bev, we are set to roll, Roni is relaxing with Will, let's open the doors and let's get them in, and the show on the road." She looked at us.

"Off... Come on, off, this is your mums' stage Jemi, go sit and watch what you have created, come on... Bugger off, some of us have a job to do."

At the far end of the hall, the doors opened, and people started to enter, outside on the field the show was coming to an end, as traders and stand holders started to pack up, the PA announced the guest speaker was starting in the hall, and people began walking off the field and down the road towards us.

Birch and I sat in our seats, and were joined by Deb's and crew. We were all sat to the left of the central aisle, the other VIP's were all sat on the right. Lillian and Celia appeared to be very excited.

I noticed at the far end of the hall, men in black shirts were setting up a long table filled with books, I was impressed at the size and scale of the whole operation. The bright purple hair of Bev stood out at the back next to the doors, she was wearing a black vest with the words 'Security' written on it, it felt comforting to know she was there, I would imagine if anyone wanted to force their way in, they would think twice if they saw her.

The room just kept filling up, and there was far more than I expected. I noticed Molly as she walked down the aisle wearing a bib that had 'Staff' on it, as she guided Marion, Marjorie, and the Vicar to their seat. Her stuck up mate Sophia was also helping, she showed Peter and Mary Saxon the way.

As always, I got a scowl from Marjorie. Mum and Dad walked down smiling, she saw me and came over.

"Abby, it looks like we could have up to three thousand, it is the biggest audience this place has ever held." I gave her a big smile.

"Good for you mum, that will show her."

She chuckled as she walked to take her seat, Deb's was getting very excited, as were Chloe and Edwina, Anthony was always buoyant in public, so it was difficult to tell. Birch sat as still as a rock; her hands squeezed together slightly. I patted her leg.

"It will be fine, stop worrying, your mum will steal the day, you have worked too hard on this for it to fail." She looked nervous.

"Really? Deads my heart is pounding, if something goes wrong..."

"Birch it won't." She took a deep breath.

"Not long now, and we will see."

The room was packed to the rafters, and the hum in the air from the hundreds of conversations sounded like a huge generator, just humming along. I felt excited as I saw Katie walk towards us, she stopped at the rope, and lifted it up to clip it to the post. She stood in front of us, and spoke on her head set.

"Okay we are set to go... Roni is in place and set.... Lights standby.... Projection... stand by.... Camera's roll.... we are going in 3.... 2....1.... and we are on go .... Go ... Go!"

She turned, and walked up the steps and onto the stage, as the house lights went down, and the spotlights came on, the stage flooded with light, and all the conversations came to an end. God my heart was pounding in sync with Birch's, why the hell did I feel so nervous? Somehow it felt like tonight would define my future, and to be honest, I was shit bloody scared about it.

Chapter 32

Food for Thought.

The room was packed to capacity, and three thousand people had arrived, and paid on the door, and there were still people outside, the lights lowered to the hum of conversations, which died slowly away as the stage lit up. The suited figure of Katie walked onto the stage holding a microphone, she stood in the centre, and waited until all was quiet, and then lifted the microphone to her mouth.

"Ladies and gentlemen, thank you for attending here this night, for you are as always, in for treat. Your guest speaker will be presenting a new format tonight, which is why you will see, we have cameras around the place. I would also like to add that at the rear at the end of the talk, we will have all of Veronica's books available for sale, and we are delighted to say, that the proceeds from every book sale tonight, will also be added to the funds for your village." She smiled at everyone in the hall.

"We will be filming tonight specifically for Veronica's web site, of which cards are available at the back, so you can look up the URL, and watch it again as many times as you like. I am honoured to say that this guest speaker is not only someone I have had the pleasure of working with, I also consider her to be my inspiration, and my best friend. Bev darling will you ensure the doors are properly closed, we would wish for no interruptions, thank you."

The crowd turned slightly to glance back, it was clear, no one was going to mess with her, Katie smiled.

"If everyone is ready, please welcome for you pleasure. Dr Veronica Gemma Dixon."

The applause was deafening, as she walked calmly onto the stage in black slacks, and a long flowing white blouse. She was wearing a head mic, and smiled as she approached Katie. Katie held up her arm as the applause continued, and backed away towards the steps, leading down to the floor, in front of where we were sat. She winked as she walked past, opened the red rope, walked through, and the reattached it, and walked towards the back of the room, talking quietly into her head set.

The noise died down, and Veronica stood on the stage, alone, behind her in large letters on the screen was her name.

"Good evening everyone, and thank you for being here tonight. I am, as introduced, Dr Veronica Dixon, and I am a therapist working in the fields of Relationships, Sexual Dysfunction and Practices, and also Conflict. I have indeed written several books on all of these, some of them best sellers, and I also run a website, blog and video channel, all of which are done out of my practice, which is based in the centre of the city of Manchester."

I looked across at the VIP's as they all watched her, Veronica started to talk about her practice and the problems she faced with others in it, and the kinds of solutions she offered, I missed some of her words, as I was too busy watching Marjorie and Marion, who I noticed would lean into each other and whisper.

My mum and dad were sat together saying nothing, my mum looked really interested, and was listening intently. Every now and again she gave a smile, as if Veronica had said something, she understood better than she had ever let on. Deb's was sat forward in her seat, hanging on every word, so was Anthony, Edwina was leaned into Chloe, and occasionally after Veronica made a comment, Edwina would nod, and then whisper to Chloe, who smiled and gave a slight nod, and yet Chloe never once took her eyes off Veronica.

I turned to Birch, and there was that look, it was total involvement and adoration. I watched as her lips silently said the words at the same time as Veronica, I was aware she had written it, but I had no idea she had memorised it. Her bright eyes moved from side to side, watching her mum, god she was so attractive, I just lost myself for a moment simply watching her, the noise in the background slipping into a dull hum.

I was so conflicted, and I wanted to know why this girl was so unlike any other I knew, and made me feel all these crazy and wild feelings, that I was apparently incapable of feeling for anyone else. Well certainly any other girl, I was not sure about guys. I had thought I loved James, but I think it was clear, it was just a fantasy, because it felt nothing like this. Oh my god am I in love with a girl?

No, I could not be, I like guys way too much, it is just friendship, deep loving friendship, it could not be anything else, that was it, we were great mates, this was a test, nothing more. I was seeking the truth of me, which is what Birch had told me so many times. I was just looking into myself, and asking the question, lost in the time and space of my mind, no longer aware of the room filled with people, as I pondered the one question, I had been asking myself all Summer. 'Who am I really.' Reality came crashing into me, and I snapped out of my head, to the loud voice of Veronica.

"WHO AM I!?"

I looked to the stage as she stood there looking right into the audience, holy shit can she reads minds? Oh hell, I hope not, Birch is her daughter after all.

"Who am I? It is a good question...." She looked out at the audience.

"Well, I am considered an expert in my field, I have sold well over ten million books, and I am the one up here talking tonight, but is that what defines me, is that who I really am? I say not, I say they are just labels, and I am more than that."

I sat motionless, transfixed by her presence, she was elegant and feminine, and yet she had an inner power that commanded the whole room. She walked slowly across the stage, and then turned to face the audience. Her tone changed and she smiled.

"I am the very fortunate daughter of a remarkable woman, who was intelligent, loving, compassionate, and most of all a maverick. She had a massive influence on me, because she was the one who taught me not to judge, but to understand. I miss her deeply, as she passed a few years ago. I am also very lucky to be married to the most amazing guy, he is my rock in every way."

She looked to the back of the hall, where I knew he was standing.

"He is the love of my life; I owe him so much." She gave a

beautiful smile, not unsimilar to that of Birch.

"My best friend in the world, is my promoter, and I have the most unbelievable and beautiful daughter, who has exceeded my every expectation. She is also a maverick, and I see my mother clearly in her as she grows. I love them all deeply, and they define my life."

She walked back along the front of the stage.

"My daughter has just aced her first university year, and I am so proud of her, she is an inspiration to me."

She had hardly said a word I had heard, and yet I was holding my breath, hanging on to everything she said. She stopped and turned to face out.

"You now know who I am, my question tonight is, who are you?"

Behind her the same words appeared in big letters on the screen. Veronica walked back to the table, sat on it, and faced the crowd, she lifted her glass and took a sip, her voice was soft and gentle, but easily heard through the PA system.

"That is a question that I ask every day in my practice back in Manchester, and over the years I have found it also one of the most difficult for people to answer. You see the problem is, we all know what we like, and what we feel, but in many cases, we are so afraid of being exposed, we hide from our feelings, hide what we like, and we never reveal our truth. Few have the power to cast off their doubts, because the majority all live by those terrible four words that can destroy your life."

The words appeared in large letters on the screen.

"WHAT WILL PEOPLE SAY?" She smiled at the audience.

"I see you are all there already, living in dread, because you know how powerful those four words can be. Would you like to know what I tell my clients? Because I have four words that I always respond with. DOES IT REALLY MATTER?" I smiled and looked at Birch.

"I absolutely love your mum." I looked back at the stage, Roni smiled as she sat there, on the table. I could see her watching the audience, just like Birch did when she watched people.

"I find it very sad, that nine out of ten people look at me, and then tell me it does, because I know for a fact, it does not.

The world is changing my friends, social media has changed everything, and as much as it can be a power for good, it also has some pretty nasty consequences. It has placed people under the microscope, and they have suffered because of it. You see it is easy to shame a person online, because you can easily hide behind a fake profile, and troll anyone. The problem is, over the years, that very aspect of social media has jumped off the page, and people have adopted it into their normal everyday lives."

She slipped off the table and walked to the front of the stage.

"The one lesson I have learned in my practice, probably more than anything else, is this." She turned and pointed to the large screen, and as she said the words, they appeared on the screen. "Grownups.... Bully...Too." I gasped when I saw it.

"Holy shit Birch, what have you done?"

Veronica calmly walked across the stage, and watched the audience, there was utter silence.

"When we say the word bully, just about everyone thinks of school, that is just where it starts, and trust me, it is not a thing for young children alone, and it has been around for a very long time. I think is it one of the biggest fundamental problems of life today."

She stood still for second, and looked round at everyone in the room, I could feel the tension in the air, and felt goosebumps on my arms. I mean holy shit, she was there in front of all of them, and calling them out for their own behaviour, I gave a slight gasp.

"Oh my god, she is brave." I could not help, but just watched, held captive by her presence.

"It is so easy to tag someone with a label, and then beat them with it, let's be honest here, it is one hell of a lot easier than being honest, or compassionate, or trying to understand another person. Fuck all that, let's call them a name, and hurt them before they hurt us.... I am not wrong, am I? It is so easy, so convenient, it just slides off the tongue."

I was ridged in my seat, the whole room was hung on her every word, and it appeared to me a lot of them felt very uncomfortable. Veronica walked back to the table, took a sip of her drink, and turned around.

"Recently my daughter had a friend, who was being bullied by grownups, and she came to me to ask my advice, as to what she could say to make her feel better. My daughter is a very loving girl, well actually she is a young woman, but she was being hurt seeing her friend suffer, and so I told her this."

She turned and pointed back at the screen; the words appeared in large letters.

"Fear... Of.... Being... Shamed." She turned back to the audience.

"We all live in fear, because people do use it, and yes, it is very wrong. They use labels, based on snap judgements, that targets aspects of a person, and they find hurtful words that are associated with them, and then use them to demoralise and belittle a person... We all know those so called flaws that people like to weaponize, don't we?"

Veronica walked back to the table and took a drink, and once again the words appeared above her.

"Gay... Lesbian... Bi.... Trans... Naturist.... Adulteress.... Kink... Whore.... Fraud.... Deviant... Slut.... Transient.... Sinner... Witch.... Embarrassment.... Voyeur.... Exhibitionist.... Trouble Causer." Veronica looked up at the screen.

"There are so many more, the list is endless, and every one of them is just so easy to access and use, and when that is done, people get hurt. Let me give you some sobering facts."

The words appeared above her on the screen, and scrolled up as she spoke, it was startling to see all of the statistics, I knew this was what Birch had created, I had seen her putting the slideshow together, but just seeing it all that big on the screen, as it scrolled slowly up, took my breath away.

"Each year, over five thousand young people in the UK kill themselves, and the number is rising. It is one of the biggest concerns of the mental health profession at the moment, and bullying is a major factor, as is isolation. Some people feel so isolated and intimidated by their communities, they kill themselves, and that is just the young."

Veronica walked slowly to the front of the stage, and looked at all of the seating before her, her voice softened.

"I knew a thirty five year old man who was into BDSM, it was his fetish, and I realise that a lot of people do not understand why someone would want to do that, but he did, it actually made him calm, it gave him a release, it made him feel good about himself, until the neighbours found out. As his therapist, and because he had no traceable family, I had to identify his body, he left me a letter saying sorry."

Veronica stopped, and just for a second, she choked, I saw a tear run from her eye, and I felt an instant restriction in my own throat, and I swallowed hard. I felt shocked, and so helpless, the thought terrified me, because of the stirring deep inside me, was it my own awareness, had I not thought about it just before leaving for University?

"Excuse me a second."

She walked back to the table and took a drink, took a deep breath, wiped her eye, and then tuned back to the audience, the impact it had was huge. Just seeing her up there alone and so vulnerable, frightened me, and my eyes filled with tears. Veronica composed herself.

"This guy was a really nice guy, but I got to witness the months of hell his neighbours inflicted on him. He literally became a prisoner in his own home. I took his letter home and read it, and I cried for over an hour, because he did not deserve the sort of things they did to him. He was bullied and isolated, the authorities did little to help him, and so he lived in adject fear. His last words in his letter was to thank me for all I had done for him, he apologised for failing me."

I wiped my eyes quickly, and looked round the audience, their eyes were glued to her, and a lot of people looked sad and hurt, it was so silent, it was unbelievable. I looked back at the stage, as Veronica came to the edge. She looked so small on the big stage, stood alone, and fragile in the spotlight, and she had that Birch like quality that just pulled everyone in to her.

"When my daughter asked me for advice for her friend, I told her, go to your friend, and let her know it is okay to be who she is, she is one of the brave ones, who does not hide who she is, and tell your friend this. What someone says about her, says far more about them, than it ever will her. Your friend has done nothing wrong."

Veronica looked down, and right at me.

"If anything, she has done everything right, and she is braver than everyone who has called her, because she chooses not to hide who she is. Tell her, as a person, she is magnificent and beautiful."

I suddenly felt a huge surge run through me, and my eyes filled with tears again. I looked down as Veronica walked away from the edge of the stage, and sat back down on the table. I had so many emotions coursing through me, I did not know what to do. Birch slid her hand over, and took mine in hers, and she gave it a squeeze. Deb's put her hand on my back, and softly rubbed it, Veronica's voice was soft, as she sat back on the table.
"That really is the problem isn't it, my friends? Every one of us has something to hide, and we all live in fear of being shamed for it, so few of us have the guts my daughter's friend did, because she owned it, and she wore it with dignity."

She jumped off the table, and clapped her hands together, and everyone jerked in their seats. There was movement on the stage, as men in all black, slid large mobile cameras to each side of the stage, and pointed them into the audience.
"Okay, as I have told you, my daughter is an amazing and wonderful person, and tonight I am going to do something that she has worked on just for me... I know, I am such a proud mum; I cannot help myself. She has no idea how gifted she is, and when she qualifies, she will be joining me at my side working in my practice. So I have allowed her to help me tonight, by changing this show a little, and I have asked two very lovely young women to help me out, so Chloe and Edwina, would you like to join me on stage please."
I looked at Birch, as I sniffled and wiped my eyes.
"What is going on?" She smiled and winked.
"You will see... Just watch."
I got lost for a moment, as I watched Birch, her dazzlingly bright green eyes were locked on the stage, this was her plan, and her invention, as I have seen so many times before, she took in every second of detail as it happened.
Chloe and Edwina got out of their seats, and walked to the stage steps, they went up and onto the stage, and Veronica smiled.
"Oh, you two, look so beautiful, are they not simply stunning everyone? I am sure their parents must be so proud. Oh, girls I

have to say, I absolutely love your hair, it is amazing, you must let me know who your stylist is?" Chloe blushed.

"He is my friend… he is called Antonio."

There was a surprised rumble in the audience, Veronica turned to the crowd.

"If you are here Antonio, let me have some of your cards, I know a few people in the celebrity world, who would love this sort of flare and talent, I will pass your cards on."

I turned to Anthony, and smiled, his eyes were wide, and he had his hands to his mouth in shock. I leaned over Deb's, and patted his leg.

"You deserve that."

He was too shocked to talk, and we giggled. Veronica looked at the audience.

"I have been here for a few days, and I must say, I have been made so welcome, and I cannot thank you all enough. You have the most beautiful village to live in, and it is a credit to you all. As with all villages, people are hiding parts of themselves, and it has not gone unnoticed, you see I have a cheated a little, because there has been someone here for a while watching for me, and so I have been able to get a very good look, and idea of village life, because I want to expand my practice at some future point, and I think this place could be an ideal location."

That was a bit of a surprise, half the audience appeared very happy, some not so much. Veronica looked down.

"Below me is the VIP section, roped off with these wonderful red ropes. All these people have played their part in keeping this village running, as they have done for a long time, and they all should be commended for their efforts."

Veronica started to clap, and the audience joined in, it was really loud.

She walked back to the table and lifted two piles of envelopes, turned, and handed one pile each to Chloe and Edwina. She turned back to the audience, and walked to the front of the stage, as the applause died down.

"My very lovely assistants have envelopes with a name on, and they are going to hand them to the person whose name is on them, and they contain a card. These are very special cards, because they appear to be black, and blank. I am a therapist after all, and confidentiality is key to my profession. When I ask you, I would like each of you to open your envelopes, and I will do a little technical magic, to make it possible for you to read them."

Chloe and Edwina came back down the steps, and handed out the cards, and I was really surprised to see my mum and dad also got one, so did Deb's and Anthony. I looked at Birch.

"Do you know about this?"

"Some of it, it looks like mum is pulling a fast one."

I looked at Veronica, she smiled at everyone in the VIP section. Chloe and Edwina looked at their last cards, and looked shocked, there were also cards for them. They walked back to their seats, beside Anthony, who was still grinning like a Cheshire cat, but they were looking worried.

I saw Chloe's face as she sat down. Birch and myself were the only two without cards. The cameras on the side of the stage tilted down, and on the screen the pictures of the VIP's with their envelopes appeared, Roni gave a big smile.

"Right, now everyone has a card, what I am going to do is show these specially chosen people, that we all have a secret we hide, and to avoid their own shame, they have joined in with others in the past, by shaming others to deflect the truth of themselves. So tonight, I will show them a part of themselves. I will again say, this is like a private session, I will be asking you not to disclose the contents of your cards, but I would like you to confirm if I am right or I am wrong. Simply that, my assistant Katie, will come down there with a mic, and all you have to say is yes or no, when I ask you."

The whole row suddenly looked very uncomfortable, as they held their envelopes in front of them, I cannot deny, I was terrified over what I thought could happen, Christ I hoped this did not backfire. I sat back in my seat and felt very anxious, Birch who was still holding my hand, gave it a gentle reassuring squeeze.

Katie came down from the back of the room with a microphone, she undid the red rope, slipped through, and walked to the front of the base of the stage. Veronica appeared very happy.

"Oops, I still have two more, she slipped her hand in her pocket and pulled out two envelopes, and smiled.

"I believe we have an Abigail and a Birch here?"

My heart froze, Birch appeared to tense up, she whispered quietly.

"Oh, Mum you bitch." I swallowed hard, and quietly panicked.

"What... What has she done, oh Christ, are we going to be publicly crucified?"

Veronica looked at both of us and smiled, as Katie delivered the cards. I felt terrified and panicked, as I looked at the envelope, and swallowed hard. Oh shit I knew it, I was going to be dragged out and exposed in front of everyone.

"I will not be asking you two anything, but I do think you both need to ask yourself something important." I gave a massive sigh of relief.

"I want you two to wait until everyone has finished, before you open yours."

She stood right at the front of the stage, and looked down at those from the village with cards.

"You can now open your envelopes, you will not be able to read them, just hold them in front of you, so only you can read them... Will darling, can you lower the lights a little more please?"

At the back William Dixon began to lower the lighting, and the room descended into almost darkness.

"Are we ready.... Alright you can read your cards."

Bright blue lights came on above the seated members of the VIP section, and I suddenly understood, it was ultra violet light, and she had written on each card in UV pen. Words appeared on every card, and those holding them read them. Veronica looked down at Peter and Mary Saxon, they were holding a card that said 'Naturists' They both looked shocked.

"Remember, I will not reveal the content of the cards, just nod or say yes, if it is true."

Peter looked at Mary and smiled, he looked up at Veronica and gave a nod, it was correct. She smiled. Next came Colin and Angela, their cards read 'Swingers' Angela laughed, and she smiled at Veronica and nodded, it was indeed right. Andrew Bosworth was next. 'Domestic Abuser' He scowled up at Veronica, she smiled. He tore up his card and sat back, glaring at her, she did not flinch.

"I will take that as a correct."

Lillian and Celia looked at theirs and Lillian gave a chuckle, it read 'Lesbian' Veronica smiled and winked, Celia actually blushed.

Tom from Jessop's opened his. 'Cannabis Grower' He smiled a dreamy smile, and gave a thumbs up. Amanda the florist looked at hers, gasped, and pulled it to her chest, 'Lonely Adulteress' She looked guilty and nodded.

Ronald opened his, and I cannot deny I held my breath for his reaction. He read it, then raised his eyebrows, and then nodded, Veronica smiled. I was a little disappointed, I had thought he would have reacted much worse.

Next was Hatty, I was surprised to see she had one, it read 'Shamed and Lonely' She looked up at Veronica who smiled, and nodded softly. Her face upset me, because Hatty looked the saddest I had ever seen her.

My dad looked at his. 'No idea of the gift, his wife is' He gave a long sigh, and nodded, but did not look up.

The silence in the room was surreal, as everyone watched the pictures on the large screen, as each person read their cards. My mum was next, 'You have the most beautiful daughter' She gave a squeak. and looked at Veronica, I saw the tears in her eyes as she nodded. What the hell was on that card that moved her to tears so fast?

My brain spun out of control, as I watched her wipe her eyes. The Vicar opened his card and looked at it, 'BDSM Fetish' he smiled, well his teeth moved. I could not believe he smiled, did he really not mind that huge thing pushed up his butt, my mind was mind spinning? Marion was next, 'Secret urine fetish, hypocrite' She squealed and hid the card quickly, then turned at looked right at Ronald.

My heart began to beat fast as Marjorie lifted her card. 'Voter Fraud, Bully' She looked up, and her eyes glared.

"This is outrageous." She spotted herself on the large screen behind Veronica. Veronica looked down at her.

"But it is none the less true, isn't it?"

Aware of the camera Marjorie tore up the card, and sat back with a hateful look on her face. Veronica moved on to us, I cannot deny I was panicked, as I saw the camera man turn his camera towards us. Roni pointed to Deb's.

Deb's gave a giggle and then showed me her card, I gasped. 'Closet lust, sexual Deviant' She giggled and raised her thumb to Veronica. Holy shit, she actually admitted it, my best friend from home, was actually admitting she was a closet pervert.

Anthony had no real need to look. 'Gay in denial for too long' He smiled at her, and flicked his hair from his face. Chloe giggled. 'Overactive sex drive'

"Veronica you have no idea how so."

We all chuckled. Edwina was last. 'Bisexual' it was true, and she smiled as she nodded.

Veronica walked back to her table, and took another drink of her water.

"All of you think about this, because it is really important. Ask the question, how did she know?"

She looked down at all of them sat there staring up at her.

"You hide, but it is not as hidden as you think it is, there is always someone who will see it, just think of that as you walk home, secrets have an odd way of revealing themselves, and it is never in the ways we fear."

Veronica walked along the stage, and the words that appeared on the screen read 'Nothing stays hidden forever.'

"As you can see, we all have something deeply private to hide, and all of you have hidden it whilst shaming others, and I feel there is room for some inner dialogue with yourselves."

She walked back to the edge of the stage and looked at Birch and myself, I noticed the large screen went blank, and the camera man slid his camera away from the edge of the stage.

"Girls, before the UV lights go out, you may read your cards."

I nervously opened mine, and was afraid to look, it read. 'In love, but afraid to admit it.' I swallowed hard and looked up at Veronica, she smiled.

"You will get there, turn it over."

I flipped the card over, and it the tiniest writing it read. 'Victim of shame.'

It was the handwriting of Birch. I nodded, it hurt to read it, it felt painful, and I lowered my head, and before I could stop it, a huge sob came up my throat, and Deb's leaned over to hug me, it was the truth, but it hurt so bad, I had no idea what to do. Deb's held me tight, I felt Birch's hand slide onto my shoulder and she gently squeezed it, and whispered.

"I am sorry Deads, but it is true, it needs to be said."

Birch looked at hers, and her eyes filled with tears, it simply read 'In love for the first time, and afraid', she looked up at her mum and smiled. "It's true."

The tears ran down her cheeks, I wanted to know what was on it, but she slipped it back into the envelope and held it to her chest. Veronica walked back to the centre of the stage.

"Every town, every village, and every city have people who suffer from being shamed for no other reason than they are different, I know, I talk to them every day. We all have problems, we all have secrets, and we all have fears, but that is not a good enough reason to victimise another person. People have become fake, two faced, and bullies, and it has to stop, because it is the main cause of emotional damage in this world, and so to all of you here tonight, I will offer this challenge to you."

She walked back the front centre of the stage, stood still, and looked round the packed room.

"It is never too late to change. Who you were, who you are now, and who you will become, are all different people. So go to those you have hurt, and apologise, or just be kind, think of how you would feel if you knew that others knew your deepest darkest secrets, and be better than you are now, become someone you want to be. Every client I have ever worked with has had the same advice from me."

Once again as she spoke the words appeared on the screen above her.

"BE YOU, APPRECIATE EACH OTHER."

"My name is Dr Veronica Gemma Dixon, and I want to thank you all, for coming and listening, and for supporting the efforts of this wonderful and beautiful village, every penny spent today will ensure its survival."

The crowd stood up and applauded, and it was deafening, whistles and cheers, crashed over the place like I had never ever seen, it was crazy. Veronica was like a rock star, as she stood and gave a bow.

I had to wipe my eyes of the remaining tears to see better. The applause lasted for some time, and eventually, she raised her hands, and asked for silence, and for everyone to stay seated. It took a good few minutes, for calm to descend. She looked so happy stood up there as she smiled, she looked in the audience and adjusted her face mic.

"I am so delighted with your response tonight, and I am deeply grateful. This is a new format for me, and I have really enjoyed doing it. I too can get stuck in the old ways, and old patterns of behaviour, we all can, and maybe change is needed. I am so lucky to have such a forward thinking daughter, because if I am honest, she deserves far more of the credit than I do. She is the reason I am here, doing this for all of you tonight, and I would like to share this with her if I may? Could I ask her to come and stand beside me, Ladies and gentlemen, I would love to introduce the future of my work, and I hope another doctor to the family."

I felt Birch tense up, and I patted her leg, Veronica looked straight at her.

"Jemi, please, will you?"

She held out her hand and Deb's turned.

"Get up there Birch, what are you waiting for?" I gave her a nudge. Veronica gave a huge smiled as Birch stood up.

"Ladies and gentlemen, my daughter, and hopefully the future Dr Jemima Dixon."

I screamed with all I had, as did all the others, as Birch walked onto the steps, and the stage, to her waiting mother. We all stood up and started clapping, and in the VIP section there were astounded gasps. Lillian and Celia were on their feet jumping around clapping and yelling, Marjorie scowled, and muttered to Marion.

"I should have known that bitch was involved, she has been nothing but bad news since she came here."

Marion said nothing, Marjorie was nowhere as in control as she thought, Marion had seen what was written on her card.

Birch looked uneasy, and almost shy, her cheeks were pink, as her mother slipped her arm round her, and stood at her side, and they looked so alike, as they faced a crowd of three thousand clapping and cheering people. Veronica covered her mic.

"You gave me a great vehicle, and so…. I got you." She giggled and Birch smiled.

"Get used to this kid, you will go much further than I have."

I had my phone out taking pictures, I knew I would never forget this, and I wanted something to look at, and just remember. Finally, Birch came back down to us, and Veronica left the stage.

Katie walked onto the stage with her mic, and waved the cheering crowd into silence.

"Ladies and gentlemen. We have books written by Roni available at the back, and as I announced earlier, all sales tonight will be going into the village fund, so by reading the books, you will be helping yourself, and by buying them, you will be supporting your community. Roni will be available to sign copies, and we are currently organising a line to her table. There will be a short break, coffee and tea is available at the back, and then shortly I will hand the mic back to Mrs Marjorie Wallace, and we will have the final prize award ceremony, and then finish this wonderful Fete. Can I just say one more thing before Roni is available to you all, we both would like to say a huge thanks to Felicity Watson, who has run this event like clockwork, and made everything so easy for us, she has worked very hard behind the scenes, and we really do appreciate it, so our thanks Flick, you earned it."

A lot of people nodded in agreement, and Katie came down the steps with a smile and hugged her, it was nice to see, although, did she just rub my mum's ass? Holy shit… The dirty bitch, she did!

I sat in my seat, knowing the rope was a little protection, Chloe, Edwina and Debs went for coffee, and five girls called Anthony to the rope. I assumed they wanted their hair doing, one of them smiled at me and, gave me a thumbs up. Birch was sat deep in thought still holding her card, I really wanted to know what was on it, but I was afraid to ask, she caught me staring at her and smiled, she lifted her hand to my face and cupped my cheek.

"You really are so very special; do you know that?"

I have no idea why, but I blushed as I smiled, she really had no idea how much that meant to me.

Deb's arrived with coffee, and we all sat down and drank. Marjorie was talking, but it looked like Marion was not even listening. The Vicar was up chatting with Colin and Peter, they were discussing the presentation, but I bet none of them mentioned the content of their cards.

Katie arrived and spoke quietly to Marjorie, on the stage Veronica's things were being removed, and long tables were being set up, with all the cups and certificates by my mum and dad, it would not be long before they started.

You have no idea how big a fete is, until you have to sit through the endless presentations. My name was finally called and I walked up to be presented with a small silver cup, and a certificate, the rosette was already on the wall above my bed at home. Marjorie actually smiled through gritted teeth, and I smiled back, said thank you very politely, and took my prize and left the stage.

I took a picture of Anthony as he held up his first place trophy, his face was so lovely, his smile, the joy in his eyes, and just the confidence he had.

Brent stood at my side and cheered for him, and I loved that, because I knew the hell Anthony had gone through, and I felt happy we would not be leaving him completely alone, when all of us headed back to Uni.

Birch was so proud as Roni and Will cheered from below the stage, she held up tiny little cup and waved it at me, her eyes sparkled so brightly, she had no idea at all, how much she had changed my life, although I still don't think curd is a jam, even if it does have marshmallow in it.

Watching mum take first from Marjorie, was the best feeling ever. I have never seen her so happy, it was nice to see my dad cheering her with us, as we snapped pictures, I am not sure, but it felt like something inside him was changing.

I had always felt a loneliness around mum, and I had felt it a little less in the last couple of weeks. I hoped things would change at home for the better, they had time until my next term break, where we would be campaigning for mum in the council elections. Between you and me, I was hoping to find the spare room empty when I arrived home.

Chapter 33

Summer Ends.

Listening to Roni speak, had a big effect on me, I had taken every single thing she said to heart. I am not certain anyone else had, but for me, a person who was deeply engaged in trying to work out who I was, and understand myself, her impact on me was seismic.

I had left the church hall that night, hoping she had resonated with many of the people who lived in the village, because it did need to change and embrace a more modern acceptance of cultures and trends.

I find it sad that I was seen as threat, I grew up here, it was my home, could they not see its beauty and nostalgia were equally as important to me, as it was them? Wotton is beautiful, my problem was never with the village, it was with some of the people.

Tuesday had been simply too busy to have enough time to think, because we had all been equally as busy, even though organising an event is a lot of work. What few appreciate is, after it is done, it has to be taken apart and packed away. Just looking at the church hall was enough to see that, as men in black shirts, unbolted everything and wheeled it back into the long truck parked outside.

Bev paid a visit on Tuesday evening with Roni, and she sat with me for a while, while Birch talked with her mother, she felt puzzled, and told me.

"These two posh old birds invited me to tea last night, whoa Deadly it was weird." I frowned at her, feeling tense.

"Posh birds, you mean Lillian and Celia?" She nodded.

"Yeah, them two, I sat in their house, and they gave me these tiny fucking sandwiches, and tea from a pot, in them tiny cups. I mean it was nice, they were proper lovely, and all that. I ate the fucking lot, they were bloody tasty, and then they sort of smiled, and it got weird."

I looked at her with suspicion, and felt my heart beat increase.

"Weird, in what way?" She smiled, and I felt an inner dread.

"Oh god you didn't?" She shrugged.

"Well, it were like this Deadly, you know the taller one?"

"Celia?" She nodded.

"Aye her.... Well, she smiles, and gets all posh like, and says to me. We really admire you, and we wondered if you would like to partake of a joining with us, we feel we would be enhanced by your womanly abilities.... I was like what the fuck did she just say?"

I cannot deny, I was already cringing, and was starting to dread what was coming next, and yet again my attraction to morbid curiosity got the better of me.

"So, they invited you for a threesome?" She smiled and nodded at me, and I knew I was going to hate myself for asking, but I had too.

"So, what did you do?"

Why do I do this to myself, I regretted asking the moment I said it, and I was hoping she would not answer, but this was Bev, what on earth was I thinking? She thought about it for a second.

"Well, I was not too sure what she had asked, you know they talk a bit posh for me, so I looked at her and said, so, you are up to fuck?" I gasped.

"HOLY SHIT BEV!" She smiled.

"They looked a bit shocked like, and then said yes, so I did what I do best, and I fucked em both for four hours."

"What?" She nodded with a smile.

"Hey I am telling you them posh birds were good, I cum like crazy I did."

And I was already regretting ever even staring a conversation with her. I cannot deny the thought of Bev, Celia and Lillian cavorting on a bed, was more than a little unsettling to me, and having witnessed her in action, I was surprised Lillian did not have a stroke. Bev sat back with a smile.

"That Celia bird, she has a really nice ass you know, when I ripped her pants off, I was like, fuck, I am well in here."

I shuddered, and my stomach gave a weird wobble, and sloshed inside me, and my legs felt all weak.

Having been exposed as Roni's daughter, Birch was happier, as she could freely associate with her mother, and so on Wednesday, she spent the day alone with her parents, before we all hugged Bev and her parents, and waved them goodbye, as they headed back home to Uppermill.

Deb's was busy at the care home, and so I spent my day stretched out in the garden, looking deeply into myself, and how I had been treated by people I had grown up knowing. That night Birch and I sat talking about everything that had happened, we sat in the kitchen catching up, and washing our clothing ready to return to Manchester.

Today was a free day, as much of what was needed to be done was finished, and here I am sat on a guy named Andrew, who is lay on my blanket, at the lake. His pants are around his ankles, my clothes are strewn across the floor after skinny dipping, and after a lot of kissing sucking and groping, I was now sat straddled across him, grinding my hips down, as I bit down on my lip, as all those wonderful feelings, and tingles, were building inside me, and my god, I needed them.

I was thrusting my hips backwards and forwards, slamming myself onto him, and with each push, those tingles sent electricity shooting through my body, and I was beathing faster and faster, gasping in air, as I rode harder, to achieve that wonderful golden moment of climax. God, I need this, I had been turned on for days, and feeling more and more frustrated. I needed the release this would bring, just to calm my libido enough to get me back to Manchester and free of the stress and frustrations of this god awful village.

Through the trees, I saw Petal, her back door was open, and a guy was stood with his pants round his ankles, as his butt slammed backwards and forwards, Birch's legs flapping either side of his shoulders, she was getting what she needed too, and I felt happy, knowing she too needed to release her inner frustrations.

I felt the buzz burning in my crotch, my legs began to tremble, and I leaned forward, gripping his shirt, as I pushed down harder, feeling every inch of him inside me. He had not looked that fat, but he was long, and it was touching parts of me that had not been touched for some time, and oh my god it was working really bloody well.

"Oh God Andy… I am almost there… Oh god…. Oh, god Andy."

He pushed his hips up, and oh my god, it pushed him just that tiny bit more inside me, and my body went wild.

"Oh my god I am going to cum… Andy… Andy…. Oh GOD!"

My vagina, and my head exploded, as the electric shot through me like lightning, and I stiffened, and leaned back, and felt that deep internal throbbing from him.

"Arrrrrrrrrgh!!!"

BOOM! It hit me like a crashing wave and engulfed me, as I shook like a spin dryer, the air flowing out of my lungs, until that moment, when I gave a huge deep breath inward, and I was spent, and collapsed on top of him.

I did not want to talk, I did not want to move, all I wanted was to gasp as much air back into me, as my legs trembled and vibrated like a tuning fork. He was breathing as fast as I was, his arms wrapped around me, but he manged to gasp out a quick.

"Hell girl, I think you broke me."

He gasped in more air and relaxed. I lay on his chest panting, my brain in sexed drunk mode, but it was just nice, as I felt him throb, then shrink, and slip out of me.

There was no way I could sit up or walk, so as his arms loosened, I simply rolled off him, and lay still, gasping at his side.

"Thanks Andy, you have no idea how much I needed that."

I raised my arm to my face, and felt the sweat rolling off my brow. Andy sat up and glanced at me.

"How long you here for?" I lifted my hand, as I smiled and patted his hip.

"Sorry…. I head back to Manchester tomorrow." He smiled, but he was clearly disappointed.

"That's a shame, I would definitely be interested in doing this again." I smiled.

"Sorry, that's the breaks." He looked saddened but gave me a smile.

"What was your name again?" I chuckled.

"Molly." He nodded.

"Cool... Well Molly I won't forget this."

I nodded back to him, and breathed in deeply to regulate my panting lungs. I thought if he wants to boast, telling everyone I was Molly would be a little more than funny, it would be absolutely hilarious in the village.

I lay on my back, looking up at the branches of the trees that surrounded me, with the blue sky behind, I was spent, as I enjoyed the feeling of slowing coming down, from the high of an orgasm, and enjoying the stillness that swirled inside my soul, and let my thoughts drift.

I read an article last week that said young people were having less sex, and honestly as I lie here, enjoying the joy of having just been screwed, I cannot for the life of me think why. It makes me feel amazing, I become so aware of parts of my body I normally never think about, and enjoy all those amazing little tingles that just ripple all over me. I love the calmness of my soul after, like I am doing now, and for me it is so addictive, why would anyone not want to feel this wonderful?

I finally had to move, so I sat up and saw the discarded condom, ew, could he not take it and dispose of it like a normal human? I looked behind me, and could see Birch's legs, hanging out of Petal, whoever had been slamming into her, had obviously gone on, to either sleep, or recover for another round.

I found the strength to stand, but my legs were still wobbly, and decided to stagger towards Birch.

I walked slowly through the trees in the direction of Petal. I passed a large pine tree into a small clearing, and saw something I never expected to see. Deb's was stood up against a tree, stark naked from swimming, her legs parted, and between them Edwina was going at it like a lap dog.

Deb's had both of her hands on the back of Edwina's head, but it was the look on her face that was amazing. Her eyes were glazed and almost closed, and she had a look of sheer lust on her face that simply shocked the shit out of me, she was gone into some sort of transcendental state of bliss, and I found it fascinating to see.

Edwina became aware I was there, and turned to me. She pulled her face out of Deb's vagina, and gave a quick smile.

"She asked me what it was like, and now she knows." She turned, and went back to work.

"Cool... I was not aware you did requests Edwina?"

She was far too busy to answer, and thought I would leave Deb's to her quest of self discovery. I made it to Petal, Birch was sat up looking knackered, I climbed in, and she lifted a bottle of beer, and flipped off the top.

"Here you look like you need one." I took it gratefully, and flopped down at her side.

"I am well and truly done."

We chinked bottles, and leaned back to rest, and watch out of the back door. I looked at Birch who was lying back on a rolled up blanket, with her eyes closed.

"Have you seen Chloe?" She lifted a limp arm and pointed.

"Over there somewhere, she was having a threesome a bit back, she seems to really enjoy the attention of two, if you cannot see her, well its Chloe, she will be at it again, I am telling you Deads, that girls vagina is invincible."

It took a while, but eventually Birch decided to go find her clothes, I followed to get mine, and the blanket. Deb's was sat against the tree, Edwina was lay on the floor smiling, so I assumed, Deb's had repaid the favour and done well.

We reached the bank of the lake, where Chloe was swimming to wash off, she was all smiles, when she walked out dripping. She grabbed her clothes.

"Are we off soon, pretty much everyone else has gone?"

I got the feeling if they hadn't, she would have stayed until she had sexually sated all of them. Slowly we made our way back to Petal, as Deb's and Edwina, grabbed their stuff and jumped in.

We set off home with Birch driving, as the three girls dressed in the back, and as is the case with Birch at the wheel, it was not long before we were back at my house. Hot sticky, and smelling heavily of sex, we once again stripped, and dived in the pool, to cool and clean off.

Anthony arrived not long after, and dived in to join us. He had changed so much; it was really quite remarkable. We all ended up gathered in the guest house, naked, and sat on the floor, as had become the norm for us.

There was a tinge of sadness to us, as this would be our last time together here. The guest house had become a sort of base camp for summer, and we were all in a thoughtful mood, as we recounted some of our adventures over the past weeks.

I sat listening, my mind once again, preoccupied with my own inner search for my identity, when Edwina made a remark about Anthony's junk.

"You know, I think you have a great dick, if you were straight Anthony, I would screw you for sure."

There were giggles all around the room. I was sat with a pillow behind me, resting on the thin section of wall between the kitchen, and the bedroom, and I looked up.

"Why is his gayness an issue?"

They all looked at me, I looked at Anthony, and saw him watching me with a puzzled expression.

"I have known you since school Anthony... I liked you back then, I saw you as a nice guy, but I did not really know you as a person, for all I knew, you screwed girls. I am looking at you now, you are naked, and you have a great body, I would defo sleep with you because of it. You know what, I know you better now, I have talked to you, and spent time with you, and really got to know you, my only real regret is I wish I had made the effort sooner." He smiled at me and nodded, and I continued.

"You are my friend, I consider you to be an amazingly good friend, and I am going to miss you, but you know what? I don't give a fuck about your gayness, I don't care that you want to sleep with guys, because to me, that has nothing to do with who you are. You are a wonderful and caring person, and I love you for that."

His eyes glistened as he looked at me.

"I love you too Abby, I really do, I love all of you, and I am really going to miss you all." Birch lifted her glass.

"Deads is right, fuck his gayness, he is much more than that."

I nodded, and raised my glass. I looked round the room, they were all staring at me. I shrugged at them all.

"I really listened to Roni, I found her talk mind blowing, and I realised something, we are no better than Marjorie."

There were gasps all around, Deb's looked at me with her jaw dropped.

"Holy shit Abby, how can you even say that?"

Birch smiled, and turned from her seat at the window.

"Because Deb's she is right, just think about what my mum said." I raised my glass again in salute to Birch.

"Listen to our master."

I laughed, and they all looked at me as if I was mad. I looked at Deb's.

"Edwina screwed you today, and you screwed her back, not because you are a lesbian, but because you were curious and had questions. So, if I was Marjorie, I would call you a whore or a slut, or even Bi sexual, it is a label she uses to put people down, like gay or queer or 'like that' which are her pet words for people she sees as like Anthony, so what are you Deb's, what label should I give you?" She looked confused.

"I don't know, I really enjoyed today, but I enjoyed being with Jimmy, so I suppose I am a bi sexual now?" I shook my head.

"NO! You are not. Deb's you are going to be a bio chemist, like Anthony is a great hair stylist, or Chloe, you are an artist, and Edwina you are a computer whizz, why do we have to be defined by our sexuality, why is it more important than anything else? Why is it more important than whether or not we are kind, understanding, helpful, intelligent, or friendly as people? Do you see what I mean, the world is so god dammed messed up with its bloody sexual identity labels, and whatever it is that it now defines us by. Why should we be only defined by who we have sex with?"

Birch smiled, as the others just stared at me trying to work it out in their heads, I needed to say this because it had been eating at me all day.

"Guys it is wrong, that is what Marjorie defines us by. Birch and me are her whores, she called Chloe a tramp, it is just wrong. Look at Hatty, her life is defined by Marjorie, who has branded her a Harlot, and yet she is an amazing artist, and a teacher. I am more than who I sleep with, I want to be known as a writer, not a fucker." I started to giggle, and Birch joined in.

I could see I hit something inside them, Birch looked at me and winked, Edwina looked at Birch.

"If it does not matter, then what am I, because I like sex, and I choose in the moment who it will be with, which can be either sex, that is Bi sexual?" Birch leaned back on the chair.

"You said it yourself, you like sex, why should that define you, why can you not just be sexual and leave it at that? Sex is a natural process, it is like eating or breathing, you need those to sustain you. Most doctors and psychologists would say that as a race, we all need sex equally as much, because mentally and emotionally it is very important. The benefits of sex are more than well documented, and all the positive effects on the body, mind, and spirit. So, answer me this, if you meet someone who has not been laid in ages, their lack of sex does not define them like it does with Anthony does it? I think that is unfair to Anthony, hell it is unfair to all of us. I think Deads is right, we should never define ourselves because of who we sleep with. Sexually deprived people, are still plumbers, artists, welders, etc, they are not classed as sexless and shunned. If Anthony was straight, he would still be a hair stylist, and yet he has been targeted because he is gay, not because he is a stylist."

I nodded and could see they were starting to understand us. Chloe was lay on the floor.

"I get where you are coming from, but for some, it is the only identity they have, so what do they do?" I looked at her.

"What if it only defines them, because that is what certain groups have campaigned for, and that small group of activists has manged to change society? Okay I get it, for them it is possibly the only important thing in their life, which is why they are activists, but what about the rest of us?"

I watched their faces as they listened to me, I could see all of them trying to puzzle it all out, and understand what I was saying, and I was glad that they were considering it, because it felt so important to me.

"I do not talk about my sex life, who I have sex with is important to me, and the person I sleep with. I see it as special, intimate, a private moment of deep importance to me. It matters to the two of us, it should not matter to the rest of the world, because it is just a moment of wonder, but it is not my whole, not the complete me."

I lifted my glass and took a sip.

"Marjorie has used it against us as a weapon, and so have activists who have not considered everyone else's thoughts and feelings, it is a selfish act based on their own agenda. We have all been labelled with it, and the rest of the world forced to accept it, because they think that is right. Isn't that exactly the same as what is happening here, Marjorie and her small group, has everything sown up for all of us? Guys this village has over five thousand people living here, and yet Marjorie, has control, and determines the way everyone has to live, she is just the same as the activists, forcing her ideals on everyone else."

Birch sat listening to me and gently smiling to herself, as I spoke.

"Does it matter if it is a pressure group in society, or one person here, those are still her standards, not mine, or any of yours, and it is the same all over the world. Small groups of individuals, use pressure groups to get things the way they want, and that is why we have all these pigeon hole titles we have to fit into, but surely one box cannot fit all? We are examined and defined by their idea of what we should be, not who we actually are as people, that is social conditioning. The naked body is shameful, this skin colour is not acceptable, yet that one is, who you sleep with picks your box. You heard Marjorie, with her Whore, Slut, Transient, Miscreant, titles for us, she is picking the pigeon holes for everyone around here. All I am saying is why can we not take that power back off her, when it comes to us? Why can we not do the same, and reject those labels completely, and all just be sexual humans, or even better, just humans?"

"I am just curious."

Everyone looked at Birch, she shrugged.

"I am…. I am curious about life, curious about people, curious about other cultures, curious about attitudes, and behaviour, which is why I want to be involved with my mums' work. I had a chance to sleep with a woman once, she really wanted me to, but I just didn't want to. I have considered it with another woman since, and if I am honest, I really wanted to, but I was afraid, so am I Bi or straight? I say neither? I say I am just really curious, because I like learning from everything I do. Every adventure in life is a lesson, and that is all I care about, learning about me and how I react to things. Personally, I agree completely with Deads. Guys there are seven billion people on the planet, and every one of us, is completely unique, so should there not be seven billion pigeon holes? I can only be me, and only I can define who that is, no one else can or should. I too hate all the labels in the world today, so I suppose if you want to give me a label, I will pick one myself, based on what I know about me, and it is neither straight or bi, it would be Curio."

Chloe sat up, and gave a huge smile as she looked at Birch.

"Oh my god, I love that. CURIO! It sounds awesome."

The others all nodded, and I smiled.

"It is a great term Birch. Curio, meaning curious about everything, curious about life in general, yeah by that definition, I am a Curio too." Deb's nodded.

"Yeah me too... I am a Curio, it really fits me, because I love science, and fashion, books and great sex, why should I be anything people in the village would call me? I am staying a Curio."

Anthony smiled and nodded his head and agreed,

"I think that is a really wonderful way to describe how I feel in general, because despite popular opinion, I don't lie around all day thinking of sex with men." Chloe lifted her drink.

"Sadly, I do, to me sex is art, and I fucking love art."

We all started to laugh, and raised our glasses to Chloe.

I sat back, and watched them all as they continued the conversation, and thought about my summer. Coming home would have been so much better if my looks had not been how I was defined by the village. My mother would not have been angered, the people in the village would not have pointed and stared, and yet they had, and as a result I had been left isolated.

I was lucky in the sense I had Birch and Deb's, without them I would have been alone and afraid, unable to leave the house, and it simply was unfair and wrong. Wotton lived by rules set by Marjorie and her cronies, and as a result of not appeasing her ideals, I suffered, and that had to change.

I understand that change can be hard for most of us, especially when we look inside ourselves, I know, I have spent a year looking at myself and trying to understand the thousands of thoughts and feelings I had locked inside.

The simple fact was, change is an evolutionary process, no matter how much we try to stop it, we cannot.

Every experience I have had has taught me something, which is why that blonde blue eyed innocent girl called Abigail Watson, has been replaced with the dark gothic Deadly, it was a natural progression of the person I would become, and no doubt there would be many more changes in the future.

Roni was right, we should not have to hide who we are for the sake of a public perception. We should all have the freedom to explore life, because when it all comes down to it, this is my life, not Marjorie's or my mother's, it is mine, and I should be free to pick and choose how I live it, and that should apply to everyone.

Be you, appreciate each other, those words were stuck in my mind. Roni was so right, and it was a powerful message to a village that hides so much out of fear of being shamed.

Growing up, I had seen how it looked to the outside was always far more important that how it was on the inside, that was the rule of living here for eighteen years, and this year, I saw how much that had eroded my own family.

Mum and dad still appeared the same to the outside world, but they were not, on the inside they shared separate rooms, and hardly spoke to each other. Bradley Wheeler was respected because he was rich, but that was so sad, he should be respected because he was a decent person, because he loved his wife and step daughter.

Hatty was suffering from grief, and made the mistake of reaching out to a man in her loneliness, but he was married, and because of that, she had been branded for life. Birch hated Bell Twats, and so when the bells were sabotaged, even I jumped to the wrong conclusion.

Jumping to wrong conclusions has left this village isolated and lost in time, and maybe it did need two strong characters like Birch and myself to walk openly down the street, at the start of summer to point it out.

Had we made a change, I really was not sure, maybe we had just played our part in starting the process? Like Birch has always said, there are times when you need to plant a seed, and watch out for what grows in your sunlight, and I think one or two seeds have been planted this summer.

It is strange how six weeks ago I had stood at the station terrified, just wanting to jump back on the train, and go back to

Manchester, and now as I sat here having endured the village, as I looked at my friends, I did not want to leave. Perhaps that was the point, I had to arrive, and then leave, and everything in between had its purpose, and now it was time to move forward again.

"Abby.... Abby... We have to go." I jerked out of my thoughts.

"What?" Chloe smiled.

"It is late, and we have to make a move."

I nodded and pulled up my legs to stand, as the others all dressed, and I gave a long sigh, this was the moment I was dreading.

The hardest part of this summer, is saying goodbye to the people who have become so important to me. At eleven thirty, Chloe, Anthony, and Edwina had to leave. I found it so hard, I was not ready to say goodbye, if I am honest, I never want to say goodbye to them. I felt a burning pain inside me, and so we arranged to meet outside the salon, before we drove home, so I hugged them all, and watched them walk happy and smiling up the garden.

Shortly after, I stood and looked at Deb's, and smiled at her, she smiled a sad smile.

"I will defo see you in the morning." She came across and hugged me so tight.

"I love you Abigail, it was the best summer ever." I felt my insides twist.

"I love you too Deb's, see you in the morning."

She turned with a smile, and made her way out. She waved goodbye until the following day, and I closed the door to the guest house, feeling the start of heartbreak, I turned, and Birch put her arms round me.

"Come on Sweetie, we knew this day would come?"

I could not help but feel so sad, and fought back the tears. I understood this time would come, but it felt so hard now. They had become such good friends, and I had really come to love them deeply. I knew it was going to be so hard to leave, even though I knew the life I was going back to, and I really wanted to get back into Uni life again.

Birch took my hand, and led me through to our bedroom, we

stripped, and curled up together, and once again, as I thought of
the two single beds, and the spare room at Birch's house, this was
the last time she would snuggle into me, and the truth was, even
though we had not been sexual, I still wanted to sleep with her.

I lay back in bed, and she snuggled into me, and I felt her
warmth against my skin. It had become so familiar to me, a part
of my life that was important to me. I lay there in the dark with
her wrapped around me.

"This is our last night sleeping together, isn't it?" She softly
kissed my shoulder.

"Not completely, I had a double bed delivered to my house.
Dad has moved the single into the spare room to create a twin.
When we get to my house, you will be staying in my room until
we go back to Uni, and I have been thinking, perhaps we should
rearrange the dorm, and push the two beds together, I want us to
keep sleeping like this too."

I lay in the dark, listening to her softly breathe, and I felt the
tears in my eyes. I had been so afraid of coming home, and now
I didn't want to leave, I wanted this Summer to last forever. I
wanted to see mum every day, and have another hug from dad,
and I wanted to watch Hatty laugh.

I loved seeing the bright happy and bubbly Deb's as she sat up
in bed, and hearing about the crazy adventures Chloe and Edwina
had experienced. I wanted to be there, just in case Anthony
needed me, but I had to go, and it really hurt. I have no idea when
I drifted into sleep, all I know is, I was reliving the Summer, and
at some point, I slipped from reality and into my dreams.

We were woken up by my mum early. Everything was already
packed, all we had to do was put it in Petal, and we would be
ready to go. We sat in the kitchen, and had a cooked breakfast;
mum had also prepared us a packed lunch for our travel back.
Like me she was trying to be brave.

Petal was not fast, and we had pencilled in a seven to eight
hour trip. Deb's wanted to come one last time before we left, and
we were expecting her when the doorbell rang. Dad pressed the
button, and walked to open the front door; he was more than a
little surprised to find Hatty. She was holding a big package, and
gave a frustrated sigh.

"Sorry, I thought you would be at work, where is your car?" He looked at her, and sighed.

"In the garage out of the way of that jeep of Birch's, if you behave, you can come in, I assume that is for the girls?" She gave a nod, and smiled.

"Thank you, Edwin, I will try to be good."

She stepped in, and came down the hall towards the kitchen, all of us were surprised when she walked in.

"Hi, I have waved the white flag... Abby, I have done this for your room, dorm, whatever you call it up there?"

I walked towards her, and she handed me the wrapped picture. Birch was really excited, as I undid the string and opened the paper. It was an oil painted canvass, and it took my breath away. Birch stared at and then filled up with tears.

"Deads it's us."

I felt the tears as I looked at it, and I realised it was from the picture she had taken, on the first day of the summer events. The picture showed Deb's leaning on the new notice board, and Birch and me, were larking around in front of it. I could not believe my eyes. It took my breath away, and I choked up.

"Hatty, this is beautiful, I cannot find the right words, except I love it."

I handed the picture to my mum, and then threw my arms around her.

"I love you so much Hatty." Birch moved in for a group hug.

We stood it against the wall, I did not want to wrap it back up until Deb's had seen it, and we had a coffee with Hatty.

Deb's like us, wept when she saw it, it was such an important day, because that was the first day we walked into the village. I had been hiding in the house, and Deb's had called me out on it, it was also the day Birch found Petal, and Deb's wore no knickers in a short skirt, and I made peace with Chloe. It was such a massively important moment in our lives, and now Hatty had frozen it forever on a canvass.

The moment I was dreading finally arrived. Petal was packed ready, and pulled onto the front. Saying goodbye was terrible. Mum wept buckets, as did I, Birch was dragged into hug by my mum, and almost squeezed to death.

"You have become a very important part of my family Birch. I have to say, I have grown to love you dearly, and I am really going to miss you two trashing the guest house. There will always be a place in my home for you, always."

Birch filled up, and pulled my mum back into her arms.

"I will be back Mum, I promise."

Birch just calling her mum, broke her heart, and my mum wept bitterly, she clung to Birch, just as she would me, and in a strange way, I could see how similar it had been when she had said goodbye to me a year ago. Birch broke away wiping her tears.

"Don't forget, flavoured sugar, and flavoured gin, always go for a wholesome flavour." My mum smiled as she wiped her eyes.

Birch stepped back, and I suddenly felt a huge pain rip through me, and just burst into tears, as she snatched me into her arms, pulled me close and hugged me tight.

"Oh Abby, I am going to miss you so much, I know it has not always been easy, but you have no idea how deeply I love you, and it has been so nice having you back home."

"I know mum, I have loved it too, and I really am going to miss you, promise me you will write every day, and promise me you will take care of dad and Hatty, you all need each other like I need Birch and Deb's."

My dad looked at Birch.

"I am going to miss not running a nudist camp in my garden, I can honestly say, I have never met anyone like you Birch, but I am so very glad I have. Take good care of yourself, and each other."

Birch leapt up, and threw her arms around him, which did indeed surprise him.

"I will actually miss you Ed, take good care of mum for me, she is a very special lady, but you know that already." She kissed his cheek. "Work a little less, and swim naked once in a while for me."

She giggled, as she stepped back and wiped her eyes. He smiled and nodded. Dad hugged me so hard I thought I would break.

"I am so proud of you Abigail, and I love you very much. Take care."

"I love you too dad, be good to mum for me, this will be hard for her."

Hatty smiled, and hugged us both at the same time.

"Not only am I so very proud of you two, I also really admire you. Stay close to each other, and look out for one and other. I hate goodbye, so I am not going to say it, but I see both of you as my children too, and I love you both. Drive safe and text me when you arrive."

She let both of us go, and I wiped the tears from her eyes and smiled. It was heart breaking, I am so glad Birch was driving, I know right, how crazy is that? I had so many tears in my eyes, I would not be able to see the road. Hatty waved goodbye.

"Stay wild girls, and don't let them dent your spirit, I am proud of you both."

Driving away was so hard, it was ten times harder than last time. We drove into the village and up to the salon, where Edwina and Chloe stood waiting. Anthony had just finished a client and was washing his hands.

Saying goodbye was too much, it was heart breaking. Delphine came out to say goodbye, and ended up with a hand full of phones, as we all stood next to Petal, and had one last picture taken of all of us together in Wotton.

Those final hugs were painful, I could not imagine what it would be like to not see each other every day.

Letting go of Deb's was gut wrenching, I just wanted to take her and the others back with me. She stood in front of me with tears rolling down her cheeks, I loved her so much, letting her out of all of them go was the hardest. I pulled her so tight I almost crushed her.

"I don't want to do this Deb's; I hate leaving you alone. We will talk every day, I promise, and we will be back at the end of term."

I kissed her cheek and we broke apart. She smiled.

"I am just going to say, I love you, and if you need me, I will be there. This is not goodbye; it is the last page of chapter one."

She smiled. Birch dragged her into another bone crushing hug.

"Fuck Goggles, I am really going to miss you. You are such a huge part of us, it will be weird not to have you beside us. I am coming back, and so yes, we will have a new chapter to start, and I am so looking forward to it. I am already planning ten times the crazy for us. I love you Gogs, I really do."

I was breaking my heart, when Birch finally guided me into the car. Pulling away was one of the hardest things I have ever done, everyone cried and wept, but we all reassured each other we would stay in touch by group video call. Birch waved out of the window.
"STAY CURIOUS, MY CURIO'S!"

Driving slowly round the green as I took a last look for the Summer, I was surprised at how many of the shop keepers came out to wave goodbye. As we reached the cross roads, Lillian and Celia waved their hankie's, and shouted goodbye, and as always, there she was scowling as normal, and I assumed glad to see the back of me.

Marjorie watched as we turned the corner onto Station Road to fill up for the motorway.

"Good riddance, to bad news and her whore. It is time this village had normality again, and I aim to get it."

I sat in the seat wiping my eyes, as Birch filled up with fuel, and as I pulled my paper tissue away from eyes, I saw three girls walking towards the main village, and all three had multi coloured hair. Birch came round the side of Petal, and saw me watching them. She climbed in with a smile.

"You were the seed Sweetie; look what is growing in your sunlight. Do you remember that first day when you were afraid to even look up, well just look how many came out to wave you goodbye, things will be very different when we come back next summer, even Wotton has to modernise."

She turned on the engine, and drove to the road, Marjorie was still watching from the top of the road, we turned away from her, and headed north towards the motorway. I slipped back into the seat.

"Marjorie is still in control." Birch sniggered.

"Do you think so? She is hanging on like the dinosaur she has made herself, but I think your mum will do very well in the next vote. Her margin was slim last time, but this time she will win it hands down, and change will come, even if only in a trickle, hell Deads, it is already happening."

I love Birch and her optimism, I wish I had her confidence,

Marjorie would play dirty, she always had in the past.

"I am not sure Birch, I am not sure she will, Marjorie never fights fair." Birch smiled.

"Oh, I think she will find her old ways will not be so reliable this time, you will see."

Felicity walked down to the guest house, and walked in; it was a lot cleaner than she expected. She stood in the living room, and looked round, it felt odd now it was not covered in women's clothes. Walking into the bedroom she saw a brown large envelope on the bed.

"Oh, what have they forgot?"

She picked it up, and was surprised to see her name on it, she frowned, lifted the flap and looked inside. It contained paperwork, she slid it out to see a letter written to her from Birch.

'Dear Flick. You will find contained within, copies of pictures taken by Hatty, and given to my mum for her to evaluate Madge for her talk. These are voting slips from the last election, and all of them clearly show votes for you. Madge replaced them with votes for herself. She could only do this because Mary at the post office was instructed to deliver all postal votes to Madge.

We think she checked those on the outskirts, who visited the village less, and replaced their votes for you, with votes for her, thus she won, when in truth you should have won. In order to win, you need to convince the council to assign an independent person to check the votes. You may or may not, find my notes on the cards I made for mum, and who is up to what in the village, mixed in with these papers. The way I see it, if you also know their secrets, and give subtle hints, you will protect them, and Madge loses her ability to threaten people. Talk to Hatty, we will be back to campaign. See you at half term. Your newly adopted daughter Jemi.

PS. Look in the top right hand kitchen cupboard, you may find these few things mum brought down with her a help.

Felicity walked into the kitchen, and opened the door, and stepped back abruptly, with a shriek.

"GOOD GOD!" She smiled.

I took a deep breath, as we crossed the county border, and approached the motorway, Birch hit the button, and the compact disk sprung into life, with Battered Taco, I looked at Birch and smiled, she burst into laughter.

"Oh.... Oh.... OH JIMMY!"

We zoomed down the slip road, and onto the motorway, and Birch looked in her rear view mirror.

"Bye bye Village of the Dammed, fuck, what an awesome summer, next year will be so much wilder!"

I settled into my seat for the long journey home, and thought of all we had done, Birch was right. I did need to look at myself and admit a few truths. I had been riddled with fear, but that was not just from the village, I had been afraid of disappointing my parents, and that had hurt me, because it had led me to think I could not change or grow up.

Veronica was right, who I was when I left home for Uni was one person, and who I was sat in Petal driving north, was another person completely, because I was so different compared to the girl who left, it was like I had transformed.

Over the coming weeks I would look at every aspect of my life, and what I felt in my heart, and what I believed my life should be about, and I felt excited about who I would become, because again that would be yet another version of me, and I was curious as to what that would be like.

Birch has always told me that life is a journey, she had often told me as we sat in the dorm, that it annoyed her that it was always referred to as a path of life, in her book, it was river, and she had dropped the sail, and was enjoying the journey, bobbing along, and going with the flow, and I thought, I could do that too.

I turned and looked at Birch, she had the window open, the music playing, and her long white hair with black patches was lifting and dancing on her shoulders. Her skin was still quite pale, almost like alabaster, her long eye lashes blinked above her beautiful green eyes, as she watched the road. Her soft lips mouthing the lyrics, of the song, 'Fuck me till I can't stand, by Battered Taco.' She was beautiful to look at, there was no doubt, but she was far more beautiful as a person, and as my best friend.

"I love you Birch." She blinked, and tilted her head.

"What Sweetie?"

"I said, this was the best Summer of my life." She smiled.

"Good, it was supposed to be. My mum told me the day I left, make it special Jemi, make it Abigail's Summer."

I smiled more to myself, she had no idea at all, but it meant everything, but there again, that was Birch, it's a Birch thing you know, and you sort of just get used to it?

Coming next in the 'The Curio Chronicles'
by Robin John Morgan.

Five years have passed, and all of the Curio's have finished College and University. Like seeds, they have all been scattered to the winds, following their dreams and careers, leaving Abigail alone, afraid and victimised, living in the guest house, which she has turned into a writers retreat, avoiding the village of Wotton Dursley.

There are signs that their summer had brought some changes, but opinion was still very much controlled by Marjorie, and Abigail had slipped into a spiralling depression, heart broken, as she realises, she has lost Birch forever.

All of the Curio's are suffering, spread apart, and struggling to cope, and all of them are praying for a miracle, and it arrives unexpectedly in a blur of lilac.

The Curio Chronicles continue, in Part Two, Curio's Summer by Robin John Morgan.

More Author's
From
Violet Circle Publishing

Mike Beale. (Children's Book)

Crumble's Adventures.
ISBN: 978-1-910299-06-7

Colin Smith (Play)

Heaven knows I'm Miserable Now
ISBN: 978-1-910299-16-6

Ted Morgan. (Poetry and verse)

Wordsmith's Wanderings.
ISBN: 978-1-910299-04-3
Peregrinations of the Wordsmith
ISBN: 978-1-910299-18-0
Silhouette Soldiers
ISBN: 978-1-910299-19-7

Robin John Morgan. (Fiction/Fantasy/Slice of Life)

Heirs to the Kingdom.

Book One, The Bowman of Loxley.
ISBN: 978-1-910299-00-5
Book Two, The Lost Sword of Carnac.
ISBN: 978-1-910299-01-2
Book Three, The Darkness of Dunnottar.
ISBN: 978-1-910299-02-9
Book Four, Queen of the Violet Isle.
ISBN: 978-1-910299-03-6
Book Five, Crystals of the Mirrored Waters.
ISBN: 978-1-910299-05-0
Book Six, Last Arrow of the Woodland Realm.
ISBN: 978-1-910299-07-4
Book Seven, Bridge Of Sequana.
ISBN: 978-1-910299-17-3
Book Eight, The Circle of Darkness.
ISBN: 978-1-910299-26-5

The Curio Chronicles.

Part One, Abigail's Summer.
ISBN: 978-1-910299-27-2

Find out more about our authors and their books at

www.violetcirclepublishing.co.uk

Violet Circle Publishing Manchester UK

www.ingramcontent.com/pod-product-compliance
Lightning Source LLC
Chambersburg PA
CBHW050958180726
48291CB00006B/1884